THE ECHO OF VALOR

CODENAME ROSE

TIMELESS AGENTS SERIES
BOOK 2

HANNAH BYRON

DEDICATION

IN HONOR OF EILEEN MARY NEARNE
MBE CDEG

Codename Rose

"It was a life in the shadows, but I think maybe I fitted it. I could be a bit hard and secret. I could be lonely. I could be independent."

Eileen Nearne.

Odile and Eileen in Torquay, 2009

Also dedicated to the memory of **Odile Maria Nearne Belladelli** *(1954–2022), beloved niece of Eileen Nearne, whose devotion to her "Aunt Didi" reflects the profound family bond they shared.*

Odile's love and care for her aunt, her tireless efforts to preserve Eileen's memory, and her role as a bridge between Eileen's incredible war story and future generations, have deeply inspired me while writing ***The Echo of Valor, Codename Rose.***

It is a privilege for me as a historical fiction writer to honor Odile Nearne, closest to Eileen in her later years, in this way. Love and devotion to family were at the heart of both her life and Eileen's.

This book is a work of fiction, inspired by real events and individuals from World War 2. Names, characters, businesses, places, events, and incidents are used in a fictional manner, even when based on actual historical facts and figures. While the narrative may incorporate real names and locations to enhance the authenticity of the setting, the portrayal of characters and events is purely fictional. Any resemblance to actual persons, living or dead, or actual events is coincidental and should be interpreted within the context of a fictional story. For more information, please see the Author's Note.

ISBN eBook: 978-90-833027-7-5
ISBN Paperback: 978-90-833027-8-2
Book Cover Design by Ebooklaunch
Editor: Amber Fritz-Hewer
Website: Hannah Byron

PREFACE

In the annals of World War II, countless stories of courage and sacrifice remain untold, but few are as compelling as those of the men and women who risked everything in the shadows. Among them were the agents of the Special Operations Executive (SOE), tasked with sabotage, espionage, and resistance behind enemy lines. Of the 39 women who served in SOE's French section, one name stands out for her quiet resilience and unyielding strength: Eileen Nearne.

Like many who served in clandestine roles, Eileen bore the weight of her experiences in silence. After the war, she withdrew from public life, spending her later years in Torquay, England, largely unknown beyond a small circle of those who cared for her. Though she spoke occasionally about her wartime service in the 1990s, she carried her memories privately. When she passed away in 2010, the depth of her heroism was rediscovered, ensuring she would not be forgotten.

It was her devoted niece, Odile Maria Nearne Belladelli, who ensured Eileen received the dignity and recognition she deserved. Odile, the only daughter of Eileen's younger brother Frederick, was deeply connected to her "Aunt Didi," especially in her later years. Along with her husband, Enore, and their sons, Fabio-John, Giulio-Richard, and Silvio-Stephen, she visited Eileen frequently, offering companionship and love. When Eileen passed away, Odile immediately traveled to England to arrange her funeral, safeguarding her aunt's legacy. A woman of quiet strength herself, Odile fought a long battle with brain cancer before passing in December 2022, leaving behind a legacy of devotion and resilience.

The Echo of Valor is my tribute to Eileen Nearne and her family. This is not a biography—those have already been written. Instead, this historical novel seeks to honor Eileen's legacy with empathy and imagination, bridging historical truth with the emotional depth of fiction. The story explores not only her wartime bravery but also the lasting wounds of trauma, reflecting on how courage endures across generations. Through the contemporary storyline, centered on Dr. Mia Thompson and journalist Sebastian Stone, the novel reimagines the way Eileen's life and sacrifices might continue to inspire.

While the real Eileen lived much of her later life in solitude, this novel envisions a world where she finds connection and recognition. I have written it with the deepest respect for her privacy and the choices she made. As someone who has endured personal loss and understands the instinct to retreat within oneself, I hope to honor her strength while acknowledging the pain that often lingers in the aftermath of great sacrifice.

To the Belladelli-Nearne family, and in particular to Fabio-John, I owe profound gratitude. His generosity in sharing reflections on his mother, Odile, and his family's bond with Eileen has guided me in crafting this tribute. His warm approval of this fictionalized portrayal—a compassionate reimagining of Eileen's later years—has meant the world to me. May this book serve as a lasting light on

Agent Rose, honoring the courage of Eileen Mary "Didi" Nearne, the steadfast love of her niece Odile, and the enduring legacy of their family.

Hannah Byron

List of Agents mentioned in The Echo of Valor.

CODE NAME	NETWORK	ROLE	*ALIAS*	LAST NAME	FIRST NAMES	FATE
Alcide	WIZARD	organiser	*Michel Richou*	Savy	William Jean	Returned
Armand	SPIRITUALIST	organiser	*Jean Conte*	Dumont-Guillemet	René Alfred	Returned
Arnaud	WIZARD, SPIRITUALIST	W/T Operator	*Maurice Faure*	Grafeuille	Adrien	Returned
Blaise	SPIRITUALIST	W/T Operator	*Henri Garnier, Jacques Gillaumin*	Diacono	Henry Louis-Antoine	Returned
Nadine	HISTORIAN	W/T Operator	*Claudie Irene Rodier*	Rolfe	Lilian Vera	Executed
Ambroise	CLERGYMAN, DETECTIVE	Courier, W/T operator	*Micheline Claude Rabatel*	Bloch	Denise Madeleine	Executed
Louise	SALESMAN 1 & 2	W/T Operator	*Corinne Reine Leroy*	Szabo	Violette Reine Elizabeth	Executed
Jacqueline	STATIONER	courier	*Josette Norville*	Nearne	Jacqueline Françoise Mary	Returned
Rose	WIZARD, SPIRITUALIST	W/T operator	*Jacqueline Duterte, Alice Wood, Marie Louise Tournier*	Nearne	Eileen Mary (Didi)	Survived capture and escaped
Odette	SCHOLAR	W/T operator	*Yvonne Jeanne Bernier*	Baseden	Yvonne Jeanne Thérèse	Survived capture

PROLOGUE

2 Lisburne Crescent, Torquay, England, 1 April 2007

The seaside town of Torquay lay dreamily quiet in the misty noon sun. The tracksuited joggers and sturdy-shoed dog walkers had returned home from their beach exercises. The two painters in white overalls, who'd been working on a scaffold on the opposite apartment block, clambered down to secure a sunlit bench in the community garden, munching their packed lunch amidst budding rosebushes and an overflowing trashcan.

The sound of the waves in the distance created a soothing rhythm of eternal life, punctuated at regular intervals by the squawk of seagulls. Bus 19 halted at the corner to let an old man with a cane descend at his leisure. It took off again, slightly creaking with each shift and acceleration.

She shuffled through her small, cluttered flat, maneuvering between her armchair, the coffee table, and a stray chair that had succeeded in blocking her narrow path.

"*Ah, Whisky, tu es là?*" she murmured, caressing the woolly ginger fur of her pet. "Stray cat, stray woman, stray chair." But as she tried to push the chair aside with Whisky on it, a sharp jolt of pain struck her left hip. The whip of the leather hit her like hot iron, whizzing through the air, deafening in her ears. She almost toppled over, gripping the back of the chair to keep from collapsing through the memory.

Un, deux, trois... Keep counting until the pain lessens and roll call is over. No tears, show no tears.

She persisted in her trek to the window, where the outside world was happening. The sisal mat felt rough and grippy under the thin soles of her slippers. The gauze curtains fluttered slightly in the breeze from the open transom window. A shadow, fleeting but full-length, flitted across the stuccoed walls, followed by another.

"*Ah non, ici les hommes d'ombre*," she murmured in French. The shadow men are here again.

Jacqui, long ago, had reassured her during one of her screaming fits. "Didi, it's only the reflection of the waving curtains on the wall. Wake up, darling, wake up." But though her mind knew her sister was right, her eyes were certain they were the men in black uniforms with long arms and even longer rifles. They never let her go, never were they silent, always hovering, always shrieking like gulls at the sight of a morsel of bread.

Her gaze fell on the clutter of papers and trinkets scattered on a side table between the two tall windows. Among them, a letter with a familiar crest caught her eye. She picked it up, squinting to read the neat type: *Special Forces Club, 8 Herbert Crescent, Knightsbridge, London.* It was addressed to *Miss E.M. Nearne, MBE.*

She placed a firm thumb over the three letters after her name, as if wanting to erase them. These letters arriving in her mailbox had caused her plenty of chagrin in recent years. Nosy postmen and even nosier doorbell-ringing reporters. Out with them all, out!

But the letter couldn't help it. It was innocent enough.

"*Mais pas encore.*" She shook her head, a soft remembrance in her voice. The letter was an invitation to a commemoration on 11 November. "What's the use?" she whispered to herself, knowing full well she wouldn't go. She hadn't gone in years. Who would she even know there? Vera Atkins was dead. And so was Odette Hallowes. Yvonne was still around, but Yvonne Baseden was so much stronger than she was. She had coped better than most. Good for her! No, there was no point in going now.

She set the letter down, her hand brushing against a yellowed photograph in a thin silver frame. She picked it up, studying the face of a young woman in a tight-fitting uniform, her mouth set with a don't-get-in-my-way look in her serious eyes beneath neatly arched eyebrows. The beret perched at the perfect angle on her wavy dark hair.

"Marie Louise?" she murmured, the name slipping out instinctively. But something didn't feel right. She frowned, staring harder at the photograph. "No... not Marie Louise. Jacqueline?" The uniform was British. That was wrong—what a fatal mistake that would have been. She should have been wearing a French dress, a hat and gloves. What was she thinking?

Then, slowly, recognition dawned. "Didi..." she whispered, realizing the woman in the photo was her, from long before she ever became Marie Louise Tournier, Jacqueline du Terte, or Rose. Before she was sent to France. When she was just Eileen 'Didi' Nearne, a brand-new member of the First Aid Nursing Yeomanry, FANY.

Her hand trembled slightly as she set the photograph back on the table. Which one was she now—Marie Louise, Jacqueline, Rose, Eileen, or Didi? The lines had blurred over the years, the roles she played overlapping and tangling together, until she wasn't sure where one ended and the other began.

No one called her Didi anymore. That part of her seemed lost, buried under layers of aliases, missions, and memories she could no longer separate. She pressed her lips into a thin line, trying to shake off the momentary confusion, but the unease lingered. The names, the identities—they all belonged to her, yet none of them felt truly her own anymore.

She let out a soft, resigned sigh. "I'm just the cat woman now. A smile played around the set mouth as Whisky padded over to her side, rubbing against her leg.

"Je suis vraiment Didi," she told Whisky. She'd been Didi for a large part of her life, the pet name given to her by her doting family as the youngest of the four Nearne children. And now she was the only one left.

"C'est impossible!" How could it be? Her siblings had never been arrested, tortured, dragged from one concentration camp to the next, starving, shoved around, staggering on their last legs. Yet they'd all died young, and she'd just kept living and living. Eighty-six in March!

It was sheer stubbornness. Being even too stubborn to die. The thought made her laugh out loud, rather shrilly, making Whisky look up at her in surprise. He rose on his four paws, arching his ginger back and yawning wide, his long whiskers quivering in the air.

What had she been doing at the table? She glanced around the room, her eyes landing on the extinguished fireplace. The faint smell of ashes, mingling with the dusty particles whirling around her, settled in her nostrils.

The scent grew stronger as she saw the burning matchstick between her trembling fingers, the quick licking of a flame around the edge of a sheet of paper with scribbled notes, coded messages. The heel of her shoe stamping the burnt remnants on the stone floor, loud voices and fists pounding on the front door, her wireless set precariously balanced on the windowsill of the open window.

Instead of jumping out that window, she had stood stock-still, her fingers jammed into her ears. But the sound never drowned out, the scent of burning suffocating her.

Exhausted by yet another flashback, she sank into her chair, waiting until, with caution, she dared to take her hands from her ears.

"Miaoww." Whisky sat before her, squinting his friendly eyes. Time for my daily portion of Whiskas, cat lady.

"It's one of those days, Whisky," she sighed. "One of those days."

As she fed the cat in her tiny kitchen, her thoughts drifted to Odile, her only niece, the only family member she still had. *Odile est gentille.* So kind, but so far away. All the way over the Alps in Italy. Maybe she would come later in the spring, bringing her Italian husband and those three adorable sons.

"*Je ne veux pas parler de ça,*" she whispered to herself, shaking her head as if to clear away the thoughts she wasn't ready to talk about. Not that Odile ever hinted or probed, but those eyes—the Nearne eyes—held all the unasked questions.

With Whisky happily waving his tail and licking his bowl clean, she moved back to her worn armchair, her apron still tied around her waist from the lunch she had half-eaten earlier. Or was it breakfast? She couldn't remember. It didn't matter. It had been toast with poached eggs and café au lait. *C'est tout.*

She settled into the chair, her hands automatically finding the rosary in her lap, entangled with the medals she had slipped into her apron pocket.

"*Vous voilà,*" she said softly, greeting the familiar objects as if they were old friends. The MBE, with its frayed ribbon now a pinkish grey, and the Croix de Guerre, square and less comforting to touch. She knew every edge, every groove of these medals. They were a part of her, just as the memories they represented.

She began her prayers, the words spilling over her lips with the ease of many decades, as natural as her breath. "*Je vous salue, Marie, pleine de grâce...*"

The prayers had always brought her comfort, a guiding light from the quietest to the most tortured hours of her life. Her fingers moved from the medals to the rosary, each pearly bead a link to her past, each word in her prayer a step closer to peace. *Maman's rosaire.*

A sudden sound outside—a motorcycle roaring past—jolted her from her peaceful state, scattering her whispered words like autumn leaves in the wind.

"*Odile sera ici bientôt*," she reminded herself. She will be here soon. "I have to prepare for her visit. I need to get dressed, have a haircut. Heavens, I've been so neglectful of myself lately." But she remained seated in her chair, the energy to move eluding her.

Her mind drifted to the Special Forces Club invitation again, then dismissed it. No, she wouldn't go. Not this year. Not any year. But perhaps she would write a letter, just to acknowledge she'd received the invitation. Or perhaps not. The world still demanded things from her, but it was getting harder to give *acte de présence*, to put on her social mask.

"Oh Jacqui, you would've known how to deal with these things. You were always so much more accomplished at socializing. I'm quite content...usually just by myself. Just dreaming away a bit, like when I was a child. And being with Whisky, of course."

As her thoughts began to drift again, her eyes flitted to the photograph on the side table. That girl, that uniform, those short, adventurous months as a W/T operator in France. The static crackle of a radio, the tap-tap-tap of Morse code, the strain, the narrow escapes, the secret meetings in shadowy Paris. Those months had held everything she longed for. They had been her glory and her downfall.

"Didi!" She closed her eyes, the sounds of Torquay fading into the background, and she was back in Bourg-sur-Mer. A picnic with her family on the beach in front of their seaside mansion.

Didi, tu es là?

Oui, je suis ici.

YES, I am still here.

PART I

~MIA~ EXETER, MAY 2007

1

FROM SHADOWS TO SPOTLIGHT

Seven weeks later - University of Exeter, May 2007

The Great Hall, officially the hub of Streatham Campus, rose as a pillar of modernist design on the University of Exeter grounds, the impressive glass and steel structure overseeing the students' triumphs and tribulations with an impassive eye.

The sun, warm and moist for springtime, peeked through the tall windows onto the heads of the assembled guests in the hall. A myriad of electric spotlights competed with the natural light from outside, illuminating the front row of graduates in their black caps and gowns.

The stage was set, a solitary glass lectern, one brightly lit spot above it, and a microphone being tested by a skittish technician. A large screen sporting the university's green and black crest was projected on the back wall: "Welcome to the Graduation Geremony of the University of Exeter, Cohort 2006-2007."

Mia Thompson, at 25, waiting to receive her Doctorate in Clinical Psychology, was sitting alone in the front row. Her fingers were laced together tightly in her lap, resting on the black fabric of her graduation gown, a tangible reminder of how far she'd come.

Her senses were attuned to the subtle details—the faint rustle of paper as the graduates on each side of her flipped through their programs, the occasional creak of a chair, a cough, whispered conversations in the row behind. And the faint scent, easily missed amidst the strong perfume of a nearby woman and the linoleum soap used to clean the floors, but to Mia, it was unmistakable. It was the scent of books, of ink, of learning—a smell that always brought her back to that small, cluttered house in Birmingham.

Mia's fingers clenched together even tighter. The memory flashed vividly before her eyes: Miss Elsie Mayhew lying in her study, on the Persian rug amidst her bookcases. Old Doctor Frisk hunched by her side, his eyes filled with concern as he looked up at her. Mia, with schoolbooks in hand, had been ready to burst through the door with news of her algebra triumph—a rare 9 that she couldn't wait to share with her foster mom.

"I'm sorry, Mia. Miss Mayhew has had a heart attack. I'm afraid she's de..."

The rest of his words faded as the image of Miss Elsie on the floor, her legs tucked beneath her in an unnatural manner, and her ashen pallor burned itself into Mia's mind. It was a sight she could never erase—from her eyes, her mind, her heart. Nor the scent of that study with its books and the lovely, white-haired, gentle Miss Elsie. Her last foster parent, almost like a granny, the only good one in a long row. Mia had turned and fled, tears blinding her as she ran and ran, away from Solihull, away from Birmingham.

Mia blinked, easing herself back to the present in the Great Hall with a steadying breath. *Miss Elsie,* she smiled inwardly, *you've come to be with me on this special day. It's thanks to you I'm here. You believed in me. And I'm still sorry I ran away. I was so afraid to go back to one of those horrid houses again. I just couldn't do it, you see.*

The painful memory lingered, as it always would, but it no longer had the power to drag Mia down into despair. Instead, she felt a deep sense of pride and gratitude. She had been fortunate enough to experience the adept tutoring and loving care of the retired schoolteacher for two full years at the tender age of fifteen.

The hum of voices around her brought Mia fully back to the present, and she refocused on the stage. Her moment of triumph was fast approaching. She'd better be fully prepared to savor every second of it.

SITTING STRAIGHT UP in her chair, the stiletto heels of her new Jimmy Choos planted firmly on the linoleum floor, Mia waited to be called forward by the broad, blond, bespectacled professor who had taken her stance behind the lectern.

"Please join me here on stage, our first graduate, Mia Elaine Thompson," came the clear, confident voice of Dr. Kirsten Ringdal. "Dear assembled, students, families and university staff, I ask your applause for the first psychology doctorate student, Mia Elaine Thompson."

Mia stood, smoothing her black gown with hands that weren't completely steady, nor sweat-free. Once on her feet, her slender frame—evidence of years spent with little more than the bare essentials—seemed to gather strength. Her long, dark hair, tied neatly back under her graduation cap, framed her delicate face, which carried a quiet radiance, much like that of a princess stepping into the spotlight.

As she made her way toward the stage, her tempered charm and graceful movements held the room's attention. The clear sparkle of her eyes briefly met those of her colleagues from Hope Haven

Community Health, seated together near the front. Alexandra Torres, her right-hand at the center, gave her an encouraging nod, while the others smiled and clapped with all their might. The presence of her colleagues was a reminder of the professional life she had built, of the lives she had touched, and of the team that stood behind her.

The spotlight above the lectern seemed to grow brighter as she approached, each step bringing her closer to the light. She was no longer a foster child on the run, hungry, with a torn Oxfam dress and grime under her fingernails. She was a woman who had carved out her place in the world, leading a health center that was already making a difference, with a bank account, a car, and a lease on her new flat.

Dr. Ringdal's smile was so appraising it made Mia walk even straighter. Pride and genuine pleasure brimmed from the fair Scandinavian face of her professor and mentor. Mia took her place beside her, her gaze briefly sweeping the audience—a blur of faces, all focused on her. She took a deep breath, folded her hands behind her back, and listened.

"Today, we celebrate the accomplishments of all our Clinical Psychology graduates, but it is a special honor to have Mia Thompson next to me here first. Mia is the only student in the 2006-2007 cohort to graduate *summa cum laude*, not only a rare accomplishment but also a testament to her extraordinary drive and excellence," Dr. Ringdal began, gripping Mia's clammy hand encouragingly. "Her journey is truly remarkable. From an extremely challenging childhood, Mia faced obstacles that would have derailed most. Yet, she not only survived but ultimately thrived, proving the incredible resilience of the human spirit if tested.

"It is an understatement to say Mia's early years were marked by hardship. Found as a baby on Thompson Road in Birmingham, her last name indicating the place she was discovered, while her first names were derived from the two caring nurses who looked after her in hospital. Despite a turbulent upbringing and the loss of her last foster parent, Miss Elsie Mayhew, Mia's determination led her to this podium today. Her story is a powerful reminder that no matter how difficult a person's past may be, they can achieve extraordinary things.

"As future psychologists, I urge you to approach your profession with an open mind. Remember that every individual, regardless of their history, may have hidden potential. Never underestimate the strength and resilience of the human spirit."

Dr. Ringdal paused, letting her words sink in. "Mia, you gave me permission to share these details about your background, not to seek sympathy, but to inspire your fellow graduates. Your achievements extend beyond academics—they reflect remarkable fortitude and a commitment to making a difference. Let us honor Mia not only for her *summa cum laude* distinction for her dissertation, *Echoes of Unspoken Valor: Assessing and Treating PTSD in the Elderly – A Study from Torbay*, but also for her dedication to helping others through Hope Haven Community Health, a care center she founded at the age of 23. The once nameless Mia Thompson stands as an example for us all. She is proof that hard work and passion can achieve the extraordinary."

A round of applause erupted from the audience as Dr. Ringdal invited Mia to deliver her speech. She approached the lectern, her chest tight with a flurry of emotions, and cleared her throat.

"Thank you, Professor Ringdal, for those kind words," Mia said, her mellifluous voice—gentle yet tinged with gravity—cutting through the applause. "I am deeply honored to be here today and to share this moment with all of you. It's true, my journey has been rather unconventional, but if it's taught me one thing, it's to never give up. We often hear the phrase 'never give up' from those who have never known real hardship. From my own experience, I know that a power you didn't know you possessed awakens when you truly hit rock bottom. It's in those moments your true colors begin to shine through. You either give up or you survive.

"I believe I was born a psychologist. Despite everything I went through, I remained always extremely curious about the workings of the human psyche. My search to understand the effects of extreme pressure and hardship on minds and souls became my secret study long before I knew it would lead to a rewarding career. My own experiences have reinforced the open perspective Professor Ringdal reminded us of. Now, as a Doctor of Clinical Psychology I can't wait to further develop my skills at the intersection of mental illness and healing. I am committed to helping people understand that no matter where you started in life or how you lost your way, what matters most is where you choose to go from here. I want to thank all my professors and fellow students, my team at Hope Heaven Community Health, and especially my mentor, Professor Ringdal, for her unwavering support. Thank you to everyone who has supported me through the long process of completing my dissertation.

With that, Mia signed her diploma, her hand steady despite the rush of emotions. Dr. Ringdal added her firm signature beneath the University of Exeter crest, and a soft murmur of admiration rippled through the audience. Mia stood tall, rejoicing in the gravity of the moment.

"It is with great pride that I award you your Doctorate in Clinical Psychology. Congratulations, Dr. Thompson." Dr. Ringdal shook Mia's hand, giving it an extra, reassuring squeeze.

The applause that followed was thunderous, reverberating through the high-ceilinged hall. Mia felt herself buoyed by the swell of acclamation, a wave of pride and joy lifting her ever higher. The roar of approval enveloped her like a warm embrace, a culmination of years of hard work and stick-to-itiveness.

The moment Dr. Ringdal handed her the diploma, Mia thought her heart would burst with emotion.

Turning to leave the stage, her gaze swept over the audience. Amidst the sea of familiar faces, her eyes fell on a towering figure in the back row—a man with a mop of unruly strawberry-blond hair and an air of casual confidence. He was staring at her with an intense, almost unsettling gaze. She recognized him as Sebastian Stone, the gossip columnist for the Torbay Weekly, known for his nickname "Slick Sebas." *What does he care about a graduation ceremony in Exeter?*

Mia's curiosity sparked for a brief moment, but she quickly shook off the distraction. This was her moment, and she was determined to embrace it fully. Waving her diploma triumphantly, she returned to the audience, her heart brimming with the thrill of her achievement.

2

THE NOSY REPORTER

The reception after the graduation ceremony flowed seamlessly from the Great Hall to the sprawling green lawns outside. The late afternoon sun, still warm and inviting, cast a golden ray of light over the festivities, while billowing white clouds drifted lazily in the distance.

A large marquee, draped in white with a scalloped edge, added an air of sophistication to the occasion. Under its billowing fabric, high tables covered in white cloths and adorned with delicate flower arrangements were strategically placed. At the far end, a long table showcased an irresistible spread of finger foods and beverages.

In the midst of the lively celebration, around fifty graduates, still adorned in their black caps and gowns, gathered for their moment of photographic glory. The University media director, wielding a camera almost as large as her booming voice, directed the scene with an authoritative flair. "Everyone say 'cheese'!" she announced, and though posing wasn't a natural skill for many psychologists, they rose to the occasion with broad smiles and eager faces.

"Hold that pose! On the count of three, toss your caps!" she instructed. "One... two... three!"

At her signal, a jubilant roar erupted as a flurry of black caps soared into the sky, creating a spectacle as if a flock of blackbirds was taking flight. The moment marked not just the end of their academic journey, but the exhilarating start of their professional careers.

Minutes later, Mia reentered the pavilion, having discarded the graduation gown and now in a simple yet elegant Jill Sander dress that complemented her understated grace. She joined her team near the entrance, their presence adding a warm glow to her special day. Their support made this celebration even more memorable.

The group quickly formed a lively circle around her, their colorfully-wrapped presents stacked neatly on a nearby table. After exchanging heartfelt kisses and hugs, Alexandra, Mia's steadfast ally at Hope Haven Community Health, raised her champagne glass with a beaming smile. "Ronald, be a darling and grab our new doctor a glass of non-alcoholic fizzies. We need to clink glasses with her!"

Alex's deep brown eyes sparkled with admiration. "If I had even a fraction of your brilliance and drive, Doctor Thompson, I'd be over the moon. Instead, I'm just thrilled to call you my friend."

Linking her arm with Mia's, Alex drew her into the circle of camaraderie. Laughter and joyous banter filled the air, celebrating not just Mia's achievement but the close-knit bond among them.

Earlier that afternoon, Mia had driven the minibus, filled with her team, the 25 miles from Torquay to Exeter. Despite their protests, she insisted. "You all know I don't drink, so it's no sacrifice for me. Enjoy what you can on the university's tab."

Ronald, ever shy with his head slightly bowed, approached Mia with a glass of Appletiser. The way Mia's 'handyman' carried himself spoke of his past struggles and trauma, and though his features were smooth, his skittish behavior showed the effects of his autism, though today his eyes radiated with a fierce loyalty and affection for Mia.

"Will this do, Mi? The waiter said it's non-alcoholic," Ronald, asked in a timid voice.

Mia took the glass from him with a wide, grateful smile. "Perfect, Ronnie. I'm so glad I talked you into coming today. You know your presence means the world to me."

Their glasses clinked in a celebratory chime. Ronald's face brightened, though a sudden twitch distorted his features. "You're the best, Mi!"

As their eyes met over the glasses, Mia was acutely aware of their past. They'd met in the fall of 1996 when she was fifteen and Ronald was just ten—a skinny boy in tattered clothes, too afraid to let her near him. His body was bruised, his front tooth missing, and he had been as frightened as a cornered deer.

Mia had reached out to him by sharing fries she'd scavenged from a bin. They had bonded over half-eaten hamburgers and unfinished milkshakes, finding solace and survival beneath Princess Pier. Ronald had become her little brother of the street, a sibling by choice, cherished as if by blood. Mia had always been his shield, protecting him from the harshness of their reality. It had been Mi and Ronnie against the world.

I love you, her eyes communicated over the rim of her glass, and he nodded, looking around him with a little more confidence in this unfamiliar world of academia and achievement with a hesitant curiosity.

As the celebration continued, Mia's attention was drawn to the tall figure of Sebastian Stone weaving through the crowd with his distinctive swagger. Heads turned, particularly those of the female students, as the gossip columnist from the Torbay Weekly made his way through the gathering. With his towering Celtic presence and charismatic aura, he was impossible to ignore.

"If it isn't Slick Sebas making his grand entrance," Alex murmured into Mia's ear, her words slightly slurred from a tad too much champagne. "Do you want me to give him the ol' one-two and steer him away if he heads your way?"

Mia chuckled. "Oh, Alex, I have nothing for him. I'm guessing his latest fling is one of the freshers here or maybe there's a scandal brewing. He probably smells an opportunity for gossip."

Alex's face darkened as she glanced nervously at the approaching reporter. "He's definitely heading this way."

"Let him come," Mia said with a touch of firmness. "I've dealt with worse cases than our local gossip columnist."

"Just be careful. Rumor has it, his eye has been roving again since Nathalia Rostova ditched him," Alex warned.

"As if 'not being free' ever stopped Sebastian Stone from making a pass," Mia muttered under her breath, rolling her eyes.

As the local Romeo made his way to their table, Alex draped herself protectively over Mia's shoulder, casting a sidelong glare at the approaching figure. Sebastian Stone's entrance was anything but subtle; his aura had the magnetic pull of a man who knew how to work a crowd and the flamboyance of someone who thrived on attention.

"Miss Thompson, may I steal you away for just a moment?" Sebastian flashed a smile that could charm the most stoic heart, his hand extended with a tattoo of an eternity sign between his thumb and index finger. "Sebastian Stone, from the Torbay Weekly. As you most likely know."

Mia shook his hand firmly, feeling an unexpected warmth rather than the slickness she had anticipated. "I could say I'm flattered," she replied with a cool composure, "but I'm really enjoying my time here with my special crew. I doubt my recent Doctorate in Clinical

Psychology would capture the interest of your... more mundane readers."

"She doesn't want you, Sebas. Mia's a doctor now," Alex sputtered, giving the nosy reporter another glaring look that left nothing to the imagination. Mia couldn't help but inwardly smile. Even Alexandra Torres, with her sanguine Spanish features, had once fallen for the dashing columnist, only to be exchanged for a tall brunette weeks later.

Ignoring Alex's protective stance, Sebastian pushed on, "Oh, but Miss Thompson, you're quite mistaken. Your rags-to-riches success story is exactly the kind of scoop I'm after. My readers will lap it up like a cat with a bowl of cream."

"I see." Mia raised a distinctive eyebrow, meeting his gaze directly. She noticed a flicker of hesitation in his eyes, as if he didn't fully believe his own pitch. Mia was aware of some of the Stones' backstory—his father's return from the war in Afghanistan and the ensuing family turmoil. Yet, she knew she had to remain firm with this man.

"So, let me get this straight: you're asking me to help you exploit my life story for the benefit of your column? I don't think so, Mr. Stone. Good day to you."

Mia turned her back on him with deliberate finality, while Alex gave him a parting gesture that was more cheeky than rude.

"You're misunderstanding me, Miss Thompson." Sebastian Stone's voice cut through the buzz of the marquee. "I'm genuinely impressed by your achievements. If you grant me an interview, I'll ensure Hope Haven Community Health gets prominent coverage in my column. It could lead to a wave of donations."

Mia's smile faltered as she turned back to face him. Despite appreciating persistence, she had little patience for invasive reporters. Sebastian's reputation as a gossip columnist and womanizer was well-earned.

"Have I not made myself clear enough? I'm not interested," she said, her voice sharp. The street-girl side of her surfaced, her gaze as resolute as a boxer ready to stare down an opponent. But Sebastian showed to be a worthy opponent.

He leaned in, lowering his voice as if sharing a secret. One of his flirting tactics, no doubt. "Actually, aside from the interview, I thought you might be intrigued by something I've uncovered about one of your clients—Miss Eileen Nearne. I've found some rather compelling details about the reclusive pensioner by the seafront."

Mia's hands clenched into fists as anger flared within her. *How dare he!* Miss Nearne was one of her new clients after the Department for Work and Pensions had referred her case to Hope Haven. Mia hadn't met the elderly woman yet, but she'd been briefed about her fragility and reclusiveness. The thought of Sebastian prying into Miss Nearne's life was unacceptable.

"Mr. Stone," Mia said slowly, her voice leaving no space for argument. "I understand you're doing your job and I'm doing mine. But let me warn you—if you make even one step toward exploiting Miss Nearne with your pointy pen, I will report you for exploitation of a vulnerable citizen."

Sebastian raised an eyebrow in mock surprise. "You're quite adamant, Miss Thompson. I must say, I didn't expect such a strong reaction."

Mia took a deep breath, her eyes briefly scanning the surroundings—the cheerful chatter of graduates, the clinking of glasses, and the festive atmosphere under the marquee. The contrast between the joyous scene and the gravity of their conversation only strengthened her resolve.

"I'm here to celebrate today," she said with careful politeness despite her firm stance. "I now want to return to my guests. I wish you good luck with finding enough fluff for your stories, Mr. Stone."

"I think you'll want to know what I found about Miss Nearne," he said, lowering his voice. "I'm not the fool you take me for. I promise I won't knock on her door, but I think you'll be intrigued by what I found."

"You're not making much sense to me, Mr. Stone. So, this request for a meeting between you and me is about Miss Nearne and not about an interview with me?" Mia remained cautious.

He gave her the sad puppy look, "I'd love the interview, but I'll settle for discussing Miss Nearne."

"I'll see if I can find time in my busy schedule," she replied, still trying to keep him at bay.

Sebastian's smile, a mix of roguish charm and genuine sweetness, had a surprising effect. It was disarming, but not enough to make Mia waver. "Thank you," he said, pressing his business card into her hand and briefly folding his fingers around hers. It felt rather intimate but not unwelcome.

"Don't count on it," Mia called after him. But she knew that when it came to serving her clients, she would even meet with someone like Slick Sebas.

As she returned to her friends, the unusual undertone of their conversation lingered. Mia couldn't shake the feeling there was more to Sebastian Stone than met the eye. And Eileen Nearne was now firmly on her radar.

3

A CLASH OF INTENTIONS

A few days later - Torquay, early June 2007

The Torbay Weekly's office was housed in a drab, 1950s building on Windsor Road, just a few streets away from Mia's beloved Hope Haven Community Health on Lydwell Road. The building exuded a tired, post-war grayness—square, functional, and frankly an eyesore, ready to be replaced by a modern colossus of steel and glass.

Mia found the front door propped open and let herself into the tiled hallway with chipped paint and crumbling plaster. Office doors on either side were ajar, bustling with activity: clattering keyboards, telephones ringing non-stop, and the low hum of conversations. Even the receptionist seemed perpetually in motion, but she paused her relentless typing to greet Mia.

The young woman's eyes widened slightly and Mia caught the recognition in her gaze. It made her cringe—a reaction she'd come to expect over the past few days from strangers who had seen the front-page article Sebastian had written about her graduation. The piece had been broadly appreciative, but Mia would have preferred to remain out of the spotlight and not see herself splashed across a weekly with such a dubious reputation.

"Ah, Miss Thompson, you must be here for Sebas? Let me buzz his office to see if he's in."

"Please do. I have an appointment, so I suppose he's..."

"Miss Thompson, glad you're here." Sebastian himself appeared, descending the stairs with a commanding presence. His casual, gray suit accentuated his tall, broad frame, while his light blue shirt, slightly rumpled, suggested a laid-back demeanor. His pale ginger hair was deliberately tousled, as if he had just rolled out of bed looking amazing.

"I'll take it from here, Monique," he said, flashing an irresistible smile at the receptionist, who blushed and quickly returned to her computer.

"Come on up," Sebastian continued, gesturing broadly for Mia to lead the way. Dressed in a tailored navy-blue suit with a figure-hugging skirt that fell just above the knee, Mia hesitated for a moment but then stepped ahead of him with confidence.

Let him look at my legs all he wants. He'll get his due from me in a minute.

"Welcome to my pen-pusher domain." Sebastian swept open his office door with a flourish but immediately tripped over a stack of files cluttering the floor. "Oops, I shouldn't have fired the cleaning lady," he quipped, not without a degree of self-deprecation.

Mia's gaze swept the room from the doorway, with a mix of disapproval and curiosity. The office was a chaotic gallery of framed Torbay Weekly covers, each flaunting sensational headlines and exaggerated photographs. Sebastian's grinning face appeared frequently alongside local celebrities, and a row of rugby trophies gleamed under the dull fluorescent lighting. A particularly striking photo of him leaning nonchalantly against his 1980 Red Triumph

Spitfire caught her eye, but she quickly dismissed it. This was a man who thrived on attention and reveled in the trappings of his own notoriety.

The room smelled of stale coffee and old paper, a backdrop to the disarray that sprawled across the carpet—newspapers and ring binders creating a labyrinth on the floor. Sebastian navigated the mess with practiced ease, finally landing in his place behind a cluttered desk, his casual stance combined with his signature hint of arrogance.

"Why did you find it necessary to publish a front page with my story?" Mia demanded, her eyes locking onto his with an intensity that seemed to pierce through the haze of his nonchalance. Her question hung in the air like a challenge, demanding an explanation.

Sebastian casually popped a piece of chewing gum into his mouth, the smacking sound punctuating his response. "I thought I wrote nothing that would offend you. I didn't even mention the troubled youth—just your degree and what you're doing for the Torbay community with your health center. What's wrong with that?" He offered her the gum package with a disarming smile. Mia declined with a curt shake of her head.

"I thought we had a deal," she said, her tone carrying a note of frustration.

"It wasn't an interview. It was... purely informational. Newsworthy for our readers."

"Sebastian Stone, if I'm not mistaken, you're the gossip columnist for the Torbay Weekly and not a news reporter. Why did you do this?"

Surprise and amusement flashed in his eyes as he faced her frustration with the article, which he clearly believed was harmless. "Miss Thompson, if I offer you a very bad tasting cup of office coffee and you agree to sit down, I'll explain everything."

His offer came with the usual dose of his charm, but Mia remained guarded. As she moved to perch on a chair amidst the chaos, her senses were assaulted by the disorder surrounding her in a way that it had not affected her when she was standing in the doorway. The room was a jumble of clutter and disarray, very different from the neatly organized workspace she was used to.

Having spent years navigating through the clutter of the streets, Mia had developed a keen intolerance for any form of chaos, which seemed almost to press in on her now that she was actually in Sebastian's disorganised office.

He seemed to pick up on the oppressive effect his office had on Mia.

"I should have tidied up before you arrived. My apologies. Believe it or not, I've been working on a PhD lately—hence the research mess. I don't usually invite people here; I prefer to meet them on location. But I had a hunch you wouldn't want me traipsing through Hope Haven."

His tone shifted as he fumbled with a small coffee machine on a side table, which sputtered and gurgled before he muttered a frustrated curse, realizing it had run out of water. "Seems I can't even manage to make bad coffee without making a mess."

Mia, still processing this unexpected tidbit about his PhD, raised an eyebrow. "You know what? Just get me a glass of water. Forget the coffee."

A flash of almost puppy-like joy crossed his lively face. "Plain or fizzy? We have one of those fancy water coolers downstairs."

"Plain, please," she said, amused by his enthusiasm over a water cooler.

"Plain it is!" Sebastian practically bounced towards the door. "I'll be back in a sec with your choice of the finest, most ordinary water!"

Returning within moments, he handed Mia a tall glass of water. It was cool and smooth against her fingers. He then dashed around his desk, flinging his jacket over the back of his leather office chair before sinking into it once again. The chair groaned under his tall frame.

Mia took a sip of the water and found it to be as plain as expected, but the man opposite her was undeniably a presence. His rugby trophies spoke to a life of physical achievement, and despite the clutter, she could see the effort behind his successes.

"So, about the article?" she prompted, cutting to the chase.

Sebastian leaned forward, his eyes the color of Tor Bay on a summer's day. "Ah, the article. It was meant solely for your benefit, Miss Thompson. I figured if I wrote a piece about you, you'd feel obliged to come and talk about Miss Nearne." He paused, a grin playing on his lips. "Our editor-in-chief, Charles Brock, was gracious enough to give it the front page. I didn't mention our meeting to him; he just thought it was a good story. And it was—credit where it's due."

Mia's gaze hardened. "In your view, perhaps. It makes me part of your dubious hall of fame, which is not my desire."

"It did bring you here, didn't it?" Sebastian countered, his tone light but his eyes sharp.

Mia leaned forward slightly. "Yes, so what did you uncover about Miss Nearne that you wanted to share?"

Sebastian set his glass down and leaned back, as if savoring the moment. "Ah, Miss Nearne. Quite the enigma, isn't she?"

Mia frowned. "I wouldn't know. You're the one who's supposed to tell me."

Sebastian raised an eyebrow. "Aha, so you really don't know?"

Mia's voice turned cool and professional. "I generally don't discuss my clients with... uh, reporters." She almost added "shady" but thought better of it.

Sebastian's demeanor shifted slightly. He fell quiet, and Mia, with her keen psychologist's intuition, sensed a crack in his confident façade. He seemed more genuine, his voice taking on a more authentic tone.

"I've been doing a bit of digging," he began, "and discovered that Miss Nearne was a secret agent during World War II. Quite the fascinating past for the reclusive old lady."

Mia's eyes widened slightly, but she quickly regained her composure. "And why are you interested in her? She doesn't seem like typical material for your sensational columns."

Sebastian's expression turned thoughtful. "Well, you've got me there. Yes, the gutter press journalist, that's me. But something's gotta pay the bills, so I write what sells."

"I'm not here to judge your profession," Mia said calmly, "but as I've told you before, I'm not letting you get close to Miss Nearne through Hope Haven."

At that moment, the phone on Sebastian's desk rang with an insistent jangle. He shot her an apologetic glance and picked it up. "Stone here. I'm busy at the moment, can't talk," he said, his voice irritated by the interruption. He hung up quickly and turned back to Mia, "Sorry about that. So, where were we?"

"Convenient interruption, huh? We were where I told you Miss Nearne is not a topic for your column."

"Who said I wanted to write about her in my columns?" Sebastian replied, his tone unexpectedly earnest. "I'm actually working on a PhD in research journalism at Leeds Trinity. Unfortunately, I've had to put that on hold due to... uh... family reasons. But serious journalism is still my passion. In the meantime, I still have to pay the bills, though."

"Everyone has to pay their bills, but that doesn't mean you do it by throwing people's private lives out on the street," Mia shot back.

"Listen, I think Miss Nearne's story deserves to be told. I hope you can help me do that in a way that honors her legacy." Sebastian's tone was serious, his sincerity evident.

"You know it's nearly impossible to even approach her, let alone make her talk?" The words escaped Mia before she could stop them, and she instantly regretted them. But Sebastian's face lit up with a broad smile, as if her comment had sparked an idea.

"Does that mean you want to work with me?" His eagerness was almost disarming.

"There's nothing to work on, Mr. Stone. The chance Miss Nearne will open up to anyone is smaller than the point of a fine needle."

"I'm not so sure. I've been watching that documentary she did with the BBC in 1997. She did talk then, albeit in French under her codename Rose and wearing a wig."

"I have no clue what you're talking about," Mia said, trying to mask her surprise.

"I have a recording of that interview. If you'd like, you could come over to my place, and we could watch it together. Pizza and drinks included."

Mia couldn't help but laugh despite herself. "I don't think so, Mr. Stone. With your reputation around here, I'd become the town's next topic of gossip, and not in a way I'd appreciate. Thanks, but no."

Sebastian didn't seem dismayed. "Would you feel more comfortable if I gave you the recording?"

"Would you do that?" Mia asked, trying to gauge his sincerity.

"Sure. On one condition."

"And what would that be?" Mia braced herself for another outrageous request.

Sebastian's eyes twinkled with mischief. "You let me interview you. Just a short one—no deep secrets, I promise. I want to prove that I can be a respectable journalist, not just the local gossip columnist. What do you say?"

Mia considered his proposal for a moment. It was a fair trade if she could trust him to keep it straightforward. "Alright, Mr. Stone. You've got yourself a deal."

"So, like now?" Sebastian's face lit up with that familiar happy-puppy look.

Mia checked her watch. "I've got another fifteen minutes. Can you manage that?"

"Sure thing! Are you ready?" He gestured towards a pair of armchairs amid the clutter. His tone was surprisingly respectful, acknowledging the formality of their interaction.

"Yes," Mia replied, navigating from her perch to one of the armchairs.

Sebastian sat across from her, setting up a small recording device. His eyes sparkled with eagerness. "I hope you're comfortable with this setup. I know it's not exactly a high-end studio, but it's what I've got."

Mia couldn't suppress a hint of amusement. "It's fine. Let's just get this over with."

Sebastian nodded, shifting to a more professional tone. "Alright, let's dive in. I promise to keep it straightforward."

As he recorded and scribbled on his notepad, Mia found herself softening. His respectful, earnest approach reminded her of her own professional sessions. The initial reservations she'd had about him began to melt away.

When the interview concluded, Sebastian leaned back with a look of relief. "Thank you for doing this, Miss Thompson. I really appreciate it."

Mia smiled. "You're welcome, Mr. Stone. I'm glad we could find common ground. You can call me Mia."

His handsome, open face brightened even further. "Oh, that's a relief. The 'Miss Thompson' and 'Mr. Stone' thing was starting to drive me bonkers."

"Informal it is then," Mia said. "I'm looking forward to the recording of the documentary."

"Not the interview?" He joked.

"That as well."

"I'll drop both off at your center, Mia. And thanks for being patient with me. You must be quite a psychologist to stick it out for almost an hour."

Mia left Sebastian's office with a half-smile. There had been a subtle shift in their dynamic. Never in her wildest dreams had she imagined Slick Sebas as someone with whom she could feel a budding, albeit cautious, camaraderie. Better not tell Alex.

4

DOORWAY INTO THE PAST

Ten weeks later - Torquay, August 2007

Seeing no other way to contact Eileen Nearne, as she hadn't responded to letters or visits to her door, Mia tried her luck with the nuns of a small, peaceful church community where Eileen still attended Mass on Sundays.

The scent of incense hung in the air as Mia entered the little parish office, the flickering candlelight casting soft shadows along the walls. It was a humble space, with a single wooden desk, a few chairs, and shelves filled with books with golden bindings and religious figurines. Mia's eyes fell on a worn crucifix hanging on the wall, its dark wood polished by years of reverent touches.

Sitting behind the desk was Head Sister Damian, an elderly nun, her small figure swathed in a black and white habit. The thick glasses balanced on the edge of her nose seemed to magnify her kind but sharp eyes. Around her neck hung a simple wooden crucifix, which she absently touched as she spoke.

"So, dearie, what brings you here?" Sister Damian asked, her voice light and warm, like her sparrow-like figure. The thin, white fingers never left the crucifix. "And don't think I don't know who you are. I was the one who regularly left hot cocoa and a bun for you and that ratty little boy under Princess Pier. My-oh-my, I still can't get over it—how well you turned out, dearie. And a PhD now! I read it in the *Torbay Weekly*."

Mia blinked in surprise. "Was that you? Oh, Sister Damian, that is so kind. Ronnie and I had no idea. Honestly, I was always a bit suspicious. I used to tell Ronnie to let me taste everything first because I was afraid someone was trying to poison us!" she laughed softly.

Sister Damian chuckled. "It was a trifle, dearie. I'm glad it gave you a spark of light. But that's not what brings you here, is it?"

Mia shook her head, her professional purpose pulling her focus back. "I'm here on behalf of one of my clients. I believe you know her—Miss Eileen Nearne."

"Of course, I know Eileen, with her funny French accent. What about her?"

"The Department for Work and Pensions contacted me about some overdue paperwork for her pension, because she never responded to them. As my center focuses on elderly care, they turned to me, but I haven't had much luck contacting her either. Then someone told me Miss Nearne still attends Mass on Sundays, so I thought you might be able to help."

Sister Damian nodded with a knowing smile. "Yes, she's ever so punctual when it comes to hearing the Word of the Lord our Shepherd. Bless her heart. But opening the door to anyone? No. No chance. But I wouldn't know about neglecting her mail. There's nothing wrong with her mind. Do you think they'll cut her pension? That would be terrible. I don't think she has many funds, and she once told me the only family she has is a niece in Italy."

Mia hesitated, carefully choosing her words. "No, Sister, I'll make sure her pension isn't cut. But apart from that, I'm concerned about Miss Nearne's emotional wellbeing. I specialize in helping people who've faced trauma."

Sister Damian's brow furrowed as she clutched her crucifix a little tighter. "Trauma, dearie? Eileen? She has her faith, and that's a mighty strong anchor. The Lord is her Guide, and I believe she's held by His grace."

Mia offered a gentle smile, mindful not to challenge the nun's deep conviction. "Faith can be a powerful source of strength," she said, "and I respect that. Sometimes, though, people who've been through hardship benefit from extra care."

Sister Damian's face softened, though her fingers still rested on the crucifix. "I don't know if Eileen needs that kind of help. Her faith has carried her through much more than you or I can imagine. But she is a private soul, and I wouldn't be surprised if she struggles in ways even her faith doesn't entirely soothe."

Mia nodded, sensing the delicate balance. "Perhaps that's why she's able to come to Mass—to find that comfort in her community."

Sister Damian's face brightened as if a light was switched on. "Oh yes, being among others in worship does seem to help her. She still keeps to herself in many ways, but I think she feels safe here. And she still does her own shopping and walks along the beach sometimes. She's friendly with neighbors, though cautious. We can't be too careful these days."

"That's true," Mia agreed. "So, you've known her a long time?"

"Oh, right from when she moved here in 1991."

"And did you ever visit her house?"

The nun fixed Mia with her magnified eyes but didn't budge. "No, and I've never insisted. Once, after Mass, I offered to drive her home in a downpour, but she asked me to let her out at the corner of the street. She didn't want me, even me, to know exactly which flat she's in."

Mia absorbed this little anecdote and wondered if Sister Damian would comment on the peculiarity of it, but she didn't. To Mia, it made clear that Eileen's isolation was more than just self-protection —it was deeply ingrained. From her professional standpoint, it told her that gaining Eileen's trust would take considerable time. Faith might be a source of strength, but Mia suspected there were wounds that required more than belief to heal.

After a thoughtful pause, the small nun leaned forward, letting go of the crucifix and placing her hand gently over Mia's. "I'll ask Eileen about her pension for you, dearie," she promised. "I can't guarantee she'll listen, but I'll do my best."

With that, she reached for a small brass bell sitting on her desk and gave it a soft ring. The gentle chime echoed in the candle-lit office, the scent of incense and beeswax lingering in the air. A younger nun entered quietly, her eyes lowered in humility.

Sister Damian whispered something in her ear, and the younger nun quickly slipped out. A few moments later, she returned with two freshly baked buns nestled in a cloth napkin.

With a playful wink, Sister Damian slid the paper and buns toward Mia. "These are for you. I might not be able to offer hot cocoa like in the old days, but I can still afford a bun or two," she said with a knowing smile. "You and that ratty boy of yours—Ronnie, wasn't it? Yes. I expect you could still share these over lunch."

Mia felt a warmth spread through her chest. Of course, sharp-eyed Sister Damian even knew Ronnie MacDowell worked at Hope Haven now. "Thank you, Sister, that's so kind. I'll have to fight Ronnie for these, or he'll eat both. At least I don't have to taste-test them first anymore!"

Sister Damian chuckled. "Ah, well, trust is earned, isn't it? May the Sweet Lord bless you and hold you safe all the days of your life, dearie."

Mia left the church with the faint scent of incense still in her nostrils and Sister Damian's kindness warming her heart.

A week later, true to her word, the nun called her with a message. "Eileen's worried," Sister Damian explained over the phone. "She didn't get her pension check in the mail this week. She'll meet you on Tuesday at 10:00 a.m, 2 Lisburne Crescent. Knock, and she'll open the door for you. I've told her all about you, dearie—so don't worry, you're not a stranger anymore."

It was Tuesday, 10:00 a.m. on the dot when Mia stood in front of Eileen Nearne's door on the first floor of a white apartment building, just a stone's throw from the seaside. Her index finger hovered for a moment over the simple doorbell, a knot of tension forming in her stomach. Then she remembered not to ring but to knock. Would she? Why would she succeed in getting inside Eileen Nearne's home when nobody else had? The hallway felt almost like that of a hotel, practical with wall-to-wall carpeting and the same brown doors spaced evenly apart.

She knocked firmly, but not aggressively. The building was wrapped in silence, as if even the stuccoed walls held secrets at bay. There was a brief pause, just long enough for her mind to race with questions. Would Eileen trust her? Would she even open the door? Mia had met countless hesitant clients before, but something about this meeting felt different—like she was stepping into a moment far more delicate than usual.

The door creaked open just a crack, enough for Mia to see the silhouette of an elderly figure with a halo of white hair. Eileen's face was partially obscured by the dim light inside, but her sharp blue eyes were unmistakable, scrutinizing Mia with quiet intensity.

"Miss Nearne?" Mia asked gently, her voice carrying even more of the careful professionalism she was trained to use. "I'm Mia

Thompson. We spoke through Sister Damian." *Don't mention 'doctor' or she might slam the door in your face.*

For a long moment, there was no answer, just the soft whispers of silence in the hallway. Then, without a word, the door opened a little wider, enough for Mia to see Eileen more clearly. She was taller than Mia had imagined, her white hair reaching her shoulders, still thick and wavy. Her face was surprisingly smooth for her age, and there was a hint of regal posture—poised yet cautious. She didn't smile, but the piercing look mellowed just slightly, enough to suggest she hadn't rejected the outreach—yet.

"You're here about my pension," Eileen said, her voice remarkably clear, with a beautiful, singsong French accent. She didn't phrase it as a question.

"Yes, I'm Mia Thompson from Hope Haven Community Health. I came to see if I could help—if that's alright with you." Though Mia's mind was already moving beyond the paperwork, she sensed this was a crucial moment, one where she needed to choose her words ever so carefully.

Eileen's grip on the door tightened, but she didn't retreat. "Help," she repeated, as if testing the word on her tongue. There was something unspoken in her tone—a mixture of hope and wariness.

Mia waited, resisting the urge to push. Trust was earned, as Sister Damian had said, and she was willing to wait for the door to open farther. Finally, Eileen stepped back, allowing Mia to cross the threshold into the dimly lit flat.

It was a moment Mia treasured, but also one that saddened her. She knew Eileen had let her in because of the money she needed to keep coming—not because she truly wanted help.

The air inside was still, the scent of old wooden furniture and faint perfume lingering, and as Mia stepped inside, she couldn't shake the feeling that she was stepping into the past as much as she was into Eileen Nearne's world.

5

EARNING THE TRUST

"Sit," Eileen ordered, her voice brisk but not unkind. "I'll see if I can find the correspondence from the Pension people, but it might take me a while. These people send so many letters and expect you to answer yesterday. After a while, I couldn't figure out which one was the last, and their dates are all over the place. But then I didn't get my money last week—or the week before. That's not good, you know. One must eat. One must always eat."

With that, she scurried away, her worn velvet slippers shuffling softly across the wooden floor, a large ginger cat padding silently behind her like a shadow. The sliding door to the back room rattled slightly as she disappeared into the dim space beyond.

Mia let out a quiet breath, the tension from Eileen's tentative reception ebbing away, and took the moment to absorb her surroundings with both curiosity and a trained eye. Though the flat was cluttered and messy, it was surprisingly well-kept. The furniture, all heavy and made of dark walnut, spoke of another era—

perhaps the 1970s, or even older—but it wasn't chipped or stained. It was as though time had stood still in this small pocket of the world, the decades folding in on each other, leaving the past very much alive.

A faint smell of lavender hung in the air, while the lace curtains, yellowed with age, billowed softly in the gentle breeze of the open transom window. Mia noticed a couple of threadbare carpets, once fine, now faded from years of use. They were worn down to their patterns, but they still retained a certain dignity, much like the woman who lived here.

Mia took a seat in one of the armchairs by the fireplace. The worn, olive-green fabric was soft under her fingers, though it had seen better days. Across from her was another chair, clearly Eileen's, its cushion sagging from years of use and draped with a well-worn but neatly folded blanket. There was something almost touching in the scene, the small details of a life lived quietly—alone, but not entirely forgotten.

A small bookcase lined one wall, crammed with volumes. Mia's eyes skimmed the titles—mostly French novels, their spines cracked and faded from use. Some were poetry collections, others classic literature. A part of Mia wondered when Eileen had last taken the time to read them, if ever. Had the books served as a refuge during the long, lonely years, or were they remnants of a different time, a different life?

Her gaze traveled farther around the room, taking in the small trinkets on a side table—a delicate porcelain cat, a crystal vase holding a single dried rose, and a few old photographs, one showing Eileen in her FANY uniform. A keen interest tugged at Mia to examine them more closely, but with Eileen's return from the back-room imminent and her strict instruction to sit, Mia resisted the urge to snoop.

A vintage quartz wall clock ticked softly, its orange second hand marking the passage of time in an otherwise still room. From the back room, Mia could hear Eileen muttering in French under her breath. She was tempted to offer help but felt it would be an intrusion on Eileen's independence.

"Ah, voilà!" Eileen finally exclaimed, followed by more rustling of papers, though she still hadn't reappeared.

Mia's thoughts returned to the history she had uncovered about Eileen. Her sister, Jacqueline, had also been an SOE agent in France, and after her career with the United Nations, she had retired to London, where the two sisters had lived together. Jacqueline's passing in 1982 had left Eileen utterly alone.

Mia glanced at the heavy wooden table in the corner, the old armchairs—were these relics of Jacqueline's life? Did they carry memories of happier days, or were they simply anchors to the past?

The thought made Mia's chest tighten. It was easy to imagine how Eileen, surrounded by these reminders, might feel like she was living in a museum of her own history, each object a fragment of a story that had long since faded.

Eileen's cat, a plump ginger creature, padded silently back into the room and settled near Mia's feet, its green eyes blinking lazily. She reached down to give it a gentle scratch behind the ears. It was a small connection, but in this place where trust was so scarce, even the cat's quiet acceptance felt like a step forward.

The rustling from the back room grew louder, followed by the sound of shuffling footsteps. Moments later, Eileen reappeared, clutching a disarray of letters. The envelopes were crumpled and creased, some half-opened, others still sealed. She looked both flustered and slightly confused as she glanced down at the chaotic stack in her hands.

"I think I found them—at least some of them." Her voice held a note of exasperation, though there was a trace of relief as well. "But they're all mixed up. I can't make sense of it anymore."

Mia stood, stepping carefully around the cat. "Why don't we spread them out on the table?" she suggested, her tone calm and reassuring. "I can help you sort through them, and we'll put everything in order. It shouldn't take long."

Eileen hesitated, her sharp blue eyes searching Mia's face as if weighing the offer. After a moment, she gave a slight nod and moved toward the dining table by the window.

"I can't find my glasses either," Eileen muttered. "That's why I'm having such trouble with these letters. I've mislaid them somewhere."

Mia glanced around the room and spotted a pair of glasses next to the photographs on the small side table. "Are you looking for these?"

Eileen's eyes lit up. "Where did you find them? I keep losing those things, and then I lose myself," she added with a quick chuckle.

"Have you ever tried one of those cords? You could hang them around your neck," Mia suggested.

Eileen's blue eyes fixed on her again, this time with a touch of amusement. "Heavens, girl, I've never thought of that. Might be something for ditsy Didi now that you mention it."

"Ditsy Didi?" Mia repeated, unable to resist.

"That's what my family used to call me. Others would say scatterbrained, but I hate that word." Eileen's smile was warm and generous, revealing a humorous and chatty side Mia hadn't seen before.

As they spread the letters on the table, Eileen observed in her French-tinged voice that didn't quite ask questions, "Whisky likes you."

"I beg your pardon. Whisky?" Mia was momentarily taken aback by the sudden remark.

"The cat, silly! Not some young *gallant*." Eileen's laughter tinkled merrily, and Mia couldn't help but laugh along.

"Oh, I see. Yes, he's gorgeous. Have you had him long?"

"Whisky wasn't always gorgeous. When I found him in the community garden, he was all skinny and full of fleas. He's been with me for two years now, but I have no idea how old he is. Now he eats me out of house and home. I always say he eats for two cats. But when I try to put him on a diet, he sits in the kitchen all day meowing so tragically that I give in again."

"Whisky's a big cat, but I wouldn't call him fat," Mia offered. She had finished putting the letters in order and looked up at Eileen for the next step.

"Tea." Eileen's voice was firm, leaving no room for debate.

"That would be nice. Thank you." Mia still held the neatly ordered stack of letters. "I've sorted these. Would you like me to take them to the Pension people on your behalf? I have a contact there, and it might save you the trouble."

Eileen froze mid-step, her back to Mia. For a few seconds, she remained motionless, then continued toward the kitchen without acknowledging the offer.

Give her time, Mia thought.

From the kitchen, the sounds of Eileen muttering in French drifted through the open door, followed by the rush of water into a kettle and the soft clatter of crockery. Mia listened as the stove was lit and more cups were placed on a tray. After what felt like an age, Eileen returned, carrying a teapot in one hand, covered by a tea cosy, and a tray with two floral cups and saucers in the other.

"I need to fetch the milk and sugar." She placed the tray on the small table by the fire and disappeared once more. Two delicate wafer-thin cookies balanced on the saucers—a small but thoughtful gesture.

"Sit," she ordered again, and Mia, leaving the letters on the table, obediently sat in the chair she had occupied earlier.

Eileen returned, adding milk and sugar to the cups. She stirred the pot once more before pouring the strong brown brew out through a small metal sieve, each motion part of a deliberate ritual she'd practiced for decades. Her movements were graceful and methodical—very different from Mia's own rushed habit of plopping a chamomile teabag into a mug while juggling work on her computer.

After handing Mia her cup, Eileen seated herself across from her, upright, poised, and vigilant. Despite the frailty of age, there was something regal in her bearing. Mia recalled Eileen's lineage—blue blood on her mother's side.

The sharp blue eyes, now framed by glasses, studied Mia with unsettling intensity. A shiver ran down Mia's spine. These were the eyes of a woman who had once been a formidable secret agent—eyes that had seen and survived things beyond Mia's comprehension. In that moment, she glimpsed Eileen Nearne's greatness, her unshakable courage, the piercing gaze of someone who refused to be fooled.

It was a humbling experience, one Mia had never encountered before. For a brief moment, all she could do was lower her eyes, feeling the weight of the agent's presence rendered her momentarily speechless.

Mia cradled her cup, letting the warmth seep into her hands through the delicate porcelain as she regained her focus. The cups, though worn, with their faded floral patterns and slightly chipped rims, held a comforting charm that grounded her, helping ease the tension in the room. Eileen pulled her shawl tighter around her fragile frame, and they sat in silence, the ticking of the clock the only sound between them.

Remembering how important it was to take small steps to build trust, Mia knew it was time to gently guide the conversation forward. She glanced at Eileen, a playful thought forming in her mind. "Miss Nearne, if it's not too impertinent, may I ask—what's the secret to your beauty? Your complexion is incredible. I can only hope to have such smooth skin when I reach your age."

For a fleeting second, Eileen's eyes darkened, that familiar shadow of mistrust crossing her features. But Mia remained composed, reading the shift as she had done countless times before with other clients. She waited. A soft smile soon followed, the warmth in Eileen's face returning. "You're flattering an old woman." Eileen shook her head softly. "These days, it's just soap and water. But when I was your age..." Her voice trailed off, slipping into French as she absentmindedly spoke to Whisky, who had nestled at her feet.

Mia allowed the pause to stretch, giving Eileen space to speak on her own terms, all the while observing, guiding gently without pushing. With a sigh, Eileen's gaze drifted toward the window. "After the war, when I was well enough again, I wanted to be a beautician. It had always been a dream of mine, even before the war." Her voice steadied, grounding itself in the memory. "I applied for an apprenticeship with Helena Rubinstein in London. Became a trained beautician... at some point."

"That's incredible, Miss Nearne," Mia said softly, her admiration genuine. "I'm sure you were wonderful."

"I was. For a while," Eileen replied, her voice quiet now, tinged with the sadness of a lost vocation. There was something unspoken in the air, a heaviness that told Mia just how much had been taken from her.

Mia had read the reports, studied the history—how PTSD,

though unnamed and undiagnosed, had slowly closed the doors to Eileen's future. If only things had been different, Mia thought, her life might have taken another path.

When Eileen remained silent, Mia took a deep breath. It was a delicate move, but she wanted to try it anyway. "Miss Nearne, I know it's no consolation, but I understand hardship more than most. I wasn't always Dr. Thompson. I used to live under Princess Pier because no one wanted me. If you'd like, I could tell you where I come from."

Eileen's gaze flickered toward Mia, the same steady, unflinching stare that rarely asked questions, yet her eyes softened ever so slightly. "Perhaps you should," she said, her voice neutral, though there was a subtle invitation beneath the words. "Just like you should take those letters for the Pension people."

And so, Mia told it all, carefully skirting around the trauma, and ending with, "...so I survived. I passed my A-levels, went to university, and finally built a life for myself. Establishing Hope Haven Community Health became my passion and my life."

"Heavens, girl," Eileen murmured, making the quick sign of the cross.

Mia smiled softly. "And I also have a cat named Mr. Spikes—completely black except for a tiny white spot under his chin. He's very naughty."

"Heavens," Eileen repeated, but then fell silent. For a moment, Mia thought she'd said too much as Eileen's eyes half-closed, but then she sat up, her voice clear when she spoke again.

"I was the opposite of you. I had a very happy youth, though we moved quite a bit." Her fingers retrieved the rosary from her pocket, and as the beads slipped through her hands with practiced ease, she continued, "Your perseverance is remarkable, Doctor Thompson. You remind me of the resilience I saw in people during the war."

Mia smiled gently. "Thank you, Miss Nearne. I suppose it's

perseverance that kept me going. I'm so glad to hear you had a happy childhood. Every child deserves that."

"Yes, every child deserves that," Eileen agreed. "I was loved and safe, first in England and then in France. We lived in beautiful houses, and we were always together. Especially my sister Jacqueline and I. Oh, we had a carefree life, full of laughter and dreams...."

PART II

~EILEEN~ FRANCE 1931-1940

6

PENELOPE'S CASTLE

Boulogne-sur-Mer, France, July 1931

The July sun bathed the sandy beach of Boulogne-sur-Mer in golden light, casting a shimmer over the waters of the Côte d'Opale. The sea was calm, its tiny waves lapping rhythmically against the shore, their soft murmurs blending with the distant jingle of a merry-go-round. Overhead, seagulls circled lazily, their cries sharp and greedy as they scanned the beach for discarded scraps.

The calm, warm air held the briny scent of the English Channel, while the sweetness of freshly spun cotton candy drifted over from the boulevard. Children, faces hidden beneath wide-brimmed sun bonnets, raced across the sand with buckets and spades, their laughter bubbling over the soft hiss of the retreating tide. A small white dog darted in and out of the shallows, yapping at the waves that curled playfully around his legs.

Families lounged on woven blankets or in deckchairs, their parasols casting welcome pools of shade, while mothers in flowing summer dresses fanned themselves leisurely, watching the world unfold with contented smiles. Fathers, in rolled-up trousers, waded into the water with children clinging to their hands, shrieks of joy rising as they dipped their toes in the cool sea.

It was a perfect Sunday afternoon, the kind where time seemed to stretch endlessly under the clear, azure sky. For now, the day was bathed in warmth and laughter, a fleeting moment of innocence soaked up in all its glory.

But in the far distance, beyond the rolling hills of the Pas de Calais, a mass of grey clouds gathered, the faintest whisper of a storm to come. No one paid it any mind. Not yet. The day was too beautiful, too filled with the simplicity of sun and sea, to be interrupted by thoughts of the evening's forecast. Now was now and now was perfect.

The Nearne family had gathered on the beach in front of their house on Boulevard Sainte Beuve. A large picnic blanket was spread out on the warm sand, shaded by a red-and-white striped parasol the children had affectionately dubbed *Can-can*, its frills reminding them of the dancers' skirts from the Moulin Rouge. They'd seen the billboard for the famous nightclub on Place Pigalle when they lived in Paris, before their move to Boulogne-sur-Mer.

Eileen, known to the family as Didi, sat cross-legged on the edge of the blanket, her wavy brown hair catching the sunlight filtering through the parasol. At ten, she was full of bright energy, her light-blue bathing suit with delicate smocking the perfect contrast to the warm sand. She had kicked off her sandals, eagerly wiggling her toes in the soft grains beneath her, a wide smile lighting up her face.

Jacqueline, her fifteen-year-old sister, was the embodiment of responsibility. Dark-haired and blue-eyed like Eileen, she had a maturity beyond her years, her movements precise and purposeful as she unpacked the picnic basket, arranging everything with quiet efficiency.

"Didi, don't just sit there dreaming. Help me with the sandwiches," Jacqueline said with her usual firm tone, softened by the affection that always accompanied her words. Her protectiveness often manifested in a bossy manner, but Eileen never took it personally—she knew her sister's love was woven into each command.

Eileen grinned, rolling her eyes in mock defiance. "*Oui, oui, Mademoiselle Jacqueline*," she teased, scooting over to help. She lifted a sandwich from the basket and began arranging it on the plate with a light-heartedness that contrasted her sister's seriousness.

Their mother, Marie—Countess Mariquita Carmen de Plazaola—sat nearby, arranging cutlery with a graceful ease that spoke of her aristocratic background. Her movements were fluid, her soft Parisian accent threaded with the melodic lilt of her Spanish heritage, making even the simplest phrases sound elegant. "Ah, *mes filles*, no bickering today. The sun is too lovely for it," she said, her gaze gentle as it fell upon her daughters.

Marie's presence exuded grace and calm, even on a casual beach day. There was something about her quiet elegance that held the family together, a serenity that made every moment feel as though it were wrapped in a warm blanket. The inherited wealth from her Spanish family had allowed the Nearnes to live comfortably, and though their father's career had never fully flourished in France as it had in England, the children never felt the weight of it. The family's life, buoyed by Marie's influence, was rich in its own way, full of small joys like these picnics by the sea.

Jacqueline finished unpacking and handed a plate to her mother. "I'm not bickering, Maman. Didi just needs direction, or she'll drift off into one of her daydreams."

Eileen laughed, taking the playful jab in stride. "My thoughts are very important, you know," she quipped, sticking out her tongue before passing out the sandwiches.

Marie just shook her head at their antics. "You two are like day and night," she mused, but with twinkling eyes. "Jacqueline, so serious and responsible. And you, Didi, always dreaming."

"Someone has to be responsible," Jacqueline muttered, settling beside her mother and brushing sand from her skirt. "Especially with Francis and Freddie off who knows where."

"And someone has to do the dreaming," Eileen retorted, her eyes scanned the horizon, searching for her brothers, who had disappeared earlier—likely off causing mischief. "At least they're not here to eat all the food before we've had a chance."

Marie smiled wistfully, her gaze drifting toward the sea, where gentle waves lapped at the shore. "Let's not worry about them today," she said softly, her voice carrying a note of quiet contentment. "We have this moment."

Their father, Jack, a chemist by trade, sat next to Eileen on the blanket, his glasses perched on his long nose as he read from a well-worn English novel, his pipe sending wisps of fragrant smoke into the air. Jack Nearne had a high forehead and wavy dark hair, now flecked with grey, giving him a distinguished, yet somewhat somber, appearance. His eyes had a sad-dog quality but held a subdued warmth. His mouth, set in a way that mirrored Eileen's, twitched with amusement as he glanced up from his reading to watch his daughters.

"Listen to your mother, girls. It's not every day we get to have a family picnic," he said in a voice of quiet authority. Though he was fully dressed, as always, in a light linen suit, there was something comfortable about his presence, like the steady rhythm of a ticking clock.

Francis and Frederick, Eileen's older brothers, were coming into view again, locked in a spirited game of catch-me-if-you-can near the shoreline, their laughter rising and falling in the air. The family's language drifted naturally between English and French, a reflection of the rich cultural blend that shaped their home.

"*Alors, mes garçons, venez manger*," Marie called, her musical voice carrying across the beach, her boys to come and eat. Frederick and Francis, still catching their breath, collapsed onto the blanket.

"I won!" Francis, the eldest, declared triumphantly.

"No, you didn't. I let you win!" Frederick shot back, his grin wide.

"Stop it, boys, you make far too much noise," their father said, though his tone was more amused than stern. He laid his book aside. "Let us pray."

Jack began the Lord's Prayer, his voice calm and steady. The family's heads bowed, and their lips murmured the words in unison, ending with the familiar sign of the cross.

"*Bon appétit*," they all chimed.

Eileen handed her father a ham and watercress sandwich. Eyes sparkling with mischief, she asked, "Papa, do you think I'll ever be as smart as you?"

Her father reached out to ruffle her hair. "You already are, ditsy Didi. You just need to focus a little more."

Eileen momentarily moped before turning to Whisky, the family's ginger cat, who smelled the ham and had wandered over to the picnic. She stroked the cat's fluffy fur gently. "You see, Whisky," she whispered, "everyone thinks I'm scatterbrained, but I have my secrets."

Jacqueline, overhearing, nudged her. "Oh, Didi, you and your secrets. Just make sure you don't get into trouble."

Eileen's expression shifted, her face suddenly serious, her set mouth firming in a way that made her look strikingly like her father. "Don't fuss, Jacqueline. I can handle more than you think."

As the words left her lips, Eileen's mind drifted back to earlier that year at the Ursuline Convent. She had been hunched over a particularly challenging math problem, her brow furrowed in frustration. She enjoyed math, but this one had her stumped, and she felt the weight of both the nuns' expectations and her own disappointment pressing down on her.

The other girls had already solved it, their scribbles neatly finished, while Eileen sat, head buried in her arms, on the verge of giving up.

Sister Benedicta had found her like that, sitting alone in the study room. "Didi, what troubles you?" she'd asked gently, placing a warm, fleshy hand on Eileen's shoulder.

Eileen had looked up, her eyes brimming with unshed tears. "I can't do it, Sister. I've tried and tried, but it's too hard."

Sister Benedicta had smiled, her eyes full of kindness and faith. "You can do it, Didi. I believe in you. And so does the Good Lord. Sometimes, we just need to approach things from a different angle. Let's work on it together."

With the nun's gentle guidance, Eileen had tackled the problem again, her frustration slowly giving way to clarity. When she finally solved the algebra equation, the sense of accomplishment had been overwhelming, and Sister Benedicta's words had echoed in her mind: *I believe in you. And so does the Good Lord.*

Returning to the present, Eileen felt Jacqueline's elbow nudge her ribs. "Didi Dreamer," she teased.

But Eileen only smiled, her expression wise and calm. She could handle more than anyone thought—because she'd learned early on that she was stronger than she seemed and tougher than her family gave her credit for.

After lunch, Eileen wandered away from her family, seeking the quiet stretch of beach that always felt like her own secret place. She found her usual spot beside a large rock she had affectionately named Nougat. To her eyes, the rock was no ordinary stone; its caramel and cream-colored streaks reminded her of the sweet treat, and she imagined that, on some faraway shore, it might even be a piece of giant nougat fallen from the sky.

The sun had warmed the rock, and its surface, though rough to the touch, felt like a comforting presence under her palm. Nougat was just one of Eileen's many imaginary friends, keeping her company when she needed a moment to gather her thoughts without being scolded for daydreaming or ditziness. Whisky had followed her and stretched contentedly in the shade by her side, his green eyes blinking lazily as if he, too, knew this was their special place.

Eileen pulled her sketchbook and watercolor crayons from her satchel, birthday gifts, and began to draw the scene before her, blending the colors with deft fingers to create exactly the hues she wanted. She drew not as it was, but as she saw it.

Her crayons danced over the paper as she glanced at her mother, who sat with perfect poise, knitting in the soft afternoon light. But in Eileen's mind, Marie wasn't just knitting—no, she was Penelope, weaving a grand tapestry during the day, only to unravel it by night. Her mother's slender fingers moved gracefully, each stitch a part of an endless cycle, forever knitting and unraveling, as if bound to a fate of making no progress at all.

Eileen imagined her mother sighing quietly as the sun went down, ready to unravel her day's work again. She saw it as necessary, as a unique kind of Nearne magic—the spell that kept her family together, protecting them from unseen fiends. There was a God-given reason her mother's work never seemed to move forward, as though she was ordained to stay trapped in the loop of creation and erasure, waiting for something—or someone—to change.

And then there was Jacqueline, Penelope's loyal maid, the one who guarded the family's secrets and would defend them with her life. Vigilant and poised, she remained at Maman's side, watching over the comings and goings in the Nearne castle with the same careful, protective gaze she cast over Eileen.

Her father wasn't Odysseus—that was a man still far away over the wild seas. No, Papa was Socrates, seated near the hearth with his book and pipe, a deep-thinking philosopher, pondering the mysteries of Penelope and her court. Eileen loved the philosopher, but she waited for her father to become Odysseus—step into the role of the hero and make Penelope finish her tapestry.

Her brothers, now sleeping off their game of chase, were Odysseus's crew, lying exhausted on a strange island far from home. But, as seasoned warriors who had braved battles and survived countless adventures, surely, they would bring Odysseus back.

Without Eileen noticing, Jacqueline had sidled up to her, peeking at Eileen's sketch. "What are you drawing this time, Didi? Let me see," she asked.

Eileen turned the sketch toward her. "I'm drawing all of us—Maman as Penelope, Papa as Socrates, the boys as Odysseus's crew... and you."

"Oh? It's a Greek tale this time? Thank God it's not a tragedy. So, who am I?"

"You're Penelope's maid," Eileen replied, her expression studious as she softened the last hard lines with her gum eraser. "You're the one who knows how to keep the secrets safe."

Jacqueline studied the sketch intently. "Heavens, is that how you see me... how you see us as a family, Didi?"

"Yes," Eileen said, sounding surprised. To her, there was nothing strange about the scene. It was beautiful and exactly how a family ought to be. Loyal, loving. And with secrets.

Jacqueline wrapped an arm around her. "And what is your role, *ma petite soeur*? Where are you in this scene?"

Eileen thought for a moment, then made a few final sketches

next to her brothers. “I’m also a warrior, part of the crew,” she replied, triumph in her voice.

Jacqueline smiled, shaking her head slightly. “You do see the world in your own way, Didi. But it’s not the reality, you know.”

“Maybe not to you, Jacqui, but it is to me. Someone has to see life the way I see it,” Eileen said, her voice filled with conviction, the picture another thread in her labyrinth of possibilities.

As the sun began its descent, Marie called the girls to help pack up the picnic. Folding the checked blanket with her sister, Eileen felt the specialness of the day in every part of her body. She knew, as sharp as the silhouette of the silver aeroplane flying overhead, that she would forever etch this family picnic into her heart.

She lagged behind on the walk home, taking one last look at the beach, still seeing her sketchbook scene. With a wisdom beyond her years, Eileen sensed the fragility of life—of family bonds, of their connection to places. This moment, stretched in time, felt like eternity.

“Are you coming, Warrior?” Jacqueline called out. Whisky meowed at her feet, trotting ahead.

“I’m coming, Head Maid,” Eileen called back, a smile around her lips.

7

THE MOVE TO NICE

Two months later - Boulogne-sur-Mer, September 1931

"Papa, do we really need to move again?" Eileen's voice trembled as she clutched the edge of her father's white coat. Her wide blue eyes, brimming with unshed tears, looked up at him, pleading for him to reconsider. "I really like Sister Benedicta at the Ursuline Convent. She's going to be devastated when I tell her we're moving to Nice. Last week, she told me, 'frailty comes with old age, my dear.' I promised to look after her when I'm eighteen." Her voice cracked with emotion as she tried to make him understand how much the move would affect her.

It would be her fourth move in just ten years—from London to Paris to Boulogne-sur-Mer, and now to Nice. Though she had no memory of the move from London to Paris as she was only two years old, she remembered how long it had taken her to adapt to Boulogne-sur-Mer at age four. She had finally settled, found solace in new routines, and now, with yet another move looming, the upheaval felt heavier. She hated it—the packing, the goodbyes, the sense of being uprooted just as she'd begun to feel at home. She clung to her father now, hoping he would come to reason, believing she could be the one to make him see.

Her father looked up from grinding white powder with a pestle in an earthenware mortar. His glasses were perched on the bridge of his nose, and a deep wrinkle of concentration furrowed his brow. Not the right moment to disturb him, Eileen knew, but emergencies broke the rules. Maman and Cassie, their help, were already packing the crates, and the furniture had been covered with dust sheets.

"Oh, Didi, Sister Benedicta will survive without you. She has so many urchins like you to look after. One more or less will not matter to her."

"What's an urchin, Papa?" Eileen, who had a great fondness for languages, was momentarily distracted from the family's upcoming move by this unfamiliar word.

"Look it up in the dictionary, honey, and let your papa do his work." Eileen sauntered over to her father's row of books in the in-house pharmacy and pulled the heavy dictionary with the golden letters U-V on the spine toward her.

"An urchin is a mischievous child who is badly dressed and dirty," she read aloud. A deep wrinkle of concern appeared on her face. "I'm not a badly dressed and dirty child, and I'm not mischievous. At least not all the time," she said with indignation.

"I meant it more like whippersnapper, Didi. Now shoo. I need to work." There was no time to grab the dictionary with W-X to check what a whippersnapper was, but hopefully, it was something more positive.

As Eileen left her father's pharmacy with Whisky at her heels, she knew there was no stopping the move to her grandmother's house in

Nice. The reality had settled in, heavy on her chest. She would have to say goodbye to everything she had grown to love, even if part of her wasn't ready.

"At least you will go with me, Whisky," Eileen whispered in a sad voice, bending down to scratch behind the cat's ears. The ginger cat blinked at her, purring softly as if to say, *I'll follow you anywhere.*

Before heading to the convent, Eileen made her way to the beach, where she found her familiar spot beside her large rock, Nougat. The sunlight bathed the caramel and cream-colored streaks of the stone, and Eileen felt sadness like a veil over her. She ran her hand over Nougat's rough surface, feeling the warmth of the sun on the age-old rock.

"Goodbye, Nougat," she murmured. "I wish I could take you with me."

To Eileen, Nougat was a magical rock, one that held the power to comfort her, even from afar. Maybe, just maybe, she could carry a little piece of it with her. Kneeling, she picked up a small pebble that had broken off from the larger rock. Already, she felt a little better. "You'll come with me," she said softly, slipping the caramel-colored stone into her pocket. "A piece of you will always be with me in Nice."

Reluctantly, she turned away from the beach and made her way to the Ursuline Convent. Whisky trailed behind her, ever her faithful shadow, as she walked the familiar path she had taken so many times before.

When she reached the convent gates, Eileen felt the weight of the goodbye settle in her shoes, her feet heavy as lead. Sister Benedicta had been her guiding light, her source of comfort through the confusion of growing up. The old nun had always been gentle but firm, her faith unwavering, and Eileen couldn't bear the thought of leaving her behind.

Sister Benedicta was waiting in the courtyard, a smile lighting her weathered face as her 'urchin' approached. "*Ma petite Didi,* you look troubled," she said in her kind, raspy voice.

Eileen bit her lip, trying to keep her emotions in check, but it was no use. "We're moving to Nice," she blurted out, her voice shaking. "I won't be able to come back to the convent anymore."

Sister Benedicta's smile changed into something more wistful as she reached out and took Eileen's hand. "Ah, *ma chère fille,* life is full of changes, but the Good Lord always watches over us, no matter where we go."

"I promised to look after you when I'm older," Eileen said, her voice breaking as the tears she'd been holding back finally spilled over. "I don't want to leave you, Sister."

The nun patted Eileen's hand gently, her eyes full of the wisdom that came with age. "Do not worry about me, Didi. The Lord has many hands, and you will always be a part of His plan. You must go where your family needs you. But I will always keep you in my prayers."

Eileen nodded, trying to find comfort in the words, though her heart still ached. She leaned in and hugged Sister Benedicta tightly, feeling the warmth of the old nun's embrace.

"Go with grace, child," Sister Benedicta said in a low, tender voice. "And always remember, you are stronger than you think."

As Eileen pulled away, she wiped her tears with the back of her hand. Whisky rubbed against her legs, his quiet presence offering some small comfort.

"Goodbye, Sister. I will think of your words—and I'll work on my algebra," Eileen promised, trying to take heart from her guardian's wisdom.

"You do that, my dear, and become a famous mathematician."

Eileen giggled despite her wretchedness. "Now that, I'm sure, is not God's plan for me."

But she felt a lot better after her goodbyes.

. . .

Back home from the convent, Eileen escaped into the backyard with her sketchbook and watercolor crayons, seeking solace in paper and color. Whisky padded beside her as she flipped to a blank page. She knew she had to face the real reason why this move felt worse than the others.

Her hands hesitated for a moment before beginning the new drawing. She wasn't ready for the move to Nice, but perhaps if she sketched the house there, it might help ease the knot of unease in her chest.

With tentative strokes, Eileen outlined the contours of the house at *60 bis Avenue des Arènes de Cimiez*—the sunlit Nice mansion where her family had holidayed every other summer for as long as she could remember. The two-storey house overlooked the famous Roman amphitheater, where she imagined gladiators with spears, though in reality, it was more like a stone pit. The windows reflected the Mediterranean sky, while the palm trees framed the avenue, standing like tropical sentinels.

The image took shape under her fingers—the white façade, the terracotta roof, and dormer windows emerged as she remembered them. As her crayons moved, she muttered to Whisky, the only one who seemed to understand her unease.

"It's a beautiful house, Whisky. There's even a garden where you can play and lie in the shade. But I don't want to live there without Abuela." Her strokes were steady but full of feeling as she shaded the roof. "It won't be the same. Not without her."

Eileen paused, biting her lip as she sketched the downstairs windows. Abuela had always sat there on the porch with her rosary, watching the avenue in a quiet manner that comforted Eileen. But that image was gone now. Her grandmother had passed three years earlier, and though time had moved on, the ache in Eileen's heart remained—a hole she wasn't sure would ever fully heal. She'd managed summers there, but living in the house full-time felt different.

"I can't live in her house without her," she whispered, rubbing a soft line into the sky with her thumb. "It feels wrong, like we're taking over something that doesn't belong to us. But if I say that, they'll just think I'm being oversensitive again."

She added a few final touches—the palm trees, herself lounging in the hammock, and her cat sitting watch at the garden gate.

"That will do, Whisky. We'll conquer Nice together." Eileen closed her sketchbook, her fingers brushing the pebble from Nougat in her pocket.

8

GROWING PAINS

Three years later - Nice, Summer 1934

Eileen drifted lazily on her stomach through the warm Mediterranean waters, catching glimpses of the sunlight filtering through the gentle waves above. The Côte d'Azur had become her playground, a place where she could leave behind the cares of school and housework and lose herself in the endless blue. Today, she'd spent the afternoon snorkeling, gliding among the seagrass meadows and watching schools of tiny silver fish dart around her, their scales flashing like quicksilver in the light.

The sea was her refuge—a place where she felt weightless and free, where the troubles of a thirteen-year-old vanished with every stroke she made. Eileen was a strong, confident swimmer, always winning contests against her brothers, though they were gone—*God knows where*—today. She had grown accustomed to her own company and often sought it out.

Tired but content, she waded back to the shore, snapping off her snorkel. The salty water dripped from her emerald bathing suit as she walked up the sandy beach, all long legs and wet brown hair clinging to her back. With a blissful sigh, she flopped down on a sun-baked rock, letting the warmth seep into her body. She surveyed the beachgoers, watching children build sandcastles, couples strolling hand-in-hand, and sailboats bobbing in the distance.

This was home now. Nice was where she belonged, where she felt most at peace. The memories she had made here felt stronger than those of Boulogne-sur-Mer or Paris. She couldn't imagine leaving the Côte d'Azur again. Her heart swelled with a silent prayer that her family would stay here for good, that she'd never have to say goodbye to this life. The good life. The peaceful life.

But goodbyes had become something of a familiar companion over the years. The memories of her grandmother's death, of saying farewell to Sister Benedicta, and the loss of her beloved Whisky had all chipped away at the naive security of childhood. And now, though she didn't know it yet, another goodbye was waiting for her.

After drying off and gathering her things, Eileen made her way back home, her skin glowing from the sun and her hair still damp in the sea breeze. She opened the garden gate, where their new pet, Moustache, a shy white cat with enormous whiskers, greeted her with a cautious flick of his tail. Moustache wasn't as loyal or affectionate as Whisky had been, but he was there, watching her from a distance as she walked up the path to the house.

Surprised to see the front door ajar, Eileen approached cautiously. The usual quiet of the afternoon was broken by the bustling noise of her mother's voice and the sound of packing.

Eileen's heart skipped a beat. *It can't be true.*

Inside, the clatter of a suitcase being shut echoed through the upstairs hall. Dropping her towel and sandals by the door, she raced toward the source of the noise.

"Jacqui?" she called, an uneasy feeling creeping over her.

Her older sister appeared at the top of the staircase, sharply dressed in a figure-hugging navy suit, her face aglow with excitement. Jacqueline held a suitcase in one hand, a mischievous glint in her eyes as she descended the steps.

Eileen's heart sank. "Are you leaving?"

Jacqueline smiled but didn't slow her pace. "Just for work, Didi. I'll be back soon."

"But you've never gone away for work before," Eileen protested, trying to mask the sudden rush of panic rising in her chest.

Jacqueline set her suitcase down by the door and turned to her sister. "It's just a week, nothing to worry about."

Eileen followed her outside, where a taxi waited at the gate, its engine idling softly. Unable to hold back any longer, she darted down the steps, still dressed in her damp bathing suit, the cool stones pressing against her bare feet. "Jacqui, wait! Am I not going to get a hug?" she cried, her voice trembling with emotion.

Jacqueline turned and laughed. "Darling, you're acting like I'm moving to Africa! And you're all wet. I can't ruin my new suit, but here's a kiss." She leaned in and planted a quick peck on Eileen's cheek. "Now be a good girl, Didi, and stop fussing."

"But where are you going? What's this work?" Eileen demanded, her frustration bubbling up. It wasn't like Jacqueline to leave her in the dark about something so important. At just eighteen, she looked so smart and grown-up, a woman with a secret.

"Someone has to sell all that office equipment for *Équipement de Bureau Riviera*, and that person is *moi, chérie,*" Jacqueline winked. "I'm a traveling saleswoman now. Isn't it grand? Don't give me that look—my taxi's waiting, and I really have to go. I'll bring you back something from Monaco."

With a final kiss on the cheek, Jacqueline's blue suitcase disappeared into the boot of the taxi, and she slid into the backseat with a quick wave.

It had all happened so suddenly, Eileen stood frozen on the curb, staring after the taxi as it disappeared down the avenue. Passersby muttered something about her state of undress, snapping her out of her daze. She turned on her heels and hurried back inside the safety of the gates, her mind racing.

Only for a week, she mumbled to herself, letting herself fall into the hammock in the garden. Staring up at the sky, her thoughts were swirling wildly. Jacqueline had always been there—her sister was more to Eileen than any other family member; she was her closest ally, even more so than Maman. Jacqui forgave Eileen's quirks, her dreaminess, and most importantly, she had always shouldered the lion's share of household chores.

Now, with her sister gone, Eileen knew what that meant. All those responsibilities would fall on her. And if there was one thing she detested in life, it was chores.

Alone in the house, she heard the distant hum of the radio in the parlor—Radio Paris—one of the constant companions that filled the quiet. Lately, the voices on the radio had shifted, talking less about jazz and new movies, and more about unsettling things: Hitler in Germany, politics in Europe, rumors of alliances and rising tension. Eileen didn't like it, but she couldn't help but listen.

One day, she thought, *I'll be tuning in not just for music but for messages from "Ici Londres." And it will be vital that I do so.* The idea lingered in her mind, though she didn't yet comprehend how close that future was.

For now, though, it was just her,the chores, and a radio filling the silence Jacqueline had left behind.

9

THE END OF INNOCENCE

Six years later - Nice, 25 June 1940

The crackle of Radio Paris filled the Nearne living room, its familiar hum a backdrop to Eileen's morning routine. She stood by the sideboard, feather duster in hand, absent-mindedly sweeping it across the polished wood. But when the static-laden voice of the announcer sharpened, breaking through the interference with sudden clarity, her hand froze mid-air.

"...Non-French citizens must leave the Côte d'Azur within eight days..."

For a moment, the house seemed to hold its breath. Eileen's heart quickened as she cast a glance at her parents, who had moved closer to the radio as if drawn by an unseen force. Her mother, Marie, perched at the edge of the sofa, hands clasped tightly in her lap, her knuckles white. Her father stood beside his wife, a tall, still figure with his glasses low on his nose. It was the silent dread on his face that alarmed Eileen the most.

As the tension in her chest grew tighter, her eyes wandered to the open window, seeking freedom. The warm Mediterranean breeze slipped through, carrying the sweet scent of oleander and jasmine. The sky was a perfect shade of blue, unmarred by a single cloud. A wide-winged seagull floated serenely above the crown of a palm tree, its flight striking something deep in Eileen's soul. Was the peaceful beauty of the summer morning real, or surreal?

Her grip on the feather duster tightened as though holding on to it could somehow keep her world from falling apart.

"...WITH France fallen, Philippe Pétain signed the armistice with the Third Reich on 22 June, dividing the country into two zones: the Occupied Zone under German control and the Free Zone under the Vichy government headed by Marchal Pétain. Today 24 June, he also signed an armistice with Italy... The Côte d'Azur, including Nice, now falls under Italian control coming into effect tomorrow.... All non-French citizens must leave immediately."

THE WORDS HUNG in the air, final and cold. Her father's face turned an ashen gray, while her mother's delicate features seemed to crumple--her lips pressed tightly together to hold back a cry. Eileen could feel the ground shifting beneath her, a hollow sensation filling her stomach. They were going to be evicted. Nice, their home, their sanctuary, was no longer open to them.

She glanced at her parents again. The weight of the moment settled like a thick layer of dust in the quiet room, erasing the sunlight and the promise of a summer by the sea.

It was the end of safety, of solace, of certainty—everything Eileen had ever known.

"Papa, must we...?"

Before she could finish, a loud pounding rattled the front door.

"Jack, you go!" Marie managed, her voice trembling. "We can't let the housekeeper..."

Eileen, her heart leaping into her throat, tightened her grip on the feather duster so much she felt it start to flex under the pressure. Though nineteen, she suddenly felt no older than ten. She slid to the sofa, seeking comfort by her mother's side as the banging echoed through the house.

Her father straightened, shoulders rigid, and with a grim expression, he strode to the door. Marie and Eileen followed cautiously, peeking from behind his back.

Two Italian soldiers stood on the porch, feet planted wide, dressed in navy-blue battledress. Their faces were hard, revolvers ready at their sides. As Moustache, their shy, white cat, bolted between their legs and into the safety of the house, Eileen's stomach twisted.

One soldier thrust a folded paper into her father's hand, barking in rapid Italian, "*Vai via tra 8 giorni.*" Leave in 8 days.

Jack's hand tightened on the doorframe as he unfolded the paper, his eyes scanning the text. "Evicted?" His voice was thick, speaking French overlaid with his native English accent. "Only eight days?"

"*Si, si*!" The soldier barked again, sticking a second notice on the door, treating them like criminals.

Eileen's chest constricted. "Eight days?" she squeaked, her voice barely audible. Could it be true? The radio had been right. Everything she feared was crashing down around them. Their home, their life in Nice—gone, with a single French signature on an Italian decree. Pétain, once France's Great War hero, had sold them out.

"But where will we go? How will we—" Marie's voice quivered.

"Hush," Jack silenced her with a raised hand. He turned back to the soldiers, pleading in his broken French, adding Italian *per favore's*. But the soldiers remained indifferent and just shrugged off his words. They were merely messengers, unconcerned with the fate of yet another foreign family. They pointed to the notice one final time, then turned and marched away.

When the door slammed shut, Eileen felt a chill creep into her bones despite the summer heat. She gathered Moustache into her arms; the cat, sensing the tension, curled tightly against her. Eight days, and everything would be gone.

"Papa, how will we reach Jacqui? Where is she even?" Her voice cracked, barely holding back tears.

"We'll reach her through *Équipement de Bureau Riviera*, Didi. Jacqueline is the least of our concerns right now." His tone wasn't unfriendly, but the weight of the situation was clear. Eileen understood. Her father, never one with the strongest nerves, was struggling under the pressure of seeing everything they had built over the past nine years in Nice unravel so suddenly.

"You two—pack what we need. Only the essentials," Jack said firmly. "I'll go to the municipality, see if I can undo this madness. If not, I'll find out how we can leave the house secure, without these Italians raiding it."

"But where will we go, Jack?" Her mother asked, voicing the question burning in Eileen's mind.

"Grenoble," he said with finality. "It's our only viable option."

Grenoble? Why Grenoble? The question flickered in Eileen's thoughts, but the world was spinning too fast for her to voice it. All she knew was that the life they had known was slipping away, and nothing felt steady anymore.

PART III

~MIA~ TORQUAY, 2007

10

A FRAGILE TRUST

Torquay, August 2007

Mia shot a quick glance at the clock and was shocked to see it was past two in the afternoon. She'd been listening to Eileen for almost four hours, forgetting all her other appointments, mesmerized by the richness and lucidity of Eileen's memories of her youth.

She'd been with Didi in France at the family picnic in Boulogne-sur-Mer, swam with her in the warm Mediterranean, and felt the terror when Italian soldiers pounded on the door.

Mia's stomach grumbled, reminding her she had skipped lunch, while Eileen began to droop ever so slightly.

"Oh, my goodness, I've kept you talking way too long. I'm so sorry, Miss Nearne." Mia stood up, grabbing her bag and stacking the letters from the Department of Work and Pensions into it. "Can I give you a hand with the teacups?"

Eileen, sitting upright with her back as straight as ever in the high-backed armchair, blinked once and smiled. "Heavens, girl, don't fuss. I can handle a couple of cups perfectly fine myself." Glancing at the clock, she added, "Dear me, I didn't know I had so many words left in me." She rose stiffly. "I'd better see you out—and get myself to the grocer's, unless it rains."

Mia glanced through the yellowed, lace curtains. The sky was overcast, but no rain fell. "Best take your umbrella, Miss Nearne, just to be sure in this typical English summer. I'll be in touch as soon as I have a definitive answer from the Pension people. I'll call my contact this afternoon, but it may take a few days before everything's in order. Please don't worry about it. I'll make sure you receive your check this week."

"Thank you, dear. You do that."

"So, same time next week? Would that work for you, Miss Nearne?"

Eileen's blue eyes fixed on Mia, a mixture of clear and unreadable emotions swimming in them. Then, with a short nod: "Alright. Now go with God's blessing." She made the sign of the cross over Mia, and the gesture took Mia's breath away. No one had ever blessed her before, let alone someone as devout as Eileen Nearne.

"Thank you," Mia stammered, momentarily feeling like a little girl.

"*Vous êtes gentille.*" With these words, Mia slipped out of Eileen's flat, a whirlwind of emotions swirling inside her. Had she handled the situation professionally enough, or had she lost perspective on how much her client could handle?

"Nonsense," she scolded herself. "Most of the time such meetings aren't cookie-cutter appointments—a client might need more time to open up." Yet she couldn't shake the feeling she'd stayed too long.

As Mia stepped outside the wind picked up. Her hand went to her hair out of habit, and she muttered, "darn!" at her realisation.

Her hairclip had come loose and must still be in Miss Nearne's chair. She'd just have to get it back next week.

THE NEXT DAY, Mia sat at her desk at Hope Haven, deeply absorbed in the file of a new client when her phone rang. The name on the screen surprised and alarmed her—*the parish office of Our Lady Help of Christians.* Her first thought was that something was wrong with Eileen Nearne.

"Hello, Doctor Thompson, Sister Damian here." The sweet, singsong voice of the elderly head nun sounded in Mia's ear.

Sitting up straight and trying to keep her voice calm, she replied, "Hello, Sister. How can I help you?"

"Mia, dear, I hope I'm not disturbing you." The nun's voice was as gentle as ever, but there was a serious undertone. "I wanted to ask you about Miss Nearne. She didn't come to Mass this morning. I can't remember Eileen ever missing our mid-week intimate service in the side chapel. It's her favorite moment of the week, so she always tells me."

Mia frowned, twisting her pen between her fingers. "Eileen didn't come to Mass? I have no idea why."

"I thought perhaps," Sister Damian continued, "well, I know you visited her yesterday. I wondered if she might have mentioned anything?"

Mia's mind went into overdrive. "No, she didn't say anything. She mentioned she was going shopping after I left. We had an incredibly open talk, Sister—it really surprised me. But now I'm wondering if I overstepped. She was a bit tired when I left, and she had talked a lot about her youth." Mia's words tumbled out, and she frowned, realizing how unprofessional she sounded. "I hope I didn't push too much."

"Oh no, no, don't worry," the Sister interrupted, sensing Mia's anxiety. "I'm sure it's nothing. She probably just needed space. Let's see if she comes to Sunday's service. I'll give Mr. Pierce, her next-door neighbor, a ring—ask him to keep an eye on whether she leaves the house. One can't be too careful, you know. If she's still absent on Sunday, then we'll know something's wrong. But I wanted to check with you first."

"Thank you for letting me know, Sister," Mia said, trying to keep her voice steady. "I'll... I'll check in on her soon, but I already promised to visit next Tuesday, so I don't want to overwhelm her any further."

"Don't do anything extra, dear, and don't fret. I'm sure there's a perfectly good reason she stayed indoors. The weather was beastly, so maybe it's just that."

After hanging up, Mia was far from reassured. She replayed every detail of the previous day's visit. Had she pushed Eileen too far? Was the conversation about her youth too stressful for her? *Did I miss a sign?*

Mia tried to concentrate on the file in front of her, but she realized Eileen Nearne wasn't just another client. For some reason, she was much more. The hours she'd spent in that cluttered apartment on Lisburne Crescent in the company of a reclusive war heroine held a strong echo of secrets and valor—something had changed in the young doctor. As a survivor herself, Mia recognized a fellow fighter from miles away.

Eileen Nearne was one of those rare human beings who had gone through the wringer, who had the odds stacked against them, and yet survived. Her fate resonated deeply with Mia's. Perhaps too deeply. They were cut from the same cloth. But it was a dangerous alliance. Eileen was a client, and Mia was her psychologist. That line should never be blurred, and yet it had been—and Mia couldn't shake off the possible repercussions.

Unable to focus any longer, she got up from her computer screen and made her way to the staff kitchen, hoping to bump into her closest colleague—her sparring mate, co-director, and best friend—Alexandra Torres. Luck was on Mia's side. Alexandra was just refilling her coffee mug, her cell phone pressed between her ear and shoulder.

"Ah-uh, Ah-uh, yes, I've got it. I'll see you Monday at ten. Bye, Mrs. Wallace."

"Hey, Alex, do you have a minute?" Mia asked, leaning against the counter.

"Of course." Alexandra quickly made a note on her phone and turned her deep brown eyes to Mia's face, a concerned look on her fine Spanish features. "Let me guess—Miss Nearne?"

Mia had to chuckle despite her worries. "Can you read my mind now, Miss Crystal Gazer?"

Alex didn't answer immediately, but countered with "coffee?" When Mia nodded, she smiled. "I don't need a crystal ball, honey, to understand you. Remember, I had to reschedule three clients for you on Tuesday because you stayed with Miss Nearne for over four hours? I knew something was up, but I wisely kept my mouth shut. So, what's going on?"

Mia quickly told her about the phone call she'd just had from Sister Damian and her growing worry about whether she'd crossed a boundary with Eileen. "I keep wondering if I missed something. Eileen was quiet when I left, but she didn't seem distressed. Now I'm second-guessing everything."

Alexandra took a thoughtful sip of her coffee before replying. "It sounds like you handled the visit well. You've been careful, and she seemed to trust you. Maybe it's just a blip, something unrelated."

Mia nodded, but the unease still gnawed at her. "I hope you're right. Sister Damian said to wait until Sunday, but something isn't sitting right with me. I think I'll go for a walk and clear my head. I have no more appointments this afternoon. Just paperwork."

Alexandra smiled. "Good idea. Sometimes stepping away helps. Take your time. And you know where to find me—unless I'm gazing into my crystal ball."

"Ha, ha!" Mia slipped out of the building, letting the fresh air wash over her as she started down the path toward the promenade. The clouds hung low over the bay—a typical English summer day.

As she rounded a corner, deep in thought, Mia almost collided with a tall, familiar figure—Sebastian Stone, wearing his usual cheeky grin.

"Whoa, careful there, Thompson," he teased, though his tone was more casual than usual.

Mia didn't smile. "Sebastian. What are you doing here?"

"Oh, just out for a stroll," he said, glancing at her with a gleam in his eye. "You look troubled. Something on your mind?"

Mia crossed her arms, feeling a sudden chill. "You didn't happen to… visit Miss Nearne yesterday, did you?"

Sebastian's expression shifted, and Mia's heart sank as she saw the guilty look cross his face.

"Well, yeah, I thought I'd drop by," he admitted, scratching the back of his head. "Just to see if she'd open up a bit. You know how it is."

Mia's jaw tightened. "And?"

"She opened the door—thought I was you, I think. She gave me your hairclip, actually." He fished into his pocket and held out the small clip. "But when she realized I was, well, me, she shut the door in my face. I tried to tell her I knew you."

Mia stared at the hairclip in her trembling hand with a sinking heart. *So that's why Eileen hadn't gone to Mass.* Sebastian had spooked her, pushed her too far. And now the fragile trust she'd worked so hard to build was shattered. *I bring reporters in my wake.*

"You had no right," she snapped, her voice laced with anger.

"You've just set everything back. Do you have any idea what you've done?"

Sebastian's smile vanished. "I didn't mean to upset her. I just wanted to give her something I'd—"

"Just stay out of it, Sebastian," Mia cut him off. "You've done enough. Leave her alone."

"Mia, wait—" he called after her in a pleading voice. But she had already turned her back on him. Tears pricked at her eyes as she walked away, clutching the hairclip in her hand. *I'm not being professional,* she brooded. *I'm too close to this.*

PART IV

~EILEEN~ TORQUAY AUGUST, 2007

11

ECHOES OF EXPOSURE

The previous afternoon - Torquay, August 2007

Eileen sat in her worn armchair near the dead hearth, Whisky, her old cat, curled up in her lap. The rain lashed against the windows, but she was content, having been to the grocer's. Now she was dead-tired, ready for a nap, yet she kept staring at the hairclip she'd found wedged between the cushions after Mia had left.

"Mia," she repeated the name softly. So that had been the skinny girl she'd often seen hunkered down beneath Princess Pier. God, when had that been—five, ten years ago? Life went so fast, and Mia had certainly changed since then. Well, Didi knew all about how life could change in the flick of a moment.

She liked Mia—she liked few people these days—but the girl had warmth, an honesty that disarmed her, and a deep understanding that made her feel... safe. Or had it been a mistake to open up to that young doctor? Eileen shook her head. *A doctor.* She still saw that skinny girl with a small, dirty boy sitting next to her under the pier. She'd often wondered why the municipality didn't do anything about it. *It wasn't my responsibility*. She stayed out of everything, didn't interfere with good or bad. *One never knew what might be revealed if one interfered.*

Eileen shifted uncomfortably in the chair, but Whisky's weight kept her in place. Her fingers traced the delicate lines of the hair-clip. *Too much.* Had she said too much? She had spoken about her childhood—sunlit days by the sea, happy memories of Boulogne, the house in Nice... but it wasn't long before those memories darkened. She hadn't meant to talk so much. But Mia had a way of making her feel she could. *Talk can be dangerous.*

Eileen's mind wandered. *She's a psychologist, after all. She has a reason to be in my house—she's assessing me.* The thought brought an old, familiar tension crawling up her spine. She didn't need help. She'd managed just fine on her own for decades. A psychologist in her house was not part of her plan.

Eileen sighed, trying to shake off the nagging worries. *Something is wrong.* She knew disaster before it struck. It had become a sixth sense. *The Gestapo won't catch me a second time. Oh no!* She was prepared. Or was she? What did it matter, anyway? Mia seemed kind enough. And at her age, maybe it wasn't so bad to have someone looking out for her. Her fingers still fiddled with the clip, and she found herself wondering how long she could manage to keep letting Mia in before it became too much.

The bell rang sharply.

Eileen flinched, her thoughts scattering. No one rang that bell these days. Neighbors and postmen knew better; she never answered. Her breath quickened at the sound. *What now?* Whisky jumped from her lap, also alerted by the unfamiliar noise, and disappeared into the kitchen. Mia had knocked as instructed. Why hadn't she disconnected the damn thing? *I really should check the fuse box.*

As Eileen stared down at her hands, she noticed the hairclip she was still holding.

Oh, it's Mia! Of course.

She stood and walked slowly to the door, her body tired from the earlier trip to the grocer's, her mind muddled with exhaustion from the long conversation with Mia. She peeked through the small crack of the door as she turned the knob, expecting to see the familiar outline of Mia.

But it wasn't her.

There stood a man—tall, broad-shouldered, with a mop of pale ginger hair. Quite attractive in a classic, Celtic way. For a moment, Eileen's mind grew even more confused. He resembled an agent she'd known—Arnaud, another W/T Operator she'd worked with in Paris, but... Arnaud didn't have this wide smile. He was a serious man.

Her mind was all in a muddle as she tried to concentrate. *Arnaud? No...* The man said something—something about being a friend of Mia's—but she barely heard it. Her stomach turned. *The grin, the casual tone... why is this stranger standing at my door?*

She blinked, dazed, as memories came flooding back. The reporters. It wasn't Arnaud.

She was thrown back to the late nineties. After her BBC appearance in 1997, they had hounded her—one after another, knocking on her door, wanting her story, her details, her secrets. She had regretted every word of that interview. They had reduced her to just another spectacle.

"Are you a reporter?" The words barely left her lips, and she wasn't sure if he heard her at all. But the answer she feared came nonetheless. He flashed a press card. Torbay Weekly.

He's one of them. She wanted to scream. Her hand shook as she pushed Mia's hairclip into his outstretched hand, not even knowing why she did it. She slammed the door before he could say another word.

Eileen pressed her back against the door, breathing heavily. *Again*, she thought. *It's happening again. And Mia's involved.*

Encore les journalistes et les thérapeutes. J'aurais dû le savoir. Never trust reporters or therapists. *I should've known!*

The fragile thread of trust she'd started to feel toward Mia snapped. Just like that.

Her legs felt weak, and she stumbled back to her chair, collapsing into it, her mind swirling with mental fog and confusion. *What has Mia done?* Had she sent a man who looked like Arnaud to trick her? Eileen was too tired to make sense of it, too tired to even feel shocked. She only knew she wanted everything to stop, to rewind back to when she could hide behind her walls without interference.

But she needed the pension. *How can I get by if I stop letting Mia in?* The thought gnawed at her, leaving her feeling helpless. Her stomach churned, and she stared at the floor, the ticking of the clock on the wall driving deeper into her frazzled nerves.

"Meoww." Whisky jumped into her lap with a wail, his ginger fur pressing into her. Eileen's mind fogged. *Whisky?* But wasn't he...?

Her heart jolted, and in that moment, the flat, the door, and the confrontation with the tall man faded. She was back in her father's old black Renault, Whisky—the same ginger fur—nestled in her lap. The scent of petrol filled the air as the car jolted over the rough road, taking her farther from Nice, from the warm Mediterranean, from everything she'd known and loved.

Grenoble, she thought, her heart sinking. *Grim Grenoble. Oh, Nice! Where my carefree life had ended—and nothing would be the same ever again.*

PART V

~EILEEN~ FRANCE/ENGLAND 1940-1943

12

GRIM GRENOBLE

Grenoble, France, July 1940

The Nearnes found temporary shelter in La Monta, an old, comfortless château on Rue Adolphe Muguet. The château's cold stone walls and drafty rooms were a far cry from their sunny terraced bungalow overlooking the *Arènes de Cimiez* in Nice, but it was a refuge from the advancing German forces.

Situated in the middle of dark, pine forests and under overcast skies, Eileen felt as though they had been banished to a spooky, medieval castle, one from which she, the princess under a spell, would never escape. Even the bars on the windows and the murky moat surrounding the sturdy building made it feel like a prison.

Still, Jacqueline was with them again, and their eldest brother Francis and his wife Theresa lived just down the road. *Small comforts*, Eileen reminded herself.

Grenoble, nestled deep within the French Alps, was nothing like sunny, cosmopolitan Nice. Every day, a persistent mist hung low over the mountains, clinging to the jagged peaks like a heavy shroud. The air, thick with moisture, pressed against the bleak walls of La Monta. The cold stone trapped the damp, making the house feel more like a tomb than a refuge. Far too large and impractical for a family of four, but in this phase of the war, choice was not a luxury they had.

Even in July, they huddled by the hearth, desperate for warmth. The damp seeped into everything—into the walls, the floors, the furniture, the beds. Fires had to be kept burning day and night, but the wood from the nearby forests was so wet that it hissed and spat in protest, sending up more smoke than heat.

Moustache, Eileen's shy white cat, lay miserably on the hearth rug, curled as close to the sputtering flames as he could manage. His fur, once clean and bright under the sun, now looked dull and dingy. He shivered, protesting the cold, longing for the warmth of Nice where he had sprawled lazily in the sun-drenched courtyard, basking in the heat. Here, in Grenoble, even summer felt like winter to him.

Eileen crouched beside the fire, poking at the embers with frustration. "It's no use," she muttered. "Everything's wet. We'll never get warm at this rate."

Jacqueline entered, dropping a soggy bundle of logs near the hearth. "This is madness," she sighed, brushing damp hair from her face. "We're surrounded by trees, and yet there's not a single dry piece of wood to be found."

Eileen glanced at her sister before turning to the window, where mist curled like ghostly fingers through the trees, clinging to the dripping leaves. She knew they were relatively safe here and tried to be grateful. Anything could have happened if they'd refused to leave their bungalow on the Côte d'Azur. Nothing good, that much was certain. She shuddered. *Better not think of that.*

But the words slipped out before she could stop them. "I miss

Nice," she whispered. "The colors, the smells... they made me want to paint. But here, I can't. It's all grey and brown and black. Damp everywhere."

Her mind wandered back to the vibrant markets on *Cours Saleya*. If she closed her eyes, she could almost smell the fresh oranges, the tang of citrus mingling with the scent of ripe figs and lavender. The stalls were alive with color—bright reds and yellows from peppers and lemons, baskets overflowing with plump red tomatoes. The scents of sweet honey and freshly baked baguettes wafted across the square. She could hear the lively chatter of vendors, the clink of coins, the buzz of life under the warm sun, and always the soft lapping of the sea, the salt breeze dancing through the air.

Jacqueline, noticing the wistful tone in her sister's voice, began sorting through the logs, finding the driest ones. "Why don't you try to paint anyway, Didi? It might help, even just a little."

"My hands are too sore from all that wood cutting, Jacqui. But you're right, as soon as we manage to dry more wood and get this ridiculous house in order, I'll try." Eileen sighed, rubbing her palms together. "I just wish Maman felt better and would leave her bed, and that Papa would find a job. It feels like the entire household is on our shoulders."

Jacqueline sank into a creaky chair and pulled out a packet of cigarettes. With a flick of the lighter, the end of her cigarette glowed in the dim light.

"Give me one!" Eileen demanded, leaning forward.

"Didi, you shouldn't smoke. You're too young," Jacqueline replied, raising an eyebrow at her sister's sudden eagerness.

"Too young. Too scatterbrained. Too clumsy. Too dreamy," Eileen shot back, her voice trembling with frustration. "I'm no longer a child, Jacqui. I'm nineteen. I can smoke."

Taken aback by her sister's outburst, Jacqueline hesitated for a moment before handing over the packet of Lucky Strikes—black market, of course.

"Ah well," she sighed. "If it can give you any comfort, might as well."

Eileen lit her first cigarette and inhaled deeply, coughing only once. The sharp taste of the tobacco hit her, but along with it came a strange, soothing calm she hadn't felt since their harrowing escape from Nice three weeks earlier.

"Oh, I want to do this for the rest of my life!" she declared, grinning as she deftly held the cigarette between her index and middle fingers, imitating Jacqueline's practiced ease.

Jacqueline wrapped a blanket around her shoulders, gazing into the sputtering fire. "We traded the sun for mist," she said softly. "And excitement for survival."

"If only I had paid more attention to life in peace," Eileen mused. "I might even have been less discontent with dusting and ironing. At least we had music, light, and sunshine for our chores. And you'd bring me lovely little keepsakes from your travels. Do you miss it much, Jacqui, working for *Équipement de Bureau Riviera*?"

"Oh, I do, Didi." Jacqueline's voice was tinged with nostalgia. "Even though I had to deal with improper remarks and sleep in dingy hotels at times, it was fun. Plus, I made my own money. I can tell you, there's nothing like the feeling of being a woman earning her own keep. It's empowering."

Eileen could only imagine what that must feel like. "Maybe, one day, if I can sell my paintings to galleries, I'll understand what you mean."

Jacqueline rose from her seat, tossing off the blanket. "Moping has never gotten anyone anywhere, so let's get back to work, sweetie. It'll be lunchtime soon, and Papa always has an appetite. But before that... I might have found a bit of distraction for us."

Eileen's eyes lit up. "What is it, Sis? Tell me!"

"I will, but only if you promise we'll finish the work and not dwell on things."

Eileen placed her hand—still holding the cigarette—over her heart, scattering a fan of silvery ash across her cardigan. "I promise I'll never mope again. Not here, not anywhere."

Jacqueline smiled, then leaned in. "Alright. I met a student from the University of Grenoble. His name is Daniel, and he studies law. He told me they have a resistance group with the students, and he asked if I wanted to attend a meeting they're holding tonight."

Eileen's excitement flared. "Oh, now that sounds like a plan! And can I come too?" She quickly extinguished her cigarette, so eager that she seemed ready to clean the entire château from ceiling to cellar.

"Only if you don't tell Maman and Papa. We have to keep it secret. You know how they fuss over you."

Eileen rolled her eyes playfully and pressed her index finger over her lips, signaling that they were sealed.

LATER THAT NIGHT - *University of Grenoble*

THE HALL WAS DIMLY LIT, more like an underground bunker than a respectable university space. The walls were roughly plastered, and simple spotlights hung from the low ceiling, casting a diffuse glow over the crowd below. The air was thick with cigarette smoke, swirling in the low light, and the constant murmur of voices thrummed like the pulse of the very room.

Along the walls, long cabinets held an odd assortment of sports trophies, while banners, team photos, and posters for recent films and theater productions added bursts of color to the otherwise dingy room. The Nearne sisters slipped through the heavy wooden door without anyone noticing them. They stood close to the entrance, their eyes adjusting to the low lights and dense atmosphere.

"It's the students' hall," Jacqueline shouted into Eileen's ear, but her words barely registered. Eileen was already swept up in the atmosphere. The energy in the room buzzed with life—groups of young men huddled together, talking in low, intense voices, their cigarette embers glowing in the dim light. Scattered among them were young women, most dressed in trousers and jackets, some with berets pulled low over their brows. They exuded an ease and confidence Eileen instantly adored.

I'll never wear a dress again, she vowed, the idea suddenly thrilling. Here, in this smoke-filled room, surrounded by people who seemed to live by their own rules, she felt something stir inside her—liberty. It was in the air, in the laughter, in the conversations she couldn't quite catch, and in the relaxed way these students carried themselves.

She took a deep breath, inhaling the scent of tobacco, sweat, and excitement. *This!* This was what she had been missing all her life. Her coveted Nice life had never exposed her to anything like this, but now it was as though she had stepped into another universe, one where anything was possible.

"See him? That's Daniel." Jacqueline nodded toward a young man standing at the front, his eyes sharp as he was engaged in an animated conversation with several others, a shock of long dark hair hanging low over his brow. "He's the one who invited me."

As they edged closer to the front, Daniel greeted them with a firm handshake. Eileen lingered behind as he introduced Jacqueline to his entourage, feeling slightly out of place. Suddenly, a voice broke through her thoughts.

"You don't look like a student."

Eileen turned to see a young man with a cheeky grin leaning

casually against the wall. His slightly protruding front teeth only added to his charm, and the mischievous glint in his eyes made her take a second look.

Mimicking his playful tone, she replied, "Neither do you."

He laughed, a light, unguarded sound that made her feel instantly at ease. "Touché. I'm Andy, student of life and bad bass player," he said, holding out his hand. "And you?"

"I'm Eileen, but everyone calls me Didi," she replied, shaking his warm, firm hand.

"Ah, Eileen, the English girl," he said, his grin widening. "I've heard about you and your sister."

"You have?" Eileen tilted her head, intrigued.

"Word travels fast around here. Two British girls hiding out in the French Alps? Not exactly a common story." His tone was teasing but kind.

Eileen felt herself relax a little more. Andy seemed genuine, his easy-going nature a welcome contrast to the tension that had been building inside her. "We're not hiding. We're just... waiting..." she said, her voice trailing off.

Leaning in, he whispered in her ear, "Waiting for the right moment, I hope. Because you know," he gestured around the room with a sweep of his arm, "waiting without purpose can turn dangerous. People here are tired of waiting. And tired of living under the Germans' thumb."

Eileen's gaze swept across the smoky hall, remembering why they had come. She and Jacqueline hadn't come just to chat with charming boys—they were here to see if they could do something to change their bleak situation. She straightened her posture, reminded of the importance of paying attention.

Jacqueline, who'd been deep in conversation with Daniel, turned toward her. "Didi," she said in a low voice, "Daniel's talking about a resistance network they're setting up here in Grenoble. They might be able to help us get the papers in case we would … you know …want to try to get to England."

Eileen gasped. They'd never even discussed that, while Andy gave her a knowing look. "So, you're not just here for the company, then?"

"No, we're not."

"Welcome to the anti-Nazi club, Didi," he said with a grin.

Just then, Daniel's voice cut through the hum of conversation. "Attention, everyone," he called out in the tone of a commander. The chatter died down, and all eyes turned to him. "First, let's make sure all the doors are locked. And everyone check there aren't any unwanted faces among us. If you see anyone unfamiliar, speak up now. These two new faces," he gestured toward the Nearne sisters, "are with me. I vouch for them."

Andy leaned closer. "It's happening," he whispered. "The resistance is growing. If you're ready, you could be part of it."

Eileen felt her heart swell with pride as she nodded. *Part of it.* The very idea was so thrilling. This was a world beyond the boredom of Grenoble, beyond the cold walls of La Monta. A world with purpose. She glanced at Jacqueline, whose eyes reflected the same excitement. They'd come looking for a distraction, but they had found something much bigger—a spark of rebellion, a chance to fight back.

Satisfied the room was secure, Daniel continued. "As we all know, Grenoble won't escape the war for much longer. The Germans are moving south, and it's only a matter of time before they reach us. We need to act. We need to prepare."

"But how?" a girl in a red beret demanded, a cigarette glowing between her fingers.

"There are many ways," Daniel replied calmly. "But as students, we should start with using our skills and resources wisely. We'll begin by forging papers. There are Jewish families, British citizens, and others who need to get out. We can help them."

"I like it," the girl in the beret said, nodding thoughtfully. "We could use the university presses to make copies."

"I'd rather focus on self-defense," a burly man interjected, his large frame more suited to a wrestling ring than a classroom. "We need para-military training if we're going to stand a chance against the Germans."

Murmurs of agreement rippled through the room, and the conversation turned to strategy and logistics. Ideas flew around like sparks from a woodfire—each suggestion more daring than the last.

As Eileen listened, her excitement grew. They would act. Soon. For the first time in what felt like forever, she wasn't just waiting. She and Jacqueline were part of something—something greater than chopping wood and filling kettles to make tea.

13

THE GREAT ESCAPE

Twenty months later - Grenoble, France, 20 March 1942

Eileen stared down at her hands, dusted with white flour, as she prepared to knead another loaf of bread. It was just one of the many endless chores that awaited her on this dreary March morning. Though it was past ten o'clock, La Monta was so deeply nestled in the forest, daylight barely reached the windows. Even the kitchen, with its view of the long meadow beyond, remained shadowed, the wet grass outside glistening faintly under the overcast sky.

The air in the house was thick, oppressive. A single candle flickered against the cold, stone walls. Electricity was a luxury they couldn't afford to waste, and the dim, sputtering light seemed to match the mood inside La Monta—bleak and suffocating.

As her hands worked the dough, her eyes wandered to the trees outside, their dark silhouettes blurred by mist. Beyond them, the Alps loomed in the distance, their jagged peaks shrouded in the same unshakable fog that clung to everything in Grenoble. The unyielding mist seemed to creep into her very soul, weighing her down with each passing day. It had been like this for nearly two years now—a life of routine and waiting, of cold and silence.

Something has to change.

The thought flickered in her mind like the spluttering candle. Too weary to even act on it, she tried to shake it off. But the more she kneaded, the more the frustration inside her grew, building like a storm she could no longer contain.

I can't stand this anymore.

The words formed before she could stop them - a raw, whispered confession. Her hands moved more furiously, attacking the dough with an intensity that mirrored the anger welling up inside her.

"Something has to change soon, or I'll break," Eileen muttered. "A life in limbo is no life at all."

Jacqueline, who was peeling potatoes at the sink, glanced up. Eileen could see the same weariness etched in her sister's face. She dropped another potato into the pan of water, dried her hands on her apron, and retrieved her cigarettes from her apron pocket. They shared a Lucky Strike—rationed like everything else.

"I agree," Jacqueline sighed, exhaling smoke and handing the cigarette to Eileen. "We're wasting away here."

The enthusiasm that had once filled them during those early meetings with the students at the university had long since faded. Weeks had turned into months, and months into years. The resistance efforts moved at a crawl, and their family remained in hiding, keeping a low profile as British citizens in enemy territory.

"We need to leave, Jacqui," Eileen said, her voice firmer this time. "This place... it's suffocating us."

Jacqueline crumpled the empty Lucky Strike package with a grunt. "I've been thinking the same thing. Maman and Papa will be alright here with Francis and Theresa to look after them. But you and I... we need to get to England. Join the war effort."

"Papa will never let me go," Eileen said sadly. The longing in her voice was unmistakable. The idea of leaving Grenoble felt like a distant dream, one that had lingered for too long.

"You're twenty-one now, Didi," Jacqueline said, a hint of determination in her tone. "That's what I've been waiting for. You can make your own choices now."

For a moment, hope soared in Eileen's chest, but it quickly faltered. Her shoulders slumped again. "But how? Even if Papa agrees, how would we leave? Where would we go?"

Jacqueline's lips curled into a mischievous grin. "I've been waiting to hear from Daniel," she said quietly. "Yesterday... he told me he might be able to finally get us forged papers. If he does, we can go, Didi. We can leave for England. We still have family in London. We could stay with them."

The mention of Daniel brought back memories of that smoky university hall—the excitement of being part of something bigger than herself. But that excitement had soured. Nothing had moved forward, and Eileen had grown tired of waiting.

"Are you sure?" she asked, uncertainty lacing her voice.

"Not sure," Jacqueline admitted, "but it's the best shot we've had so far. This war is dragging on forever. No one expected it to last this long, and it's getting worse. And here we are, two strong young women, idling away in the Alps. What good is that?"

"No good at all," Eileen grumbled.

"I'm meeting Daniel this afternoon," Jacqueline continued. "He said he'll know more by then."

A smile finally broke across Eileen's face, lighting up her features. "Fingers crossed!"

Later that evening, the Nearne family sat around the kitchen table. The silent tension that hung in the air was as smothering as the smoke from the damp logs smoldering in the AGA cooker. Eileen's hands shook slightly with trepidation as she stared hard at the worn tablecloth, waiting for Jacqueline to speak.

Their father puffed on his pipe, brow furrowed as he remained engrossed in one of his beloved English novels. Eileen thought he looked tired—worn down by years of uncertainty, yet still fiercely protective of his family.

Jacqueline was the first to break the silence. "Papa, Maman... Didi and I have made a decision."

Jack's eyes narrowed, and their mother looked up from her knitting, her hands stilling over the half-finished grey sock. The gravity of the moment hung in the air, clear to everyone at the table.

"What decision?" Jack asked, his voice tight.

"That we're leaving," Jacqueline said firmly. "We're going to England."

"Absolutely not!" Jack slammed his pipe down, scattering ashes across the table. "You girls are not leaving. It's far too dangerous."

Eileen held her breath. She had expected this reaction, but it didn't soften the blow. "Papa," she said quietly, "Jacqui and I are wasting away here. Don't you and Maman want to see us happier than this? We want to join the war effort. Sitting here in the Alps isn't going to change anything." She stopped herself from saying they were "rotting away"—such words were forbidden in their strict Catholic household.

Her mother's face paled. "Didi, you're too delicate for such risks. What if something happens to you?"

Eileen felt Jacqueline's reassuring hand squeeze hers. "We're not children anymore, Maman," Jacqueline said softly but firmly. "I've seen enough of the world to know how to protect Didi. I'll always look after her."

Jack's face was stern. "You don't understand the dangers out there," he insisted. "The journey alone is filled with risks, and once you're in England, there's no guarantee of safety."

"There's no safety here either," Jacqueline countered. "The war is closing in on all of Europe. We're like rats in a trap. Hitler won't rest until he's squeezed the life out of every one of us."

Eileen swallowed hard. "Papa, we need to make a stand. You were young once. You fought in the Great War. Now let us do our part in this one."

Her father's expression softened at that. She could see the weight of her words sinking in. He glanced at Marie, who had slowly resumed knitting with trembling hands.

"What do you say, Marie?" Jack asked in a quieter voice. "The girls seem determined to go."

Marie's eyes glistened with tears. "Oh, Jack, I don't know how we'll manage without them. But I do see their point. Life isn't getting any better here. And Frederick is already doing his bit. You tell us what to do."

Jack looked between his daughters, seeing their resolve. His gaze softened even further as he recognized the determination in their faces. "Promise me you'll be careful," he said as the fight in him died down.

Eileen nodded with a heavy heart. "We will, Papa. We promise."

Tears rolled down her mother's cheeks as she dropped the knitting once again and reached across the table, taking both her daughters' hands in hers. "May God protect you both," she uttered in a voice thick with emotion. "Go and make us proud."

Jack's voice cracked as he gave his final consent. "Then go. Do what you must. May the Good Lord protect and guide you."

"God always protects us, Papa," Eileen said in a trembling voice. "Always."

14

THE LAST EASTER DINNER

Two weeks later - Grenoble, 5 April 1942

The Easter Sunday meal at the Nearnes was a subdued event, more a farewell gathering than a celebration of the Resurrection. Yet, Eileen, with her fervent belief in life over death, prayed with all her soul for peace—that the sacrifice Jacqueline and she were about to make would help lead the way to freedom from the fetters of the evil German Reich.

The family sat around the wooden table in a kitchen lit by more candles than usual—a small luxury they could scarcely afford, but one that cast a faint sense of festivity over the somber gathering. The rich scents of roast lamb and rosemary, mingled with the ever-present smoke from the wet logs in the Aga, were the result of more luxury obtained with weeks of saved ration cards.

Even the traditional Easter dishes and the small glasses of sherry Jack had poured did little to lift the heavy mood. Every bite felt, to Eileen, like a reminder of what she was about to lose—her family, the only constant she'd known her whole life.

In her twenty-one years, Eileen had never spent a day away from her parents and siblings. As the youngest and most babied member of the family, she had no idea what life outside her sheltered existence looked like. Yet the freedom of it tugged at her, like the open field beckons a dog still held on a leash.

As the sisters sat side by side, Eileen was more aware than ever that they were in this together. Without Jacqueline, she wouldn't have even considered leaving her family. But inwardly, she resolved that it was time to grow up. She wouldn't completely depend on her elder sister—she would make her own mark, carve out her own path. How, she didn't know yet, but that it would happen, of that, Eileen was sure.

Across from them, their mother tried to keep her hands steady as she ladled out portions of mashed potatoes and gravy. But her skin was pale and taut, the dark rings under her eyes betraying sleepless nights spent with the fear of losing her daughters to the folly of war.

Eileen cast furtive glances around the table. Her father, seated at the head, eternally puffed on his pipe, the lines on his face deeper than she remembered. Francis, her eldest brother, sat to their father's left, his nervous, twitching mouth and restless eyes betraying his anxiety. He kept one arm draped protectively around his wife, Theresa, who stared silently into her plate. Their three-year-old son, Jack II, sat beside her, pushing a small wooden horse back and forth over the white damask tablecloth. Even he was quieter than usual, sensing the tension that hung in the air.

When their plates were filled, her father's sonorous voice began the Lord's Prayer, and the familiar words carried an extra layer of meaning for Eileen. She blessed God, her family, the safety of the house she was leaving behind, and the unknown path ahead.

After a solemn Amen, they ate in near silence, the clinking of forks on plates the only sound breaking the stillness.

Marie looked at her daughters, blinking away a tear that constantly threatened to spill. "You'll write to us, girls, won't you?"

"Of course, Maman, as soon as we can. But you know how it is—things may not be straightforward with the war. Postal services are unreliable," Jacqueline assured her. "But we'll try to send word as soon as we arrive in England."

"And if we can't, please don't assume the worst," Eileen added, though her voice was smaller than she intended. "We'll be fine."

Despite the care Marie had taken to prepare a lavish meal, Eileen struggled to swallow. The reality of leaving her family squashed any appetite she had. She caught the faint sound of her mother's rosary beads slipping quietly through her fingers under the table.

Jack put his fork down and cleared his throat. "Girls... just know we'll be praying for you every day, asking God to keep you safe."

Eileen forced a smile. "Thank you, Papa. I'll say my prayers too."

Little Jack, sensing the tension, looked up from his wheeled horse. "Aunt Didi, where going?"

Eileen hesitated, then ruffled his dark hair. "We're going on an adventure, Jack. A very important adventure."

Jacqueline, more composed, added, "But we'll be back, Jack."

"I come?"

His childlike enthusiasm softened the strain in the room.

"No sweetie, not this time," Theresa explained.

"You must stay here and take care of everyone while we're gone, alright?" Eileen teased gently.

Little Jack thought about it, then nodded solemnly. "Okay, Auntie."

The meal ended quietly, and as they gathered in the parlor for a final moment of prayer, Marie led them in reciting the Hail Mary. To Eileen, the familiar words felt like a lifeline in the uncertainty she was facing. Never had her beads felt so important, her whispered words so potent.

THE NEXT MORNING, the first light of dawn broke over the mist-shrouded Alps as Eileen and Jacqueline Nearne embarked on the most dangerous journey of their lives. Clutching her suitcase, Eileen glanced back at the rugged mountain range that had both sheltered and imprisoned her for the past two years. Grenoble, once a refuge, had become her prison—a prison she was finally breaking free from. But at what cost?

Her parents' final embrace felt like something out of a dream—her entire being suspended in a surreal mix of fear and determination. The forged papers tucked inside their coats claimed they were French citizens, the De Bonville sisters. But in their hearts, they were still British, carrying their true identities as a hidden weight. Their parents didn't even know the full extent of the danger--arrest with false papers was a constant, looming threat.

As Eileen called out a final *au revoir* to her parents, huddled together in the dimly lit entrance of La Monta, her mother's whispered prayers lingered in the still morning air. A cold shiver ran through her as a sense of finality settled deep in her chest. Would she ever see them again? The chill of the early morning was nothing compared to the dread creeping through her veins, the sharp awareness of life's frailty—and the strength of their family bond.

Her father's parting words— "May God protect you"—echoed in her mind as they boarded the Lyon-bound train at Gare de Grenoble.

Had Eileen known what lay ahead, known that it would be seven long years before she saw her family again, would she have had the courage to board that train?

Would she?

PART VI

~ EILEEN ~ TORQUAY 2007

15

WAKING FROM THE PAST

Torquay, August 2007

Eileen woke with a jolt, her breath coming in sharp gasps. The choice—safety or the brutal fight for survival—loomed in her half-conscious mind. *La baignoire*, the barbed wire. All she had endured for "going on an adventure." The cool air of her flat felt stifling, as oppressive as the foggy mountain air she'd left behind so many decades ago.

For a moment, she couldn't place where she was. Her hand flexed as if still clutching the small brown suitcase. Her body trembled with the chill of that April morning in Grenoble. But instead of frost underfoot, it was the sagging familiarity of her old armchair that met her.

The rhythmic ticking of Jacqueline's clock—like her sister's steady heartbeat with her everywhere—brought Eileen back to Torquay and 2007. Her fingers tightened around her rosary, not the suitcase. *I'm safe again*, she thought. *Safe for now*.

She sat up, gripping the armrest, steadying herself from the emotional shock she'd just endured. Her heart pounded in her ears, while the past swept over her in waves—the crunch of frozen ground beneath her best shoes, Jacqueline's urgent voice telling her they couldn't miss the train.

"I am Elle de Bonville. No, Jacqueline Duterte." So many aliases, so many names. They blurred in her mind, but one image remained crystal-clear: the moment she left her family behind, burned into her memory as though it had happened yesterday. Her father's soft, resigned blessing. Her mother's tear-streaked gaze. The way they'd stood in the dim light of La Monta, huddled together as if still trying to shield their Didi from the cruelty of the world outside.

Seven years.

The knowledge that it had taken seven long years to be reunited with her beloved Papa and Maman still sliced through Eileen like a bitter wind, even now. Had she known—had she realized how long that separation would last, how much she would have to endure just to survive—would she have had the courage to board that train?

Eileen shuddered. The answer wasn't in the young girl who left, but in the old woman she had become—an answer she could never have known at the time. Thank God she hadn't known. Neither had her family. If they had, it never would have happened. A blessing and a curse, tangled together like the threads of her life, all lived by the grace of God's mysterious ways.

She gazed around the small flat, where shadows gathered in the corners like old secrets. Night had fallen, the blurry light of the street lantern in front of her house shining through the gauze curtains. Her eyes flicked to the clock. It was past eleven. She'd been in her chair since late afternoon.

Stiffly, Eileen rose to close the heavy curtains. Whisky meowed and curled his tail around her legs.

"Sure, you're hungry, you little monster. *Tu as toujours de l'appétit.*" On legs that refused to move as quickly as she wished, Eileen shuffled to her kitchen—and then stopped, forgetting why she'd come.

They're all gone.

She'd lost them all—Maman first, then Francis, Frederick, Papa, Jacqueline, even little Jack and Theresa. Only Odile, Fred's daughter, remained. But she was far away. For a moment, Eileen let the familiar ache seep into her, the hollow pain of losing everyone—her family, her childhood, the safety net that had once cradled her. *How terrified I was, that day in the Alps.*

Until then, her parents had kept her so small—out of love, because they cared. But in that final goodbye, she hadn't just left them. She had left behind delicate Didi, the God-fearing, scatterbrained dreamer of a daughter they had raised. In her place was the wartime agent who would do whatever it took to survive.

That wrenching goodbye had been the crucible, forging her into something stronger than anyone had believed she could be. A quiet, fierce determination had rooted itself in her, a need to survive, no matter what came her way. And God knew the war had thrown everything at her. The war, and the aftermath.

"Meow, meow."

"Alright, my dear. Feed you and put the kettle on."

Eileen rubbed her eyes, exhaustion blending with a dull ache in her chest. But she was still here, wasn't she? After all the suffering, after the Gestapo interrogations, after the cold and hunger of the camps. They had almost broken her—almost. But not quite. When it came to survival, she had one compass: God would see her through. And He had.

But Whisky cared more about food in his bowl than his mistress's musings and made that loud and clear.

....

With Whisky fed and contently curled up on his cushion near the hearth, Eileen settled back into her armchair, tucking her blanket around her legs, the warmth of her tea seeping through the porcelain cup. The ticking of the clock seemed to mark the time she had left, which wouldn't be long, she thought. She took a sip, letting the heat soothe her throat, and tried to focus on the present, on what needed to be done.

Mia. She liked the young woman, more than she cared to admit. She'd even started to trust her, just a little. That slight urchin from beneath Princess Pier, so much like the ravaged children she'd seen in Ravensbrück. But look at her now—all poshly dressed and a doctor. Quiet determination, the kind Eileen admired. A survivor.

But now... *Sebastian.* Eileen grimaced, the memory of his intrusion at her door still raw. How dare he? How could Mia have allowed him to get so close? They knew each other. He'd rung her bell because Eileen had let *her* in. *Reporters... always after the war story.*

But Mia should have known better than to let him approach. Or... was it an accident? Something Mia hadn't anticipated?

Her hands trembled as she placed the cup back on the saucer. *I'll have to stop seeing her now,* Eileen thought. But the implications gnawed at her. She needed Mia's help with her pension. And despite everything, she didn't want to push the girl away. Not completely. Maybe... maybe if she told Mia what had happened, they could fix this. *But could she be trusted again?*

Eileen sighed, staring into the steam rising from her tea. The past and present swirled together in her mind, impossible to separate, like smoke curling into itself. Mia—her hands stretched through the gates, begging for a crust of bread, her dress in tatters, lice crawling through her matted hair. Eileen blinked, trying to banish the images, but they were only replaced with worse feelings —the worry, the anger, the betrayal. But the fear clung to her, like the mist that had always shrouded Grenoble.

As she finished her tea, even its warmth couldn't dissolve the cold that had settled inside her. Exhaustion weighed down her bones. Eileen placed the empty cup on the side table and stood, her movements slow and deliberate as she prepared for bed. Whisky followed, weaving between her legs as if sensing her unease.

In the bedroom, she lay down, pulling the covers up to her chin, her body aching with fatigue. She closed her eyes, hoping for dreamless sleep but knowing that the past would come, as it always did.

And sure enough, it came. In the darkness, the train's whistle shrieked in her ears, the cold Alpine air nipping at her cheeks as she and Jacqueline boarded that fateful train. The weight of her suitcase was back in her hands, the fear a knot in her stomach as she left behind all she'd ever known. And ahead of her... the unknown.

PART VII

~ EILEEN ~ FRANCE/ENGLAND 1942-1943

16

AN ARDUOUS TRIP

Grenoble, April 1942

The first leg of the journey, from Grenoble to Marseille, was a quiet storm of anxiety. Eileen sat stiffly in her seat, her fingers clenched around the armrest, her false identity papers tucked securely in the pocket of her coat. Every screech of the train's brakes sent a jolt through her body. She exchanged tense glances with Jacqueline, who appeared outwardly composed, but the slight tremor in her sister's hand as she lit a cigarette betrayed her unease.

"*Ça va*?" Eileen whispered, already wondering if they'd done the right thing. Normally, on a morning like this, they would be chopping wood or baking bread. Now, every mile that separated her from La Monta felt like a trip into the abyss.

"*Biensûr*," Jacqueline whispered back, retrieving two old copies of 'Marie Claire' from her bag and handing one to Eileen. "Read," she instructed, "or at least pretend to."

Eileen did as she was told, though inwardly she rehearsed her new identity: Marie de Bonville, traveling with her sister Elle to visit their ailing Spanish grandmother in Madrid. Though Eileen had always enjoyed role-playing, the stakes felt much higher now. Her life more or less depended on it.

"I'll just be myself," she decided, glancing down at the magazine but not seeing the pages. "After all, we did have Spanish grandparents, and Jacqui is my real sister. And I can speak Spanish if they test me."

The only thing different was her British nationality – the lack thereof - which now felt almost as foreign to her as Great Britain itself. Apart from short family visits, her life—at least the last nineteen years of it—had been thoroughly French. She even spoke English with a French accent.

When the train finally rolled into Gare Marseille-Saint-Charles, where they would change trains for Barcelona, Eileen's heart constricted at the familiar sights—the Mediterranean coastline glinting in the distance, the scent of salt and citrus in the air. Though Marseille wasn't Nice, the sea was the same. But now, fear overshadowed any fondness she had for the region. France had become just another obstacle, another prison to escape from.

As they disembarked, scanning the station for the international train to Barcelona, Eileen tried to relax. At least they were outside of Italian-occupied France and could communicate more freely now. Jacqueline kept her pace steady, whispering instructions as they neared the exit gate.

"Stay calm, Didi. We're French, remember?"

Eileen nodded, though her heart pounded in her chest. The lie tasted bitter on her tongue, but it was their only protection. When they approached the checkpoint, a French police officer stood before them, his eyes cold as they flicked from Eileen to Jacqueline.

"Passports, travel papers," the officer barked, holding out his hand.

Jacqueline handed over their forged papers, her voice steady. "Elle de Bonville," she said, "and my sister, Marie."

The officer narrowed his eyes, flipping through the documents. His gaze lingered on Eileen's face for a moment before returning to the papers. He hesitated, his lips pursed under his black moustache. Eileen could hardly breathe. Why was he taking so long?

"Where are you going?" the officer asked, after a thorough inspection.

"We need to board the train to Barcelona. Could you tell me the platform, Sir?"

The man looked at Jacqueline as if she'd spoken in a foreign tongue, his eyes still fixed on their documents. *Hurry up,* Eileen thought. *There's nothing wrong with them.*

"These papers..." the French gendarme muttered, signaling to another officer. "Charles, have a look."

The other man, tall and menacing, stepped closer, taking his time flipping through the papers. "There's something off with them, Jean," he said. Turning to the sisters, he barked, "Follow me."

Eileen's throat tightened as they were ushered aside.

"You cannot continue to Spain with these papers," the second officer finally said, his voice cold. "You lack the proper exit permits."

Jacqueline's face remained calm, though Eileen could feel her tension. "There must be some mistake, Sir," Jacqueline replied politely. "We've traveled from Grenoble, and our papers should be in order. We're French citizens—"

"I can see that," the officer cut her off. "But no proper exit papers, no train. Understood?"

Eileen felt panic rising in her. What were they going to do? They couldn't return to Grenoble, not after coming this far. She looked to

Jacqueline, whose calm façade was beginning to crack. The forged papers had been their only ticket out, and now they were stranded.

After what felt like an eternity, the officer waved them off. "Resolve it with the authorities. But for now, you're not leaving."

The sisters were left standing in Marseille's station with their suitcases, watching the crowd ebb and flow around them.

"What now?" Eileen asked in a small voice.

Jacqueline's jaw tightened. "We can't stay here. If we try again, they might get suspicious, and suspicion is the last thing we need."

"But how do we leave without the proper permits? How could we have the wrong exit papers?" Eileen muttered, frustration creeping into her voice.

Jacqueline hesitated for a moment before her eyes lit with sudden determination. "I don't know, Didi. Something must've changed. But we'll try our luck at the American consulate. Daniel told me if anything went wrong, we should head there."

Eileen blinked in confusion. "What? Why the American consulate? We're, you know..." She didn't finish, wary of being overheard.

"The British consulate closed in 1940, after the Armistice. But the Americans are still operating. They might be able to help us." Jacqueline was already heading toward the exit, and Eileen quickly followed. "We show them our real passports, tell them who we are, and hope they can get us out," Jacqueline added in a hushed voice.

"But our French identities..." Eileen began, her words trailing off.

"We won't involve the French authorities," her sister replied firmly. "We'll use our real papers. The Americans might be able to help us."

Eileen swallowed hard, a fresh wave of nerves crashing over her. What would happen if they abandoned their French aliases and revealed their true identities? They still had to cross part of France to reach Spain.

The American consulate was tucked away in a leafy suburban part of the city, a modest building guarded by two sentries, the American flag fluttering proudly above. Jacqueline strode up to the door, her back straight and determined. Eileen followed, trying to mimic her sister's calm exterior, though her heart pounded in her chest.

Inside, they were greeted by a tired-looking, balding consular officer. His desk was cluttered with papers, and a large, framed photograph of a solemn woman in a black dress sat prominently on his desk—probably his wife.

Jacqueline wasted no time, explaining their situation in English, tinged with French. "We're British subjects, Sir, and we urgently need to leave France to get back to England. Can you help us?" She carefully avoided mentioning the forged papers.

The man raised an eyebrow, his tired expression growing a bit more skeptical. "You're just now trying to leave? Most Brits cleared outta here in '40. I thought everyone had gone by now." He let out a long sigh. "Look, if I can get you the right papers, it's gonna be a hassle. Things've changed a lot these past two years. We're about to shut this post down too. It's getting real dicey around here." He looked at them pointedly. "You got your passports?"

Jacqueline nodded, and with steady hands, she retrieved their real identity papers from behind the double lining of her suitcase. Eileen followed, her fingers trembling as she handed over her documents.

The officer didn't say anything, but his raised eyebrow spoke volumes. "Well, alright then," he muttered, flipping through their passports. "Here's how it works—you're gonna have to get to Barcelona first, then on to Madrid. After that, you'll wanna head for Lisbon. Once you hit Lisbon, you'll be on safer ground—maybe catch a plane or a boat to the UK. I can get you papers to get as far as Madrid, but from there, you're gonna have to hit up the consulate in Spain. And just so we're clear," he added, leaning forward, "I can't guarantee squat. If the French or the Spaniards decide to get fussy, they will. You follow?"

Eileen nodded, a flicker of hope rising. "So... we can leave?"

"Yeah, you can leave," he replied, tapping their documents. "But move fast. Like I said, no guarantees. Once you're across the border into Spain, though, you'll probably be alright."

With quick, practiced movements, he drew up the necessary papers, stamping them several times and adding his signature. "Good luck, ladies," he said, handing them back with a nod. "You're gonna need it."

At the Spanish border, the precariousness of their situation became all too clear to the sisters. Spanish soldiers with hardened faces and stiff uniforms boarded the train, barking orders in rapid Spanish and scrutinizing every passenger's papers with military precision.

Their fluency in the language, thanks to their mother, was their lifeline as the soldiers, in their haste, took apart anyone who didn't immediately comply.

Eileen kept her eyes lowered as she handed over her British passport, bracing herself for the worst—half-expecting to be dragged off the train and marched back to France, where imprisonment likely awaited. Beside her, Jacqueline's steady breathing provided a calming anchor, and Eileen clung to her sister's composed demeanor.

"Where are you going?" the soldier demanded in a gruff tone, barely glancing up from their documents.

It had already become an unspoken rule that Jacqueline

answered for both of them. “We’re on our way to Madrid to obtain our next exit papers,” she responded in flawless Spanish. “From there, we’ll continue to London, where our cousin is waiting for us.”

The soldier’s eyes flicked between the two of them before grunting something unintelligible and stamping their papers. With a curt nod, he moved on. Jacqueline allowed herself the briefest smile of triumph, but neither sister exhaled until the train finally pulled away from the border.

“That went alright,” Eileen whispered, her voice shaky with relief.

“We’re not safe yet,” Jacqueline reminded her. “Spain isn’t exactly friendly to people like us.”

She was right. The journey through Spain felt like one long held-breath. At every stop was the feeling that the train could be stopped, the tension palpable. Rumors about travelers being sent to the infamous *Miranda de Ebro* internment camp rippled among the few international passengers. Eileen remained silent, lowering her head each time soldiers patrolled the platform, their boots echoing like a warning.

Maybe I’m not built for this life of adventure, she thought bitterly. *Maybe I am too naive for this, as everyone always tried to tell me.*

Sensing her unease, Jacqueline nudged her lightly. “You’re doing great, Didi,” she whispered. “You’ll get used to living without certainties. It’s all about going with the flow.”

Eileen managed a weak smile. “I’ll try. I want to.”

Finally, in Madrid, hope flickered to life. The British Consulate, operating quietly behind thick doors and with hushed voices, provided them with their proper exit papers. The road ahead remained uncertain, but they were one step closer to freedom. Lisbon, their next destination, lay in neutral territory. For the first time in two years, the Nearne sisters wouldn’t be hunted, wouldn’t be viewed as *persona non grata*.

. . .

THEY ARRIVED IN LISBON, where sleepless nights in cheap, drafty rooms became their new reality. The uncertainty of how they would ultimately make their passage to Britain left them despondent until, finally, a stroke of luck arrived in the form of Captain George Thompson, a burly sailor with a heart of gold and a weathered face to match.

Eileen's spirits instantly lifted as they were introduced to him on the docks. The captain stood well over six feet, his broad shoulders filling the cabin doorway of *The Highland's Lass*. His salt-and-pepper beard looked as though it hadn't seen a trim in years, and his sun-worn skin gave him the look of a man who'd spent more of his life at sea than on land.

"Well, what have we here? A pair of British lassies, eh?" Thompson's voice was as gruff as his appearance, with a thick Scottish burr. He eyed them both, his steel-blue gaze softening as he noticed the weariness in their eyes. "Don't worry, I'll get ye to Gibraltar safe and sound. Been sailin' these waters since before ye were born."

Eileen exchanged a glance with Jacqueline, both suppressing their nervous laughter at his confidence.

Thompson patted the railing of his merchant ship, which, while sturdy, looked like it had seen better days. "She ain't no luxury liner, but she'll hold her own," he said proudly, thumping his chest. "I've never had passengers before, mind ye, especially young ladies. But don't fret, lassies. I'll make sure yer comfortable."

As he led them aboard, Eileen noticed the mismatched flowers that adorned the captain's quarters—wildflowers placed haphazardly in old bottles and cups. "Thought ye'd appreciate a wee touch of color," Thompson grinned, scratching his beard. "Not much for decoratin' but figured lassies might like it."

Eileen stifled a giggle, touched by the odd, kind gesture. She could tell that beneath the gruff exterior, Captain Thompson had a gentle side. His booming voice might have sounded intimidating at first, but there was a kindness in his eyes, an understanding of the toll the war had taken on everyone, even those like them who were running from it.

"Thank you, Captain," Jacqueline said in English. "We're so grateful for your help."

"Ach, it's nothin'," he waved it off, "just doin' my bit for the war, same as anyone. Ye'll be fine with me." He winked at Eileen. "Just sit tight and don't go wanderin' the decks too much. The sea's a temperamental mistress, she is."

"I won't, Captain," she promised, feeling a welcome measure of comfort in the warmth of his presence. For the first time in weeks, she felt a sense of safety. Captain Thompson was a person she knew she would always remember. And they were finally moving forward, step by step, toward Britain—away from the shadows of war-torn France.

When they finally set foot on the Rock of Gibraltar, Eileen's legs nearly gave out from sheer relief.

"You've got a fine pair of legs, lassie, but they're not sea legs," Captain Thompson chuckled.

Eileen couldn't agree more. The rocky terrain beneath her feet felt solid and safe, like a fortress after the endless days on the rough sea. The seaman, with his gruff but kind smile, thrust the now-wilted flowers into their arms. "I ain't got use for these anymore, girls. Now, ye take care of each other, and when ye get to Glasgow, say hello to Scotland for me."

He handed them the final papers for their last leg across the waters. "You'll sail on HMS Britannia—one of the Navy's finest."

Eileen and Jacqueline thanked him, feeling extremely grateful. Captain Thompson had been their unlikely savior, and Eileen knew his kindness would stay with her forever.

"Good luck to ye, lassies," Thompson called after them as they walked down the dock. "You'll do fine. Fight for what's right, and don't let the bastards grind ye down."

Over 2 months since departing Grenoble, finally in late June 1942, the passenger ship from Gibraltar eased into Glasgow's dock like a tired old lady, having withstood German attacks from above and below—Messerschmitts in the sky and U-boats lurking beneath the waves. The passengers, as weary and shaken as the vessel herself, heaved a collective sigh of relief as they reached the freedom of Great Britain.

The morning sky over the port of Greenock was a muted gray, heavy with low-hanging clouds that released a gentle drizzle onto the green hills and dark-grey rooftops. The Scottish summer was a far cry from the sun-drenched shores of southern France Eileen and Jacqueline had left behind, but it felt more open, more welcoming than the gloomy Alpine forests.

The rain glistened on the cobblestones of the quay, and the air was filled with the scent of salt and fish. Eileen, still on deck with her suitcase and her sister beside her, scanned the unfamiliar landscape stretching before them. A knot of contradictory feelings twisted in her stomach—hesitancy, homesickness, and a flicker of hope for a more useful life.

Stepping onto British soil, she reminded herself. *We defied the odds.* For the first time, coming to her fatherland felt somewhat like an adventure. Freedom was now within reach—no longer the constant fear of being sent back gnawing at her. She took a deep breath of the brisk Scottish air.

I'm no longer the sheltered girl from home, she told herself. *I'm my own person now—I'll get a job, help in the war effort, and finally step out of the shadows of childhood.*

"*On l'a fait!*" she said aloud in French, slipping naturally into her mother tongue. *We made it!* Who cared what language she spoke—French, English, Spanish? She was free.

Jacqueline smiled, wrapping an arm protectively around her shoulder. "Don't cry victory yet. The real fight begins now."

"True," Eileen replied, her eyes gleaming with fierce determination. "But this fight—we will win!"

17

ARRIVAL IN ENGLAND

The port pulsed with frenetic energy—dockworkers shouted orders, seagulls shrieked in the gray sky above, and the sharp whistle of a distant train pierced the air. Eileen, with legs still shaky from the long sea voyage, followed Jacqueline as they joined the line of weary travelers snaking toward the Immigration Office. Rain misted down, beading on their coats and dampening their hair.

Ahead of them, a stern-faced officer with a thick mustache and sharp bark waved them forward, his uniform darkened by raindrops. He looked more like a soldier than a simple immigration officer, his eyes scanning each face as though any one of them might pose a threat.

Eileen clutched her British passport tightly, wondering whether the forged French papers tucked into their luggage might raise suspicion. But why would they check? She had grown weary of inspections and endless stories. After crossing half of war-torn Europe, dodging border guards and fabricating countless lies,

Eileen's nerves were frayed. Her eyes drifted to Jacqueline, whose calm exterior didn't quite mask the tension in her jaw.

Inside the Immigration Office, the air was thick with the smell of damp wool, cold sweat, and the ever-present bite of tobacco. The room hummed with nervous energy—dozens of travelers clutching their papers, their eyes fixed on the uniformed officers stationed along the walls. It felt more like a checkpoint than a welcome.

"Next, please!" A narrow-faced woman's clipped voice called from behind a counter. Her fingers tapped the desk impatiently. The sisters stepped forward, their shoes scuffing the worn floorboards.

"Passports," the woman demanded, barely glancing at them as she snatched their documents. Her eyes flicked across the pages with the precision of someone who had processed a thousand faces before. No warmth, no hint of welcome, just cold, detached efficiency.

Eileen cast a quick glance at Jacqueline. The silent exchange between them said it all—stay calm, show no fear. They were back on British soil. No one was sending them back. Or would they?

The officer paused, her eyes narrowing as she examined their passports more closely. Eileen's mind raced. Was something wrong? Had they overlooked a detail?

The woman straightened, her tone flat. "Everything seems in order," she said, shuffling the documents back to them. "Proceed to the next room for the security check."

The second room was colder, illuminated by the sterile light of overhead lamps. Armed police officers stood watch as each traveler's belongings were searched with meticulous care. Every item in their suitcases was pulled out, examined, and set aside—soap, a photograph of their parents, a small prayer book. Eileen stiffened when one officer flipped through her well-worn Bible, but after a brief inspection, he returned it without comment.

"It feels like we're still on trial," Eileen murmured in French.

"What's this?" another officer demanded, holding up Eileen's forged *Marie de Bonville* passport.

Jacqueline stepped forward. "Please don't hold it against us, Officer. As British citizens, we had little choice but to ask for forged papers in case we needed them to escape France. Fortunately, we didn't have to use them. The American consulate in Marseille helped us secure proper exit papers. We traveled as British citizens."

The man gave them a skeptical look. "You can explain that to the authorities in London," he grumbled, before handing the passport back. "It's none of my business."

Their belongings were finally returned, and with a curt nod from the officer, they were escorted outside to a waiting train. The gray drizzle continued as they boarded the train bound for London.

"It's not over yet," Jacqueline muttered through clenched teeth.

"What did he mean by 'the authorities in London'?" Eileen wondered aloud, her voice weary. She was tired. All she wanted was for someone to smile and welcome them home.

As the train crossed the border into England, Eileen sat up straighter, taking in the rolling green hills and mist-covered valleys.

"England," she murmured, tasting the word on her tongue. "Our fatherland."

Jacqueline folded her arms, her gaze also fixed on the passing countryside. "Feels strange, doesn't it? To finally be here... yet it doesn't feel like home. I mean, I was only seven, and you were two when we left."

Eileen nodded, watching the rain splatter against the glass. England was supposed to be their safe haven, the land they had longed for during their harrowing journey. But now they were here, it felt alien, distant. She wondered if it was a place that would ever truly feel like home.

With the police officers hovering across the aisle, Eileen couldn't shake the uneasy feeling that no matter where she went, she would always be seen as an outsider, a stranger, a potential enemy. It wasn't a pleasant thought, and she tried to push it away, but every time she glanced at the two dozing Bobbies, her heart ached for France.

By the time they reached Euston Station, the sun had dipped below the horizon, leaving London draped in dusk. The city was lively enough. Despite the blackout restrictions, there was no curfew and pedestrians and cars thronged the streets. People moved briskly, gas masks in hand, soldiers in uniform mingling with civilians, all shouldering the ever-present threat of war with heads held high. Posters plastered the walls, urging the populace that "Your Resolution Will Bring Us Victory" amidst the air raid warnings and ration queues.

The air was thick with coal smoke and exhaust fumes.

"Quite different from the Alpine air," Eileen remarked with a cough as they stood waiting for the bus, the two policemen like silent sentinels on either side.

"True," Jacqueline agreed, "but maybe we'll get used to it. I still recognize some of the buildings, but I didn't realize London had been hit this hard by the bombings."

Sandbagged doorways and gaping craters marred the cityscape--remnants of the Blitz.

"So different from France," Eileen observed quietly. "At least we didn't have bombings in the south."

Jacqueline glanced at her sister. "Didi, I think we'd better start speaking English together. It might help us blend in faster."

Eileen bit her tongue. They had never spoken English together before, but Jacqueline was right. She cast a glance at their guards and nodded reluctantly.

"I will try," she agreed, the foreignness of her own words settling uneasily on her tongue.

When the double-decker bus, commandeered for refugee transport, arrived, they climbed aboard with a crowd of other displaced souls. French and Polish voices mingled with English as the bus veered through the darkened streets of the city.

Eileen's heart lifted slightly at the sound of her native tongue. They weren't the only French refugees seeking shelter in London. *Isn't General De Gaulle here with his Free French?* she mused. *Maybe I could offer my services to him.* But another thought quickly followed. *No... I'd better try to become more English, find work with an English firm.* The desire to blend in warred with the comfort of her French identity.

As they crossed Wandsworth Road Bridge, the towering silhouette of the Royal Victoria Patriotic Building loomed ahead, its Gothic spires rising ominously against the night sky. The weathered facade spoke of its long history—once a school, later a hospital. Now, it seemed a purgatory for those like them, caught between war-torn homelands and an uncertain future.

Inside, the corridors echoed with the sound of footsteps on the flagstone floors, the chill air tinged with the sharp scent of carbolic soap. Eileen and Jacqueline were marched down the hallways by the ever-present Bobbies, the shadows of their escorts flickering under the sparse overhead lights.

"Leave your belongings here and follow us to the interview rooms," one of the officers barked, pointing to a nearby room, which must have been a former dormitory as beds still lined the walls in neat rows.

The sisters exchanged tired, resigned glances. *Again?* Eileen thought, her weariness sinking deeper. *When will this end?* But there was no choice. They obediently placed their suitcases beside the simple cots and followed the officers.

By now, Eileen's heart thudded in her chest like the pounding hooves of a dozen horses. *Not another interrogation.* She wasn't sure how much more of this she could endure. Her mind felt dulled from the relentless stress, her body fatigued, her stomach gnawing with hunger. But none of that mattered. There was no room for failure now. No time for tiredness, hunger, or the desperate need for the bathroom. She steeled herself, pushing aside every biological need, and focused entirely on one thing: giving the right answers.

The room was sparsely furnished, containing only a table, a few chairs, and a glaring overhead light. Officers from MI5 and all branches of the British forces—the Navy, RAF, and Army—lined the opposite side of the room, their expressions unreadable. The image blurred before Eileen's tired eyes, and she felt a small wave of relief when one of the uniforms called them over.

"Please, have a seat." He gestured to the chairs across from him.

Eileen perched on the edge of the hard chair, bracing herself for the barrage of questions that followed. They dove deep, probing into every detail of their lives: family, friends, and the perilous journey they'd undertaken through occupied Europe.

"What can you tell us about German troop movements in the Free Zone?" an officer asked, his pen poised above his notebook. He nodded at Eileen, waiting.

She paused, choosing her words carefully. "They are constantly shifting," she said. "Always moving, like shadows. Most of the Jewish people have already been arrested. And they're sending any capable men to work in factories in Germany."

"And the conditions in France?" another officer chimed in, his tone laced with skepticism.

"Dire," Jacqueline interjected quickly. "We were constantly asked to show our 'safe conduct' papers. That's why our parents decided to move to Grenoble—our British passports were becoming a real problem. There aren't many German troops in the French Alps."

"Not yet," Eileen added quietly. "But we moved out just in time."

"Do the French resist?" The next question came more sharply, the officer's tone demanding.

"Openly?" Eileen asked, her blue eyes wide.

"In any way," he barked.

"Yes," Jacqueline answered, "the French still hold hope that the German occupation won't last. But there are many collaborators too. People are hungry. They'll betray their neighbors for extra ration coupons or a little money."

An officer with dark eyes, peering over the rim of steel-rimmed glasses, spoke next, his tone almost accusatory. "Why do you speak English with a French accent if you're British subjects?"

"I… I'm sorry, Sir," Eileen stuttered, taken aback. "I moved to France when I was just two years old. But our parents insisted that we keep up our English fluency. Maman even hired a tutor for us when we lived in Nice. It's just the accent… I assure you, there's nothing wrong with my English…"

The officer waved a hand dismissively. "I've heard enough. Your father's British, hence the passports."

As he turned to his colleague, Eileen overheard him mutter, "Darn frogs."

His colleague, catching her eye, offered a brief, apologetic look. Eileen stiffened slightly, recognizing the slur. "Frogs" had long been a derogatory term used by the British for the French. The officer's disdain wasn't directed at her specifically, but it stung all the same.

The interrogation stretched on for hours, the officers relentless in their pursuit of information. They questioned them about political allegiances, their views on leaders both foreign and domestic, even the jokes whispered in the shadows of occupied streets.

Despite the pressure, Eileen and Jacqueline held their ground. Their answers were steady, consistent, though exhaustion gnawed at their edges. The hours bled into days, the monotony broken only by cups of watery tea and plates of soupy potatoes, brought by ample-bosomed nurses who whispered words of encouragement.

Finally, after two grueling days, the verdict came: the sisters were deemed trustworthy enough to enter British society. Their courage and honesty had convinced the interrogators that they were not spies but genuine refugees—fellow allies in the fight against tyranny.

Issued gas masks and ration books, they were free to leave the Victoria Patriotic Building, but Eileen knew their journey was far from over. As she stepped out into the London air—thick with coal smoke, but also now tinged with hope—she realized she'd taken her first true step toward freedom.

She glanced at her sister, the spark of relief returning to her eyes. "I think the worst is over now, Jacqui. They don't think we're spies. We're not going back to France."

A tired smile spread across Jacqueline's face. "Yes, we're here. Now, bed and board. And tomorrow, we'll start looking for work."

"Board, bed, and a bath," Eileen yawned, "and maybe some bread with jam."

Jacqueline chuckled. "Sounds like a plan."

Two young women, two suitcases, standing on the edge of a new life. The war wasn't over, but they were just beginning.

18

A MOMENT OF REST

Walking away from the Victoria Patriotic Building as fast as their legs would carry them, Eileen struggled to keep pace with Jacqueline. Her legs ached, nearly giving out under the weight of exhaustion.

"Where are we going, Jacqui, and at this speed?" she panted, stealing glances at the bustling streets around them, her suitcase bumping against her thigh with every step. It felt as if it was filled with lead.

"Let's see if we can find rooms with Papa's old friend on Stamford Hill," Jacqueline suggested. "I've got the address somewhere. Papa assured me we could knock on his door any time."

Eileen frowned, glancing up at the gloomy sky. She hadn't slept properly in days. "I just hope he's home," she muttered. She couldn't take another disappointment—not now.

The bus ride to Stamford Hill passed in a blur. The sisters stared out at the ravaged city—buildings damaged from air raids, sandbags piled high around doorways, and blackout curtains drawn tight across windows. The German attacks were like open wounds in a defiant city.

When they arrived at their destination, they found themselves standing in front of a modest red-brick townhouse on Darenth Road. The house seemed untouched by the war, with ivy creeping up the walls and the windows sealed off from the world outside. Eileen felt a flicker of hope as they approached the front door.

Jacqueline knocked firmly on the oak door, and the sisters waited, exchanging nervous glances. After a few moments, the door creaked open, revealing a man with kind eyes and graying hair at the temples. His face wrinkled in confusion at first, but recognition dawned as soon as Jacqueline introduced them.

"Heavens, girls, I wouldn't have recognized you after all these years. Have you come all the way from France?" Mr. Bennett opened the door wider, his voice filled with warmth. "Do come in. What a surprise!"

Eileen let out a sigh of relief, stepping into the house as though she had just been saved from drowning. She had never felt so grateful for the familiarity of an English accent, a friendly face, and the smell of home-cooked food. Mr. Bennett, George, was everything her father had described—a tall, tawny man with a bristly mustache, and the kind of calm demeanor that came from years of military service.

The interior of the house was just as comforting. The air smelled of homemade soup, and the warmth from the fireplace embraced them. Odile Bennett appeared from the kitchen, her face pinched but kind. Her eyes flickered with surprise as she took them in, but there was also hesitation in her gaze.

"Welcome, dears," Odile said, though there was a slight quiver in her voice. "You must be exhausted."

Eileen could sense the uncertainty, and for a moment, she feared they had overstayed their welcome before even stepping foot inside.

Jacqueline gave her a reassuring glance, quickly stepping in to smooth things over. "Thank you, Mrs. Bennett. We're so grateful to you. It's been a long journey."

Odile's gaze softened, and she offered a small smile. "Let's get you settled and then we'll see about feeding you."

Eileen clasped Jacqueline's hand as they followed Odile inside. The walls were lined with books, and a few paintings—George's own work—added splashes of color to the otherwise muted room. She felt her muscles relax, the tension easing slightly now that they had found a safe place to rest.

But beneath the surface of their relief, Eileen couldn't shake the weight of uncertainty. The war wasn't over, not even in London, and they were far from settled. They had left one danger behind, only to face another—a life in a strange city, where nothing was guaranteed.

"Now, George has told me you've escaped from France and need a safe place to stay, and I understand," Odile continued, leading the sisters through the house. "You're welcome to stay with us as long as you need. We have a spare room upstairs—it's not much, but it's comfortable. Since our boys, Gilbert and Frank, left to join the service, it's been empty. No grandchildren to spoil yet, you see."

The room was modest but welcoming, with two single beds neatly made with crisp white linens. A simple vase of paper flowers sat on the nightstand, their faded colors a small effort to brighten the blackout-draped window that showed nothing of the outside world. The air was filled with the faint scent of lavender that seemed to permeate the house. Though the space was small, it felt warm, a refuge from the chaos of war.

"It's perfect," Eileen murmured, her voice thick with gratitude. The weight of weeks of uncertainty and sleepless nights settled deeper into her bones.

"Thank you," Jacqueline added softly.

"Alright, dears. The bathroom is down the hall, and I'll leave you some towels and soap. It's not much with all these shortages, but we'll manage." Odile smiled, her eyes kind despite the shadows of worry. "Make yourselves at home and then join us downstairs for tea. It's simple fare with the rations, but we'll share what we've got."

The sisters nodded, exchanging a glance filled with silent relief as Odile left them to wash up.

"Of course, we were given ration books. We will bring them down to contribute," Jacqueline assured their new host, while Eileen ran a hand over the neatly folded towels, appreciating the softness of clean fabric after the rough journey. The water, though cold, felt refreshing on her face as she rinsed away the grime of travel.

When they returned downstairs, they found the dining table set for four, with two extra places neatly laid out for them. George sat at the head, his military bearing still evident in the way he carried himself, even as he spooned out the modest portions of tomato soup. Eileen and Jacqueline took their seats, feeling shy and overwhelmed in the warm glow of the simple household. The sound of cutlery against china filled the silence as their stomachs rumbled in anticipation.

"Food, then rest—I prescribe it," George said with a gentle smile. "But first, we must give thanks. Let's Praise the Lord."

George's voice, strong and resonant, filled the room as he said grace, blessing the meal and their new guests. His words, though simple, carried a weight of faith that reminded Eileen so much of her father. She bowed her head, her heart swelling with a bittersweet mix of homesickness and gratitude.

After the prayer, they quietly began their meal. The taste of the warm soup was a small comfort after so many days of hunger and stress.

Jacqueline, her gaze still fixed on her plate, broke the silence with a practical question. "Will there be a possibility for us to find work?"

George opened his mouth to respond, but Odile, ever the motherly figure, gently interrupted. “There will be plenty of time to discuss your plans in the morning. Tonight, we’ll sort nothing. Don’t worry, love. Everything will fall into place.”

Eileen’s thoughts drifted to her brother, Frederick, and a flicker of hope ignited in her chest. “Have you had any word of Frederick? We haven’t heard from him since he left France.”

George shook his head solemnly. “I didn’t even know he was in Britain. He never contacted us.”

“That’s a pity,” Odile added, her brow furrowed with concern. “We consider any of John’s children as our own.”

Eileen’s heart sank a little. She had hoped, even expected, that Frederick would have reached out to family friends by now. “He supposedly joined the RAF,” she said quietly, “so perhaps he’s with his regiment.”

“We’ll find him,” Jacqueline assured her, a note of determination in her voice that made Eileen feel a little lighter. She glanced at her sister, grateful for her strength, and the sisters shared a brief smile, finding solace in each other’s presence.

For now, they were safe, fed, and cared for. Tomorrow would bring more challenges, but tonight, they could rest.

19

LOOKING FOR A JOB

The next day – London, July 1942

Clad in their best dresses, hair carefully styled, and shoes polished to a shine, the Nearne sisters stepped out into the London streets the next morning. Uncle George and Aunt Odile— as their hosts had warmly insisted they call them—had provided them with a city map and packed them a simple lunch wrapped in brown paper. The comfort of their hosts' hospitality still lingered, but today they were on their own, ready once again to face the uncertainty of the day ahead.

The war-torn city buzzed with relentless energy. Buses and cars rattled by, the air hummed with the distant rumble of fighter planes overhead—Spitfires and Hurricanes, no doubt, patrolling the skies. Pedestrians bustled along the pavement, many in military uniforms, while civilians carried gas masks slung over their shoulders, an ever-present reminder of the war.

The contrast between the quiet, rain-soaked mountains of the

French Alps and the chaotic vibrancy of London was overwhelming. Everything jarred Eileen's nerves, the sights, sounds, and unfamiliar smells assaulting her senses all at once. Yet beneath the noise, she felt a flicker of excitement. It was thrilling, this bustling, war-hardened city where she'd been born two decades earlier but could hardly remember.

As they walked, Eileen's gaze was drawn to the smartly dressed women hurrying by in military uniforms. It seemed as if every other woman was in some kind of service.

"What are these uniforms?" she asked, her curiosity piqued by the sense of purpose they radiated.

Jacqueline glanced at the women passing them. "Uncle George told me the blue ones are WAAF, and the khaki ones are FANY."

"What's WAAF?" Eileen asked, her eyes following a group of women in perfectly tailored blue uniforms. "I'd like to join them. Their uniforms look so much nicer than the rough khaki ones."

Jacqueline gave a wry smile. "The WAAF stands for Women's Auxiliary Air Force. And we don't have any connections to the RAF, except for Frederick, and I doubt that'll help us."

Eileen sighed, disappointed. "And the FANY? Maybe I could join them if the WAAF's out of reach."

"FANY stands for First Aid Nursing Yeomanry. They've been around a long time, but it's mostly for women with nursing skills or those who can drive ambulances."

Eileen's face fell. "No nursing or driving skills here." She let out a resigned breath. "I suppose we'll have to look for office jobs, then. I hope they don't make us wear something dreadful." Her eyes lingered on an elegant woman in a WAAF uniform walking just ahead of them, her dark curls peeking out from under a perfectly angled blue beret. The seams of her stockings ran straight down her legs, as immaculate as the sharp cut of her jacket and skirt.

"I suppose we'll just wear the only good dress we own," Eileen added with a sigh, still imagining herself in one of those smart blue uniforms.

"Don't lose hope just yet," Jacqueline said to sound optimistic. "With the war going on, who knows what opportunities are out there?"

"So, where do we start?" Eileen wondered.

Jacqueline's perfectly arched brows furrowed as she thought. "I'd love to be a driver for the Women's Royal Navy Services," she mused. "But without any experience driving on the left side, I doubt they'd even consider me."

"You should try!" Eileen encouraged, her voice filled with genuine admiration. "You're a brilliant driver, Jacqui. You know that. I wish I could say the same, but Papa never let me practice once the war started."

Jacqueline's lips curled into a slight smile. "Thank you, sweetie, but driving in Nice or Paris is one thing. The roads here are different, and the traffic..." She sighed. "Besides, with my sales experience, I don't know what I could do in London. I don't have any connections here."

"Well, where shall we start, then?" Eileen asked again, the question hanging between them. Then, as if a forgotten idea resurfaced, she added, "What about the *Bureau Central de Renseignements d'Action*? We're bilingual, Jacqui. De Gaulle could find us useful, don't you think?"

Jacqueline's frown deepened. "Maybe. But we're British, Didi. He's looking for French citizens, and no matter how French we feel, our passports say otherwise."

Eileen's heart sank at her sister's words. "It's always the same," she murmured. "We don't belong in France because our passports say England, and we don't belong in England because we sound French. We're almost like stateless people."

"We're not stateless," Jacqueline said sharply. "We're lucky, Didi.

We have two countries we love and call home."

Eileen bit her lip as she held back a bitter thought. She didn't want to admit it, but she wasn't sure how much she liked England. It was foreign, unfamiliar, and far from the home she had known. Here they were, two foreign girls in a sea of war refugees, and the prospect of a much-needed job as yet an elusive dream.

"Let's try the Ministry of Labour," Jacqueline suggested, clearly determined to lift their spirits. "Britain needs women like us—young, single, and ready to work. There must be something for us."

Eileen nodded as they made their way through the throngs of people, dodging bicycles and the occasional military truck, until they reached the imposing brick building of the Ministry of Labour and National Service. The Union Jack fluttered above the entrance, a poignant reminder of "everyone doing their bit" as the nation came together for the war effort.

Inside, the ministry was a hive of activity. Long queues stretched out in front of various desks, each staffed by stern-looking officials in pressed suits or military uniforms. Eileen and Jacqueline joined the line, their excitement dimmed by the sheer volume of paperwork and bureaucracy unfolding before them.

"Next!" A clerk's voice rang out from behind a wooden desk. The man, without looking up, gestured for them to sit. His black hair was thinning, and the deep lines on his face spoke of the exhaustion of processing hundreds of cases a day. "Names, please?"

"Jacqueline Nearne. And this is my sister, Eileen," Jacqueline replied, her voice clear but with a distinctly French accent that made Eileen wince inwardly. She worried the sound of their accents might make their chances slimmer.

The clerk flipped through their papers, his pale-blue eyes narrowing behind dark-rimmed spectacles. Finally, he looked up. "And what skills do you bring, ladies? This country needs workers—

factories, offices, military services. If you have any of these skills, you'll be called upon soon enough."

Jacqueline straightened her back. "I have experience as a saleswoman, but I was hoping to apply for a driver's position with the Women's Royal Navy Services."

The clerk raised an eyebrow, unimpressed. "Recently arrived from France, I see. Any experience driving on the left?"

Jacqueline shook her head. "Not in England, Sir."

He scribbled a note on the form. "We're recruiting drivers, but you'll need to pass a test here first. And you?" He turned to Eileen.

"I have no formal experience," Eileen admitted, "but I'm bilingual—French and English. I'd like to work somewhere I can use my language skills."

The clerk gave a distracted nod. "Plenty of need for interpreters, clerks, and typists. We'll see what opens up."

They moved through several more desks, some conversations bringing hope, others frustration. Some clerks were encouraging, others bluntly told them to wait—their names would be added to a long list of women eager to serve. But no definitive path emerged.

Hours passed, and as the afternoon sun dipped behind the tall buildings, they found themselves still without a clear direction.

"Let's hope something comes from this soon," Jacqueline muttered as they left the building. It was finally time to eat their packed lunches—though it was already past teatime. "We can't afford to wait forever. Our funds are running out."

"I know," Eileen agreed, biting into a dry, sardine sandwich. "At least some of the clerks seemed hopeful."

"Some, yes. And some, no," Jacqueline replied, taking a sip of the cold tea from their thermos as they sat on the steps of the Ministry of Labour.

Unknown to the sisters, while their official requests languished in a pile of papers at the Ministry of Labour, their names—and their fluency in both French and English—had already caught the attention of someone watching from the shadows. The war had its own way of finding those who could be of use. And for the Nearne sisters, it would soon come calling.

20

THE INTERVIEW AT SANCTUARY BUILDINGS

A few weeks later - London, early August 1942

The house on Darenth Road was unnervingly quiet. Jacqueline had left early that morning, her face tense and purposeful as she'd slipped out the door, refusing to answer Eileen's questions about where she was heading.

"Why are you taking a suitcase, Jacqui? Where are you going? Don't leave me here on my own."

"It's just for a training up north, Didi. Don't fret. I'll be back before you know it. Now be a good girl and get yourself a job, just like me."

"What training, Jacqui? And where in the north?"

"Honey, I haven't got time for all your questions. Now be a good girl and give Aunt Odile a hand."

"How long will you be gone?"

"Just a few weeks..." Jacqueline had replied, her voice too casual for Eileen's liking.

"Weeks!?" Eileen had planted her hands on her hips. "Why didn't you tell me before?"

"Bye, Didi, darling," Jacqueline had said, giving her a quick peck on the cheek before disappearing out the door.

"Where's she going, Uncle George?" Eileen had stormed into the dining room where Uncle George sat with his breakfast and the paper.

"I don't know, Eileen. But your sister has a job, so we'd best be pleased for her. She's a smart girl, won't run into trouble. It's probably the Services if she's going on a training." He had lowered his newspaper to take in Eileen's pinched face.

"Remember this, my dear girl: in a war, we don't ask too many questions." The paper had gone up again, leaving Eileen to slink back upstairs.

She had slumped onto her bed, already missing Jacqueline. Her sister's presence had always been like a protective layer of soft wool —sometimes tight and prickly, but always warm.

Eileen listened to the silence. Aunt Odile had gone out to run errands. Uncle George was off to his Bridge club. She sat alone in the small bedroom she, until now, had shared with Jacqueline. The blackout curtains barred any view of the world outside. The familiar scent of lavender soap lingered in the air, but even a smell that reminded Eileen of home couldn't dispel the melancholy that clung to her like a second skin. The bedside lamp cast a ring of light on the table, leaving the rest of the room in gloomy shadows.

She sat on the edge of her bed, fingers nervously toying with her rosary beads. The familiar rhythm of prayer brought her little comfort today. Her thoughts drifted back to her parents in France— her mother's pale face as they'd said their final goodbyes, her father's soft, sad eyes. Would she ever see them again? A knot of homesickness twisted in Eileen's stomach.

A sudden clatter at the front door startled her from her reverie.

The letterbox flapped noisily, its metallic echo ringing through the hallway.

Mail? Eileen stood up, her heart giving a quick, unexpected lurch. It probably wasn't for her, but any excuse to do *something* was welcome, even as boring as gathering the mail. She hesitated for a moment. Should she leave the mail for Aunt Odile? But curiosity got the better of her. Smoothing her skirt and brushing a stray curl behind her ear, she headed down the narrow stairs to the front door.

A single, brown envelope lay on the hallway floor. Its size and stiffness seemed out of place, too official. With a jolt, Eileen saw her name scrawled across the front. She picked it up, feeling the weight of the paper, and turned it over. The embossed crest made her breath catch—it was from the Ministry of Pensions.

"Pensions?" she muttered, perplexed. "I've never worked a day in England..."

Her fingers fumbled for Uncle George's paper cutter on the vestibule table, carefully slicing open the envelope. A folded sheet of parchment slipped out, the edges rough and official-looking. The letter was brief, almost cryptic.

War Office Room 055

Dear Miss E. Nearne,

We believe you might be of some use to the war effort and therefore invite you to attend a meeting in Sanctuary Buildings on 27 August at 14:00. Please treat this letter with the greatest confidentiality and do not share the information with anyone.

E. Potter

. . .

EILEEN BLINKED, her pulse quickening. "Of use to the war effort?" She read the letter again, and then once more, as if its meaning might become clearer. Sanctuary Buildings... that was somewhere official, wasn't it? *The Ministry of Pensions has a War Office...?* The embossed crest confirmed this wasn't some hoax, but the letter's secrecy unnerved her.

"Why can't I tell anyone?" she whispered, glancing over her shoulder instinctively, as if someone might overhear her in the empty house.

Was this some sort of military enlistment? But why her? She had no experience. And why such secrecy? Jacqueline would be suspicious if she kept this from her, and Aunt Odile would surely ask questions. Keeping secrets wasn't in Eileen's nature—yet something about the letter's tone commanded her to make the vow of confidentiality it asked for. Perhaps it was a blessing in disguise that Jacqueline wasn't here, because she would have gotten it out of Eileen with one stare.

Eileen raced upstairs as she heard Aunt Odile's key in the lock and tucked the letter into her handbag, quickly snapping the closure shut.

"Are you upstairs, Eileen?"

"I am, Aunt Odile."

"I'll put the kettle on."

"I'll be down in a minute."

Eileen sank back on the bed, needing a few more moments to process the strange invitation. She'd go to the interview with E. Potter first and decide afterward whether to tell anyone. Just in case it was some kind of misunderstanding.

But deep down, Eileen already had the eerie feeling that this was "it." The terse wording, the official crest—this was her chance. The

War Office needed her, and she was ready to show she wouldn't disappoint them. After all, hadn't she come to England to do her bit in the war? Hadn't she longed to prove herself? This was her opportunity, and maybe, just maybe, it was something she'd have to face alone.

A few weeks later – London, 27 August 1942

Eileen arrived well in time for her interview, gazing up at the imposing office block on Great Smith Street. She'd taken extra care ironing her best dress, curling her hair, and fending off Aunt Odile's persistent questions.

"A job at a translation bureau. Somewhere on Great Smith Street."

No, she had no idea what the work entailed. She'd explain when she came back. Yes, she'd be back in time for tea.

Finally, Aunt Odile had stopped asking.

As she arrived at Sanctuary Buildings, Eileen took a deep breath before ringing the bell. She smoothed the invisible creases from her green, summer dress, a nervous habit she couldn't seem to shake. The door opened to reveal a somber-looking man in a dark suit and bowler hat. Eileen suppressed a flicker of surprise at his full attire indoors, wondering if he'd simply forgotten to take off his hat or if this was all part of the mystery surrounding her interview.

"I'm here to see—"

"Follow me," he interrupted before she could finish.

It was clear she wasn't going to get any further conversation out of him, so she let her eyes wander around the entrance hall. It felt impersonal, like the lobby of a well-respected hotel—spacious and sturdy, with a large, carpeted staircase and a gleaming mahogany banister leading to the upper floors. The scent of wood polish, tobacco, and well-hidden secrets lingered in the air.

The man in the bowler hat led the way up the staircase to the first floor, stopping in front of a nameless, numberless door. He knocked, and a hoarse male voice from inside called, "*Entrez!*"

Eileen tried to steady her nerves as the whole situation seemed more like a scene from a movie than a simple job interview. As she stepped into the dimly lit room with blacked-out windows, she blinked against the haze of blue smoke, gradually making out the figure of a middle-aged man sitting behind a simple kitchen table.

"*Entrez, Mademoiselle Nearne. Fermez la porte et asseyez-vous,*" he instructed, his French accented but clear.

Assuming this was the E. Potter for the interview, she obeyed, closing the door behind her and taking a seat across from him. The air in the room was stifling and hot, while the dim lightbulb over the table cast a circle of pale-yellow light over the man's lean features. His intense scrutiny in the smoke-filled air made Eileen avert her eyes, her face heating up beneath her carefully styled curls. No gentleman stared at a woman like that.

The situation became stranger by the minute, and for a moment, she wondered if coming here had been a mistake. But having come this far, she knew there was no turning back now, this could be her chance to matter.

In the silence between them, Eileen cast furtive glances around the room, mentally preparing herself for a way out, should it come to that. The man's desk was cluttered with files and an overflowing ashtray, the smell of stale smoke thick in the air. An empty coffee cup, rimmed with a dark stain, sat among the mess, alongside a crumpled brown paper bag that likely held the remnants of his lunch. Filing cabinets lined the walls, their cold metal surfaces adding to the sterile, impersonal atmosphere. One window had a section of its blackout board removed, offering a bleak view of an empty stone courtyard below.

Eileen focused on the man's hands instead of his face—pale and slender, they moved with practiced precision as he filled his pipe. The rasp of tobacco against the pipe's bowl was the only sound breaking the silence. When he struck a match, the sharp smell of sulphur filled her nostrils. He puffed slowly, blowing lazy circles of smoke toward the ceiling, thickening the already hazy air.

When she dared another glance at his face, she found his sharp, probing eyes still fixed on her. He seemed to be gauging her through the cloud of smoke he'd created, his expression stern and unreadable. The hard set of his thin lips gave no hint of warmth, no suggestion of kindness. He had the look of a hard-nosed spy—unyielding, calculating.

Is this what they expect me to become? Eileen wondered.

TRYING TO STEEL HERSELF, Eileen held the man's stony gaze for a few seconds before her nerves began to fray. Shifting in her seat, she smoothed another invisible crease from her skirt, struggling to maintain her composure. If only Jacqueline were with her. Jacqueline would have broken this awkward silence, maybe even given this man a piece of her mind. But Eileen had promised herself she would face this ordeal alone. Clearing her throat, she finally spoke up.

"*Êtes-vous Monsieur Potter*?" Though her voice was soft, her French was flawless—much better than his, she was sure. He couldn't hold that against her.

But the man ignored her question completely, leaning forward as he spoke in that grating voice that cut through the smoke like a dull knife.

"Where in France did you live?"

"Paris, Boulogne-sur-Mer, Nice, and Grenoble, Sir," Eileen responded quickly, wondering why these British officers always seemed to ask the same questions. Surely, all of this was already in a file somewhere?

"Why did you move so often?"

Eileen paused. "Family reasons, I suppose. We moved from London to Paris because my mother wanted us to be bilingual and closer to her family. Then she wanted to live by the sea, so we moved to Boulogne-sur-Mer. When my maternal grandmother passed, my mother inherited the house in Nice, so we lived on the Riviera for a time. But when the Germans occupied France, we had to leave, and my father thought Grenoble would be safest."

"Your family members?"

"My father and mother, my older brother Francis, then Jacqueline, Frederick, and finally me," she answered. "Jacqueline and Frederick are also in England."

"Who is married? Who isn't?"

"My parents are married, of course. Francis is married—he has a family and they are all still in Grenoble."

The questions came at her like rapid-fire, each one probing, testing her resolve. Eileen felt the pressure building, her mind racing to keep pace.

"What do you think of Pétain?"

"He is a collaborator," she replied, her voice tinged with anger.

"Hitler?"

"A tyrant."

"De Gaulle?"

"A symbol of hope for France."

"Churchill?"

"A leader with strength and resolve."

The man leaned back in his chair, continuing his relentless study of her, never breaking eye contact. Despite his average height, his presence was imposing, and his silences were as unnerving as his questions.

"How did you get out of France?"

"My sister and I traveled through Spain and Portugal to Gibraltar," Eileen answered carefully. "From there, we were able to board a British ship. It wasn't easy, but we managed."

"Are you willing to go back?"

Eileen blinked, unsure she'd heard him right. "Back to France, Sir?"

"Where else?" His eyes narrowed.

"But... I've just arrived here, Sir. As long as the Germans occupy France, it's too dangerous for British citizens."

"Why do you think we're speaking French?" he shot back, leaning forward again. "Answer the question."

Eileen felt flustered by his harsh tone but realized what he was implying. She would go back as a Frenchwoman. But how? With false papers again, like the flawed ones Daniel had provided in Grenoble? Despite her anxiety, the idea intrigued her.

Her heart pounded as she nodded. "Yes. If I could help in any way, I'd go. But how would I go back?"

"You jump."

"Jump?" Eileen was confused. "You mean from the sky?"

"Yes. You jump."

"Oh." A rush of images—parachutes, night skies—flashed through her mind, but she didn't dare ask for further clarification.

"Do you or don't you want to make the Germans' lives hell?"

"I do," she replied, still in shock but meeting his gaze.

"Are you willing to face danger?"

"Yes."

"Extreme danger?" His voice dropped to a low, menacing tone.

"Yes."

"Even to die for France?"

Eileen hesitated, the question needed careful consideration. If she was anything, she was honest and serious. Her mind flicked back to her recent journey through enemy territory, to the dangers she and Jacqueline had braved to get to same shores. The Nazis, the stories of torture and disappearances—it all came rushing back. She knew what could happen to her. But still...

"I suppose so," she said in a quiet but resolute voice.

Her interrogator paused, his face unreadable. He scribbled something on his notepad, checked his watch, glanced at the large calendar on the wall, and jotted down a few more notes. A flicker of concern crossed his features before his expression turned neutral again. "What we ask is not easy-breezy, Mademoiselle Nearne. It requires courage, sacrifice, and utmost secrecy. I don't think you're ready for that yet..."

"Oh, but you see... I am," Eileen stammered. "If I've given the impression—"

The man waved his hand. "Stop right there, Mademoiselle. You'll do your bit, don't worry. Just in England for the time being."

"In England?" Eileen's confusion was evident. Why had he gone on about the dangers, only to tell her she'd be staying in England? *It's not fair.*

"I'm not saying 'never France.' I just want you to get proper training and experience as a wireless operator first. We're in dire need of coders and decoders on both sides of the Channel."

"Oh, I see." Disappointment must have shown on her face because her stern interrogator mustered a small, faint smile.

"You're an intelligent woman, Mademoiselle Nearne, I can see that. I assure you, your work will be as vital to the war effort here as it would be anywhere else."

"I understand," Eileen murmured, squeezing her hands in her lap as they grew damp with sweat. "I just want to help." Then, remembering this was a job interview, she quickly added, "Will I be paid? Even if... uh... I'm not going to France?"

"Of course."

She wanted to ask more about what a wireless operator did and how she'd learn coding and decoding, but she didn't want to give this cold man the satisfaction of ignoring more of her questions. *He is only the interviewer; he won't be my boss. I hope.* She would learn everything in time.

Another thin smile brushed his lips as he tapped his pipe in the ashtray, then waved her off with a gruff, "Welcome to the Org, Mademoiselle Nearne. Mrs. Bingham will take good care of you. You'll receive further instructions in the post—how to join the FANY... uh... First Aid Nursing Yeomanry, and when and where to go for your training."

The Org? Mrs. Bingham? FANY?

Eileen was tired, her head aching. She stood up as the man, already filling a fresh pipe, showed no further interest.

"Thank you, Mr. Potter, and goodbye."

"The name's Jepson. Selwyn Jepson."

Whatever, Eileen thought as she closed the door behind her, finding the man in the bowler hat already waiting to escort her out.

At least the interview had landed her a job of sorts, but a tinge of disappointment nagged at Eileen for not having secured the real job —the one, once she was forced to consider it, she had hoped would take her back to France.

PART VIII

~EILEEN~ TORQUAY, 2007

21

CROSSROADS OF MEMORY

Torquay, August 2007

Snapshots of memories, like photographs in faded colors, flickered behind Eileen's eyelids, as the reel of an old movie unwinding. She was there, sitting in a dimly lit room with Gershwin's *Rhapsody in Blue* playing faintly in the background. Dressed in a light-blue summer dress with a white collar and a thin belt, white lace gloves fastened neatly at her wrists.

She fumbled with a string of rosary beads that lay nestled in her lap, their rubies glinting. Jacqueline, her hair perfectly styled in lush, loose curls, sat across from her in a Chesterfield armchair, slender legs crossed at the knee, laughing as she sipped bourbon and smoked. The way she held that elegant cigarette holder, balancing it between two fingers—only Jacqui could pull that off.

Where was this? London? Her birthday? Or was that a year earlier...or later?

The echo of their laughter blurred into a faint hum, and suddenly, Eileen awoke. Her eyelids lifted, only half-open, barely aware of the dim room where no music played, as unfamiliar as the scene of her dream. An unpleasant heat pressed around her, making beads of sweat cling to her skin and dampen her nightgown. As always upon awakening, the first thing she did was listen. Was it safe here? A dull ringing in her ears gave way to the sound of her own ragged breathing.

She was in England… in Torquay… in a bed. Safe, but her sister was gone. Gone so long now.

"Oh, Jacqui," she murmured in a raspy voice, the sound of it foreign even to herself. "I'd trade a year of my life for just one more day with you. To hear your laughter again."

"Meeooww." The cry startled Eileen, bringing her to full consciousness. Turning her head, she squinted as the flick of a ginger tail slipped through the half-open door. Moustache? No, that wasn't right… The name of *this* cat drifted just out of reach.

"Meeooww."

Her dry voice stumbled out in French, "*ah, c'est toi, Whisky, n'est-ce pas*?" Her throat was so parched it made her voice creak. "I'm coming, dear. Give me a moment… I need to put these scattered brains of mine back in order."

The cat padded over, leaping onto the duvet and curling beside her. Stroking Whisky's warm, soft fur, Eileen let the present settle around her. She was in her Torquay flat, not in London. Her bones felt heavy, and her hip was sore. She'd probably been lying on it again. It was a stubborn ache—a souvenir from the SS interrogation in the *Rue des Saussaies*.

Outside her window, the warm hum of summer carried through, bringing with it the vibrant voices of children--a high, light sound that slipped through the cracks of her shrouded memories.

Footsteps rushed by on the pavement, followed by children giggling. Eileen stiffened, her ears pricking as she registered the sound. A whistle—shrill and haunting—the same one from the camp, the one that meant... No, it was only a bus braking on the hill, then the smooth rattle of a bicycle passing.

"Didi, you have the hearing of an African elephant. You'd catch a blade of grass shifting." Maman's voice, faint and teasing, drifted into her mind. True enough, her eyes may have faltered, but her ears were sharp, catching every soft sound that crept around her. Always on alert.

Never trusting the silence—programmed by fear to always be listening—she never completely got used to the contrast of sounds mingling with the silence around her. The balance of what she heard and what she *thought* she heard struck her as fragile, temporary. She closed her eyes, longing to drift back to her dream—sitting with Jacqui in that smoky London club, bourbon in hand, her birthday, perhaps, or maybe only the last time they'd laughed together.

Their London mornings had held so much promise, something richer than the tea and toast on a tray in solitude that she was accustomed to now. But then the image warped—her spoon clinking against a thin tin bowl filled with gray, watery slop. Soup, they called it. The taste, metallic and bitter, cut into her memory.

"No." She forced herself to blink away the images, swallowing hard against the sourness in her throat.

Outside, a mother called to her children, her voice soft and tender, guiding them to lunch. "Almost lunchtime," she'd said, as if everything were perfectly in place. Eileen lay still, unmoving, listening to the echoes of a life she'd once dreamed of—a husband, her own family, perhaps. Instead, she had chosen this life, the life of an agent, a warrior. And now? Now she was only Eileen, the lonely woman lying in her narrow bed, with a ginger stray purring beside her.

"If I had listened and stayed at my dull job as a coder at Station XII, this would never have happened. *I* would have been a wife and a mother, calling my children to lunch."

But the excitement had worn off. After 365 long nights and days across 1942 and 1943, her optimism had faded into endless hours spent coding and decoding messages from agents who led the *real* life of war effort. Her own dreams of heroism had faded into what she could only think of as 'invisible contributions.' For a time, she managed to console herself with the notion that every message cracked, every order relayed, was still a lifeline—a tool for victory. But those justifications felt thinner and thinner, and the idea that *she*, Eileen Nearne, wasn't deemed good enough for fieldwork, for the life of danger she so craved, made her tumble into a dark depression.

ON THIS AUGUST morning in 2007, Eileen's mind was suddenly clear as a cloudless sky, clearer than it had been in years. She was standing at the crossroads of her memory. This was what Jepson had warned her about, what Jacqui had tried to spare her from.

Had she been wrong to beg Baker Street, over and over, to send her to France? Had God himself tried to protect her by keeping her at Aston House in Herefordshire? Was it her own stubbornness that had delivered her to this life? If she had known her relentless pursuit of being a *real* agent would lead to endless sleepless nights, to the wrenching loss of friends, to a solitude so vast it often felt like a fog settling in her bones...

Oh, the unanswered questions! She'd been young, she'd been foolish, she'd been reckless. And yet, in her innermost self, Eileen knew that not even a pack of wild horses could have stopped her. The five glorious months of being a secret agent, before her arrest, washed over any regrets of a life wasted in the years afterward.

Eileen pushed her hands over her face, shielding herself from the weight of her life's decisions. Perhaps a simpler life could have spared her this loneliness. Perhaps, without the scars, she might even have married, might have filled her home with the warmth of a family.

But that wasn't the life she'd chosen. Or, rather, the life she'd accepted. So here she lay, Eileen the lonely warrior, nothing more than a faded photograph tucked away, remembered but rarely seen.

In the distance, the sounds of laughter continued, and she felt a fresh pang—a longing for a life that could have been, perhaps should have been. A gentle knock at the front door cut through her reverie. Though her ears registered it, she ignored the sound, until there was another knock and something stirred in her—an instinct, or maybe the faintest glimmer of hope.

PART IX

~MIA~ TORQUAY, 2007

22

THE DOOR AJAR

Torquay, August 2007

Mia sat at her desk in Hope Haven Community Health, staring down at a brown envelope in front of her that bore her name but no return address. A soft knock sounded at the door.

"Come in," she called, lifting her gaze.

Alexandra sauntered in, her dark eyebrows knit together in a frown as if she'd just walked through a thundercloud.

"What is it, Alex? Something wrong?"

"Not with me, but perhaps with you," Alexandra replied, her tone uncharacteristically sharp.

Mia blinked, taken aback. Her friend and coworker was usually as warm as sunshine on a summer's day.

"With me? Care to explain?"

Alexandra pointed to the brown envelope lying unopened on Mia's desk. "That, my dear, is what's wrong." She practically spat the words out.

"How so?" Mia picked up the envelope, studying it, but then she caught on to what Alex was implying. With a gasp, she dropped it and took a quick step back.

"You mean it's...a letter bomb?" Grabbing her colleague's arm, she tugged her toward the door.

"No, silly!" Alexandra pulled her arm free, exasperated. "It's from Slick Sebas. I thought I warned you to stay clear of that pickup artist. The man's broken enough hearts as it is, and I won't stand by and let him add yours to his collection."

"How do you know it's from Sebastian Stone?" Mia asked, ignoring the implications about his amorous attempts.

"Because I saw him drop it in the mailbox when I got here. He even had the nerve to say you'd love what was inside! The man thinks it's Valentine's Day every day of the year. Cut him off, Mia—I'm begging you!"

"Thank you for your concern, Alex, truly. I'm sure it's nothing personal. But I agree; it's inappropriate to keep sending things after I made it clear I want nothing to do with him. Especially after what he pulled with Miss Nearne."

Alexandra folded her arms across her chest, her face scrunched in a scowl.

"Are you sure you're over him, Alex? You seem awfully riled up," Mia teased.

"Oh, I'm over him. I just know he can turn on charm like a faucet, and I can't bear seeing you become his next victim."

"Not a chance." Mia eyed the envelope with renewed determination. "Let's see what he's got to say for himself."

She tore open the envelope, and a flat, round metal box fell onto the desk. The label read, "Original copy: *School for Danger*, 1947. Directed by Teddy Baird, starring Captain Harry Rée and Jacqueline Nearne."

Alex leaned in as Mia turned the metal box in her hands. She wondered what it was. Jacqueline Nearne, for sure, was Eileen's sister. She'd been in the SOE as well, that much Mia knew. And apparently, she'd appeared in this docu-drama after the war. Carefully unfolding the note tucked inside the envelope, she read.

> Mia,
>
> I was able to purchase this original copy of School for Danger at a very reasonable price. This is what I'd wanted to give Miss Nearne, but through my own foolishness, I blew that chance. Can you please give it to her?
>
> Sebastian

MIA WHISTLED THROUGH HER TEETH, glancing over at Alex, who stood with a dubious expression. "Does he really think this changes anything?"

"In a way, it does, to me," Mia admitted. "I genuinely believe he wanted to surprise Miss Nearne with something thoughtful. But why does he have to be such a dork?"

"Because he was born a dork," Alexandra grumbled.

"Well, if I ever get a chance to restore Miss Nearne's confidence, I'll pass along this *School for Danger* copy. But first, I need to make sure she knows I've secured her pension." Mia slipped the note and the round box back into the envelope. "I was just on my way to try my luck with her again. Third time lucky, I hope."

"If you do get her to open the door, maybe hold off on giving her that movie. It could just set her off again," Alexandra warned before heading to the door.

"I agree. No Sebastian Stone, in any form, for Miss Nearne for the foreseeable future."

"Believe me, he's always scouting for soft spots in women," Alexandra muttered as she closed the door behind her.

Mia sighed, whispering to herself, "Maybe he does have a nice side." It had been a thoughtful gesture from Sebastian, though she wasn't entirely sure what he expected to gain by giving it to Miss Nearne.

An hour later

Mia checked her watch before knocking on Eileen's door. A quarter to twelve. Would this be an appropriate time, or would she be interrupting an early lunch? If she was going to try today, she had no other choice; back-to-back meetings filled her afternoon. Eileen would be counting on her pension money to arrive tomorrow.

Her heart pounded almost as loudly as her knuckles against the brown door. She could almost feel the tension through the thin wooden barrier between them.

"Miss Nearne," she called, leaning close. "It's me, Mia. Are you in? I have good news about your pension."

The door opened just enough for Mia to catch a glimpse of Eileen's expression—worn, cautious, a flicker of betrayal lingering in those myopic, blue eyes. But before she could say a word, the door shut again with a firm, defiant click. Still, it was a step in the right direction. The door had been ajar. If only for a second.

Taking a steadying breath, Mia began again, keeping her voice soft and calm. "Miss Nearne, please. I didn't know Mr Stone would come here. I promise, I had nothing to do with it. He shouldn't have intruded; it wasn't fair to you."

Silence. Mia hesitated, wondering if Eileen was even standing there listening or if she'd withdrawn deeper into her flat. She pressed on, hoping her words would reach through the door, if not to Eileen's heart, then at least to her ears.

"I only came to bring you this." She held up the letter, even though Eileen couldn't see it, as if the gesture might somehow bridge the divide. "I've sorted things with the pension office. They confirmed everything. It's all fixed and official now." She paused, steadying herself. "I thought it might bring you some relief."

She waited, listening to the sounds from Lisburne Crescent below—people chatting, a car honking, a bus rattling by—the world alive around Eileen and the silence from within. The moments dragged, and Mia finally turned on her heel, accepting she'd likely lost her chance of mending things. It felt like a defeat, not only professionally for the young, ambitious psychologist but personally, too. She'd grown fond of the old, warrior woman.

But as she reached the end of the corridor, she heard the door creak open behind her. Mia turned to see Eileen standing there, her gaze wary, surrounded by an aura of loneliness that made Mia's heart ache.

Eileen stood there, a slight tremor in her stance, shoulders slightly hunched, her wary gaze peering out as if deciding whether to give any hint of approachability. Mia instinctively softened her posture, taking in the scene with careful, measured calm.

She knew one wrong move or word would send Eileen retreating back into her fortress, so she took one careful step forward, then paused, holding steady, her gaze warm and gentle, as if she were coaxing a skittish animal. Every muscle in her own body was relaxed but controlled, her hands hanging loosely at her sides, her face open, welcoming. She sensed that Eileen, though standing there, was poised to pull back at any moment.

"It's good to see you, Miss Nearne." Her voice was barely above a murmur. *Dear God, let no one come out of one of these other doors,* she prayed inwardly, knowing that any sudden noise could break this fragile moment. "I brought the confirmation for your pension. I'm so glad I managed to sort it for you. There will be no more delays in payment of your cheques."

I'll one day show you how to set up online banking, Mia thought as she kept her friendly gaze on the trembling woman, *so you don't have to cash your cheques in all weather at the post office anymore.*

She lifted the envelope just enough for Eileen to see it, not reaching out or making any sudden movements. As she took another small step, Eileen's eyes shifted toward the envelope and then glanced back at Mia's face, searching, as if to read her intentions. Mia felt her own heart thrum, urging her to close the distance faster, but her mind knew better. She'd met clients who had shut themselves off from the world before, but Eileen's isolation felt deeper, like a wall that had been cemented over many decades. Rushing could destroy everything.

Slowly, she took another step, watching for the smallest flicker of retreat, but instead, she saw a trace of curiosity—even defiance—something of the real, strong Eileen Nearne shining through. This woman wasn't done living yet; she had a power in her that had survived the worst, and here she still stood.

"I'll leave this with you," Mia continued softly, lifting the envelope a little higher. "I'm sorry I can't stay longer. I just wanted you to have it today and know everything's been settled for this week's payment. And every other week, as well."

Eileen's gaze remained observant but less resistant, her hands opening slightly at her sides as if she were debating reaching for the envelope. Mia noted the weariness that lingered in her expression, the hollow shadows under her eyes that hinted at sleepless nights and memories that clung too tightly. A wave of compassion washed over the young psychologist—she would recognize the loneliness in Eileen's gaze anywhere. It was a state she knew too well herself.

Every instinct told her to reach out, to close the distance and offer the comfort she knew Eileen craved. But she stayed rooted, letting the silence stretch as gently as she could manage, so that Eileen might find her own way to reach out. It was as if Mia were planting a seed—one that would grow not out of her own urgency but from Eileen's inner longing for connection.

Carefully, she extended the envelope, her face brightening into an encouraging smile, her movements slow and deliberate. "I'll let you be, Miss Nearne," she said, adding a gentle warmth to her words. "But I'll be around if you need anything… even if it's just to talk."

In the long, narrow corridor, Mia was acutely aware of every detail—the slight shift in Eileen's posture, the way her hand, thin and frail-looking with blue veins shining through, finally reached out to accept the envelope, her gnarled fingers curling around it as if it were a lifeline. Mia held her position, offering a slight nod of encouragement, making sure Eileen knew she was not asking for more.

In the stillness, Mia sensed she had opened the smallest of doors to Eileen's guarded heart. She took a small step back, maintaining a respectful distance.

"Goodbye, Miss Nearne—or, as I'd prefer to say in your native tongue, *au revoir*."

"*Au revoir*." The voice was creaky but strong, followed by the smallest of smiles. "*Et merci beaucoup*."

"You're very welcome, Miss Nearne. Helping like this is what I do for a living."

She turned, moving down the hallway with a calm, steady pace, not wanting to break the delicate balance they'd just established.

I'll be back, she thought as she walked away, hoping that Eileen, in the quiet moments that would follow, might feel the first stirrings of a desire to open that door again—perhaps even a hope to one day find a friend on the other side.

23

THREADS OF CONNECTION

The Blockbuster Video on Market Street was nearly empty when Mia entered, and she realized it must be nearly closing time. Blockbuster wasn't a retailer she often visited, and she felt rather lost among the rows of videos on display. A couple snickered in a corner as she inadvertently wandered into the erotica section. Quickly, she turned and made her way to the counter, where a young woman with heavy makeup was chewing gum and watching a sitcom on a tiny television set.

Without taking her black -rimmed eyes off the screen, the girl asked, "Wha's up?"

"I'm looking for a docu-drama from the 1940s. *School for Danger*?" Mia asked politely.

The girl's eyes flicked to her for a second, then back to the TV. "Yer lookin' for what now?"

"Do you have *School for Danger*?"

With a sigh, the girl pointed a black-lacquered nail toward the back of the store. "Try the special offer section. Nothin' before the sixties is for rent, mind. But ya can buy 'em for a quid if ya find anythin'," she muttered, letting her gum pop as she snorted at something on the screen.

Mia followed the assistant's vague direction to the back of the store, scanning the dimly lit shelves for the documentary section. She didn't hold out much hope, already wondering if she'd need to find someone who could help her view Sebastian's original copy. But then, after a few minutes of browsing, her fingers brushed against a VHS labeled *School for Danger*, subtitled *Now It Can Be Told*. Mia couldn't believe her luck. The box looked in excellent condition—a 1984 copy, thankfully compatible with her old VHS player, which she'd held onto despite everything moving to DVD.

She clutched the box with a sense of reverence, thinking of what this film might mean to Eileen and her sister, Jacqueline. Tonight, she'd watch it alone, hoping to gain some insight into the life Eileen for a period in the 1990s had been rather eager to share.

Back in her cozy flat on Torbay Road, Mia stood at the window, as she did every time she came home, with her black cat Mr. Spikes nestled in her arms. The evening was sunny and golden, the light shimmering over Tor Bay, casting a soft glow on Princess Pier as the lights had yet to turn on. Below, people strolled down the wooden planks, eating ice cream or stealing kisses from one another. The merry-go-round hummed its endless jingle, and white yachts bobbed in the harbor, a scene that always stirred a quiet joy in her.

She loved this view, yet there was another reason she'd chosen this flat. It gave her a constant, unobstructed glimpse of the pier, not far from where a scrubby, restless teenager had once camped beneath it. That girl—the one she'd been—had needed sanctuary, a haven, something no amount of scenic beauty could truly provide.

Holding Mr. Spikes closer, Mia felt the familiar pang that grounded her. This view reminded her daily of who she was and where she'd come from, and of all the small, improbable steps that had led her here. For all her success, it was this small ritual of looking back that kept her steady, like a compass she couldn't afford to lose.

After feeding Mr. Spikes and preparing a Cup-a-Soup for herself, Mia drew the curtains and slid the video tape into her VCR. Her laptop sat open beside her on the couch, a half-typed search query on Jacqueline Nearne lingering on the screen. As the grainy black-and-white film began, the crackling narration introduced the SOE agents, their bravery, and their critical missions in occupied France. The two main characters were real former agents, Harry Ree and Jacqueline Nearne. Mia absently stroked Mr. Spikes as he curled up in her lap, but soon found herself entranced by the unfolding story.

Jacqueline was movie-star beautiful, moving with a graceful swiftness, her lush, wavy dark hair framing an expressive face. Her English was elegant with a strong French lilt. Though taller and more slender than Eileen, Mia could see a resemblance between the sisters—a shared poise, a fierce determination, and perhaps something of the Spanish aristocracy from their mother's side.

As Mia watched, she found it almost unbelievable that Jacqueline was not a French actress but a true SOE agent who, just four years before the film was made, had been in the field like her sister. Jacqueline re-enacted scenes from their wartime past, slipping into Eileen's role as a W/T operator as though she'd been born to it.

The line between performance and reality blurred, drawing Mia deeper into the world the sisters had known, making her feel she was glimpsing not only history but a hidden, shared strength that ran through both sisters' veins.

After the docu-drama ended, Mia typed "Jacqueline Nearne SOE" into the search bar of her internet browser and clicked through articles, biographies, and mentions of Jacqueline's wartime courage. Halfway down a page, a byline caught her eye: *Sebastian Stone, National Heritage Daily*, dated three years earlier. Surprised,

Mia clicked, scanning the opening lines of the article, her pulse quickening as she read.

"The sacrifices of SOE agents are often discussed with a sense of admiration and mystery. But Jacqueline Nearne, sister to Eileen Nearne, has largely remained in the shadows. For Jacqueline, the mission was about more than strategy or covert operations; it was about protecting her sister, about loyalty that extended beyond any orders or directives..."

Mia's eyes skimmed further, noting Sebastian's sharp but respectful tone as he recounted Jacqueline's missions, her tenacity, and her bond with Eileen. A bit of reluctant admiration seeped in. This wasn't written for mere sensation—he had clearly researched the Nearne sisters' story with a careful, if unpolished, hand. *Could he have been serious about wanting to shift from gossip to research journalism?*

On impulse, Mia pulled out her phone, typing a quick message before she could second-guess herself.

"Received the film copy. How did you manage to get it? Watched it yourself?"

She hit Send, feeling the faintest stir of curiosity mingled with skepticism.

What have I done? Her finger hovered over the delete button as Alexandra's warning replayed in her head. But before she could retreat, her phone chimed with a response.

"Always on eBay for SOE paraphernalia. Here's a link to an article I wrote on Jacqueline Nearne after watching School for Danger myself. Bit dated, though."

There was no trace of his usual charm—just a straightforward response, almost as if he were keeping a respectful distance after their last encounter.

Mia glanced at the link, her thumb hovering over it before deciding to respond.

"Yeah, I read it. It was thorough & interesting."

A few seconds passed before her screen lit up again.

"Thanks. Always wanted to write pieces like that. But National Heritage Daily doesn't pay enough."

She hesitated, choosing her words. *"Why are you still with the tabloids?"*

"Yeah. It's temporary. But taking too long, I'm afraid."

She could almost hear the restraint in his words, the careful tone, as if he didn't want to push further than she'd let him. Mia felt a flicker of understanding, remembering her own compromises to stay afloat.

After a pause, she typed, *"Well, you've got talent. Hope it will work out for you."*

This time, his response took longer. *"Thanks, Mia. Means a lot, especially from you. Can you please give Miss Nearne the film reel for me if you have a chance?"*

His tone of respect, underscored by caution, was enough to allow a small sense of trust to inch forward.

"I'll try. Good night."

"Good night, and thanks."

Mia set her Blackberry down and stared at the gray flickering screen of her television, which had reached the end of the video. She got up to switch it off, stirring Mr. Spikes awake. The cat rounded his back and stretched luxuriously.

"Time for bed, Spikey."

As she brushed her teeth, Mia felt a curious sense of connection with Sebastian through Miss Nearne, almost as if the old lady were giving her a knowing wink. Catching sight of her reflection in the bathroom mirror, mouth full of toothpaste, she shook her head. Yet, the alarm bells Alexandra had tried so hard to instill in her stayed silent.

It's not like I'm dating him. He has more than enough dates to last him a lifetime. But a new thought surfaced, cautious yet curious: *What if he really does know something valuable about the SOE women?*

From a caregiver's perspective, as an advocate for healing and honor, Mia felt compelled to uncover Eileen's past. She needed to understand the context of those war years, to piece together the missing links that might help with Eileen's treatment and in honoring her experiences. And Sebastian—perhaps drawn by the historical significance and the often-overlooked valor of these women, and maybe even their forgotten struggles after the war—might just offer the perspective she needed.

They approached Eileen's story from different angles, yet Mia couldn't ignore the potential for partnership with Sebastian that tugged at her thoughts. Could they actually find common ground here—to do some good for Eileen's mental health and legacy?

She rinsed her mouth vigorously, shaking her head once more. "Nope! No reporters near Miss Nearne. I'll have to do this alone."

24

A CALL FOR HELP

Three weeks later - Torquay, early September

The phone rang at Hope Haven just as Mia was about to leave for lunch. Surprised, she picked it up, recognizing Sister Damian's warm, familiar voice on the other end.

"Good afternoon, Dr. Thompson. I hope I'm not interrupting?"

"Not at all, Sister. What can I do for you?" Mia replied, her curiosity piqued.

"Well, I've had a message from our dear Miss Nearne. She mentioned there was something she could use your help with—she was a bit hesitant to say much, but it seemed important enough for her to ask directly."

Mia felt a stir of anticipation. "Did she say what it was?"

"Only that it has to do with... a task that requires a computer. Perhaps it's best if you discuss it with her yourself. She sounded quite keen, in her own way."

The thought of Eileen reaching out willingly felt like a step forward, and it stirred both Mia's professional curiosity and personal empathy. Whatever Eileen needed, Mia knew this request carried a significance that might go beyond a simple online task. Perhaps this was Eileen's way of opening a new door. Then again, it might be something as practical as online banking.

"I'll check in with her. Thank you for letting me know, Sister Damian."

"Well done, Doctor, and good luck."

Later that day

MIA CLIMBED the narrow steps to Eileen's flat, noting the polished brass on the door handle and a hint of lavender, which seemed to greet her before she even knocked. She'd barely lifted her hand to knock when the door swung open.

There stood Eileen, her cheeks flushed, her blue eyes bright as winter stars. Her white hair, though in dire need of a trim, was brushed and neatly held in place. She wore an old-fashioned navy dress with long sleeves and buttons down the front. The apron was gone, and two medals—gleaming and carefully pinned to her chest—caught Mia's eye.

"Miss Nearne," Mia greeted warmly, registering the transformation, wondering what might have sparked it.

"Oh, Dr. Thompson, do come in, do come in," Eileen replied quickly, her voice rapid with that singsong French lilt. She ushered Mia inside, her words tumbling out almost too fast. "I've tidied up a bit, even found some biscuits in the cupboard, *langues de chat*, you know, heavens, what do you call them in English? Is it cat tongues? Anyway—just in case."

"Please just call me Mia. Dr. Thompson sounds so formal. And there was no need to do all that, though I love cat tongues. Haven't had them in years."

"There, there! I thought so. A bit of sweetness never does any harm, now does it?"

Mia stepped into the flat, noting the meticulously arranged sitting area, a freshly dusted tea set laid out on the small table with perfectly aligned cups, and Eileen's hands, fidgeting ever so slightly, smoothing the fabric of her dress. As Mia took a seat, she observed the energy radiating off Eileen—a kind of brightness she hadn't seen before, though it bordered on frenetic.

"I see you've put on your medals," Mia said softly, her eyes meeting Eileen's with a smile of appreciation.

Eileen's hand flew to the medals almost self-consciously, her fingers lingering on the familiar metal. "Yes, yes, thought it was the thing to do," she replied, her voice brisk but with an undercurrent of vulnerability. "A little reminder, you know, of... well, the past. I never wear them these days. The occasions have gone."

It was on the tip of Mia's tongue to mention that she'd seen a photograph of Eileen wearing them back in 1993, at the unveiling of the Ravensbrück plaque for the female agents who had perished there. In it, Eileen stood looking very serious in a white jacket, side-by-side with Odette Hallowes, whose impressive row of medals contrasted with Eileen's modest two. But Mia thought better of it. No mention of concentration camps. Stick to the now.

"Tea? Sugar?" Without waiting for an answer, Eileen dropped a generous scoop of sugar into the porcelain cup and poured the tea. Being used to chamomile without any additions, Mia noted the milk that was added before she could reply.

"Thank you." She accepted the cup gracefully, sensing the pride and hesitation mingling in her host as Eileen took the other armchair but quickly scooted up again, reminding Mia of the girl she'd pictured during her family's picnic in Boulogne-sur-Mer.

"Oh, shoot, *les langues de chat*! I promised them and then completely forgot. My head is a sieve these days."

After she offered Mia a biscuit, Eileen perched on her chair again, still restless and fidgety. With her trained eye, Mia noted all the subtle signs in Eileen: the tapping of her foot, the flushed blotches on her cheeks, the quick, animated gestures. She recognized these signs—often seen in clients on the edge of a breakthrough or, sometimes, of pushing themselves a bit too hard.

"This is such a warm welcome, Miss Nearne," Mia said gently, keeping her tone steady. "You've gone to a lot of effort, I can see that. Why don't we just sit and enjoy the moment?"

Eileen nodded, seeming almost relieved at Mia's suggestion, and sat a little deeper in her chair, folding her hands primly in her lap with the ever-present rosary never far from her fingers.

In a soothing voice, slowing the room's energy, Mia continued, "Sister Damian mentioned you'd asked for my help with something on the computer?"

Eileen didn't seem to hear her. Mia noticed her lips moving—she was praying Hail Mary's in French, likely to steady herself. Quietly, Mia took her laptop from her bag and placed it on the coffee table without a sound.

"What was that?" Eileen shook herself from her silent prayer and stared at the silver rectangle on her table. "You're not going to record me, are you?" The fear returned to her eyes as her gaze darted between Mia and the laptop.

"No, of course not, Miss Nearne. I just wasn't sure whether you had a computer, so I thought I'd bring my own."

"Is *that* a computer? Good heavens, they were massive in my day."

"Actually, it's what we call a laptop, but it works the same way. Whatever you need, I can look it up online and help you with it. Is that a deal?"

"Yes, yes... now I remember. It's the Special Forces Club in London. They want us to register online. They always have a special dinner around November 11, but I think I need to fill in renewal forms and payments and the like—I can't make head or tail of their letter."

"Do you have it here? May I take a look?"

With quick, brisk movements, Eileen got up and opened a drawer beneath a table with her photos, mumbling to herself in French, "*Mon Dieu, c'est où? J'ai ma tête en l'air.*" She let out a satisfied "*ah, voilà*" and held the envelope up with a triumphant look. Her medals tinkled on her chest as she handed the letter to Mia.

"Thank you for your trust, Miss Nearne. Let me see if I can make heads or tails of it. I understand the Special Forces Club has something to do with your war work?"

As Mia scanned the instruction letter, her focus remained on Eileen, who launched into a lengthy discourse about the SOE club, founded in 1945, which had brought both comfort and gaiety to her and to Jacqueline.

"But you see, I haven't been going for the good part of ten years," Eileen said, almost sheepishly. "I'm surprised they're still sending me those letters, considering I've been so rude as to never even let them know I wouldn't be coming. Just shows they're truly good people."

Mia hesitated but decided to take a chance. "And are you reconsidering the invitation now?" She held back the urge to ask why, knowing it was not yet the time.

"Well, I don't know, but I'm not getting any younger," Eileen replied with a girlish giggle, her wrinkled face lighting up with a youthful radiance that revealed the beauty she still carried at eighty-six. "Perhaps my manners have improved a bit, and it's time I give them a sign of life."

Mia returned the smile. “Let’s go through the paperwork, step by step, if you’d like.”

“Just don’t promise them anything.” Eileen’s blue eyes took on a stern look, and Mia shook her head.

“Just the essentials so you’re in the loop, right?”

“Yes.”

Eileen’s hands, so animated earlier, began to calm, and her shoulders lowered a fraction. As they worked through the form together, Mia noticed Eileen’s breathing slow, her initial nervousness easing as they settled into the rhythm of the task. She responded to each question with patience, gently redirecting any of Eileen’s jittery energy back to the present moment. Every so often, Eileen would dart back to the drawer to find her passport, her bank details, and finally, her Special Forces Club card.

Halfway through, Eileen let out a small, self-deprecating laugh. “I’m absolutely useless with this newfangled technology. And to think I was trained to work a wireless transmitter under the Nazis’ noses! Now I can’t even get through a payment form.”

Mia smiled, sensing the tension lift. “We all have our strengths, Miss Nearne,” she replied warmly. “And today, we will tackle this one step at a time, together.”

As they completed the final steps, Mia felt a newfound calm settle over the room, the earlier tension receding, replaced by a gentle quietude. The moment felt like a bridge between them—a balance of Eileen’s courage to reach out for help and Mia’s empathy, supporting her while respecting her boundaries. The camaraderie they had felt so strongly on Mia’s first visit seemed to return.

The cat purred, the tea grew cold, but they talked, time slipping away unnoticed. Eileen’s gaze softened, drifting absently to the medals on her chest, her fingers tracing the familiar edges.

After a few minutes of silence, Mia asked gently, “Were there other times like that, when you felt alone but still carried on?”

Eileen's hand stilled on the medals, and her gaze grew distant. The question lingered in the air, drawing her inward, back to memories she had tried so long to keep locked away.

"Well," she began, almost to herself, "I suppose it was when I finally got the green light to train as a secret agent. It was at the end of 1943. That was when I really began to wonder what I'd gotten myself into."

MIA STAYED SILENT, vigilant, watching Eileen falling deeper into memory.

PART X

~ EILEEN~ ENGLAND/FRANCE NOVEMBER 1943- JULY 1944

25

CALLED TO DUTY

London, November 1943

Eileen was on leave from the listening station at Aston House, Hertfordshire, where she'd spent the past year coding and decoding messages from agents in France. It was grueling work, and Mrs. Bingham ran a tight ship. Eileen's role was vital but unrewarding, leaving her feeling like one of Bingham's many anonymous FANY girls—on the periphery of the real action. The buzz of messages from the field surrounded her, but it was never hers to feel firsthand.

She'd applied for the "real job" at SOE three times now, each attempt dismissed on the basis of age. No one under twenty-five, Colonel Buckmaster had insisted, was to be sent behind enemy lines. Eileen was only twenty-two, a fact that grated on her each time she received another rejection. How often had she pleaded her case, only to be told that rules were rules?

As she sat at the Bennetts' round breakfast table in London, stirring her tea, her mind drifted once again to France. Her sister

Jacqueline had left for the field in January of that year, and her subsequent silence had been deafening. Eileen had no way of knowing if the encrypted messages she handled were Jacqueline's, and she feared the worst. They were all faceless voices on the wireless, and her work was to decode but never understand, to pass along each message like a slip of paper over the counter, never knowing the meaning nor the outcome.

"You're awfully quiet, dear," Aunt Odile observed as she poured Eileen another cup of tea. "I do hope you're not coming down with something. Mrs. Henderson, the baker's wife, says there's a terrible flu going around."

Eileen forced a small smile. "No, Aunt. Just tired, I suppose. It's very good of you to let me stay here during my leave. It helps me rest."

"Oh, the war's hard on everyone, my dear. Just getting the ingredients to cook is like foraging in the forest these days. You rest up all you need."

Eileen absently crumbled a piece of toast between her fingers, feeling her aunt's gaze on her. She kept her own eyes lowered.

"I just... miss Jacqueline." The words slipped out before she could stop them.

"Ah, we all do," Aunt Odile sighed, patting Eileen's hand. "But that girl always lands on her feet."

Before Eileen could respond, the letterbox clattered. She rose quickly. "Shall I get it, Aunt?"

"Oh, go on then. It's probably just another bill."

On the doormat lay a plain brown envelope with no return address. Eileen's name and address were scrawled in neat, unremarkable handwriting. Her hands trembled as she slit it open, half-dreading and half-hoping it might be something about Jacqui. Instead, she found a brief, official-looking invitation requesting her presence at the Hotel Victoria on Northumberland Avenue the following day. No reason was given, nor was there a signature. Eileen blinked at the paper, her heart racing.

It couldn't be SOE. Could it?

As she passed back through the Bennetts' cozy kitchen, her mind spun. What if they were reconsidering her application? The idea filled her with a fierce sense of hope—and fear. She glanced out the small kitchen window at the overcast November sky, feeling a pull as sharp as ever to leave behind the routine safety of Station XII. Rumors were circulating of an imminent Allied invasion of Mainland Europe; surely they'd need skilled operators like her in the field. *If only Buckmaster would give me the chance.*

Returning to the table, she tucked the letter into her pocket and forced herself to finish her tea, though her mind was already making up all sorts of ideas about the Hotel Victoria. Aunt Odile, noticing the light in her eyes, remarked, "What was in the post, dear?"

Eileen managed a tight smile. "I received an invitation for another interview tomorrow. Here in London. So, it's just as well I'm back in London after my exile in Hereforshire."

"Let's hope they'll offer you something better since you're clearly not enjoying this translation work," Uncle George chuckled, oblivious to her true role as a decoder for the French resistance.

Eileen's heart twisted slightly as she nodded. "I hope so, too."

"Tomorrow may be your chance, dear," Aunt Odile said, getting up to clear the breakfast table.

Eileen hoped so with all her heart, though it certainly wasn't the kind of work the Bennetts would wish for her.

. . .

The next day

Eileen stood outside the Hotel Victoria, gripping the brown envelope as she took in the building's grand, weathered facade. A relic of another era, its ornate stonework and tall windows whispered of a time when London had been the heart of an empire. Now, it exuded an air of war and secrecy. Men and women in various uniforms, as well as plainly dressed civilians, hurried in and out, their faces tense, their movements deliberate.

Taking a deep breath, Eileen stepped inside. The contrast between the opulent lobby and the grim-faced people passing through it struck her immediately. The air hummed with a quiet urgency that heightened her own unease. People passed each other like strangers in a busy station, heads down, focused on missions known only to them.

At the reception desk, a young man with a clipboard barely glanced up when she gave her name. "Room 138, second floor," he muttered, already answering the phone as he dismissed her with a wave.

The lift creaked as it carried her upward, the metal gate clattering shut behind her. When she stepped out onto the second floor, the grandeur of the lobby gave way to a more utilitarian space. The carpet was worn and threadbare, and the wallpaper had started to peel in the corners. Eileen's footsteps echoed down the dimly lit corridor until she reached Room 138.

Eileen knocked, and the door opened to reveal a smartly dressed woman with sharp, assessing eyes in a rather haughty, yet striking, face. She appeared to be in her thirties and exuded authority. As she regarded Eileen with her piercing gaze, a curl of smoke from her cigarette drifted lazily toward the ceiling. A string of pearls gleamed at her throat.

"*Entrez, Mademoiselle Nearne,*" she said in impeccable French, her voice nasal, betraying the rasp of a heavy smoker.

The room was even more of a stark contrast to the luxurious lobby and the utilitarian corridor—sparsely furnished, the sterile lighting softened only by the haze of smoke.

At the window stood a man with his back to them, puffing on a pipe. For a moment, Eileen wondered if this was Mr. Potter, but before she could ask, the woman took control of the conversation.

"I am Miss Atkins, Intelligence Officer," she said, gesturing for Eileen to sit. "I will be conducting your interview today."

Eileen perched on a worn armchair. The man at the window turned slightly, acknowledging her with a nod before returning to his quiet observation of the street below.

"We have a few matters to discuss," Miss Atkins continued, her eagle eyes never leaving Eileen's face. "I trust you understand the importance of discretion in all our operations?"

"Of course," Eileen replied, though the question "what operations?" hovered at the tip of her tongue.

In rapid French, Vera probed gently yet insistently into Eileen's background, motivations, and mental resilience. Eileen was ready this time, having answered similar questions often since arriving in England. But then Miss Atkins caught her off guard.

"Are you romantically involved with anyone?" Her sharp blue gaze held steady.

Eileen shook her head, puzzled. "I'm not, no."

"Good." Miss Atkins' tone was approving. "Relationships can be liabilities in our line of work. We need people who are focused and undistracted."

The intelligence officer leaned forward, tapping her Craven A cigarette into an ashtray. "You understand the risks involved in being sent behind enemy lines? The strain you might face being in German held territory?"

"I understand some of it," Eileen replied hesitantly. "Mr. Jepson told me about the risks in my first interview more than a year ago." She looked unhappy. "When I wasn't selected to go to France but instead went to Bingham's Unit."

"Well, that's changed now," Vera nodded. Eileen took a deep breath, relieved that dreary period was behind her now.

"I'm still not entirely sure what I'm supposed to do when I'm back in France, but I've thought about it, and I'm willing to do whatever is necessary."

Miss Atkins nodded again, clearly satisfied. "Very well. I will make sure you're transferred from Bingham's Unit to SOE Section F. You will receive further instructions soon. Notify no one of this interview, your assignment, whereabouts, nothing. You'll be enrolled at a training school under the code name Rose. Upon arrival, use that name at all times and speak French exclusively. I will be monitoring your progress regularly."

"Thank you, Miss Atkins." Eileen rose, unsure whether to offer her hand, but the officer kept hers firmly by her side.

"Good luck, Rose. We're counting on you." A faint, approving smile played on Miss Atkins' lips.

26

TRAINING AT BEAULIEU

A few days later, December 1943

Be at Waterloo Station at 10:00 a.m. Bring only necessities. Instructions will follow.

Eileen folded the note and tucked it away in the pocket of her FANY jacket. She was so excited about the message that she thought she might burst, but there was no one to share the news with, not that it was allowed—Miss Atkins had been very clear about maintaining strict confidentiality, even with family. And she certainly couldn't tell the Bennetts that she was on her way to becoming a secret agent in France.

Luckily, the Bennetts were out for the day, visiting their son and daughter-in-law in Guildford. Eileen left them a short, nondescript message on the kitchen table: *I've been enrolled in a translation course out of town and hope to return in a few weeks.*

An hour later, dressed in her stiff FANY uniform, Eileen found herself standing on the bustling platform of Waterloo Station. Steam billowed from the trains, thickening the air with the familiar scents of coal smoke and oil. The noise was nearly overwhelming: whistles blew, engines chuffed, footsteps clattered against the platform, and hurried voices mingled with the sounds of departure. Soldiers and civilians jostled through the crowd, each searching for their carriage, their faces a mix of determination and weariness.

In one hand, Eileen clutched the small suitcase that had carried her few belongings from Grenoble to London; in the other, her fingers curled around the rosary in her pocket, grounding her amidst the whirlwind of noise and emotions. She scanned the platform, searching for anything, a familiar face, a hint of what was to come, something that might make this feel real. She lingered near the Third Class section, unsure which class she was meant to travel in, though she forced herself to stand tall.

If Jacqui can do it, so can I, she reminded herself, though she had only vague hints of what the secret agent training might involve. Jacqueline had let slip that there would be physical drills, Morse code, and various other skills. Well, Eileen was fit, young, and willing. And Morse and coding were skills she already had under her belt. Miss Atkins had said she'd be trained further as a W/T Operator, so she expected more coding and decoding, along with who knew what else.

At exactly ten, a voice jolted Eileen from her thoughts. "Rose? Follow me."

A tall, broad-shouldered man in uniform, with a puffy red face, was already making his way through the crowd, not waiting for her answer. Eileen, along with two men and two women, joined him as he led them toward a second-class train car, his movements brisk, his eyes focused. They climbed aboard, and as the train pulled out of the station, she felt the thrill of forward motion—she was finally on her way.

The hours to Beaulieu in Hampshire passed in relative silence, each passenger seemingly lost in their own thoughts. Eileen resolved that she wanted to pass the training with flying colors, so she wouldn't befriend anyone, but instead remain as aloof and secretive as she could manage. It would be a challenge; she loved to chat and laugh, but this was too important. She wanted the instructors to see her as determined and serious, not as some silly girl craving adventure.

Her eyes flitted from the passing scenery to her fellow passengers, assuming the other four were trainees like herself. Across from her sat a young woman, also in FANY uniform, with strong, intelligent features and striking dark eyes that held a quiet intensity. Her brown hair was neatly styled, and she sat very erect, her expression focused and thoughtful. She looked nice, and Eileen found herself wondering whether she was French or English. They seemed to be about the same age, perhaps with only a year or two between them.

Now and then, they exchanged brief glances, but each time, Eileen quickly averted her gaze, reminding herself of her promise not to socialize without purpose. She needed to keep her focus on her inner resolve. Make her family proud, make Jacqui proud, make SOE proud.

Sitting tall, she willed her posture and hands to remain still, letting a quiet determination settle over her like a soft blanket. She prayed God would help her prove her worth through her actions, not through being a friendly scatterbrain.

As the train began to slow, Eileen caught sight of the dense woods and open fields of the New Forest, their wintry hues softened by a gentle fall of snow. As they disembarked at a quiet rural station, thin snowflakes began to swirl down, settling noiselessly on her shoulders and dusting the brim of her duffel coat. She shivered slightly, the chill cutting through even her warm layers. Underfoot, the fresh snow crunched softly, adding a quiet rhythm to their footsteps as they followed a waiting officer to an unmarked military truck.

"All aboard!" The officer's voice cut through the winter air like a cold chisel. They quickly obeyed, scrambling into the back of the truck, the girls hoisting up their narrow skirts with a touch of embarrassment. Their luggage following.

The drive was a jostling journey down a winding road lined with skeletal trees, their branches stripped bare by winter's touch. The snow began to fall more heavily, muffling the sounds around them, and Eileen felt herself pulled into a profound silence. The canopy of the forest gradually closed them off from the outside world, wrapping the small group in a shroud of quiet and isolation. Her thoughts, usually racing, began to still, drawn into the calming rhythm of the snowfall.

There was a stark beauty in this solitude, a calmness in the silence that mirrored her own resolve. It felt as though the whole world had gone still, focused, and she took a steadying breath, finding comfort in that quiet.

Her fingers yearned for crayons, an ache she hadn't felt in ages. Whenever the incessant chatter in her mind quieted like this, her desire to draw and paint returned. She couldn't capture the scene here and now, but she inhaled the stillness of the landscape, storing it in her mind. One day, after the war, after her mission was over, she would sketch and paint again. This moment—hung in the balance between war and peace—would find its way onto her canvas. It would be a memory of a time when she was on the precipice of her mission.

As the baby of her family, Eileen had never done anything this daring or isolated before. She was utterly alone, unknown, with her future as shadowed and uncertain as the forest secrets around her. And yet, in the heart of the quiet, she felt a newfound strength within her. With God's protection and her own resolve, she was ready to face whatever challenges lay ahead. In this stillness, she sensed that she would be tested to the very fabric of her soul—and she knew, deep down, that she would face it.

Within the sprawling grounds of the Beaulieu estate, the truck rolled to a stop outside a low, plain-looking building with a faded sign reading *Training Wing 27*. The officer grunted, "*Descendez!* Out you go. This'll be your quarters for the next few weeks. There are no men and women's dorms anymore—too many of you to bother with that."

Eileen exchanged a wide-eyed look with the pretty FANY who'd sat opposite her on the train. *A shared dorm with men?* She could practically hear her mother's horrified gasp. But the other girl's eyes sparkled with amusement, and she gave Eileen an encouraging nudge.

"We'll look out for each other," she whispered. "Odette. Code name, of course."

"I'm Rose," Eileen whispered back with a grin. "And thank you."

They followed the officer through a narrow hallway into a large, open room lined with metal bunk beds. On each bed lay a pile of military-issued blankets and a small, scratchy-looking pillow. The air was tinged with the smell of shaving cream and eau de cologne, mingling with the faint dampness of woolen underwear.

Eileen took it all in with a mix of excitement and disbelief. It seemed she and Odette were the only two women in a room with at least a dozen men. But there was little time to dwell on the arrangement as they followed the grumpy officer to the last two empty beds, side-by-side in a corner of the room.

"These are yours. Unpack as fast as you can. I'll be back for you in ten. And remember—*français seulement*. French only!"

Around them, the male recruits were already settling in—some adjusting their beds, others rummaging through their belongings.

Eileen even spotted a pair of men's boots hanging off the top bunk by a precariously thin shoelace.

"Looks like we've joined a pack of wolves," Odette murmured in French.

Eileen smirked. "At least they seem rather tidy wolves. My brothers' rooms back home were certainly worse."

A gruff, middle-aged man with a bushy mustache and piercing blue eyes under a high forehead sauntered over with an amused look on his face. "Don't worry, ladies," he drawled in French, his strong English accent unmistakable. "We won't bite. Not unless we've missed our morning tea, anyway."

Odette snorted. "Good thing I brought my own tea bags, then. Never know when you might need a bargaining chip."

The man chuckled. "Just make sure you don't take them to France, ma'am. You wouldn't be the first to get caught by the Gestapo with British tea or cigarettes."

"Noted," Odette replied curtly as she set her suitcase on the bed and unbuckled it.

Eileen followed suit. "I'm glad we're not in bunk beds. This way, we can keep an eye on each other—and on those men."

Odette grinned. "We'll come to no harm, Rose. As he said, they don't bite."

Eileen eyed the rough blankets with a rueful smile. The bed and the room offered little in terms of privacy or comfort, but that wasn't what she was here for.

Odette was already making herself at home, laying out a comb, a small mirror, and—to Eileen's surprise—a tube of red lipstick on the bedside table.

"Didn't think we'd need glamour here," Eileen said, unable to suppress a chuckle as she nodded toward the lipstick.

"Ah, *chèrie*, it's not for glamour," Odette replied with mock seriousness. "It's for morale." She tucked the lipstick under her pillow with a practiced, endearing flair.

Eileen gazed at her new roommate, both amused and strangely comforted. This wasn't at all what she had expected—a dorm full of men, a spirited roommate with a light-hearted view on their austere situation—but she felt she could adapt. She may not have brought her lipstick, but she was more than capable of holding her own.

"Well, Rose, I'm prepared for our first night in the wolves' den. What about you?" Odette winked.

Eileen smiled back at her, shoving her suitcase under the bed and smoothing her skirt. "I guess so. Though I could do with a bit of luncheon."

She realized she hadn't eaten since breakfast at the Bennetts', and it was now late afternoon.

"I'm starving too, but I think we'll have to settle for a quick ciggie." Odette nodded toward the grumpy officer who was zigzagging his way through the beds toward them.

Instead of a cup of tea and a sandwich, they had a quick drag on their cigarettes before being ushered into a makeshift classroom that had probably once been a cozy sitting room in The Drokes building at Beaulieu. The original character of the room lingered in the faded wallpaper, patterned with ivy vines, and the elaborate, slightly chipped cornices near the ceiling.

Now, it was starkly furnished with two rows of wooden desks and chairs that looked hastily repurposed for military use. A chalkboard on a metal stand stood at the front, and the windows, frames frosted with snow, cast dull, pale light into the room. Electric lamps dangled from above, their bulbs dim, barely pushing back the shadows that clung to the corners.

About twenty men and women were already seated, each looking tense and focused, as Eileen and Odette quietly shuffled in to take seats. The scent of damp wool and tobacco lingered in the air, mingling with the slightly musty smell of old carpet.

At the front stood their instructor—a terribly tall, skeletal man with a white rim of hair around his otherwise bald scalp and sad, drooping eyes that reminded Eileen of an old hound dog. His ill-fitting suit hung loosely on his frame, sleeves a touch too short, and he clutched a clipboard in one hand while gesticulating with a pointer toward a set of chalked-out rules on the board.

As Eileen and Odette settled in, his gaze flicked toward them, his somber eyes resting briefly on Eileen before he resumed his address.

"*Asseyez-vous et faites attention*," he ordered in precise, unaccented French, directing his pointer to the two empty seats at the front, right under his gaze. They quickly moved to take their places.

Once seated, Eileen retrieved her notepad and pen from her handbag eager to record everything there was to learn from this man.

"I am your security instructor," he continued in French delivered in a low and solemn voice, "and as you lot will be trained as wireless telegraphy operators, your security is even more paramount than that of other members of the network." He tapped the pointer against the board with a rhythmic intensity. "Rule 1: You operate alone, unseen, and unheard. Make no mistake; the success of your mission—and your life—will depend on how well you learn to blend in, to avoid notice, and to stay silent. This isn't about making friends or companions," he continued, his sad eyes sweeping the room. "In fact, it's quite the opposite. Each of you must be prepared to work alone, possibly for months at a time. No contact with anyone in the circuit. Just receive and send messages through mailboxes and couriers you don't know."

Eileen scribbled notes furiously, feeling the weight of his words settle over her like the heavy snow outside, blanketing any sense of comfort or companionship. She cast a sidelong glance at Odette, but she seemed absorbed in her own thoughts, her expression serious, pen poised. The somber reality of their roles was sinking in, layer by layer.

The instructor's tone sharpened as he continued, detailing the essentials of wireless operation and the life-or-death importance of keeping transmissions brief. "You'll have to find a place where you can blend into the sounds of the environment," he instructed, his voice grating with urgency. "You'll need trustworthy people nearby, people who can drown out the sound of your tapping. In a city, that means blending into the din—finding civilians who will unwittingly shield you. Over a café, or a busy workshop, anywhere you can vanish into the noise. But in rural areas, it's another thing altogether. Then you must get as far away from people as possible. Complete isolation."

Eileen's pen hovered for a moment. *Where will I go?* she wondered, her mind drifting briefly to the countryside, to fields and streams untouched by war. If she had to be on her own, she'd rather avoid the challenge of securing people to protect her while she transmitted. Better to rely completely on herself. But of course, she knew her wishes held no sway. Her placement, her mission, her entire future—all were out of her hands.

After what felt like hours of severe instruction on security, they were finally dismissed. The instructor tapped his clipboard with a long, pale finger. "That will be all for today. Tomorrow, it's Morse code and more Morse code. Swiftness is everything. For now, you're expected in the dining room at seven sharp. Don't be late."

The group shuffled out of the classroom, silent and thoughtful. Six weeks—that was their life expectancy in the field. The tall man hadn't minced words. Eileen's legs felt stiff from sitting for so long, and a sadness settled in her heart, pressing down on her chest. She didn't want to die. But what about Jacqui? Was she...?

As she and Odette made their way down the dim corridors of

The Drokes, Eileen noticed the same tension and fatigue etched across her fellow trainees' faces.

"We'll do well, Rose!" Odette said, attempting to cheer them both up. "I think women are actually better at this than men. We can blend in more, you know."

"Yes, of course!" Eileen took a deep breath. "We'll survive! Both this course and our mission."

But as they neared the dining room, the laughter and clinking of cutlery within seemed like sounds from another world. Survival was far from a guarantee—it was a gamble, one that held stakes neither of them could yet fully grasp.

27

FINAL PREPARATIONS

Three months later - London, late February 1944

The small fitting room, hastily arranged in one of the back rooms of the Hotel Victoria, was icy-cold, with only a faint beam of late-winter sunlight filtering through the high window, casting a muted glow over the dusty corners. Eileen clasped her arms around her torso for a bit of warmth as she stood before a tall mirror. A French seamstress pinned the hem of a plain gray skirt with pursed lips, a row of needles and pins held between them.

Eileen studied her reflection, telling herself she was Jacqueline du Tertre, a shopgirl from Nice, headed to Paris to find work. Jacqueline, a name she both treasured and dreaded, would be her role for the coming months. In the mirror, she practiced her new identity: a quiet, slightly clumsy, rather naïve girl, nondescript and easily overlooked.

Acting had always come easily to her, and she'd thrown herself so fully into this role since Miss Atkins had first described it to her that she even dreamed as Jacqueline—adding her own backstory. In her mind, Jacqueline had worked at a post office briefly; that might explain why she'd picked up some Morse code. Surely, that was innocent enough, wasn't it?

"*Mademoiselle, tournez, s'il vous plaît.*" The seamstress's voice broke her concentration, and Eileen realized she'd been lost in character. She turned, giving the woman a slightly sheepish smile, giggling as Mademoiselle du Terte might.

She had already tried on two dresses, a blouse, and a coat—all simple, French-cut clothing that would help her blend seamlessly into the sea of Parisian women. The clothes were neither new nor particularly stylish, just as they should be.

"Parisian women have had to let their standards fall very low," Miss Atkins had explained earlier. "There's hardly any fabric to be had in the cities anymore, and people are making do with pre-war clothes. Yours can be whole, but they should look well-worn. The same goes for your shoes and handbag."

The reality of her departure from Eileen Nearne began to settle. She would leave behind her English identity, her FANY uniform, and even her name. In a few days, she would step off the Lysander in France as a Frenchwoman with a mission, a life, and a past as carefully constructed as the hem on her skirt. Codename Rose but also with two wireless code names: Petticoat and Pioneer. Yet the codenames had little identity for her, far less than Mademoiselle du Terte.

"It's just a simple mending stitch that's needed," the seamstress muttered, oblivious to the bigger mission her needle and thread were contributing to. "No one will look twice at a girl with a proper hem. I'll have it done by tomorrow."

Back in her FANY uniform, Eileen exited the fitting room only to bump into a familiar figure. The broadly-built man of ordinary height, dressed in a smart dark suit, was Alcide, her organizer. He gave her a warm smile from behind his gold-rimmed spectacles, his sharp, intelligent eyes taking her in with a mix of jest and joviality.

"Rose, I gather you had your final fitting? Now come with me so you and I can finalize things for our mission as well. Let me show you a part of Hotel Victoria that's already famous—or perhaps rather infamous among us agents. I'm taking you to the bathroom."

"The bathroom, *Monsieur*?" Eileen didn't know whether to laugh or be alarmed. She'd met with her future boss a few times, always under the watchful eye of Colonel Buckmaster or Miss Atkins. She'd liked and trusted him immediately; he had a warmth and humor that put her at ease. But was he making a pass at her now?

Alcide stopped, still grinning, and took her in with an amused look. "Just testing you, *Mademoiselle*. I promise you, the black-tiled room with a black bathtub is the most secluded and secure place in all of Hotel Victoria for secret rendezvous. And don't you think the WIZARD organizer can have such a rendezvous with his W/T operator? Come on, Rose. I was told you love role-playing. Here's your chance—with me in the bathtub, and you pretending to wash my hair." He ran a hand through his thick salt-and-pepper hair.

"Alright," Eileen giggled, "show me the bathroom."

They made their way down the narrow corridor until they reached what Alcide had called the famous bathroom of the Hotel Victoria. As he opened the door, Eileen took in the sight with awed amusement.

The room was cloaked in elegance, the walls and floor gleaming with glossy black tiles that cast a soft, reflective sheen under the dim lighting. In the center, a deep, black, porcelain bathtub stood, as though inviting any conversation within its embrace to remain cloaked in secrecy. The ambiance was almost theatrical, the shadows settling over the room in a way that felt both alluring and secure. The black tiles gave the room an intense intimacy, creating a pocket of hidden space away from the hotel's bustling exterior.

But what caught her attention even more was the young man sprawled in the empty tub, his boots propped up over the edge, a copy of an SOE sabotage manual held aloft as he read, lips moving with concentration.

Alcide rolled his eyes and sighed. "Sullivan, surely this tub can survive a minute without your presence. Can't you study railway sabotage elsewhere?"

Sullivan didn't even look up, flipping the page. "All due respect, Alcide, but nothing beats the peace and quiet of this porcelain haven. Besides," he smirked, lowering the manual, "I heard this tub was supposed to be shared."

Eileen stifled a laugh, and Alcide fixed her with a mock glare. "Don't encourage him, Rose. It'll only make him worse."

Sullivan finally sat up, his gaze landing on Eileen with a playful grin. "Ah, *Mademoiselle*! I suppose you're here to take over the official lounging duties. Be my guest." He climbed out of the tub with exaggerated gallantry, offering her a mock salute before strolling out, manual still in hand.

When he was gone, Eileen giggled. "I see this is a very serious SOE facility, *Monsieur*."

Alcide chuckled, gesturing to the tub. "It may not be conventional, but even agents need a break. Now, sit if you like—though not to read a manual on sabotage, I hope. I have other plans for you."

Eileen perched on the edge of the tub, still grinning. "No, no sabotage for me. But perhaps a little practice on my Jacqueline du Tertre act?"

"Excellent idea," Alcide said, gesturing to the room's theatrical shadows and elegance. "And this couldn't be a better stage. Surrounded by black tiles and safely out of sight, we can speak freely. I'm here to give you the good news: a date has been fixed for our departure to France. The night of the 2nd of March."

"Oh, how exciting!" Eileen jumped up from sitting on the edge of the bath. "Are we parach—" She stopped mid-sentence, glancing quickly at Alcide's malformed right arm.

He kept smiling, unruffled. "I'm afraid not, Mademoiselle. Can't take the risk with an arm like mine, though I must say I've learned to live well with my 'mishap.' I can ride, shoot, even sail a yacht, but a parachute jump in the dead of night, with the Gestapo lurking in the bushes and my precious W/T operator's life in the balance? No, I'm not going to risk that."

Despite Alcide's jocular tone, Eileen felt the weight of his words. He'd been in occupied France as a resister and was held in high esteem by 'the Firm,' as the agents called SOE.

"Rose?" His voice softened, a low warmth in his tone as he studied her face. "Buck may say you're ready, but are you truly?"

Eileen met his gaze with steady eyes. "Yes," she replied, calm but charged with the thrill of knowing it was real. "I've been waiting for this day since I left France as a *persona non grata* with my sister in 1942. It's been almost two years of waiting. I am ready."

"Your sister is in France too. For SOE." He said it casually, and Eileen felt a flash of curiosity. Did he know more about Jacqueline?

"Yes. I'm glad Buck told me she's all right and will be back on leave soon. It's a pity I'll miss her, as I'll be gone."

"Well, let's hope this blasted war is over soon, and you'll reunite with your sister. Her praises are sung as a devoted courier through all the halls of HQ."

"Yes, Ja—my sister is fantastic," Eileen corrected herself, suppressing Jacqueline's name. She didn't know her sister's codename but was imprinted with the importance of codenames only.

Alcide closed the lid of the bidet and sat down, carefully arranging the pleats in his trousers. "The weather may still be an obstacle. Early March's temper, they say, is hardly promising." A grimace flickered across Alcide's face, and Eileen sensed his own eagerness to return to his homeland.

"Can you prepare yourself for delay if necessary, Rose?"

As she met his dark, steady gaze, Eileen felt an unexpected bond. He was her superior, her colleague, but also her protector. "Of course, Alcide. I'm ready when the weather is ready."

He inclined his head, his warm yet guarded smile never wavering. "I hate to say this, Rose, but going into France at this point is far more dangerous than even a year ago. It's a double-edged sword. Because of the imminent Allied invasion, the Firm is sending ever more SOE agents into the field. Hundreds by now. At the same time, the Germans have honed their skills at catching us and are growing more nervous—and dangerous—with every hint of resistance and sabotage. To put it simply: our chances of survival are far lower now."

Eileen nodded, prepared. She'd known this would be the case. She was ready.

"I'll do my utmost to watch out for you, Rose. And though I'm honored to have such a skilled operator, I'd rather you be stationed in the countryside and not in south-west Paris as is planned. Paris is crawling with risk. So, promise me you'll do nothing to compromise yourself." He paused, his expression softening slightly. "I know I'm supposed to say 'don't compromise the network,' but truly, I mean you. You'll be out there with only a handful of contacts to rely on. I have my network, my friends and colleagues, but you... with that wireless set. It's a lonely and extremely dangerous position."

Eileen took in the seriousness of his words. "I'll be vigilant at all hours, Alcide. Don't worry. People often think me frail and unworldly, but I can blend in. I won't take unnecessary risks. I can be solitary, stealthy, and safe. I'm certain of it."

He rose from his perch on the bidet, and Eileen stood as well. He gave her one last, piercing look.

"See you at RAF Tempsford in a couple of days, Rose."

"See you there, Alcide."

He turned to open the door, pausing to let her pass first. She turned back, hesitating. "And thank you. For everything. I... I like you." She smiled, almost girlishly.

"I like you too, Rose. And I hold your skills in high esteem. Now, enjoy your last days in London and be merry."

OUTSIDE, snow flurries swirled down from a darkening sky, the cold air biting at Eileen's cheeks as she departed Hotel Victoria for the last time. She watched Alcide's figure in his navy overcoat disappear into the crowd. Northumberland Avenue seemed suddenly foreign, knowing these were her last moments on London's familiar streets. In just days, she'd be walking the bridges over the Seine in Paris—a Paris occupied by the enemy, full of all the warnings instilled in her.

As she made her way to the Underground station, anticipating a final evening at the Bennetts', Eileen realized she'd spent her life waiting for this moment. To do something meaningful, to prove her worth, to be as brave and capable as her sister.

And now, with her life packed into Jacqueline du Tertre's small case, a new name, and the image of war-worn France imprinted in her mind, she felt herself poised on the edge of something monumental—a leap into an unknown fate as inevitable as it was terrifying.

28

FLYING TO FRANCE

A few days later - RAF Tempsford England, 2 March 1944

The bitingly cold, low hanging mist swept across RAF Tempsford as Eileen stood on the edge of the tarmac, her worn French suitcase in one hand, while her other clutched a handbag. White plumes of breath escaped with every exhale, her stockinged legs barely able to resist visible shivering in the unfamiliar French shoes on her feet.

The looming Lysander gleamed dully under the dim lights, its curved wings cutting a silhouette against the overcast sky, the underside freshly painted in black varnish to keep it out of sight from any patrolling Germans below.

"Rose, could you step into the hangar a moment?" Miss Atkins's voice sounded behind her. "Last-minute checks."

Eileen followed the Firm's spymistress into the hangar, grateful to escape the icy breeze, if only briefly. The intelligence officer's expression was serious, her blue eyes sharp as she took in Eileen's shivering figure and the thick layer of tension that hung about her. She extended her hand toward Eileen's handbag.

"May I? Just routine." Her voice carried the authority of someone who left little room for objection.

"Of course." The inspection was routine, but Eileen knew it was a final test of her readiness.

Vera searched the bag methodically. "Just making sure there are no British rail tickets, ration cards, or other such items." She glanced up, satisfied. "This is all in order. Now, let's check your pockets and labels—anything British that might give you away."

Eileen nodded, holding steady as Vera quickly, precisely, and respectfully examined Mademoiselle du Tertre's belongings and the insides of her clothes. The check was over in seconds, obviously a well-practiced routine.

"All is well," Vera said, standing back. She paused, then leaned in slightly, her voice softened. "One last thing, Rose. I'm sure your instructors at Beaulieu mentioned what we call the L-pill?"

Eileen nodded, eyes steady.

"I understand you're a devout Catholic, and there is no obligation to carry it if it goes against your beliefs. But I offer it to you nonetheless." Vera held up a gold ring inset with a small ruby, discreetly designed to open and reveal the capsule concealed inside.

Eileen accepted it without hesitation, her expression neutral. She'd known this would come. Sliding the ring onto her middle finger, she replied evenly, "I will not take it unless I am on the verge of betraying a fellow agent. So yes, I'll keep it, Miss Atkins."

"Good, that's settled, then." Vera nodded, seeming almost relieved.

Eileen quickly pushed the thought away. *Just don't get caught,* she reminded herself.

"The ruby ring is a gift," Vera added. "You may keep it."

"Thank you, Miss Atkins."

They moved outside, where the roar of the Lysander's engine had grown louder. Eileen spotted the familiar outline of Alcide in his overcoat, and a wave of reassurance settled over her. His presence, solid and steady, reminded her she wasn't entirely alone in this.

Alcide's gaze lingered on Eileen with a paternal warmth. "I'll do what I can to keep her safe, Vera," he said gently.

"Buck and I expect nothing less." Vera gave Alcide one of her rare smiles.

The familiarity between the French lawyer and Miss Atkins gave Eileen an unexpected boost of confidence. After all, Miss Atkins was considered Buck's right hand.

A stocky man in RAF overalls approached, his face slightly shadowed under his helmet.

"Flight Lieutenant Murray Anderson, at your service. But everyone calls me Andy." He gave the two agents a no-nonsense grin. "It's time. The lady's ready!" He nodded toward the Lysander. "Weather's holding steady for now, so let's get airborne. If you're all set."

"Is my wireless set aboard, Flight Lieutenant?" Eileen asked, suddenly realizing she hadn't seen her precious cargo since disembarking from the taxi.

"Sure is, Miss. All taken care of. You'll be tapping away happily in a day or two."

They exchanged final handshakes, with Miss Atkins's last words lingering as a reminder of the gravity of her mission.

"*Bon courage*, Rose. We'll be waiting for your first message with bated breath."

"I'll send it as soon as I can."

Following Alcide and the pilot to the plane, Eileen climbed aboard, feeling the chill of the metal through her clothing as she settled into the cramped space. Every inch of her was tense with anticipation, the thrumming of the Lysander's engine reminding her that this was it—the beginning of something immense.

As the engine roared to life, a deep, vibrating thunder filled the cabin, reverberating through Eileen's bones. She'd never been aboard an airplane before, and the tumultuous start made her grip the sides of her seat, bracing for what was to come. Part of her was terrified, a raw instinctual fear rising within her, but another part urged her to throw caution to the wind.

Bring it on. The words formed on her lips, unspoken. No one would have heard her over the drone anyway. To live on the edge, to feel the thrill of daring, to trust her instincts—this was her moment to show both mankind and her Maker what she was made of.

She clutched her handbag tightly in her lap, feeling the ruby ring with the L-pill pressing into her finger as the plane lifted off into the darkened sky.

I am Jacqueline du Tertre. Eileen "Didi" Nearne remains in England. She no longer exists.

A sense of calm, deep and profound, settled over her, like the serene stillness she'd felt in the truck ride to The Drokes only three months earlier. It felt like a lifetime ago. Yet, the calm seemed eternal, an unexpected gift from God as she faced the unknown.

Both she and Alcide sat in silence, each wrapped in private thoughts. Now and then, Alcide unscrewed the lid of a tin flask and took a swig, offering it to her once, but she shook her head with a small smile. She wrapped her coat tighter, using a storage bag as a cushion and a rough blanket draped over her legs.

The steady drum of the engine lulled her, and she must have dozed off because when she opened her eyes, red lights flashed up from the ground below. Instantly alert, she sat upright, staring down at the signaling lights. Had they arrived already? She'd missed the entire flight over the Channel and most of France.

Feeling the descent, she looked over at Alcide, who met her gaze in the dark.

"Yes, we're almost there, Rose," he shouted over the drone of the engines. "Ready?"

"Yes." She stared out the window at the flashing lights below, the fields barely visible in the moonlight.

Flight Lieutenant Anderson's voice crackled through the speaker. "Prepare for landing. You've got two minutes to disembark. Take all your belongings. Good luck and stay safe."

Eileen's heart pounded as she clutched her suitcase and handbag even tighter.

"I'll take the wireless set," Alcide shouted into her ear. "Don't worry about that."

"But..." Eileen hesitated, glancing at his disabled arm, knowing he had his own baggage to carry.

"I'll climb the ladder twice. Done it before."

As the Lysander glided down, touching down smoothly in the quiet field, Eileen felt her nerves tingle with anticipation. She knew they were in the *département of Indre*, north of *Châteauroux*—French soil, German-occupied, and, from now on, her new world.

After that, everything went so fast. Eileen had barely clambered down the steep ladder when two shadows appeared by her side, speaking in rapid French, their voices tinged with the unmistakable accent of Paris.

"Are you alright? We have to be quick, or we'll all be caught." Relief flooded through her—Frenchmen, good allies. She instantly felt as though she'd come home.

One of the men hoisted her wireless onto his shoulder, but he paused, giving her an intense look.

"Wait," he signaled to Anderson, who was already revving up the engine. "You're too young. Go back, *Mademoiselle*, now you still can. This is madness."

The other man nodded in agreement, his voice low but urgent. "The Firm must be desperate, sending such young ones. These female W/T operators get younger by the day. Miss, turn back now, while you still have the chance."

Eileen glanced at Alcide, seeking his support. She hadn't endured all the training and sacrificed her life in London to be sent back now.

"I'm older and more prepared than you think," she protested firmly. "I know the risks, and I'm ready."

The two men exchanged a look, then the one with the wireless shrugged. "Very well, *Mademoiselle*. It's your choice. Just don't say we didn't warn you." With a final nod, he turned and strode across the dark field, her wireless set balanced on his shoulder.

As Eileen moved to follow, she glanced back at the Lysander. Anderson, already on his way to London, raised a gloved hand in salute before the plane's roar filled the night, its wide wings lifting into the darkness.

Home! The word hovered briefly in her mind, but she shook it off as she took careful steps across the frozen grass, feeling the finality of her decision. *Home is here,* she reminded herself resolutely.

They stopped at a small inroad where one of the Frenchmen lowered their luggage onto a waiting cart.

"Keep your revolvers ready," he hissed in a low voice, "the road is always the trickiest."

Eileen removed her Welrod from her handbag, watching closely as the men carried their Sten guns, trying to mimic their confident grip. Shooting hadn't been her strong point during training, and the weight of the metal felt strange and unwieldy in her hand.

"Take off your glove, *Mademoiselle*. It'll hamper your precision, if needed."

She slipped the glove off, feeling the cold bite into her skin but grateful for the advice.

"Where are you taking us?" she whispered.

"*Hotel La Grange*," he replied, a hint of mischief in his voice, as his companion stifled a chuckle.

"Don't test her," Alcide's voice cut through, sharp and direct. "It's a nearby barn, Rose. The best we can do in the middle of the night. We can't risk being seen with our luggage before curfew ends."

"Alright." Eileen suppressed a shiver, both from the chill and the sudden awareness of their vulnerability on the open road. The frost, the dark, being in France—all were pressing in, but if Alcide could manage it, then so could she. She would manage.

They set off again in silence, Eileen inhaling the crisp French air, the night's stillness broken only by the crunch of their steps and the slight creak of one of the cart's wheels.

The barn was dark and drafty, filled with the earthy scent of old hay and burlap sacks.

"We'll leave you to it," one of the Frenchmen said, his bearded face barely visible under his black beret in the moonlight. "There's a thermos with coffee on the rack and some ham sandwiches wrapped up. Hope you brought your own booze to stay warm. *Bonne nuit*."

"*Bonne nuit et merci,*" Alcide replied. They shut the barn door behind them, and the only light was a thin sliver of moonlight slipping between the slats.

"Afraid we can't use a torch," he added. "If you want to smoke, just be careful not to set fire to the hay."

"Understood." Eileen's teeth chattered. "I could really use a cigarette, though I didn't have any French ones to bring along."

"Here you go. *Gauloises*." He handed her a crumpled pack with a grin.

"Perfect," she replied, taking one and gratefully inhaling as she lit the end. Then she poured them cups of lukewarm coffee.

Side by side, they sat on the hay bales, smoking and sipping quietly. The ham sandwiches were very welcome.

"You're in France, Rose," Alcide said after a moment. "How does it feel to be back?"

She was silent, letting the question settle as she looked around the shadowy barn. Gratitude filled her—the chance to do something meaningful—and with it, the weight of responsibility that now rested on her shoulders.

"Important," she said finally, a smile in her voice. "I feel important, really important, for the first time in my life."

"Ah, yes," Alcide nodded thoughtfully. "Important isn't quite how I'd put it for myself. Necessary, perhaps. If we do it right, we change history, you know. Win the war, end fascism, restore democracy. I suppose that's... important."

Eileen chuckled. "You think big, Alcide. I was only thinking selfishly—of myself, being part of all this."

He extinguished the end of his cigarette against the sole of his shoe, pulling out his flask with a smirk.

"Care for a last drink? It'll help you sleep."

"What is it?"

"Nothing but the best. *Courvoisier*. Never travel without it."

Eileen took a swig, feeling the warmth of the cognac spread through her, easing the chill in her bones.

"Try to get some sleep," Alcide said, resting back against the hay. "Tomorrow, we part ways, but you'll be in good hands. Our reception team will take you to *Orléans*."

Eileen yawned, nestling into the rough hay and feeling, at last, a bit of calm. Her first night in France wasn't comfortable, but it was real—the beginning of an adventure she'd dreamed of for so long.

29

THE TRIP TO ORLÉANS

The next morning, Vatan France, 3 March 1944

Eileen awoke to the gray dawn filtering through gaps between the barn's wooden slats. She shifted uncomfortably, stiff from a night on the rough hay. Jolted by her own movement, she sat upright, suddenly alert. *Where was she?* But the memory soon returned: she was in France, on her first SOE mission.

Stretching her stiff limbs, she looked around her, trying to catch sight of Alcide's familiar figure among the shadows, but there was only stillness. A movement on her dress caught her eye—a black spider scurrying across the fabric. She flinched, brushing it away and standing up quickly. She wasn't fond of insects, especially spiders.

With a sigh, she smoothed her dress, noticing how crumpled and travel-worn it appeared. If she wanted to blend in among the French, she'd need to look the part, and right now she felt far from the poised image of Jacqueline du Tertre, shopgirl on her way to a new life in Paris. She instinctively reached for her hair, knowing it was tangled, and no mirror or pins to help fix it.

She whispered Alcide's name into the quiet, but there was no response. Then her eyes caught sight of a folded piece of paper on top of her suitcase. As she reached for it, she recognized Alcide's neat, meticulous handwriting: *La rose fleurira—The rose will bloom.* So, he'd left without waking her. It was a bittersweet realization; she'd thought they'd say goodbye in person but hopefully they would meet up in Paris soon. The note was his keepsake, an uplifting message to help her through moments when she'd be low.

In the stillness of the barn, Eileen took a moment to absorb her dusky surroundings. Here she was, alone in France, freezing in a barn, on the brink of her twenty-third birthday, but this was what she'd wished for. Now she had to make it work. She finished the last of the cold coffee from the thermos and unwrapped the remaining ham sandwich. Hardly a feast, but it would do.

Just as she took her last bite, the barn door creaked open, and two young men stepped in, their silhouettes outlined by the morning light.

"Good morning, *Mademoiselle*," greeted the taller of the two, a sandy-haired fellow with a wiry build and an easy smile. "I'm Marc. We were your reception team last night, and we're to escort you to Orléans today." He looked very youthful—beardless and fair—almost too young to be a resistance fighter. But hadn't the Firm said the same about her?

"Frederick," introduced the other, stepping forward. He was dark-haired and wore a black gabardine coat with the collar up and a black beret pulled low over his forehead. His cautious eyes scanned the barn, noting every detail.

Eileen rose, relieved at the sudden company. "I'm Rose." Her voice was steady, and she gave her guides a careful smile. "Officially, I'm Jacqueline du Tertre from Nice, on my way to Paris." She took her forged travel permit from her bag and handed it to Marc. "My... uh...boss issued these, but I'd rather double-check they match the area. We don't need any problems en route." She avoided mentioning SOE aloud, even in this remote barn.

Marc examined the papers. "They look in order. The Germans keep changing the *Reise Papiere* format, but these should get you to Paris."

Frederick gave Eileen a skeptical look. "As I said when you arrived, you seem rather young for someone in this line of work. You sure you're up to it? France isn't exactly cloud-cuckoo-land these days, especially not Paris."

Eileen straightened, squaring her shoulders. "I'll be twenty-three on the fifteenth of March," she replied firmly, perhaps more for her own reassurance than theirs. "I'm ready for this."

Frederick raised an eyebrow, still unconvinced. "Almost twenty-three is still young for what's ahead. You know what happened—"

Marc cut him off. "Drop it. If Rose says she's prepared, she's prepared. None of us are safe, whether we're fifteen or eighty-five."

Eileen wisely decided not to probe further into who or what Frederick was referring to.

"Let me gather my things."

"I'll take the heavy case." Marc had already hoisted her wireless set onto his shoulder. "Though you know you'll be carrying all your luggage yourself once in *Orléans*."

"I know. I can handle it." She was grateful the Firm had fitted her with the latest version, the suitcase-sized Type A Mk.III, weighing just under 40 pounds—compact and manageable compared to earlier versions.

Eileen quickly collected her things, following Marc and Frederick out of the barn and into the frost-bitten morning. The air was sharp, the world around them quiet and dim with the pale light of early March.

"We'll walk to Vatan Station and board the train to Orléans. It's about ninety miles north. There we'll take you to a safe house, where we'll part ways," Marc explained as they moved along. They soon found themselves in the deserted streets of the small Centre-Val de Loire town, where they passed only a handful of farm workers and black-clad elderly women, their empty shopping bags flapping softly against their sides—likely on their way to the baker or butcher.

The setting was strikingly ordinary: no Germans in sight, only the quiet pulse of rural life. Eileen could see how smoothly the system of dropping and retrieving agents worked here, concealed within the routines of small-town France. A rooster crowed, a dog barked, shutters opened with a creak. An ordinary day in seemingly ordinary France. Just three young people with their luggage, blending into the morning as they headed to the station.

In a playful tone, Frederick remarked, "Though you're not here for sightseeing, Rose, you have to admit—even occupied France has a certain charm in the morning light." They were just crossing a medieval stone bridge that arched gracefully over a winding, frozen river. The banks were adorned with glistening icicles that caught the first red light of dawn as the sun peeked over the horizon.

"It does," Eileen replied, taking in the delicate beauty of the countryside that had been hidden in the night's cover. Even the scent of smoke drifting from chimneys brought back a wave of nostalgia. French wood fires smelled different from English coal fires—more fragrant, with a sprucy sharpness. "It feels good to be home, in a way," she added, though a shadow crossed her eyes.

Marc glanced over, seeming to catch the wistful undertone in her voice. "Together we'll free France from the yoke of tyranny, Rose," he murmured, "and one day, all of France will be pretty and homey again."

Eileen nodded, her lips forming the words, "*Vive la France.*"

The easy camaraderie of her companions felt comforting, and for a brief moment, she felt as if the three of them were simply setting out on a shared adventure. But she corrected herself. *Don't make friends, work alone, avoid others as much as possible. Disappear into anonymity.* She wasn't here to make friends.

At the station, Frederick motioned toward a small cafeteria. After some discussion, he insisted on buying breakfast, returning with fresh rolls, butter, jam, and a pot of hot coffee.

"Consider it a welcome-home meal," Marc said with a grin, sliding a steaming cup toward her.

"*Merci beaucoup*!" Eileen immediately set out savoring the warmth of the coffee. They ate in companionable silence, exchanging occasional smiles but careful not to draw too much attention to themselves.

Yet, beneath the light-heartedness lay an undercurrent of vigilance. Eileen noticed how Frederick's eyes roamed the station, noting every passerby and exit. Marc, too, maintained a relaxed posture, but his gaze scanned the room with practiced ease, taking in every detail.

It was a reminder that these men were not merely companions on a journey; they were allies on a mission, united in the unspoken awareness that their lives—and many others—depended on each move they made. And like Eileen, each was invisibly armed, ready for whatever lay ahead.

The train journey to Orléans passed smoothly, but the moment they stepped onto the platform at *Gare d'Orléans*, Eileen's heart jolted. Her gaze was drawn, almost unwillingly, to the sight of several German soldiers strolling the station in their crisp, gray-green uniforms, rifles casually slung over their shoulders, shiny black boots clomping on the pavement.

A wave of anger washed over her. The sight of them, arrogant and at ease on French soil, made her fists clench at her sides. Her breath came short and sharp as she stared, unable to tear her gaze away. It wasn't until she heard a hiss at her side that she realized she was glaring openly at them.

"For God's sake, don't stare at them!" Frederick's urgent whisper cut through her shock. His hand gripped her elbow tightly, guiding her forward as Marc threw her a worried glance. "If you want to get to Paris without being arrested, act like any other Frenchwoman under occupation—look past them, ignore them, or stare down at your feet!"

Marc added, the urgency never leaving his voice. "Yes, blend in, *s'il vous plaît,* Rose. If they single you out, that's when the trouble starts."

Eileen forced herself to drop her gaze, but her cheeks burned with embarrassment and anger. She hadn't realized how unprepared she was for this part of the mission—the reality of sharing public spaces with the enemy, even breathing in the same air. In Nice and Grenoble, in the early part of the war, the German presence had been distant, something she'd known about but never truly encountered. But now, as they walked through the streets of Orléans, Germans were everywhere: chatting in groups, smoking on the corners, laughing outside cafés with commandeered French waitstaff, as if the city belonged to them.

Her pulse quickened with each step as she became acutely aware of the foreignness of her surroundings, of the eyes that might fall on her if she wasn't careful. Even her cover story, Jacqueline du Tertre from Nice, suddenly felt thin and vulnerable. She'd worked so hard to become this invented self, but Jacqueline du Tertre would need to learn how to live under the German gaze without a hint of anger or hatred.

They wove their way through the narrow streets, keeping to quieter paths until they reached *Rue du Jardin Vert*, a small residential street flanked by middle-class houses. Marc nodded to a modest gray building with blue shutters slightly ajar. "Here we are," he said, his tone calming as they stepped up to the door of the safe house.

Eileen felt the tension finally ease from her shoulders as he tapped the door three times and they were allowed to enter, though her heart was still hammering from the close encounter. She'd been training for months, memorizing her cover and learning her new life as Jacqueline, but nothing had prepared her for the sight of Germans in the heart of France.

The world outside might have felt alien and hostile, but now, behind closed doors, she could breathe again—at least until she reached Paris. And this first lesson was seared into her mind: she would have to hide every instinct, every truth about who she really was if she wanted to survive.

30

FINALLY PARIS

The next day - Orléans France, 4 March 1944

The morning air in Orléans was hazy with fog as Eileen stepped out of the safe house, taking leave of Marc and Frederick, who were to return to their own GREY-HOUND Network. She gave them a brave smile, knowing this might be the last time she'd see familiar faces for a while.

"Take care, Rose, *et au revoir*," Marc said, shaking her hand firmly.

"Stay out of the Gestapo's clutches," Frederick added, giving her an intense look.

"I will. And thank you for everything. You've already helped me adjust to my French life."

"You've seen nothing yet," Frederick warned. "Just stay vigilant, night and day."

Armed with her two suitcases—one containing the cumbersome wireless set—and her handbag with her concealed gun, Eileen set off for the *Gare d'Orléans*. A thin bag of French banknotes was wrapped around her waist, beneath her dress and winter coat.

As she made her way through the station hall, bustling on this Saturday morning, her pulse quickened. Her gaze swept over other travelers with sharp focus, searching for any hint of abnormal activity. With all the confidence she could muster, she directed her feet to the ticket office, praying she wouldn't give herself away by asking for the wrong thing and hoping her forged papers would pass scrutiny.

"*Un aller simple pour Paris*," she asked for a one-way ticket to Paris.

"*Quelle classe*?"

Eileen thought quickly. First Class would give her more privacy but might single her out; Second Class would help her blend in, but meant more people around her. She took the chance.

"*Première classe, s'il vous plaît*."

The instant she said it, she felt she'd made a mistake. The ticket master scrutinized her—the second-hand clothes, the worn suitcase. A shopgirl with a first-class ticket. But the official merely grunted, grabbing her francs with his pudgy hands.

Her cheeks flushed as Eileen hurried away, seeking out her platform. She was acutely aware of every German soldier she passed, of each stern-faced officer milling through the crowd. This time, though, she kept her gaze low and focused, her expression neutral. The weight of her suitcase grew heavier with every step, but she forced herself to forget its physical burden, reminding herself instead of its immense significance.

She boarded the first-class compartment, choosing a seat close to the exit and by a window, from where she could keep watch on each station they passed. As the train picked up speed, she felt relieved by the comparative silence around her. Only one man sat at the far end of the compartment, reading *Le Figaro*. In the corridor, German voices echoed, but they didn't enter.

While keeping her eyes on the passing scenery, Eileen mentally rehearsed every nuance of her Jacqueline du Tertre persona. The practice calmed her. Now that she was truly on her own, responsible for herself, she felt steadier. All her life she'd been a bit of a loner, the one others felt the need to guide or instruct—but she knew better. When left to herself, she could show her real strength.

She looked down at her suitcases, felt the weight of her handbag, the money, and the forged papers. Inwardly, she affirmed her resolve:

This is right. This is what people do who truly want to achieve something—they take on a persona to help them reach their goal and believe in it with all their heart. I can do this as well as any other dedicated agent. I was born for this, and I will see it through.

Arriving at the *Gare d'Austerlitz*, Eileen braced herself before stepping onto the platform with her luggage. It had been at least fifteen years since she'd been to Paris, the city where she'd lived with her family as a young child. She hadn't returned since the war began, and everything she'd heard about Paris under occupation had been grim and desolate.

Stepping onto the *Quai Saint-Bernard*, the grand city unfolded around her, alive yet deeply troubled, like a beehive disrupted, each bee scrambling to escape. Something was terribly wrong with the City of Light in March 1944.

On the surface, the familiar cacophony of voices, roaring traffic, and hurried footsteps seemed unchanged. But the city's heavy atmosphere told a different story—one where the German presence loomed everywhere. Swastika flags adorned Parisian landmarks, and feldgrau uniforms filled the streets, mingling with the gleam of black Mercedes Benzes.

Yet it wasn't just the overbearing German presence that struck Eileen; it was the exhaustion of the Parisian population. Apart from the few well-fed and loud collaborators, the French looked weakened, wary, and desperately hungry. Everyone seemed fettered by a kind of fatalism, acutely aware of the looming threat of the cornered occupiers, unpredictable and increasingly ruthless. She had been prepped with current events and was fully aware that razzias, public arrests, and betrayals were part of daily life now, with friends turning traitor for a piece of bread or a ten-franc note.

With her intuitive nature, Eileen sensed the contradictions straining Paris, the capital caught between silent resistance and weary survival. The weak March sun struggled to hint at spring, casting a pale light over streets where tension simmered, and she, newly arrived, felt like a fresh messenger in a city holding its breath.

Adjusting her grip on her suitcases, she glanced briefly up at the *Jardin des Plantes*, its botanical beauty jarringly out of place in this tense, incognito version of her beloved city. Her destination was simple but vital: she had to find Louise, the only lifeline she had in Paris, the one person who could help her establish a safe point to send that crucial first message back to London.

With each bridge she crossed, each glance she cast, the city revealed itself in painful colors—a lady tattered and bruised after a brutal siege. Then, rising unblemished and pristine, the iconic Notre Dame came into view, its spires reaching solemnly toward the pale-blue sky.

Eileen longed to feel comforted by the sight of the cathedral, so meaningful to her and to all French Catholics. But as she gazed up, she felt that God seemed far-removed from this Paris. Yet, in her heart, she knew she must not give up her faith. Wasn't God precisely there, where people were subjugated, where the innocent suffered? She murmured a quick Hail Mary as she passed by Our Lady's House, her footsteps determined as she moved through the city she both mourned and loved.

The Seine shimmered darkly beneath her as she crossed the *Pont Neuf*, where only a solitary merchant ship sailed underneath.

No rowing boats, no canal barges, no pleasure yachts—just German patrol boats and cargo vessels. Another sign that all joy had been sucked out of Paris.

The suitcase containing the wireless seemed to grow heavier with each step as she approached the *Île de la Cité*. Her eyes scanned all the people she passed, hoping to catch sight of Louise, who was supposed to be waiting for her at the bridge's end. If her contact failed to appear, she'd be utterly alone in an enemy city, with nowhere safe to rest, no way to send her message to London. The realization hit Eileen hard—the precariousness of being alone in such a vast and hostile place. She gritted her teeth and kept moving, switching the suitcase between her hands every few steps to ease the weight.

Pausing briefly to gaze up at the bronze statue of Henry IV on his horse, Eileen put down her luggage to flex her aching fingers and blew on them to warm them against the creeping chill of late afternoon. The sky grew overcast, and a thin veil of snow began to fall, softening the edges of the statues and streetlamps in a spectral haze.

Then, her breath caught—a young woman, about her own age, stood on the lookout, scanning the passing crowd with a careful eye. Could it be? Eileen's pulse quickened, and a faint relief seeped in as she realized this must be Louise. The woman was at the appointed spot, standing and waiting. Thank God.

As Eileen approached, she steeled herself, pulling her posture upright and maintaining a calm expression. She'd reached her first destination, and here her mission truly began. Louise's face lit up with a welcoming smile, her features delicate yet strong, with that refined French elegance. Dark hair framed her oval face, curling gently beneath a red woolen beret, and her brown eyes sparkled with a hint of optimism. Despite the war's toll, she retained the understated beauty so often celebrated in Parisian women.

"*Ah, ma chère Rose*. How wonderful you have arrived. Come with me," Louise's voice was warm yet calm, light and musical, but grounded in a quiet strength. "Let me help with that." She reached for the suitcase carrying the wireless set, taking it with a brisk, practiced movement. Eileen hesitated—shouldn't she keep the compromising equipment in her own hands, in case they were stopped? But Louise seemed well-versed in the arrival of agents and added in an undertone, "Don't worry, dear. I won't endanger you. This is the perfect time to move about. The Germans are getting hungry and are looking for restaurants. They dine much earlier than we do."

"Thank you, Louise. I already feel lighter," Eileen replied, relieved to share the load—both literally and figuratively.

"Of course," Louise quipped with a smirk, "your type never seems to travel light."

Eileen couldn't help but laugh, despite herself. Louise nodded toward the left bank, and they crossed back over the bridge in companionable silence. Snow swirled around them, settling softly on their shoulders, while Louise's quiet confidence and steady pace calmed Eileen's nerves. At some point, Louise even tucked her arm through Eileen's, offering her a small bit of warm support in this strange city. Eileen leaned into the warmth, feeling an instant bond with the Parisienne, but bit her lip. *No friends, no ties*, she reminded herself. It would be difficult to keep up her guardedness in this unyielding environment.

They walked briskly through the cobbled streets, Eileen feeling the strain of the day's journey. The slippery snow made each step a delicate balance, but Louise's arm provided unexpected stability. She savored the feeling of not being alone. At least, in this moment.

Soon, they reached an unassuming apartment building at Place Saint-Michel. Louise led her up the narrow, winding staircase to the second floor, where she unlocked a plain wooden door and gestured for Eileen to enter first.

The apartment was modest but radiated warmth. Simple furniture filled the cozy main room: a threadbare couch, a wooden table set with well-used but polished plates and cutlery, and a small sideboard with carefully arranged china. The smell of fresh bread and broth hung in the air, and a petite elderly woman—Louise's mother—greeted Eileen with a welcoming nod, her eyes kind but cautious. Eileen noticed immediately how much the family resembled one another: the mother and two younger sisters shared Louise's dark hair, expressive brown eyes, and the same determined look that hinted at strength despite the family's simple life. The sisters, though younger, wore the same gentle but perceptive expressions as Louise, their gaze respectful.

"Rose," Louise said, closing the door behind them, "you'll stay here tonight. Tomorrow, we'll find you a place of your own. It's too dangerous for my family to keep you here long-term, but you'll always be able to use our address to collect or drop off messages." She spoke softly, her gaze unwavering, conveying both kindness and the necessity of their caution.

Eileen nodded, her gratitude overwhelming her. "*Merci*, Louise. You've already done so much for me."

They moved into the small dining area, where Louise's mother offered Eileen a bowl of vegetable soup and a slice of crusty bread and a modest portion of camembert cheese. The meal was simple but filling, and as delicious as if Eileen was dining in a Michelin-star restaurant. No questions were asked of her, no probing glances exchanged—only silent understanding and respect for whatever burden she carried.

The sisters regarded her with quiet admiration, carrying out small chores around the room without interrupting. Louise's mother gave Eileen a blanket and a pillow, gesturing to a cot near the small hearth.

"*Bonne nuit, Rose*," Louise said quietly as she tucked a shawl around Eileen's shoulders. "You'll be safe here tonight."

Eileen settled onto the cot, feeling the warmth seep into her weary bones. As she lay down, the familiar sounds of a family home soothed her—the gentle murmur of conversation, the faint clatter of dishes, the soft shuffle of feet on the floor. It reminded her of her own family in better times. She closed her eyes, grateful for this pocket of warmth in an otherwise hostile city. Wrapped in the security of their quiet hospitality, she drifted into sleep. Real sleep.

31

THE REAL WORK STARTS

The next day – Paris, 5 March 1944

Louise poured Eileen a cup of black coffee and placed a jam-filled baguette on her plate. In her singsong voice, tinged with an undertone of apology, she said, "You know, Rose, I didn't want to spoil your arrival yesterday, but finding accommodation in Paris is quite the challenge these days. Since the war, so many rural people have poured in from the countryside, hoping to find work, like your alias, so they can survive. And the Germans have seized all the decent apartments for themselves and their mistresses."

Eileen put her cup down. "I'd guessed as much. So...you haven't found anything for me?"

"It's not as bad as it sounds," Louise reassured her. "I've found you a room near *Porte de Champerret*, in the 17th *arrondissement*."

"Is that the northwestern part of the city?"

"Yes, exactly. It's close to a Metro station and not as heavily occupied by the Germans as the city center."

"Sounds good," Eileen replied with relief. "Thank you so much for going through all that trouble on my behalf."

Louise smiled. "That's my role in the resistance, Rose, so don't worry about that. I wish you could stay here, but it's just too dangerous, and my family's cramped as it is. But there's still one crucial issue—a place from which you can safely send and receive your messages. The room I found isn't suited for that, plus it's best not to transmit from where you live."

"That's what we were taught," Eileen agreed. "Unless, of course, you're in the countryside."

"I've been searching for locations around Paris where you could transmit," Louise explained, "but the risk and time it would take to travel across the city a couple of times a day would be too dangerous and, honestly, impractical."

"So, what do I do, then?" Eileen finished her breakfast, ready to start moving. "I need to notify London of my arrival as soon as possible and get into my regular 'skeds'—the schedule for sending messages—at ten in the morning and five in the afternoon."

Louise stood up as well. "I promise I'll keep looking, and since you'll be coming by here regularly, we can keep each other informed. If you're ready, let's make our way to *Porte de Champerret* now."

"I'm ready," Eileen replied, feeling the first threads of a plan coming together. "I'll keep my eyes open. We'll find something."

"We will, *ma chère Rose*. And in the meantime, remember—you're not alone in this. Together, we'll make it work."

Eileen wondered if assisting British agents was Louise's full-time role in the resistance, but she didn't ask. As it was, they had already shared enough information that could not leave the confines of the apartment at Place Saint-Michel.

Louise hailed a taxi, and the two *femmes de la résistance* rode in silence, Eileen gazing out the window at the passing scenes of Paris under the German jackboot. The car crossed the Seine, then wound through narrow, grim streets, finally reaching Porte de Champerret.

It was quieter here, less crowded, with fewer German patrols and more sparsely populated, with locals keeping to themselves. Though it wasn't a particularly scenic part of the city, it seemed just the place to blend in without suspicion.

The taxi pulled to a stop outside a modest building with chipped paint and narrow windows. Louise helped her with the suitcases and led her up a dim stairwell to the second floor, where a simple wooden door opened to Eileen's new room.

The room was small, with faded wallpaper and a single window overlooking the street. A narrow bed sat against one wall, along with a small dresser and a wooden chair. Louise placed Eileen's suitcase by the dresser and handed her the keys.

"The landlord, *Monsieur Breton*, is one of us, just so you know," Louise said. "But best to keep your distance from everyone else in the building."

"I will," Eileen replied, her eyes sweeping over her new abode. She didn't feel any particular connection to it, but she needn't. Jacqueline du Tertre, her alias, wasn't fussy. She imagined the dingy flat her cover identity had rented in Nice was likely worse than this spartan space.

"So, will it do?" Louise asked, sounding slightly hesitant.

"It's perfect," Eileen replied with gratitude.

Louise handed her a shopping bag, her eyes warm with encouragement. "These should get you through the first day, Rose. There's a loaf of bread, butter, coffee, jam, and a few apples. Even what you Brits call your 'fags'—French ones, of course."

"Oh, Louise, aren't you a dear? But here, let me pay. I've got enough francs to last a year. I'm sure your family needs it more than I do."

"Are you sure?" Louise's eyes glinted, clearly not wanting to refuse.

"More than sure." Eileen detached the money belt from around her waist and plucked a ten-franc note from the bundle. Louise's eyes widened at the sight of so much money.

"Never hesitate to ask if you spend money on my behalf," Eileen explained. "I know I can't throw it around, not knowing how long I'll be here, but I want you to know."

"Thank you, Rose. *Vous êtes gentille.*"

"Before you go, I have one more question," Eileen said. "I'll need to get in touch with my organizer Alcide when he arrives in Paris. Any idea how I can do that?"

Louise gave her a reassuring look. "Don't worry about that. I'm a French courier for WIZARD, though I never had the British training. Alcide will contact me, and I'll let you know. Come by tomorrow night, and I should know more." She gave a conspiratorial wink. "Oh—and there's a small piece of chocolate at the bottom of the bag. To lift your spirits."

Eileen smiled, wanting to embrace this kind Parisienne but kept her hands by her sides. She shouldn't become too friendly with anyone. "Thank you, Louise. I can't tell you how much this means."

The courier squeezed her hand. "You'll do fine. See you tomorrow."

After Louise left, Eileen closed the door and took a deep breath. She scanned the room, taking in the worn but clean sheets on the bed, the chipped paint on the walls, and the narrow window. It wasn't much, but it was hers, and for now, it was safe. She left her luggage where it was for the moment and lowered herself onto the mattress, feeling it sag under her weight.

For a long moment, she sat in silence, her rosary slipping through her fingers, letting reality settle over her. She was in Paris, on her own. The vastness of the task ahead loomed, but so did a small flicker of pride—she'd made it safely this far.

She glanced at the shopping bag Louise had given her, its small provisions tugging at her emotions. *Abuela*, her Spanish grandmother, would've done such a thing. Carefully, she reached for the piece of chocolate, savoring the rare sweetness as she let it melt on her tongue. She lit one of her cigarettes, the smoke, sharp but familiar, grounding her.

This was where the real work started. As Eileen sat on that narrow bed in her modest room, she felt as if she'd journeyed through four long years to reach this point—to be needed, to help end a war that had already cost far too many lives. And now she would do her part.

Thinking she should get started as soon as possible, Eileen made her way downstairs to find Monsieur Breton, the trustworthy landlord.

32

THE FIRST MOMENT OF DANGER

Three weeks later - Paris, 26 March 1944

On one of the first, true, spring mornings in the capital, Eileen left her room in the north of Paris, her suitcase containing the wireless set clutched tightly in hand and set out toward the Gare de Porte de Champerret.

It had been nearly a month since she arrived in France, and still, no message had been sent to London. That would change today. With the help of Monsieur Breton and Louise, she'd finally managed to find a safe house from where she could transmit—belonging to the trustworthy Monsieur and Madame Dubois, in Bourg-la-Reine, in the southern suburbs. All she had to do was reach her destination without arousing suspicion.

Though she would have preferred to walk, that would have taken her all day. After buying her second-class train ticket, she carefully selected an almost-empty carriage, hoping to keep to herself. The plan had worked from Orléans to Paris, so perhaps luck would be with her again. It had crossed her mind to ask Louise to place the wireless set in another carriage or ask someone from WIZARD to transport it on her behalf.

"In these last stages of the war, wireless operators are worth their weight in gold. Never compromise yourself for your equipment. That can be replaced. You can't." She recalled her instructor's words from The Drokes. But she didn't want to burden someone else with carrying her set, and she was adamant about sending that critical first message as soon as possible—she couldn't risk being delayed any further. Better to keep an eye on it herself.

Settling into a corner seat, she kept the suitcase close and positioned herself so she could look out the window. With each breath, she practiced the poise she'd drilled into herself, willing her nerves to stay steady. But her pulse spiked the moment the carriage doors slid open again just as the train was about to depart. Three young German soldiers stepped inside, their heavy boots thudding against the floor as they sauntered down the aisle.

Eileen's stomach clenched as the soldiers took seats across from her. She quickly looked away, fixing her gaze out the window and pretending not to have noticed them, but her hand instinctively tightened around the handle of her suitcase.

They could have chosen any of the empty seats, yet they dropped into the row opposite her, settling in with the casual confidence of men who knew they commanded the space. Though her eyes were focused on the window, she felt their gaze on her, her mind in turmoil. Ignoring them entirely might be as dangerous as acknowledging them.

Reluctantly, she cast a quick glance at the one nearest her—a tall soldier with spiky blond hair barely concealed under his cap, a clean-shaven face, and a neatly pressed feldgrau uniform, his revolver tucked casually in his belt. He looked too young to be occupying someone else's country, yet his face was set with a hardened authority that suggested he'd been thrust into adulthood too soon.

Before she could look away again, he caught her eye and greeted her in broken French, flashing a friendly, if not overly confident, smile. "*Bonjour, mademoiselle. Il fait beau, n'est-ce pas?*"

Discussing the weather with a German was the last thing Eileen wanted. She managed a brief, polite smile and gave a quick nod before turning back to the window, praying he'd lose interest. But she was wrong. She felt him lean slightly toward her, his attention more fixed.

"*C'est quoi, ça*?" he asked, gesturing at her suitcase. *What is it?* Her heart jumped. She couldn't ignore him without raising suspicion, especially with his companions snickering beside him. Forcing herself to meet his gaze again, if only for a second, she answered carefully but with racing pulse.

"*Un gramophone.*" The lie came out without a hitch in what she hoped was a steady enough voice.

The soldier's eyes narrowed, skepticism flickering in his expression. Eileen's pulse now spiked, and she felt a blush spreading from the roots of her hair. *This is it,* she thought, *he doesn't believe me.* But he didn't ask to see her gramophone. Instead, he leaned back, studying her with amused curiosity, before reaching into his pocket above the gleaming revolver and pulling out a package of Sturm Zigaretten.

"*Fumer*?" he offered, holding a cigarette out to her between his fingers.

She stammered, "*Non, merci... je ne fume pas.*" Her words came out too coldly, perhaps even haughty. She wasn't that, but her bewilderment made her act unlike her real self.

As he let his gaze drop to her fingers stained with nicotine, the smile vanished and was replaced by an insulted scowl. Why did she reject his friendly offer? Too late, Eileen realized this had been a careless lie, one that undermined her Jacqueline du Tertre façade.

The shop girl was nice and pliant and didn't have an opinion on the occupiers.

Racking her brain to correct her mistake, she heard the other two soldiers chuckle, muttering jokes in German at the expense of the gallant blond one. Eileen didn't understand what they were saying but she picked up the word "Fräulein" so knew it was about her. The harshness of their laughter conveyed enough, and she knew she was in serious trouble now. They were all looking at her, and now she was the center of their attention. Just what she had tried to avoid from happening.

She stiffened, her eyes fixed on but seeing nothing of the passing scenery outside the window. Every fiber of her being screamed to flee with her suitcase in tow. Yet she couldn't. She was cornered. She forced herself to remain still, refusing to show how deeply shaken she was. Outside the train window, people went about their lives, free to move as they pleased. Oh, if she could only be like them!

The next station came into view and the train slowed. Eileen knew she couldn't bear the tension a moment longer. She got up, trying to offer the soldier a small, appeasing smile, but his glare cut through her. She lifted the heavy suitcase, struggling to make it appear lighter than it was, and moved toward the door, willing her legs that felt like stiff rubber to carry her down the corridor.

Her back prickled as though any moment she'd feel his hand on her shoulder. To arrest her. She barely dared to breathe until her feet finally hit the platform. The train lingered for a moment, long enough for her to feel the heat of their stares through the window, then it pulled away, taking the soldiers with it. Her knees felt weak, her heart pounding with relief. She vowed never to select an empty carriage again.

It was still a long way to Bourg-la-Reine, but she couldn't risk getting back on another train, not with this suitcase. Bracing herself, Eileen began to walk, muttering a constant prayer of gratitude now that she'd skirted so dangerously close to the edge without going over. No empty carriages, and no transportation of her set herself. This sort of run-in could not be repeated.

For now, she could only pray the house in Bourg-la-Reine was truly safe and that the next step of her mission would go as planned.

When Eileen finally reached the house in Bourg-la-Reine, it was late afternoon, and she would have to hurry to send her first 'sked' at 5 p.m., which would be 4 p.m. in London. Relief washed over her, though her legs still felt shaky and her hands trembled from the tension of the journey.

The Dubois' modest house stood behind a low, ivy-covered wall with a small garden just beginning to show signs of spring. Eileen noted the simplicity and secluded charm of the place—a quiet, unremarkable home on a sleepy street. Perfect!

The door opened before she could knock, revealing Monsieur Dubois, a kind-faced man with silver hair and wire-rimmed glasses. His chestnut-brown eyes crinkled warmly as he extended a hand in welcome.

"Mademoiselle Rose, you're here at last. Come in, come in. You look as though you've had quite a journey."

Beside him stood Madame Dubois, a petite woman with salt-and-pepper hair pinned in a neat roll at her neck, gentle eyes, and pearl earrings in her earlobes. Their friendly faces immediately softened Eileen's weariness. Monsieur took her suitcase, while Madame Dubois guided her inside, her voice warm and motherly.

"You look exhausted, *ma chère*. Let us fix you a proper tea. Even we French know the comfort a cup of tea brings in times like this."

They led her to a cozy sitting room, simply furnished with a worn sofa, a small table with a lace doily, and a glass-paneled cabinet filled with delicate, floral crockery. The faint aroma of rosewood soap and old wood filled the air, giving the house a homely, inviting feel.

With a sigh, Eileen sank onto the sofa, her tense muscles finally relaxing. The train ride and the long walk faded into the background as Monsieur Dubois set down a steaming cup of tea before her.

"Here, drink this. It'll settle your nerves."

"*Merci beaucoup*."

"And please, have a slice of cake," Madame Dubois insisted, placing a flowered plate before her with a generous slice of marble cake.

Eileen looked a bit embarrassed, knowing how severe the shortages were for Parisians. "Are you sure you won't have anything yourselves?"

"Oh no, my dear, we've already had our tea," Madame assured her with a warm smile.

Eileen took a grateful bite. "This is heaven," she said, savoring the moment of warmth and calm after the day's narrow escape.

She sipped her tea, glancing around the room, comforted by the small signs of normalcy in a world upturned. When she'd picked the last crumbs from her plate and drained the last drop of tea, Monsieur Dubois gestured toward a narrow corridor at the back of the house.

"Come, dear. I'll show you the room you'll be using. It's quiet and overlooks the garden, so you'll be undisturbed." Both he and Madame seemed aware of the work she was about to do, though it remained unspoken.

Eileen followed her hosts to a bedroom on the second floor. A small wooden desk stood against the wall under a window with a view of the garden, where daffodils and violets were just beginning to bloom. The room was otherwise sparse, with only a sturdy chair and a simple cot along one wall—perfect for resting between transmissions.

"Thank you," Eileen whispered, taking in the peacefulness of the space. It felt almost like a sanctuary, shielded from the dangers outside.

"There is another room at the front with some loose floorboards. Let me show you where you can leave some parts. And others in that cupboard," Madame added. Everything had been thought about beforehand.

Monsieur Dubois placed a key to the front door on the table. "You'll be safe here, Mademoiselle Rose, and can come and go as you please. My wife and I are staying with my son and his wife down the road, so you'll have the place to yourself. We'll stop by regularly, but for now, you have it all to yourself. We'll be leaving shortly, so please make sure you lock the front door carefully."

"I will," she replied, grateful but a bit self-conscious about taking over their home.

"You're not robbing us of anything, my dear," Madame assured her. "Sometimes we'll be here, sometimes not. Now, please settle in, and don't hesitate to ask if you need anything."

They bid her good evening, leaving Eileen alone with her thoughts and her wireless set.

Sitting on the cot in the quiet room, she let the events of the day drift through her mind. And with a deep breath, she unbuckled the case, ready to finally send her first message.

33

CONTACT WITH LONDON

The room was still as Eileen took a final moment to survey her surroundings. She peered out the window, scanning each detail: a narrow, secluded garden with a fence at the back. There'd be no chance of escape through the window, only through the front door if anything went wrong.

"Ah well, nothing's going to happen. I can hardly believe the German direction-finding vans would come to this part of Paris," she reassured herself, though a small voice in her head reminded her not to assume safety. Her aerial would show she was on the air, and she'd been told the Germans' detection systems could pinpoint a transmission to within a radius of two miles—maybe even closer these days. Speed was key, just as they'd drilled into her at training. And fast she would be.

Focused on the task, she moved with practiced care, uncoiling the aerial wire and discreetly hanging it outside the window, as high as the room allowed. It felt surreal, and she checked it again, her mind ticking off every step, second-guessing herself. Would the set work? Would she be able to get through to Thame Park, or would interference ruin her first attempt?

We'll have none of that, Rose, she reprimanded herself. *It will work.*

She placed the Type A Mk.III wireless set on the small wooden desk, inserted the crystal, and carefully tuned to the right frequency. Her Welrod gun lay nearby, and for a brief moment, her gaze lingered on the ruby ring on her finger, with the L-pill nestled within.

This was the moment when all the lines in her life converged—she was about to make the final step into her SOE secret agent life, shedding the shadow of 'ditzy Didi,' to fully become *La Rose*, occupation: resistance fighter. The thought almost caught her breath, but her nimble fingers twisted the dial, a wave of nervous anticipation washing over her—followed by immense relief as a clear, familiar signal came through. *See? It worked.*

The static faded, and she knew she'd connected. She'd coded her message that morning, entered her security and bluff codes—*Petticoat is pleased*—and then typed out her coded message: "Alcide and I arrived safely. Met Louise, my contact. Ready to start."

The clicks of the Morse code filled the room, each dot and dash carrying her message across the airwaves. Until now, she'd always been surrounded by the cacophony of other operators, so it felt surreal to hear herself alone in the stillness. She finished the message, her hands trembling as she swiftly dismantled the equipment and stored it away, just as Madame Dubois had instructed. Every movement felt heightened, her nerves tingling, attuned to every sound and shadow around her.

Once the set was safely tucked away, Eileen allowed herself a quiet smile. She'd done it. She'd sent her first message to London, marking her place in this dangerous, unseen network. Pride surged through her, almost giddy. Standing in the middle of her transmission room, she let the thrill of accomplishment wash over her—she was here, in the heart of it, where she belonged.

Now hope for the best! On her way back to Porte de Champerret, Eileen would stop by Louise's place to listen for—hopefully—the BBC broadcast's confirmation of her message.

As Eileen let herself out of the Dubois' house in Bourg-la-Reine, a familiar, insidious dread settled over her. *Germans.* Her heart didn't pound wildly anymore, nor did her hands tremble—she was prepared now. Almost with a deadly calm. With her first transmission completed and the knowledge that what she'd done was punishable by death, she was acutely aware of her surroundings. Every shadow seemed darker, every footstep behind her louder.

Walking cautiously, Eileen kept her gaze sweeping along the narrow street. She checked her reflection in shop windows, using them as mirrors to ensure she wasn't being followed, while taking care to avoid looking over her shoulder. After passing by Louise's house once, just to make sure she hadn't picked up a tail, she finally approached the door and rang the bell with a quick, discreet movement, slipping inside when the door opened a crack.

Inside, Madame welcomed her with a quiet, motherly smile. "Come in, *ma chère Rose*. You must be hungry."

The meal was simple but welcome: mashed potatoes, cabbage, and a small slice of liver, rationed out with a care that spoke volumes about the scarcity of food. Eileen ate with gratitude, feeling both the warmth of the food and the care of the family around her.

Once they'd finished, Madame drew the blackout curtains tightly around the windows, while Louise discreetly unlocked a cabinet in the backroom. The hidden radio sat neatly inside, waiting.

Eileen felt a thrill of anticipation as she sat down beside Louise, her eyes on the radio, her nerves taut. They adjusted the dial, catching a faint, crackling static.

And then, finally, the familiar cadence of the BBC broadcaster's voice announced the news in French, followed by the coded messages for agents in the field.

"*Le Père Guillaume fête son anniversaire.*" Père Guillaume is celebrating his birthday.

Louise's mother gave Eileen a quick, supportive smile, her knitting needles clicking softly in the background.

"*La grenouille saute deux fois.*" The frog leaps twice.

Eileen's eyes stayed glued to the radio as they continued listening.

"*Tante Betty accueille sa nouvelle nièce.*" Aunt Betty welcomes her new niece.

Finally, the voice came over the airwaves with the message Eileen had been waiting for. "*Heureux de savoir que le canard a fait un bon voyage.*" Happy to know that the duck has had a good trip.

"That's me," she couldn't help uttering. "My message made it through."

"Well done, Rose." Louise sounded equally relieved. "And this message arrived for you today." She handed her a folded note. Eileen's experienced decoder eye easily understood the message.

"I'm to meet Alcide tomorrow. In *Le Jardin des Tuileries*. What can that be about?" For her security she never directly met up with her organiser. They communicated only through couriers like Louise.

"It must be important, Rose, or he wouldn't summon you. It's a risk for both of you." Louise's face grew serious. "Let me know if there's anything I can do after you've met."

Eileen read the note again. Seeing if she'd missed anything. But she hadn't. It was Alcide, the Jardin des Tuileries, 1 p.m. A place of quiet paths and open spaces—good for avoiding eavesdroppers during lunchtime, but still this meeting was not without danger. What could be pressing enough for Alcide to meet her in person?

Something urgent, perhaps even perilous, if he was willing to take such a chance.

"*Merci*, Louise. I'll be careful."

Memorising the contents of the message before destroying the note, Eileen took her leave, imagining all sorts of scenarios but also looking forward to seeing Alcide, whom she liked a lot.

34

WITHOUT AN ORGANISER

Eileen spotted Alcide waiting under the arching plane trees of the Tuileries Garden, his good hand tucked deep in the pocket of his dark overcoat. He nodded when he saw her, but his usual warm smile was missing, replaced by a somber, distracted expression that immediately worried her. Something was wrong. She joined him without speaking, furtively glancing around to make sure no one was watching them.

"Good of you to come, Rose," he greeted her in a flat voice.

"Of course. And it's always nice to see you." She tried to cheer him up, but it didn't work. They began walking side by side along the gravel path, keeping their pace casual, careful not to draw attention. As it was a warm spring day, the park was busy with Germans parading around with French girls on their arms. Eileen still couldn't get used to the sight but averted her eyes, keeping her attention on Alcide.

"Is something wrong?" she whispered, stealing a glance at his face. His brow was furrowed, and his gaze distant, as if his mind were already a hundred miles away.

He took a breath, as though gathering his thoughts. "I need to leave for London, Rose. Urgently. I've come across some critical information—plans of a new German weapon. It's a type of rocket they're developing to destroy British cities." He paused, letting that sink in.

"But...but I can code that and send it to London. No need for you to..."

"You don't understand. It's... devastating, Rose. I can't entrust the details to anyone but Buck himself."

The words struck Eileen like a shock of cold air. "You're leaving? But... what about me? ...the network? ...the messages?"

Alcide nodded sadly. "I know it complicates things, but the situation demands it. London needs to be informed immediately, and I can't predict when I'll be back." He stopped and looked at her with a serious intensity. "Listen to me, Rose. Until I return, I want you to be careful. Extremely careful."

Her chest tightened. "Alcide, you're worrying me. What's going on?"

His face softened a fraction, but she could see the weight behind his eyes. "A close friend of mine was taken by the Germans, and a string of operators have been arrested in and around Paris recently. Skilled ones. Brave ones. Women, like you." His voice threatened to break, but he regained control. "They're being captured at an alarming rate, and I can't shake the feeling the Germans have found a new way of tracking signals. And infiltrating our networks."

Eileen felt the blood drain from her face. She could tell the news was affecting him deeply, and she placed a comforting hand on his arm. "Alcide, I understand. But you don't need to worry about me. I'll be cautious. Night and day."

"Good." He nodded, but didn't seem convinced. "There's another thing. Just now I'm leaving, the Firm is sending another W/T operator to join WIZARD. It's unfortunate but I need to rely on you to help him while I'm gone. His name is Arnaud. Louise will arrange your connection with him, and I'd like you to make the best of it. Use each other for backup and coordinate carefully. There's no harm in having you both here, as I'm sure our work will only increase." He gazed around to make sure no unwanted ears listened in. "The Allied invasion is imminent."

Eileen's mind worked hard to absorb all the new details. "I appreciate the help of another operator, truly. But I've only just started myself and what am I supposed to do if you're not here? I came to France to work, not to sit around and twiddle my thumbs. Without your messages I have no work."

Alcide gave her a sympathetic look. "I understand, Rose. And believe me, I'd rather keep you fully occupied. I'll do my best to convince London to connect you temporarily with another network until I return. But," he added on that sad serious tone, "if I'm honest, this situation might be a blessing in disguise. With less work for you, you'll stay out of harm's way. Go to public places, keep your eyes and ears open, stay informed. There are other ways to contribute and build a network."

Eileen shook her head. "I wasn't trained as a courier, Alcide, but I promise I'll do my best and just hope you're back in a week or so."

He paused, searching her face. "I can't promise anything but just make sure that if you start transmitting again, change your location as often as possible, avoid patterns, keep your head down. No shortcuts."

They reached a cluster of flowerbeds, both of them falling silent as they pretended to examine the blooms, just two Parisians out for a stroll. After a long pause, Alcide spoke again, his voice no more than a whisper.

"You need to send a message today to arrange a date and place to have me picked up. Tell them it's urgent. Can you do that for me,

Rose? Let Louise know the details when you hear back. *Au revoir and bonne chance*!"

With one last glance, he took his leave, blending into the crowd as they parted ways.

"Goodbye, Alcide." Eileen said it to the budding blooms. Her shoulders sagging. With her sharp intuition she knew she would not see Alcide again. At least not until the war was over. Perhaps if they both survived. But she felt it was over with him as Organiser and she his W/T Operator. It had been a short but sweet connection.

Three days later

In an inconspicuous café near her safehouse in Bourg-la-Reine, Eileen arrived early, scanning the tables as she waited for her new, fellow W/T operator. She chose a seat in the corner with a clear view of the entrance. Across the room, a waitress with platinum-blonde hair and overly-red lips was laughing at the bar with a German officer.

"Un café, s'il vous plaît," Eileen ordered when the waitress finally sauntered over, her large dewy eyes lingering a moment too long on Eileen. Then, with a dismissive "coming," the waitress glided back toward the officer, giving him an exaggerated wink.

Eileen lit a Gauloise and inhaled deeply, savoring the temporary calm it offered. Smoking filled her stomach, however slightly, and helped soothe her nerves. Maman had always hated her smoking, but Eileen couldn't imagine getting through days like these without it. Through the smoke, she kept her expression neutral, forcing calm even as her gaze stayed fixed on the entrance.

Just as her coffee arrived and she wondered if they'd missed each other again, a tall man entered. Broad-shouldered, with a mop of dark hair, and sharp, intelligent eyes that swept the room before he gave a barely perceptible nod in her direction. He walked over to her table, sliding into the seat across from her. His clean-cut appearance contrasted with a scruffy coat, which added to his unassuming air.

"Rose," he said softly, covering her hand with his in a gesture that, to anyone watching, would seem affectionate. "Don't worry," he whispered, his voice calm and warm. His back was turned to the German and the giggling waitress, shielding them from view.

Eileen's eyes met his, and she nodded subtly, signaling she understood. Playing along, she leaned in and kissed his cheek, feeling a slight blush rise to her cheeks—she wasn't used to kissing men, much less in public.

"Arnaud. You've arrived," she said with a subtle smile, both relieved to meet another operator and tense with the awareness that meeting together was doubly dangerous.

They sat quietly for a moment, sizing each other up, before Eileen leaned in, her voice soft and intimate, as if speaking to a lover. "Alcide told me you're here to help me out. I've got a place nearby where I can work, but with Alcide gone, it's mostly just the routine checking for messages from the Firm."

The waitress interrupted, and Arnaud released her hand, leaning back as he ordered coffee and breakfast. Once she was gone, he leaned forward again and whispered, "Good to know. I'm looking for a place to transmit from myself, though I know it won't be easy around here. I saw so many Germans patrolling this *département Haut-de-Seine*. Don't you think this area's grown a little... unsettling?"

Eileen nodded, her lips pressed into a thin line. "I've noticed it too. The streets feel different, even from a month ago. But I'd hate to give up what I have—transmissions are super clear from here." She glanced around, then added, "I can help you look. I have little to do right now, and we could start scouting other areas, just in case."

Arnaud met her gaze with a hint of caution. "I'm not sure it's wise to be seen together too much. If anything happens to one of us, it puts the other at risk."

Eileen's face fell, though she saw his point. Solitude had been a constant struggle in the five weeks she'd been in France, and with so little to do lately, the isolation was more acute.

"Good point," she replied, her smile fading. She could see that the mission was still new and exciting for Arnaud. For her, though, it had quickly become a routine filled with little excitement and no friends to lean on—especially with Alcide gone.

He wolfed down his breakfast and finished his coffee in a single gulp. "Got to dash. So, Louise is our contact?"

Eileen nodded, leaving a few francs on the table for the waitress, with just enough tip money to ensure she could return without drawing attention.

Outside, the two operators exchanged a quick farewell, and she watched Arnaud's tall back disappear into the busy shopping street before directing her steps toward the Dubois house. Perhaps today, at last, she'd be lucky enough to receive a new assignment.

35

THE PLAYBOY ORGANISER

Three weeks later, April 1944

Eileen tugged her beige trench coat tightly around her as she waited on the sidewalk of the Boulevard Haussmann, one of Paris' grand boulevards, which was not her natural habitat these days. The road was filled with Black Mercedes sporting black and red swastika flags upfront, black-clad, high-ranking German officers behind black-out windows. The overall mood was black. Wherever she looked.

Despite the sunny late April morning, Eileen felt as if someone had draped a black veil over central Paris. The few French passing by held their heads down and hands shoved into pockets. They looked haggard, hollow-eyed with their clothes faded and thread-bare, shoes unpolished and with holes.

Still, Eileen had been summoned here, so she scanned the tree-lined boulevard for any signs of what might be her new boss. She checked her watch. Just past nine. Louise had arranged the meeting for exactly nine-thirty, yet Eileen had arrived early due to her uncertainty as to what to expect.

The name Armand had floated through the resistance ranks like an almost mythical figure, a 'former playboy' who now ran operations with an energy as infamous as his past adventures. She'd imagined someone polished and reserved, but she sensed the truth was more complicated.

A sudden roar of an engine broke her thoughts as a sleek, charcoal-gray car whipped around the corner and came to a smooth halt just in front of her. The car gleamed in the sunlit morning, looking more suited to the winding roads of the French Riviera than the occupied streets of Paris.

The door flung open, and a man with an easy, rakish grin leaned out. A crest of dark-blond hair, with a small scar on his chin and a sharply tailored coat in new herringbone fabric, he was both rugged and refined. His blue eyes held a mischievous glint that instantly threw her off balance.

"*Ma Rose*, I assume? Golly, my assistants are becoming younger and prettier by the day," he quipped, his accent a smooth blend of Parisian and something distinctly his own. Before she could respond, he was out of the car and extending his hand, practically sweeping her off her feet with his energy. "*Je suis Armand, a votre service*!" he introduced himself with a wide smile and a small bow, pumping her hand in an iron grip. "But you knew that already?"

"Yes, yes... Armand, I was waiting for you." Eileen managed a smile, feeling her cheeks warm a bit, afraid they'd attract far too much attention from the Germans. This certainly wasn't the typical hush-hush meeting in a dimly lit café she'd grown used to in the resistance.

"Perfect. Climb in." Armand seemed unperturbed by the Germans passing by to admire and comment on his Renault 104 E. With a sweep of his long arm he gestured to the passenger seat. "I'll give you a lift to our rendezvous spot. We've got a few people I think you'll want to meet."

She barely had time to respond before he held the door open for her with a flourish, as if she were stepping into a chauffeur-driven car rather than what should be an inconspicuous ride through occupied-Paris. The door shut with a satisfying thud, and the car practically leapt to life as Armand took the wheel, navigating the streets with the kind of ease only someone who loved speed could possess.

As they left the city center for the suburbs, Eileen found herself instinctively clutching her handbag, where her documents lay tucked beside her Welrod pistol. A small voice in the back of her mind warned her of the dangers of such flamboyance—especially now, with the Germans tightening their grip in every *arrondisement*. She shot the SPIRITUALIST organiser a sidelong glance, studying his calm, almost amused expression as he swerved around a slow-moving truck with casual ease.

"Are we meeting other agents today?" she asked, trying to gauge how much this rendezvous might expose her, even as she was swept up in the pace of his energy.

"Yes, *ma chère*, three others," he replied without taking his eyes off the road. "One is Blaise—another W/T operator who's just arrived. We're expanding, you see. Getting you and Arnaud up and running was only the first step." His smile was wry, edged with something unreadable. "You know how it goes, *ma petite*—an ambitious man needs ambitious hands."

Eileen wasn't sure if his statement was meant as praise or an invitation to trust him fully. She forced herself to relax, though a hint of apprehension lingered. His easy confidence felt foreign in the strictness of resistance operations, yet he had that effect she'd heard about, putting people at ease with his charm, despite the risk. She sensed, however, that under his playboy grin and sharp gaze was a mind tuned to the quicksilver changes of their situation.

"You seem quite at ease, even in... challenging times," Eileen ventured, choosing her words carefully.

"Oh, I am, Rose." Armand's tone softened, if only briefly, as he navigated around a group of German officers in dark uniforms. "Paris may be bruised, but she's still my city—and you are about to discover why we'll fight for her until the very end."

As they pulled up to their meeting spot, Eileen decided to trust him. For the time being at least. Whatever Armand's past, he seemed determined to press forward with their mission, certainly at high speed through the shadowed streets of Paris.

"Enter my domain." Armand held open the backdoor to what looked like a warehouse but turned out to be a secluded corner of one of his garages, reeking of gasoline and rubber tyres and filled with an array of cars and trucks.

A rough wooden crate in the middle of the room served as a table and around it stood a set of mismatched chairs. Eileen immediately spotted Louise and went over to kiss her cheeks. She was also glad to see Arnaud was present. The third man, whom Armand had said was also an operator codenamed Blaise, was a smooth-looking man with olive skin and pronounced dark eyebrows over a serious glare. He shook hands with Eileen without a word.

"Sit, Rose!" Armand ordered, pointing to a rickety looking wooden chair with a wicker seat. It wobbled slightly as Eileen sat down. Armand retrieved a flask from his coat pocket and collected some dented enamel tankards from a shelf.

"Ladies and gents, now we're all here, let's drink to SPIRITUALIST, which is the name of our new network. I thought some real spirits might do us good, to kick off the job." He poured generous portions into the tankards and handed them around. Here's to us!" He put the flask to his mouth and drained the contents. Eileen took a tiny sip from the unclean tankard and felt the cognac burn in her throat.

"Now," Armand continued, leaning against the garage wall and observing his team with a blend of seriousness and humor. "The Firm has tasked me... us...with rebuilding two of the collapsed networks in this region. Most of our comrades were arrested by the Gestapo. I'm talking of PROSPER here in the Paris region and FARMER near Lille."

He paused, a sad and serious shadow darkening his features. He cleared his throat, "I knew some of them, for God's sake! Well, the job won't be easy with the Nazis breathing down our necks, even I'll admit that much. But if we put our weight behind this, we can resurrect enough of the once-glorious networks before the Allied invasion—which, if the whispers are to be believed, is coming soon."

Eileen felt a rush of excitement and trepidation. Could it be true? Though a far cry from the serious, steady professionalism of Alcide, this flamboyant organiser seemed to have access to equally vital intelligence. She held her breath, realizing just how serious—and close—the stakes had become.

"London always believes agents in the field are miracle workers," Armand said, folding his arms across his chest. "And who am I to disagree? With three W/T operators on my team, I'll divide the tasks as best I can. Louise, I'm entrusting you with managing the couriers. As for myself, I'll be heading to Lille and the surrounding district over the next few weeks, and I'll take Blaise with me. Rose and Arnaud, you stay in Paris, but I urge you to keep moving your sets to various locations. I know it's cumbersome, and I know interference can be a headache in some parts of the city. But for your safety, deal with these nuisances and keep yourselves secure."

His face took on a somber, almost melancholic look, and it struck Eileen that this man truly cared about his team—certainly as much as Alcide had.

She shared a glance with Arnaud, noting that he seemed to be on the same wavelength, both recognizing the importance of Armand's warning. She would start searching for new transmission locations immediately, despite the reliable Dubois household and its clear transmissions.

Armand continued, his voice softening. "On a personal note, I have another mission: finding an old friend of mine, a man code-named Felix. Some of you may have heard the name. He's gone off the map, and I'm determined to locate him. So, if you ever ask London for updates, see if there's any mention of Felix. If you hear anything, make sure it reaches me."

Louise nodded, and Arnaud leaned forward. "I've heard the name. Whatever we can do, we'll do it."

"Thank you, Arnaud." With a quick nod, Armand's demeanor shifted back to his usual upbeat tone. "That's all for today. We'll leave separately. Rose, Louise, you two can travel by metro together. Good luck, agents!" And with a brisk turn, Armand disappeared through a door at the back of the garage.

As they left, Eileen turned to Louise, letting out a small laugh. "Well, our new organiser certainly brings a bit of flair to the job, doesn't he?"

Louise grinned. "He's a character, that's for sure. Hard to imagine him in a resistance network—seems more like he should be skiing down the slopes of St. Moritz or drinking champagne with the likes of Coco Chanel."

Eileen chuckled, feeling a bit of the tension ease. "But he's clever. And I think he actually cares about what happens to us."

Louise agreed. "True. Just make sure you keep that set moving, Rose. The last thing Armand wants is to lose a talented operator to a German tracking van."

A spark of determination showed in Eileen's eyes. "He won't lose me that easily."

Back in the center of Paris, the two 'femmes de la Resistance' parted ways amiably, their spirits lifted by the odd charm of their new organiser and the promise of their next mission.

36

THE FINAL COUNTDOWN

Six weeks later - Paris, 6 June 1944

A week of oppressive heat had finally broken into a thunderstorm, drenching Paris as tension simmered across the city. News had spread quickly of Allied forces landing along the Normandy coasts, and on this 6th day of June, the city felt like a coiled spring, ready to snap.

Eileen, however, had no time for speculations or weather reports. Her days were filled with frantic messaging, sending and receiving a flurry of messages from London, each transmission carrying vital updates on German troop movements, sabotage efforts, drop zones, and supply routes.

By now, Eileen had already sent more than seventy messages since her arrival three months earlier, working at a speed that even surprised herself. Her hand danced on the key with practiced ease, tapping out in Morse the lifeline of intelligence that had supported the long-awaited invasion. But the war was far from won.

Even as she worked tirelessly, a small part of her knew she was pressing her luck by still operating from Bourg-la-Reine, despite her organizer Armand's express instructions to keep changing locations.

In a rare break, she slipped into the small café near her safe house, where she'd first met Arnaud. The blonde waitress was still there, though her demeanor had cooled toward her German customers—something Eileen took as a sign that even Parisians were feeling the winds of change. It meant, however, that she felt slightly less stressed sitting there in plain daylight, a secret agent amidst the shifting loyalties of the city, meeting another in her line of work.

She spotted Arnaud at their usual corner table, already nursing a cup of coffee and tapping his fingers with restless energy. Leaning in as if they were lovers, she greeted him with a quick peck on the cheek and slipped into the seat opposite.

"Ah, Rose," he began with a smirk, "you look like you're carrying the weight of the world. That bad?"

"Feels like it." She managed a faint smile. "I don't know how many more transmissions I can fit into a day without my fingers going numb."

Arnaud raised an eyebrow. "Still at the Dubois' house?"

Eileen hesitated. "I am, yes. The interference there is minimal, and I can keep up with London's skeds without any issues. They expect updates almost constantly now." She didn't mention she'd been too busy—or too stubborn—to search for a new location.

Arnaud leaned forward, lowering his voice. "Rose, I've found a place in *Le Vésinet*, a west Paris suburb. A bit of interference, but the house is out of the way, and the landlady is sympathetic. You could transmit from there with a lot less risk."

She considered his suggestion, her gaze drifting to the café window. "It sounds good. I know I need to move. Soon."

"*Le Vésinet* isn't perfect, but it's safer than where you are now, and it's about the same distance from *Place de Champerret*." Arnaud glanced around to ensure no one was listening, though the café patrons seemed wrapped in their own conversations. "You know Armand's orders, Rose—rotate locations, don't stay put too long. It's only a matter of time before the detection vans trace your signal if you keep transmitting from the same place. They might already have."

A shiver ran through Eileen. She knew he was right, but part of her still felt invincible, fueled by the adrenaline and urgency of her work. "I'll consider it," she replied, meeting his gaze. "But right now, I'm swamped. And let's be honest, the Germans won't catch me. I'm careful enough and never stay on the air longer than ten minutes."

Arnaud nodded slowly, but his concern didn't fade. "Just remember—you're worth more than any equipment or message. I don't want to lose a friend because of overconfidence."

Eileen smiled at the mention of friendship, feeling a warmth she rarely allowed herself. "Thank you, Arnaud. I promise I'll consider the move to *Le Vésinet*. Just... not today."

After a pause, Arnaud leaned in closer, his tone shifting. "Speaking of London... Have you heard anything about that friend of Armand's, what was his name again?"

"Felix?" Eileen filled in, "though he apparently also used the name Elie."

"So, you got an answer?"

Eileen's face grew serious as she reached into her handbag, pulling out a small, coded note from her last message. "I do. London confirmed Felix, or Elie, was arrested in Paris in November last year. Apparently, a double agent betrayed him, someone from within our own lines. London has no updates on his whereabouts since."

Arnaud's brow furrowed as he listened. "So, he's been missing all this time? It's hard to imagine—he's the one who brought Armand into the resistance. I'm sure our organiser is just holding onto hope."

Eileen nodded. "I sent word to Armand, just as he asked. But he didn't take it well, understandably. He's out there looking for answers, trying to find out where they have taken his friend, but we both know how dangerous it is to chase after someone when the Gestapo is involved. London says they suspect someone who uses the name *Le Boiteau*, was responsible for the betrayal. He probably also works for the Germans, so we'd better look out ourselves."

Arnaud's expression darkened. "It's terrifying, isn't it? Knowing that we're not just fighting the Germans, but also have to watch out for our own. Someone who would sell out their fellow agents—how could they live with themselves?"

Eileen looked down, gripping her coffee cup. "It's beyond me. It's hard enough keeping up our own spirits, carrying on, and pretending to be ordinary people every day. But to intentionally turn someone over to the Gestapo? It feels like the worst betrayal."

"It makes you wonder who you can really trust," Arnaud agreed.

Eileen met his gaze. "You can trust me."

He squeezed her hand, then gave her a faint smile. "I know. So, that's why I keep telling you to move. You're braver than any woman I've ever met. But stay smart too, alright? Courage and caution—that's what will keep us alive in this business."

"Agreed. And you, too, Arnaud. With this kind of knowledge, we all need to watch each other's backs."

37

ONE FAUX PAS

Six weeks later - Paris, Bourg-la-Reine, 22 July 1944

Eileen adjusted the belt around her summer dress as she stepped out of her room near Place de Champerret, savoring the warmth of July settling over the city. She felt good. The Allies were advancing through Normandy, and the German resistance had already been broken in Caen. Armand had said it was only a matter of weeks before they'd reach the French capital, and then, surely, the Nazis would surrender.

She was proud of her role in it all, even if it meant her glorious work would soon come to an end. And then what? Back to England for some dull office job? She lived on the pulse of these messages across the Channel, fueled by the praise she could sense in London's acknowledgments. Today would be message 105, and she'd have to hurry, given Armand's insistence to send it *tout de suite* with his usual gusto.

Still, she couldn't help savoring the day—the thrill of it all, the scent of summer air, the looming victory she could almost taste. She missed her family, especially Jacqueline, but since learning her sister was safely back in England after fifteen nonstop months in France, she felt lighter, as if Jacqui were watching over her from the other side of the Channel.

Even the Welrod in her handbag and the coded message ready for London felt like delicious secrets tucked away from the Germans she despised more each day.

"I might as well pop by Louise on the way back," she murmured to herself. "It's been almost a week since I visited *Place Saint-Michel*, and it's always so nice to catch up with her."

With a spring in her step, Eileen headed toward Porte de Champerret Station to catch the train to Bourg-la-Reine. The warmth of the sun and her own buoyant mood softened Paris's bleakness, casting a gentler light over the streets and adding a hint of vibrancy to her world. Glancing at her reflection, with her hair swept back neatly and her handbag over her shoulder, she felt almost comforted, lulled by the deceptive ease of the moment.

But any sense of peace vanished as soon as she boarded the train. She found herself hemmed in by rowdy German soldiers eager to harass young women like her. Her bright mood sank like a stone.

Before she'd even settled into her seat, they surrounded her, demanding to see her papers, asking impertinent questions, and snickering among themselves, their behavior humiliating and demeaning. No one stepped forward to intervene.

"Calm down, Jacqueline du Tertre," she reminded herself, summoning her alias for strength. "You've put up with this for almost five months; you can bear it a little longer. They don't know what you know—that victory is near." She ached to snap back or simply ignore them, but neither option was hers.

As the train emptied out in the quieter suburbs, she finally relaxed. But then came the nagging doubts. She'd told herself countless times she'd move her set to Arnaud's place in Le Vésinet, yet somehow, she'd postponed it again and again. Armand had urged her to relocate several times. So had Louise. Even Blaise, who rarely ventured an opinion, had voiced his concern. "Go to *Le Vésinet* with Arnaud, Rose," he'd told her the last time they met. "You've stayed in *Bourg-la-Reine* too long already. The Germans must be closing in on you."

"Oh no, they're not. I haven't seen a detection van near the place. Ever." She'd waved off his worries, feeling a certainty that everything was under control. But now, in the quiet moments of the journey, her own doubts echoed back at her. Why did she cling so stubbornly to the safety of that familiar house? The Dubois family, the clear signal—everything about Bourg-la-Reine felt safe. Nothing had ever seemed out of place. Her transmissions blended into the city's haze, folding into the static of occupied Paris.

So?

She knew there was stubbornness in her decision, maybe even a hint of pride. It was that flicker of resistance, that reassurance in the familiar. Or was it more than that—a belief that she would notice any threat, any danger? Surely, she'd see it coming. She knew every sight, every corner, every nuance of the street like the back of her hand. Every checkpoint, every minor change had become part of her routine.

And she was most effective here for the Firm. Every message she'd sent had come through, thanks to her choice of such a reliable, secure place to transmit. Since the invasion, her coded messages had informed London of German troop movements, rail disruptions, and resistance contacts. She'd heard London's appreciation in their coded acknowledgments. Her work here was invaluable.

So, she pushed aside the doubt that seeped in each time she neared her 'office.' But the arguments tugged back and forth in her mind. What would Armand say if he found out she'd ignored his orders again?

She could almost hear his voice: *You're putting yourself in unnecessary danger, Rose. You are worth more than any equipment or place. And you're worth much more sending messages than being arrested.*

Eileen shivered. What in God's name held her back? It would be so easy to pick up her set, take it to Le Vésinet, and be done with it. Just one day of moving, of letting go of the Dubois house, of trusting the unknown.

And yet, in her tangled logic, moving felt like a risk all of its own. In a new place, she'd have to re-map every step, every shadow. Here, she knew every creak and corner. She could focus entirely on her work, not on getting comfortable in unfamiliar surroundings.

Nothing will happen today, she reassured herself. *I've been careful. I've kept my skeds short and sharp, just as they trained me.*

But deep down, her intuition warned her that this insistence on staying today would haunt her.

Okay. It's settled, then. This one message, and no more stalling. I'll dismantle everything, pick up the suitcase, and go! And then I'll go see Louise, just to see the relief on her sweet face when she hears Rose has finally seen sense, she told herself, suddenly feeling much lighter.

As she reached Bourg-la-Reine and approached the Dubois house, the comforting ivy-covered walls and the small garden greeted her, giving her that fleeting, all-too-familiar sense of security.

"No, no, no!" she murmured, steeling herself. "This is the moment of no return. You say goodbye to this place and leave today. Hopefully, it will be 'au revoir' when Paris is ours again."

And she stepped inside, feeling as safe as a hunted wolf in its own lair.

38

IMPASSE

One hour later

Eileen leaned back in her chair, releasing a quiet sigh of relief as she tapped out the final characters of her message: *Disruption Evreux rail line successful; Scheduled supply drop Falaise confirmed.* Satisfaction surged through her as her transmission cleared. London was now in possession of the knowledge it needed, so this day had been worth the risk.

Just as she removed her headset, ready to dismantle the set, a murmur of voices reached her through the open window at the front of the house. Then footsteps, followed by more talking. Her hand froze mid-air.

No, they won't come here, she calmed herself. *It's just some people passing by, that's all.* But a cold knot began to form in her stomach. The footsteps didn't fade; instead, they grew louder, echoing on the pavement, accompanied by the scrape of boots and low voices, speaking...French? German?

As quickly as she could she raced to the window in the front room, stealthily hiding herself behind the gauze curtains. Her eyes scanned the street below and she gasped. A pair of plainclothes men stood on the pavement, their gaze fixed on the Dubois' house. Then, two more appeared from around the corner, moving with unsettling precision toward the walkway leading to the front door.

Eileen's blood ran cold. Her mind seized up for a beat, her body frozen, but then, a fierce calm washed over her. *It was the Gestapo. No question about it.* This was the moment she'd dreaded for the past five months, but somehow, she was ready for it. If she couldn't escape, she could at least hide the set, play along, and pray they wouldn't find anything.

Innocent Jacqueline du Tertre with her wide blue eyes and clumsy manners. What did a former shopgirl from Nice know about the resistance? *Rien du tout*! Nothing! She cast the men another quick look before jolting into action. Maybe—just maybe—they would pass by.

She dashed to the backroom, ripping down the aerial from the window, folding it with shaking hands, and tucking it under the floorboards. She took the wireless set apart with swift, practiced movements, hiding the components in various corners of the cupboard. If they entered and didn't look too closely, it would be concealed well enough to buy her precious time.

Her codes. The message draft. She sprinted down the stairs, heart hammering in her chest, and shoved the papers into the Dubois' unlit stove. Her trembling hands flicked a match, striking it against the grate once, twice. The third time, it sparked, the edge of the paper catching fire and curling as smoke rose.

Hurry, hurry, she prayed, her eyes locked on the growing flames. If any part of her work remained, it would expose the entire network, putting countless lives in danger. She stirred the burning papers with a poker, praying the embers would swallow every trace, every letter, every name. As she ground the ashes into dust, she could already hear the footsteps ascending the front steps.

Then came the sharp, insistent knock, each blow against the wood hammering home the reality that there was no escape.

Eileen wiped her sweaty palms against her summer dress, her breath coming in short, shallow gasps. *Stay calm, stay in character.* She drew Jacqueline du Tertre's persona around herself like a protective veil, gripping onto every eccentric mannerism that would distance her from the truth. *Jacqueline is your shield.* She forced herself to open the door, only to be met with the cold glint of a gun pointed directly at her.

She staggered back, her heart leaping to her throat, but she clung to her role, lifting her hands as if to push the gun away. "*Monsieur, qu'est-ce que c'est*?" she gasped in shrill indignation, her voice pitching higher in faux shock. "What on earth do you mean by this?"

Only one plainclothes man entered at first, his face shadowed under his cap as he barked something harsh in German. Eileen didn't understand the words, but it was clear he meant business. He shoved her aside, barging past her into the house with an air of brutal authority.

With her nerves wound tight and adrenaline fueling her, Eileen seized her chance to erupt. She followed close behind, waving her hands in a frenzy, her voice rising to a fever pitch. "You have no right to barge into my home like this! *C'est scandaleux*! How dare you stomp into a respectable house without so much as a *Bonjour*! Do you think you're the law around here, pointing that filthy gun at a helpless woman? I demand you leave at once!"

Her shrieking caught the German's attention, and he stopped, turning back to look at her with furrowed brows as if assessing her sanity. She raised her voice even louder, bordering on hysterical. "Who do you think you are, huh? What do you want from me—a poor, innocent woman just minding her own business? You think you can just come in here, throwing your weight around like some —some buffoon!"

His face twisted in confusion as he took in her loud, erratic behavior, seemingly caught off guard by her reaction. She met his gaze with a wild-eyed, accusatory stare, letting her expression slip further from composure, all the while gauging his response.

As she noted his hesitation, Eileen stared hard at him, calming down slightly but still muttering to herself, "idiots with guns" and "disgraceful treatment." Her future, her survival, depended on him seeing her as nothing more than a harebrained, naive young woman, too silly to be a threat.

They stood there, locked in a tense moment of mutual appraisal, until finally, in an icy, clipped tone, he said in French, "You don't fool me, *Mademoiselle*. We know you've been sending messages from this house on an illegal wireless set. You have been working against us, and that is a crime. I'll find the set if I have to turn this house upside down, so temper your tone and let me get on with it."

Feigning acute surprise, Eileen let out a small, scornful laugh. "What are you babbling about? An illegal wireless set? I don't even know what that is! Aren't wireless sets just things people listen to? You can't send messages with a wireless set. That's unheard of." Then, shrugging, she added with a sneer, "Pah, your boss must be mad to give you such silly orders! But be my guest, go on, find that illegal wireless set you're so keen on."

The German, who she could now see was not the brightest button, was getting more bewildered by the moment, and a flicker of hope ignited in her chest. She even gave him a coy smile, though he was middle-aged, with sour breath and a rotund belly.

"Well then, tell me what this extraordinary wireless set looks like, *Monsieur*," she said in an almost friendly, softer voice. "Perhaps I'll help you look for it—I wouldn't want anything unlawful in this house. Though I have no idea how such a thing could've ended up here, I have every confidence we'll find nothing at all. So, where do you want to start?" She added, practically bubbling with mock cooperation.

She was grateful now for the hours she'd spent slipping into the guise of Jacqueline du Tertre. Over time, the persona had become second nature—unintelligent, loud, erratic, overly emotional. All the things that neither Eileen, nor Didi, Nearne were. The part felt like a shield, and she wore it with all the conviction she could muster.

Had she fooled him? The German's face bordered on something close to irritation as he turned and made his way back toward the front door. For a fleeting moment, hope blossomed in her chest.

But it shattered the next instant.

The officer bellowed a command in German, his voice cutting through the quiet like a knife. Within seconds, three more armed men rushed into the house, fanning out with swift, military precision. They moved through the space like predators, each step radiating control and menace. Eileen felt real fear now, but she held her ground, summoning every ounce of Jacqueline's volatile energy to hide the terror beneath her skin.

One soldier held her firmly by the arm, forcing her into the downstairs parlor. Her heart pounded so fiercely it was almost deafening, but she kept her expression locked in exaggerated frustration. *They can't know,* she told herself. *Just a madwoman with nothing to hide.*

But the Gestapo's efficiency was terrifying. Each man moved with purpose, throwing open cabinets, tossing drawers onto the floor with a crash. The Dubois' belongings scattered like autumn leaves, furniture groaned as it was upturned, and one officer even ripped the cushions from the sofa, slicing them open to search for hidden compartments.

The house she had come to trust, her sanctuary, was being torn apart, shredded by suspicion. She could feel panic rising like a wave. A few feet away, the lead officer watched her closely, as though waiting for a crack in her facade, his eyes glinting with a mixture of cold amusement and distrust.

Eileen kept her breathing steady, standing still, a picture of flustered outrage, while inside her mind screamed with fear. She could only hope her act would hold out against their brutal, unyielding search.

"Aha! I've found something!" Though spoken in German, Eileen understood well enough. Her heart plummeted. The voice, filled with satisfaction, echoed through the walls like a death knell. She listened helplessly as another grunt of approval followed, each sound driving home her loss. They were piecing together the set, unearthing each component she had so desperately tried to conceal. They weren't fools; they knew exactly what to look for, and they wouldn't stop until every part was uncovered.

But there was still a shred of hope—they had nothing linking the set to her. Unless… unless she had been betrayed. The thought filled her with cold fury, making her almost dizzy. She recalled the conversation with Arnaud about Armand's friend, Felix, who'd been betrayed by a double agent. The traitor known as *Le Boiteau.* But that couldn't be. She'd kept her distance from everyone, operating alone, meticulously, precisely.

Before she could process the thought further, the heavyset officer with the cap and smug belly burst back into the parlor, a satisfied grin plastered across his face. He held up a piece of the wireless set like a prize.

"And tell me, *Mademoiselle,*" he sneered, his eyes narrowing, "what do you make of this?"

Eileen's face twisted in exaggerated shock, her voice pitched in shrill disdain. "Heavens, man, what on earth is that? Is that the precious device you've been tearing this poor house apart to find?" She scoffed, but her act was cut short as the Gestapo officer holding her gave a vicious tug on her arm, forcing a yelp of pain from her lips.

The officer leaned in close, his eyes glinting with triumph. "Oh, we'll see if you keep that mouth running once you're in questioning," he growled. From his coat, he produced a pair of iron handcuffs, snapping them open with an almost theatrical flourish as another officer stepped forward, clutching her loyal suitcase with pieces of the wireless dangling from it, damning evidence she couldn't deny.

Eileen said nothing as her mind spun, weaving story after story, testing the strength of each one, her mind a flurry of desperate plans.

Outside, the afternoon sun hit her face as she stumbled forward, manacled, and held firmly by her captors. She blinked, momentarily blinded, trying to take in the scene—no less than seven cars lined the street, and Gestapo officers littered the sidewalk like dark shadows. A handful of stunned neighbors had stopped to gawk, watching as she, the innocent shopgirl, was roughly escorted to a waiting car.

One last gulp of fresh air, one last look at the house, and then the car door slammed shut, the street spinning into motion around her. She felt the rumble of the engine beneath her, vibrating through her bones as they sped off, the familiar streets of Bourg-la-Reine slipping away, leaving her destination as dark and unknown as the men around her.

PART XI

~MIA~ TORQUAY, 2007

39

A FIRM AND SOOTHING HAND

Lisburne Crescent, Torquay England, August 2007

Though Mia had perched on the edge of her chair for the past fifteen minutes, Eileen's sudden forward collapse still took her by surprise. She was just quick enough to catch the frail woman, guiding her gently down to the worn carpet with a practiced, soft fall. Whiskey darted in, meowing urgently, his green eyes wide with concern, but Mia extended a calming hand to him, setting the loyal cat aside. Her attention snapped back to Eileen, assessing her as only a trained psychologist would.

The fainted woman's head lay in Mia's lap, her face pale against the dim light filtering through the lace curtains. Eileen's skin, lined with years of wisdom and resilience, was nearly as translucent as the clock ticking softly on the wall—its hands paused at 4:17 p.m., marking the time of her fainting. A crystal glass of water shimmered on the table, catching a stray beam of afternoon light. Mia noted it, mentally reminding herself to offer it to Eileen once she came to.

Eileen's eyelids flickered slightly, and though Mia wasn't a medical doctor, she felt reassured by the steady pulse beneath her fingers. The old lady's breathing, however, was shallow, as though she'd been holding her breath on some terrifying precipice.

The memories she'd been sharing with Mia had stirred up the past in a way neither had anticipated, even though Eileen had been clear about her intentions: she wanted to purge this story from her mind, to shake off the cobwebs and let her wartime memories rest at last. Not for praise or glory, not for the prying eyes of the press, but for a kindred spirit who understood trauma like no other.

Keeping her voice soft yet clear, Mia kept talking to the unconscious woman in a steady, grounding rhythm.

"Miss Nearne, Eileen, Didi... it's me, Mia. You're safe now, right here with me. And Whiskey's here too; he needs you like I do. Do come round, please."

With gentle hands, Mia retrieved the woolen stole that had slipped from Eileen's shoulders during their discussion and wrapped it back around her, tucking it snugly to provide both warmth and comfort.

She felt a tremor beneath her fingertips as she rested a calming hand on Eileen's arm. Gradually, the rapid, shallow breaths began to ease, and Mia could see Eileen's features soften, each breath guiding her back to the present moment. Slowly, the eyes fluttered open, her gaze finding Mia's with a hint of confusion.

"Take your time, Miss Nearne," Mia murmured, keeping Eileen's body firmly settled against her. "I'm right here with you. Just breathe slowly and easily." Stretching her arm, she picked up the glass of water and brought it gently to Eileen's trembling lips.

"Take a sip. It'll do you good. Look, Whiskey's here too, rubbing against you. He wants your attention," she added softly.

"Whiskey?" Eileen's voice wavered, slipping into French. "*C'est toi, mon chérie?* How did you end up in prison with me?" she babbled, half in French and half in English. Mia could tell she was still trapped in the shadowed recesses of her memories.

"You're in Torquay, Miss Nearne," Mia explained, helping Eileen ground again. "It's 2007. You're safe, sound, and free. How does that feel?"

Eileen blinked, disoriented, struggling to sit upright. She pushed the water glass aside, but as Mia helped her back into the chair, the blue eyes sharpened, a faint, coy expression crossing her face.

"I'm sorry. I'm confused. One moment, I'm in a car, on my way to be interrogated by the Gestapo. And the next, I'm... it's sixty years later...an old woman, *ramollie du bulbe*, as the French say."

"My French isn't so good," Mia smiled. "What does that mean?"

"Well, what I am," Eileen replied dryly. "Soft in the head."

Mia shook her head. "You're anything but. Miss Nearne. I was on the edge of my seat listening to your arrest in Paris in July 1944. How brave you were—and if I may say—how you kept your wits about you. You even burned the evidence that could've led to more arrests."

Eileen waved a hand dismissively, a glimmer of irritation crossing her face. "Don't judge too quickly, my dear. I sometimes think it was sheer luck I never betrayed anyone. I came close. And the Germans didn't need my coded messages to track people down."

Mia nodded, careful not to probe too quickly. "I... I know most of the details. I've read the statements you gave after the war—now publicly accessible in the National Archives. I'm here to help you through them, step by step, but only as much as you're comfortable with."

Eileen's fingers clenched unconsciously at the fabric of Mia's sleeve. "I don't know if I can—or if I must. I've told it all before, you know. Not just in the debriefing when I returned from Ravensbrück, but time and again, to historians, biographers, the press."

Mia placed the glass of water back in Eileen's hands, watching her take a sip, then another. "I know, and I understand. But this time, we're approaching it differently. I'm not here to extract your story or add it to some public archive. I'm neither a historian nor a journalist—I'm a therapist. My focus is on you and your well-being, not on the story's historical value or anyone else's gain."

Mia hesitated, sensing the need to address a lingering question Eileen might have about her intentions—especially considering her unintentional role in bringing Sebastian Stone to her doorstep.

Eileen's lips tightened slightly. "I know what you're thinking, about that reporter from the Torbay Weekly who sniffed me out the other week." Her gaze softened a fraction. "But I also know that wasn't your fault, dear. I can see your intentions are genuine, not to exploit or expose me. But... going over these old wounds, it doesn't stop it from being painful."

"I can see that, Miss Nearne. It's such a heavy burden you carry. But I truly want to help you find a way to live alongside the past—without its grip always suffocating you. I know the details, so I'm not asking for anything new. Instead, we'll explore the emotional hold it still has over you and see how we can loosen it, even a little."

Eileen looked at Mia, a flash of irritation in her eyes. Her voice took on a hard edge. "It's useless, Dr. Thompson. Frankly, rubbish. And you know it. I've been through all the therapies. Nothing can erase the horrors from me."

Mia remained calm, meeting Eileen's gaze. "I understand, and I don't want to suggest I have a magic wand. But today, there are methods like EMDR that can ease the grip traumatic memories have on us. These approaches don't remove the past, but they help reshape the way our brains respond to the emotional triggers. Back then, these kinds of therapies didn't exist, and I wouldn't bring them up now if I didn't believe they could offer a way forward."

Mia paused, then added, "I've specialized in what we call PTSD today—and I've also personally tested many of these methods for my own traumas. I can tell you they've helped me in ways I never expected. Trauma may always be a part of us, yes, but with time, it doesn't have to dictate everything about us anymore."

Whiskey, ever the attentive companion, leapt onto his mistress's lap, curling up with a contented purr. Eileen's hand drifted to his back, stroking him gently as she murmured, "You know, he's my therapy. My pets always have been. All that talk of advanced methods and clever techniques...well, at my age, I'm not quite in the mood to jump through hoops with therapists. No offense intended, Mia. I'm sure you're very good at what you do."

Mia gave a warm smile. "None taken, Miss Nearne. This has been a long session anyway, and it's best if we part ways for today. You've given me a lot to think about, and I hope I've given you something to consider too."

Eileen's lips quirked, a wry smile creeping in as she fixed Mia with an amused look. "Smart cookie, aren't you, calling it a 'session'." She chuckled lightly, her gaze softening. "Perhaps you do have a magic wand after all. I feel... lighter. Stronger somehow." She paused, the faintest shadow passing over her expression. "Maybe even strong enough, eventually, to tell you about 11 *Rue des Saussaies*, at the French Gestapo Headquarters. What they did to me there."

"Only when you're ready, and not a moment before." Mia glanced at the clock. "Do you have something for supper? It's late, and it's been quite an intense afternoon."

Eileen waved her hand dismissively. "I'm fine, don't you worry. I've a bit of soup in the fridge. I'll be just fine."

Mia stood up, gathering her bag. "May I suggest an early night, then? After a conversation like this, you'll likely be quite worn down. When would be a good time to check in with you, just to make sure there's no backlash from today?"

Eileen paused before giving her a considering look. "You know what? Why don't we just leave it loose? I'll let you know if I feel the need. And if I do... I think I'd like you to call me Didi. That name," she added quietly, "it vibrates with a sense of belonging."

Touched by the intimacy of the request, Mia hesitated, then smiled. "Alright, but let's meet in the middle—how about 'Aunt Didi'?"

Eileen's eyes twinkled. "Aunt Didi, then." She gave Mia a rare, unguarded smile. "Goodnight, Doctor Mia."

"Goodnight, Aunt Didi."

As Mia left, she glanced back at Eileen, who was still stroking Whiskey, a slight smile lingering on her lips. For the first time, she looked as though she was ready to release a part of the past—no magic wand required.

40

AFTER HOURS

When Mia left Eileen's house, the summer evening was already settling over Torquay, casting the seaside town in a soft, muted glow. The day had been hot, and families were making their way home, still in bathing suits, trailing bath towels, inflatable swim gear, and tired children behind them.

The salty tang of the ocean mingled with a faint, earthy coolness as the day's warmth faded with the light. A light breeze stirred skirts and hairdos, carrying the occasional snippet of laughter and the clink of glasses from nearby pubs, where locals and tourists had gathered for an evening meal or a pint.

As always, Torquay gave Mia a warm, fuzzy feeling. This was her town; these were her people. One day soon, she'd ask Aunt Didi why she had settled here, of all places she'd lived: London, Paris, Nice, Boulogne-sur-Mer, Grenoble. Why Torquay? And why the longest time here?

As Mia made her way home, Eileen's vivid account of her initial training as a secret agent, and then her tense months in Paris until her arrest, echoed in her mind. She hadn't expected the guarded old lady to open up so fully, to reveal her inner self, and finally to reward her with the intimacy of her family's pet name, Didi.

Tonight had been a turning point, but one that had taken its toll on the young psychologist. This was no ordinary client, no ordinary story, and finding relief for Aunt Didi would be neither an ordinary nor an easy journey.

As Mia rounded a corner, lost in thought, she nearly collided with a familiar figure leaning casually against a wall, reading a tabloid, his face partly obscured by a Nike cap.

"Mia!" Sebastian straightened, a half-smile forming as he recognized her. "Sorry—I didn't mean to startle you."

"Sebastian," she replied, surprised to see him in this quiet part of town. She noticed the slight slump to his shoulders, his usual polished, devil-may-care attitude dulled somehow. He looked... unsettled.

"On your way home, I take it?" he asked, his voice carrying a hint of something strained.

She nodded, giving him a thoughtful look. "I was just with Miss Nearne, actually. Were you waiting here on purpose?"

"No, I wasn't. What gave you that idea?" He pushed his cap up, revealing an innocent expression, though his eyes didn't quite meet hers.

Mia looked straight up into his squinting green eyes. He was tall, but she straightened on her heels, holding her ground. "Don't lie to me, Mr. Stone. I have a sixth sense for liars."

"Oh, alright. I had hoped you'd come this way." He looked sheepish, scratching his head beneath his cap. "I figured you'd gotten access to Miss Nearne again, and I just wanted to ask... if you'd been able to tell her I didn't mean any harm and only wanted to give her that tape of her sister in *School for Danger*?"

"I don't like being spied on," Mia replied, arching a brow before adding with a faint smile, "And no, the matter of 'Sebastian Stone' hasn't quite come up."

"Okay, but... at some point, it will, right?" he ventured hopefully.

Mia wondered what Sebastian's true motivation was. Why was he so fixated on giving Eileen this old film? Was it really about her, or was there something more he was after? Her perhaps? But she'd made it perfectly clear she wasn't interested in his advances—surely, he couldn't be this persistent?

She paused, studying him for a moment. His expression was distant, distracted; his usual charm slipping into something more vulnerable. Unable to ignore her professional instincts, she asked, "Are you alright, Sebastian? You seem... not quite yourself."

He shrugged, but the gesture felt loose, unconvincing. "Nothing that concerns you, really." He started to brush it off, but Mia crossed her arms, her gaze unyielding.

"Try me."

He sighed, glancing away. "Alright, if you really want to know—I've managed to make a royal mess of my life. Again. Incorrigible, really. And it's entirely my own fault." His voice was laced with bitterness.

She raised an eyebrow. "Why are you playing the victim card, then?"

He blinked, taken aback by her directness. "Touché." A wry smile flickered across his handsome face, but there was no hiding the self-reproach in his eyes. "You, of all people, have seen real hardship, and you never complain. And here I am, feeling sorry for myself, making a mess of what could have been a perfectly good life." The bitterness in his voice was replaced by something closer to regret.

Mia bristled, a defensive edge creeping into her voice. "And what exactly do you mean by 'you of all people'?"

Sebastian dropped his gaze. "Forgive me. That was clumsy." He hesitated as if to choose his words more carefully. "I'm not great at keeping my curiosity in check, especially around people who intrigue me. And, well... let's just say I did a little search on you. It's also an occupational hazard, you know. I dig too deep—no harm meant."

Mia narrowed her eyes, torn between irritation and reluctant amusement. Then, the corner of her mouth lifted into a half-smile. "My own occupational hazard, I suppose, is wanting to help people whether they want it or not."

Sebastian looked directly at her now, and she caught a flicker of admiration—and something else, a hint of longing—in his gaze. He seemed on the verge of confiding whatever weighed on him, and she felt a moment of shared understanding pass between them, a softening of the edges of their exchange.

"How about I buy you a drink?" he suggested. "In exchange, I'll give you the rundown on how I've managed to ruin my life this time."

Mia didn't immediately reply; the earlier tension still lingered between them like a thread not quite cut.

"Or... are you hungry?" he added, quickly. "I'll buy you mussels at No. 7. Unless, you don't eat seafood?"

Sebastian's usual vivacity seemed to spring back, and his pleading expression made her relent. "Tempting offer," she replied, tilting her head thoughtfully. "Alright, but only if you promise to hear me out when I tell you why this 'victim' act doesn't suit you."

His grin returned, a touch more genuine this time. "Deal."

Together, they walked toward the famous seafood restaurant on Beacon Terrace, where warm light spilled onto the street and laughter floated into the cool evening air.

. . .

The clinking of silverware and low hum of conversation filled No. 7 Fish Bistro, where Sebastian and Mia sat at a small corner table overlooking the harbor. The restaurant exuded cozy charm, with brass fixtures casting a warm glow over dark wood tables and nautical decor.

The scent of garlic and fresh seafood wafted through the air as servers bustled about, balancing steaming pots of mussels and vibrant plates of shellfish. Outside, the setting sun sparkled on the water, its reflections dancing along the shoreline.

Mia watched as Sebastian absently twisted his fork, nudging a stray mussel shell across his plate. His usual extroverted, overbearing attitude was noticeably absent as he stared into his wine glass, lost in his thoughts.

"You mentioned putting your PhD on hold for family reasons," Mia prompted gently, though she wasn't sure she should reopen the subject. The long, emotionally charged session with Eileen had left her drained, and she had been looking forward to savoring her favorite seafood without playing the therapist again. She kept her tone neutral, deliberately avoiding an open invitation.

Sebastian exhaled, running a hand through his thick hair. "Yeah, I did. And since you're asking... I might as well tell you the whole story. Though, fair warning—the little esteem you might've had for me will be completely shot after this."

He glanced around, as if checking for eavesdroppers, before meeting her gaze. His expression wavered between self-deprecation and something darker.

"I was at university in London back in 2002, studying journalism. Thought I had it all figured out, you know? At twenty, I was going to be the next Ed Miliband or Fraser Nelson." He scoffed, swirling his wine. "Until I got involved with a waitress. Cindy. By far the sexiest woman I'd ever laid eyes on." He let out a humorless laugh. "What did I know, huh?"

He took a small sip his wine before continuing. "Cindy was lively, unpredictable, larger than life. And me? I had more testosterone than sense. Won't be the first bloke to pay the price for that, nor the last."

Mia detected the thread of self-pity creeping in and interrupted, her tone cutting through his rambling. "Can you come to the point, Sebastian? It's been a long day."

"Sorry, I'm at it again, aren't I? Sebas the victim. Bad habit." His tone was apologetic, but the self-recrimination was clear. "Cindy got pregnant. I hadn't graduated, no job, no prospects. I tried to suggest we... consider other options, but Cindy wouldn't hear it. She was determined."

Mia maintained her steady, attentive presence, though inwardly not surprised that gallivanting "Slick Sebas" had fathered a child. "And you stayed involved with her, with them?"

Sebastian's jaw tightened. "Not really. I mean, I tried, but Cindy didn't want a relationship, and I wasn't exactly ready to be a dad. She had Adam, and I've been financially supporting them ever since. That's part of why I ended up working for the tabloids—better pay than freelancing or serious journalism. It wasn't what I'd planned, but Cindy always wanted more money, and I felt responsible. Like I'd somehow failed my son by not being there."

"So, you took on whatever job kept the money flowing?" Mia kept her tone neutral.

"Exactly. And it didn't stop there." The frustration was thick in his voice. "I had to give up the PhD too. Cindy's demands for more money kept piling up, and I couldn't manage both paying them and the tuition fees. It's not like I got much time with Adam, either. Cindy's always been with someone else, and I... well, I just kept paying. I'm on the birth certificate as his father, but I barely know my own son."

Mia leaned forward, thinking fast. "Did you formally acknowledge him as your son? What last name does he have?"

"Yes, he's Adam Stone, or so he was." Sebastian's expression darkened. "But that won't mean anything now. I let all my chances slip long ago."

His voice took on a bitter edge. "Yesterday, I got a letter from Cindy's lawyer. Turns out she's married now—to some rich American guy named Benson Bennison III—and they're moving to Michigan. It was a formal statement that there was no need for me to pay for Cindy or Adam anymore, that I'm 'free of them.' All I have to do is sign the paperwork so Adam's name can be changed to Bennison. Just like that."

Mia noted the conflicting emotions in Sebastian's face—anger, guilt, and something that looked like regret. "So, in some ways, you feel free to pursue your PhD. But in others, you feel more trapped than ever?" she observed.

He looked up at her, surprised. "Yes, that's it. Exactly how I feel. I mean, I'm finally off the hook financially, but it's as if I've... I don't know, lost the little boy all over again. Though I never really was his dad. He probably barely knows who I am. But now... now he's gone, and I blew that last chance."

Mia's voice was kind but direct. "Sebastian, are you angry with yourself for never building a relationship with him?"

He swallowed hard, his gaze dropping to the table. "Yeah. What kind of father does that? What's wrong with me that I never tried to bond with my own son?"

"There can be many reasons," Mia replied. "Overwhelmed by responsibility is one. Fear of doing the wrong thing—whether for the child, the mother, or even yourself—is another. It's not uncommon for people to feel distant when they're unsure of their place or whether they can live up to their own expectations."

Sebastian's green eyes searched her calm face, as if looking for some confirmation that he wasn't as terrible as he felt, then said softly. "Little Adam didn't ask for any of this."

Mia paused, considering her words carefully. "You don't have to sign the contract. You can fight it."

Sebastian sat as still as a statue, absorbing her words. "Can I? Should I?"

"That's up to you, Sebastian. But if you want to explore your options, I can ask Mirtle Brown, a solicitor who works with me at Hope Haven, to take a look at the document. She'll know if you stand a chance."

His voice carried a thread of hope. "You'd do that for me?"

"Sure. But on one condition: ask for the bill now and let me phone a cab. I'm too exhausted to drive and I have to be around the corner here tomorrow morning."

Sebastian glanced at his own untouched glass of wine and for the first time that evening he smiled. "I forgot to drink, so I'm stone sober. Can I offer you a lift? The MG's parked just around the corner."

Mia arched a brow, her grin faint. "Did you plan this entire evening, Mr. Stone Sober? Because it's starting to feel like you did."

He laughed, the sound warm and unguarded. "I honestly didn't, Mia, and by now you must know I'm a terrible liar. But I don't regret one minute of it. You're one of a kind."

"Let's leave it at that," Mia quipped, tossing an after-dinner mint into her mouth as she grabbed her bag and made for the door.

She paused at the doorway, glancing back at Sebastian as he settled the bill with a quick word to the server. He caught her looking and flashed a crooked grin, his usual bravado returning.

"Thanks for listening," he said as he joined her. "Sorry for making you work overtime, but I appreciate it. I'll make it up to you somehow, I promise. Now let me grab the MG. I won't be a minute." He dashed off into the twilight.

As Mia waited for his return, her thoughts drifted away from Sebastian's troubles and back to the afternoon with Eileen. The next session, about Eileen's interrogation by the Gestapo, would demand her full attention. She needed to talk to Alexandra to see if the other staff could take on some of her clients, allowing her to focus entirely on Eileen Nearne. But was that fair to her colleagues? Would they be able to carry out the extra workload? Or should she hire extra staff?

The rumble of a speeding engine snapped her out of her thoughts. The red MG pulled up to the curb, gleaming under the streetlights, and came to a neat halt at her feet. Sliding into the passenger seat, Mia closed the door as the car hummed to life. She leaned back, letting the cool night breeze wash over her face.

You're done for today, Mia Elaine Thompson. Tomorrow is another day. These decisions can wait.

She let the sea air tousle her long dark hair as the handsome driver beside her, for once, kept politely quiet, leaving her alone with her thoughts.

41

GETTING READY FOR THE HARD TIMES

One week later - Lisburne Crescent, Torquay, September 2007

The click of Mia's high heels echoed in the dim hallway of Lisburne Crescent as she approached Eileen's flat. The air carried the herby scent of geraniums from the plants lining the windowsills. Afternoon light filtered through the frosted glass panes, creating dappled patterns on the floor.

Mia balanced a small bag of groceries in one hand, the items chosen with Eileen's delicate appetite in mind: tea biscuits, a fresh loaf of bread, and a few tins of her favorite soups. She had stopped at Hope Haven Community Health earlier in the week to shuffle her caseload, enlisting Alexandra's help with some of her clients. Now, with practicalities set aside, she tapped gently on Eileen's door.

"Miss Nearne? Aunt Didi?" she called softly, unsure if today would bring the same warm reception as last week. One never knew with a vulnerable client like Eileen.

A strong voice answered from the other side of the door, though

Mia didn't miss the undertone of weariness. "Is that you, Mia? I wasn't expecting you so soon."

The door creaked open, and Mia stepped inside, closing it behind her. Eileen, already retreating to the sitting room, barely turned as Mia entered. She slipped into her favorite armchair, wrapped in a soft cardigan, and clicked her tongue for Whiskey to jump onto her lap.

The clock ticked its steady rhythm on the wall, filling the otherwise silent room.

"I thought I'd bring you some groceries. I hope you don't mind?" Mia set the bag on the coffee table.

"Of course not, Mia. That's very kind of you," Eileen replied but her voice was distant. Her French accent was more pronounced than usual, and Mia noticed the shadows under her eyes and the heaviness in her demeanor. It was clear she'd had another stretch of bad nights and difficult days.

"I'm so sorry," Mia said as she perched on the edge of the chair opposite Eileen.

The tired war heroine offered her a wan smile. "No need to be sorry, my dear. You've done nothing wrong. I've survived, though Whiskey here seems to think I'm in need of extra attention." She stroked the cat's back absently, her sharp eyes flicking toward Mia. "You look tired, too. I hope it's not me keeping you up at night, or is it something—or someone—else?"

Mia blinked, caught off guard by Eileen's perceptiveness. "I'm managing," she replied lightly, hoping to steer the conversation away. Mentioning Sebastian wasn't right for this moment. "I was thinking about our next session, Aunt Didi. That is if I may still call you that?"

Eileen chuckled, the sound light but sincere. "I don't bestow favors to take them away, my dear. In fact, come over and give your old aunt a kiss. There, that will do."

Mia leaned forward, her lips brushing Eileen's soft, papery cheek. The faint scent of lavender soap and lanolin lingered, far from unpleasant. More importantly, it was a subtle reassurance—Eileen was taking care of herself again.

As Mia settled in her own chair, she said, "Last week was... intense. For both of us. Though I don't mean to compare myself to what it must do to you."

Eileen studied her closely. "Last week was hard," she agreed. "But it was necessary. Just as you told me. I've noticed a change in how I feel about this endless story that winds through my mind. I don't know if you've already applied your so-called advanced techniques, but I've noticed things are different. The nightmares are still there, and they're far from pleasant, but they seem... contained, somehow."

She paused, her expression tightening, before continuing in a stronger voice. "Ah, I know what it is," Eileen said, her voice steady but laced with emotion. "All these years, I've blamed myself for my arrest. I told myself I deserved it—refusing to leave the Dubois house, ignoring the risks and the orders from my superiors. I've been harder on myself than anyone in SOE ever was. Nobody said it was my fault. Not a single person. But still, I believed it. I've carried that guilt as if it were fact. That guilt and blame have cast a shadow over my entire life."

Mia marveled at her candor. "What an incredible insight, Aunt Didi. And you're absolutely right—you are not to blame. Not even one percent. The Nazis carry all the blame. Every last bit of it."

"Now that calls for a good English cuppa and one of the delicious biscuits you brought, doesn't it?" Eileen chirped, gently lifting Whiskey from her lap and rising to put the kettle on. On her way to the kitchen, she smirked over her shoulder. "Now, what's this 'someone else' business I'm sensing with you, Mia? Let me play the shrink for once."

Mia smiled, shaking her head. "Nothing here to analyze, Aunt Didi."

Eileen giggled, a surprisingly girlish sound, and began whistling *La Marseillaise* as she disappeared into the kitchen. Mia sat back, letting the warm, familiar sounds of the flat wash over her. Aunt Didi, when she was in full health, was one of a kind. *Who had said that of her? Of course, it was Sebastian Stone.* The man seemed to be occupying far too much of her thoughts lately. Maybe she should consult Aunt Didi—after all, she had an uncanny ability to see through people.

As the whistle of the kettle mingled with Eileen's cheerful humming, a memory crept into Mia's mind, uninvited but vivid.

Miss Elsie Mayhew. Her small, book-filled house in Birmingham. The scent of tea and old wood that filled the cozy space where Mia had spent two of the happiest years of her life. Miss Elsie, the teacher, with her kind eyes and sharp mind, had been the one to see past Mia's troubled exterior, to recognize her intelligence and urge her to study. Miss Elsie had been the first—and only—person to love Mia unconditionally.

She'd only been fifteen when she'd found Miss Elsie on the Persian rug in the sitting room, her heart stopped forever. Grief had hit Mia like a tidal wave, washing her out to the streets because she couldn't bear to go back to the foster system and face another round of indifferent strangers. Those two short years with Miss Elsie had been her only sanctuary, her only home. And now, sitting here with Aunt Didi, the faint echo of that love stirred again in her chest.

Her breath hitched. Loving someone like that—deeply, vulnerably—meant risking unbearable loss. She hadn't let herself feel that way in years. And yet, here she was, watching Eileen whistle *La Marseillaise* with a tea towel slung over her shoulder, the image so heartbreakingly vivid that Mia felt herself tighten against the ache.

Thank you, Miss Elsie, Mia thought, her chest constricting as she blinked back tears. *You've sent me another guardian.*

The sound of the tea tray being set down snapped her back to the present. Eileen reappeared, looking down on Mia with a triumphant smile. "Right, tea's up. Now, tell me—what's got you looking so serious?"

Mia forced a smile, taking the offered cup. "Nothing to worry about, Aunt Didi. Just thinking."

"About that 'someone else', I bet," Eileen teased, her sharp eyes glinting. "And might you perhaps be so daisy-eyed because of that dashing reporter from the Torbay Weekly?"

Mia stiffened, nearly spilling her tea. "How... how do you know?"

This sent Eileen into a peal of laughter, her head tipping back in delight. "Heavens, girl! I may have shooed him away from my doorstep—as the last thing I want is a nosy reporter sniffing around—but I was young once myself. And I've still got a good pair of eyes in my head. That man is what we'd say in French, *il est canon, lui*. How do you say it in English? He's hot."

Now it was Mia's turn to burst into laughter. "Aunt Didi," she exclaimed, setting her cup down before she spilled it, "you're hopeless!"

Eileen smirked, clearly pleased with herself, but Mia's laughter faded quickly, leaving her thoughts spinning. She felt the pull of too many emotions at once: the intensity of her work with Aunt Didi, the undeniable attraction to Sebastian that she'd been trying to ignore, and the unexpected pang of grief that had surfaced over Miss Elsie. It was too much. She needed to straighten herself out.

Clearing her throat, Mia smoothed her skirt, determination flickering in her eyes. "Alright, Aunt Didi. Playtime's over. Let's talk about how we're going to approach our next session."

Eileen raised an eyebrow but said nothing, her expression softening. She seemed to sense Mia's need to refocus, and she didn't protest.

"I've always found humor to be one of the best ways to cope with life's greatest tragedies," she said, her voice lowering as her gaze shifted. "But humor can only carry you so far. Some memories are devoid of humor."

PART XII

~EILEEN~ PARIS, 22 JULY -15 AUGUST 1944

42

A MASTERFUL ACTRESS

French Gestapo Headquarters Paris, 22 July 1944

The black Mercedes-Benz, its swastika flags fluttering upfront, lurched forward with a growl, the engine roaring as it tore through the streets of Bourg-la-Reine. It weaved recklessly through traffic, the driver taking impossible risks, horn blaring as pedestrians leaped for safety. Inside, every jolt and sway reverberated through the leather seat, offering Eileen no comfort, only amplifying her unease.

Her summer dress clung to her back, the oppressive heat in the car mixing with her own perspiration. The stale, suffocating air reeked of sweat and cigarette smoke, clinging to the enclosed space like an unwelcome extra passenger.

Eileen was wedged between two silent Gestapo officers in their black uniforms with faces as blank and impassive as stone. Their presence made it impossible for her to move even an inch, leaving her swaying helplessly as the car careened around sharp corners. One moment she was pressed against the heavyset man on her left;

the next, the thinner man on her right. Each unintentional brush against their uniforms sent a prickling wave of dread through her skin.

She risked a glance at the man to her left. His thick fingers rested casually on his knees, but there was a coiled menace beneath his calm demeanor, a predator-like stillness. The man to her right stared straight ahead, his jaw rigid, the angle of his cap deliberate and precise, as though rehearsed for intimidation. Neither spoke nor issued threats, yet their silence was suffocating—more oppressive than words ever could be.

The car skidded around another corner, throwing Eileen sharply against the heavyset man. His bulk absorbed the impact without so much as a glance in her direction, yet she felt the chill of his presence radiate through her. She gripped the edge of the seat with both hands, her knuckles white as she fought to steady herself.

Outside the window, the world was a blur. Vaguely familiar buildings of Paris loomed and vanished in a heartbeat, their façades distorted by the car's relentless speed. The city she'd known and loved so intimately now felt like a surreal, nightmarish landscape, warped beyond recognition.

Eileen had no idea where they were taking her. All she knew was that she had been caught—and the game of survival had begun.

A mantra pounded in her head, keeping time with the frantic rhythm of her heart. *Don't show fear. Never be afraid. Never let them intimidate you.* These words had been drilled into her during training, and now, repeating them was the only way she could stop her body from trembling.

Her throat was parched, her breath shallow. She prayed silently—to the Holy Mother, to God, to Jesus—to save her, or at least to grant her the strength to endure whatever awaited. Her training had stripped away any romantic illusions about what might come. She had endured the cold baths, the brutal interrogations under harsh lights, even the occasional strike. Would they do all that? And worse?

Buck had told her she'd endured the brutal part of the training better than most. Well, she would prove him right. For the sake of her foolishness in being caught, for the agents in the SPIRITUALIST network who were depending on her silence, she would withstand it all—without a crack in her armor.

Eileen glanced down at her hands, now clasped tightly in her lap. How she yearned for the familiar feeling of her rosary in this moment, the smooth pink quartz beads slipping through her fingers, anchored by the cool silver chain with Jesus on his cross, rubbed smooth by her touch.

But Jacqueline du Tertre wasn't particularly the God-fearing kind of girl, so Eileen's rosary wasn't there. Still, she didn't need its physical presence to summon its strength. She could feel the memory always and everywhere, solid and steady in her hands, the act of prayer alone manifested comfort. And she needed that. God alone could save her now.

Willing herself to appear calm, Eileen adopted the role of the wrongly arrested shopgirl. A harmless civilian who, once heard out, would surely receive a sheepish apology from the Germans and be promptly released.

From now on, you're not Eileen Nearne. Not one shred of her remains, she swore to herself. *You are Jacqueline du Tertre. Jacqueline du Tertre. Jacqueline du Tertre.* The name repeated in her mind like a drumbeat, anchoring her.

The car slowed as they approached the city center. The convoy of black vehicles crawled behind them, an ominous procession that made bystanders stop and gape. Eileen caught a brief glimpse of her reflection in the window: pale skin, tight jaw, but a face devoid of emotion. It was the mask she'd trained herself to wear, and it held firm.

Inside, however, Jacqueline began to rise, her fiery indignation bubbling to the surface. She was furious, indignant, ready to spit a string of rapid French accusations at her captors. How dare they arrest an innocent Frenchwoman? How dare they disrupt her life? Jacqueline was a storm brewing within, coiled and waiting, an untamed animal ready to leap out and show the Nazis the full force of her fury.

Outwardly, she remained perfectly still, her visible composure unshaken, but inside roiled and burned, preparing to spring into action.

The car turned sharply, pulling into a gravel courtyard. The towering façade of the French Gestapo headquarters at 11 Rue de Sausaisses loomed ahead, its cold, gray walls and iron gates standing like the maw of a great beast, swinging open as if to swallow her whole.

As the car rolled to a halt and the door was yanked open, Eileen felt Jacqueline solidify within her—a protective force, her armor. She let the mantra echo in her mind one final time:

Don't show fear. Never be afraid. Never let them intimidate you.

With her head held high, Eileen stepped out of the car, walking into the unknown with the poise and determination of the masterful actress she had become.

THE DOOR SLAMMED SHUT behind her, leaving Eileen alone in a small, dimly lit room. The walls were bare, the air stifling, and the wooden chair she sank down on wobbled under her weight. A metal table sat in the center, with two more chairs on the opposite side and a tiny, barred window high up on the wall. It was her first encounter with a prison cell.

The room reeked of sweat and cigarette smoke, just like the car had, but there was also a faint metallic tang that she couldn't place.

A thin bead of sweat trickled down her spine, settling between her shoulder blades, as her mind wandered to a cigarette. She longed for one with every fiber of her being. Instead, she stared down at her nicotine-stained fingers, thinking ruefully that, for the first time in years, she might be forced to give up smoking.

"Oh no, you don't!" she reprimanded herself silently. "You'll be out of here in no time and can smoke to your heart's content."

Minutes passsed. The rhythmic ticking of her wristwatch—a treasured part of her cover, given to her by Buck at RAF Tempsford on the evening of her deployment—seemed to mock the silence.

At last, the door opened, and two Gestapo officers entered. They were different from the rowdy men who had arrested her. These two were calmer, their demeanor more formal.

The older, with lined features and a carefully polite expression, addressed her in very passable French, though the clipped edges of his German accent were unmistakable. "*Mademoiselle*, sorry to have kept you waiting. I need to ask you a few questions. If you answer them truthfully, you will come to no harm. They concern your presence at the house in Bourg-la-Reine, owned by the Dubois family."

Eileen's stomach twisted at the mention of the Dubois family. Panic threatened to surge. *Oh no, please don't let them arrest that sweet elderly couple. I'll tell them they had nothing to do with it.* But outwardly, she remained composed.

She inclined her head politely, as Jacqueline would, carefully studying their movements. One adjusted his cuffs methodically, while the other placed a notebook on the table with deliberate precision.

Politeness. A ploy, she thought, her mind sharpening as she watched them. *They want me to drop my guard.*

Jacqueline took over the scene without a hitch, an edge of boredom creeping into her pretty young face as she folded her hands primly on her lap. Her large blue eyes held an innocent expression as she responded with feigned politeness.

"Of course. I've nothing to hide, Herr Major Gestapo." The earnestness in her voice belied the calculated performance.

The older officer's brow twitched, and his colleague shot him a quick sidelong glance. For a moment, they seemed unsure whether to correct her or let it slide. The Eileen inside the Jacqueline was triumphant. *Let them think I'm an ignorant fool.*

"What's your full name?"

"Jacqueline du Tertre, Herr Maj—"

"Don't address me like that, *Mademoiselle*, it's incorrect!" the officer snapped. Eileen caught the flicker of irritation in his eyes. She stored the moment away with quiet satisfaction.

"Are you French?" he continued.

"Am I French?" she repeated, her tone rising with indignation as she met his gaze. "Of course I'm French! What else would I be?" She let the question drip with absurdity.

The two men exchanged a brief glance before continuing.

"Do you have a job, *Mademoiselle*?" the younger officer asked, still fiddling with his cuffs.

Eileen blinked, giving him her wide-eyed, slightly vacant Jacqueline stare. She hesitated just long enough to suggest she was gathering scattered thoughts. "Yes," she said vaguely. "I work for a businessman."

"What kind of work?" the older one pressed, his voice calm but with an undercurrent of suspicion.

Her expression shifted into a look of bewilderment, as if she didn't understand why he was so insistent. "I transmit messages," she said plainly.

"What kind of messages?"

Her lips pursed, and she gave an exaggerated shrug. "How should I know? I only send them. They're always coded."

The Germans glanced at each other again. Eileen caught the flicker of confusion in their eyes—exactly what she had intended. They hadn't expected her to admit to sending messages. It was a calculated risk, since these were not the men who'd arrested her, and therefore wouldn't know of her initial denials. But it was a risk worth taking.

"You don't know what's in the messages you sent?" the elder officer asked, his tone skeptical but also intrigued.

"Not a clue," she replied breezily, tilting her head as if the question were beneath consideration. "When I was first hired, they tried to teach me to code. But I was absolutely hopeless at it, made such a mess of things that my boss decided it would be best if he handled the coding himself. I just transmit what he writes. That's it. So don't ask me."

She threw her hands up in mock exasperation and offered them a tight, conspiratorial smile. "To be honest, I think it's much better that way. My boss is very secretive, you see, always worried about competition. I didn't want to be blamed if anything went wrong."

To emphasize her point, she wiped her hands against each other in a gesture that said *no mistakes here,* her face a picture of innocence.

Again, the officers exchanged a glance, their confusion deepening, while Eileen, with all her might, remained composed, her heart pounding beneath her calm exterior. The trap she was setting for them was working—for now—and Jacqueline, as always, was one step ahead.

"Listen here, little lady. You were arrested in a house where wireless equipment was found," the older man said, his tone growing sharper, his words meant to cut through her composure. "Are you trying to make us believe you see nothing unusual about that?"

"Unusual?" she repeated, letting the word linger as if it tasted bitter. "You mean the wireless set? Oh, that's my boss's equipment, of course. I never questioned it. He writes the messages, I send them. It's hardly my concern what's in them. I assumed it was business."

"And you didn't ask any questions about the messages? Ever?" The younger man sprang to his feet, his movements agitated, the chair screeching across the floor. He began to pace the small room, each step of his heavy boots working on Eileen's nerves. But she stayed in her role, her wide-eyed naiveté holding firm.

"Why would I?" she replied, tilting her head as though puzzled by his intensity. "My boss wouldn't appreciate it, and I didn't want to risk my job. I'd come all the way from—"

"Shut up!" the younger man barked, his fist slamming onto the table. The sharp sound startled even his colleague, and the force sent his undone cufflink clattering to the floor. It tinkled across the tiles, the metallic sound fading into silence.

This is it, Eileen thought icily, feeling her pulse quicken. *This is where it starts. But by God, you're not going to get it out of me.*

She allowed herself to appear shaken, her lashes lowering just enough to glance hopefully at the older officer, who remained seated and studiously jotting notes in his notebook. He offered her a small, placating smile, the sort one might give a child or a frightened animal.

Eileen wasn't comforted in the slightest. If anything, her stomach twisted tighter. She had tried dispersion—now, they would try dispersion on her.

The arsenal of Gestapo interrogation techniques was opening before her, one weapon at a time. The fight ahead would be grim, and it was no longer a game of wits. It was war.

43

WINNING AND LOSING

Hours later, the air in the interrogation room was thick and stifling, the tension mounting with every word exchanged. Eileen sat hunched forward on the battered wooden chair, her hands folded tightly in her lap. She was terribly thirsty and at the same time needed the bathroom, but she willed her body to stay calm and not show its needs. Letting them see weakness licking at the edges of her resolve? No, Eileen wouldn't give them that satisfaction.

The two Gestapo men loomed over her, their contrasting approaches as deliberate as they were predictable. The older one, who'd introduced himself politely at the start, leaned against the table, his voice calm, almost gentle.

"*Mademoiselle* du Tertre," he began again, with a slight sigh as if he regretted the need for further questioning. "You've clearly been tricked. This man, your boss, has taken advantage of you. He's using you to further his espionage. Think of what kind of man would do that. Would he really care what happens to you now?"

Eileen kept her expression blank, forcing herself to meet his cold eyes as if considering his words. He tilted his head, adopting an almost fatherly tone.

"You're a clever woman, *Mademoiselle*. Surely you must see the danger he's put you in. You don't need to protect him. If you admit the truth now, we can help you. You can avoid..." His voice trailed off, leaving the implied threat hanging in the air.

Eileen didn't respond, sensing her window to reply had already closed.

"You're lying, you dirty bitch!" the younger officer snarled suddenly, lunging toward her. His voice thundered through the small room, echoing off the bare walls. Before she could react, his hand cracked across her face, snapping her head to the side and sending her tumbling off the chair.

She hit the floor hard, the cold tiles biting into her skin, but she didn't cry out. Instead, she pressed her hands flat against the ground and forced herself up, her movements deliberate and steady.

"What's wrong with you people?" she snapped, her voice loud and indignant. Her cheek throbbed, but she ignored it. Instead, she focused on appearing outraged. "I've told you the truth, and this is how you treat me? A Frenchwoman? An innocent woman? I'm not a spy!"

Her voice carried such conviction, her tone so biting, that both men froze for a moment. The younger officer took to pacing with angry steps, but his aggression faltered. The older officer straightened, letting his pen hover over the notebook as he regarded her closely.

Eileen caught the flicker of uncertainty in their eyes, and a small spark of satisfaction burned within her. *Keep them off balance. Keep them doubting.*

The older man pressed on, his calm demeanor returning, but with an effort. "*Mademoiselle*, your boss has abandoned you. He's left you to take the blame. If you confess now, we can help you. We can protect you from the consequences of his betrayal."

Eileen leaned back in her chair, tilting her head as though considering his offer. Then she crossed her arms, her voice dripping with exasperation. "I've told you the truth! How many times do I have to say it? My boss writes the messages. I send them. I don't ask questions because it's none of my business. If you don't believe me, then why are you even asking?"

The younger officer whirled around, slamming his fists on the table. "Because you're lying!"

"And what do you want me to say?" Eileen shot back, her voice rising, her frustration raw and fiery. "I keep telling you the answers, and you keep asking me the same questions! If you don't believe me, why bother? If you already know what you want me to say, just tell me, and I'll say it!"

Her outburst left a stunned silence in its wake. Both men stared at her, the younger one bristling, the older one tapping his pen furiously against the table.

Eileen's chest heaved, and tears wanted to well in her eyes, but she forced them back as she met their gaze with defiance. The truth was, she was buying time. With every passing minute, word of her arrest would spread. The other members of the SPIRITUALIST network would get alerted, giving them precious hours to hide or escape. She had been trained to endure this, to withstand interrogation and even torture for at least twenty-four hours. If she could hold out, others might avoid her fate.

The older officer leaned back in his chair, shaking his head. "You're either the most naive woman in Paris, or the most stubborn liar I've ever met," he said coldly.

Eileen didn't flinch. She let Jacqueline's indignant mask harden over her, her voice steady and biting. "Maybe I'm both. Or maybe, I'm just telling the truth, and your ears are blocked."

The room fell quiet again. The men exchanged their umpteenth glance, and the older man gave a small nod. Eileen braced herself for what was to come.

They dragged her down a narrow corridor, her feet barely keeping up as she was hauled along by two Gestapo officers, one gripping each arm tightly. The air grew colder as they descended into what felt like the depths of the building. Eileen could hear the faint echoes of water dripping, the sound sharpening her awareness of what was coming.

La baignoire. She'd endured waterboarding before at Beaulieu during training, but this wasn't practice anymore. This time, there were no limits, no instructors ensuring she survived.

The small room they entered reeked of dampness, mildew, and desperation. A bath sat at its center, filled with water so clear it mocked the darkness around it. The officers' boots echoed on the stone floor as they moved with grim purpose.

Eileen's eyes darted around looking for escape, but there was none. Her breath quickened despite herself. *Don't show fear. Never be afraid. Never let them dominate you.* The mantra steadied her, pulsing in time with her pounding heart.

The older officer stepped in front of her, his eyes cold as steel. "For the last time, *Mademoiselle*," he said in an eerily calm voice, "who are you working for? Where are those messages being sent?"

She met his gaze with defiance, her lips pressed tightly together. *Say nothing.*

Before she knew what happened, they lifted her bodily off the ground and plunged her into the bath. The icy water struck her like a shock of electricity as they pushed her under. Her body seized against the cold, her mouth and nose filling with water before she had the chance to take a breath. She thrashed instinctively, her arms pinned by the men on either side, the weight of their hands pressing her down further.

Stay calm.

The water roared in her ears, every cell in her body screamed for air. Her chest burned as she struggled, her mind frantically repeating her training: *Don't panic. Never panic.* But her body was rebelling, choking on the water, demanding relief she couldn't give it.

Suddenly, she was yanked out of the water, gasping and spluttering, coughing violently as water spewed from her mouth and nose. The room spun as she fought for breath, her drenched hair plastered to her face, the icy chill sinking into her bones.

"Who are you working for?" the older officer demanded, his voice cutting through her haze. "Where are the messages going?"

Eileen didn't speak. Instead, she looked him in the eye with a defiance that masked the terror clawing at her insides.

Back into the water she went. This time, a heavy hand pressed her head firmly under the surface, ensuring she couldn't move. Her arms strained uselessly against their grip as her lungs burned. The edges of her vision darkened, and panic threatened to take over. *They won't pull you up. This is it. This is where you die.*

Just as her body began to give in, they dragged her up again, coughing and retching. She tried to protest, but the only sound that escaped her was a choking gasp.

The questions came again, sharp and relentless, but still, she said nothing.

One last time, they thrust her under. This time, she felt the edges of herself slipping away. Her struggling ceased; her body quickly went limp. *This is it,* she thought, her mind unexpectedly calm and clear. *But they won't win. I've held out. I've done what I was trained to do.*

She barely registered being hauled out of the water, the sharp thump of a hand on her back forcing the liquid from her lungs. She spewed water over herself and the men holding her, each breath a painful, rasping gulp of air.

The room blurred around her as she was dropped onto a chair, her body slumped forward, water dripping from her hair and clothes into the growing puddle beneath her. Her ears buzzed, muffling the sound of the officers' voices. They were speaking in German, the words indistinct, but their tone carried frustration.

Through the fog of exhaustion, she realized the truth: they had failed to break her. Her refusal to answer had infuriated them, and for now, they had given up.

Despite the nausea rolling through her and the weakness in her limbs, a small ember of triumph burned in her chest. She had endured. She had remembered her training, and though she had been terrified, she had not let them dominate her. And she had betrayed no one.

Her lips twitched into a faint, bitter smile as she stared at the floor. For now, she had won.

44

MISLEADING THE GESTAPO

The Gestapo men escorted Eileen back to the dingy interrogation room, the same oppressive space where they had begun their questioning hours earlier. She sank onto the rickety chair, her body trembling uncontrollably from the cold and the effects of their maltreatment. Her nose was blocked, her throat raw, but the stifling, hot atmosphere of the interrogation room still managed to invade her senses, mingling with the metallic tang of blood.

Her dress clung to her soaked skin, her hair dripping onto her shoulders in dark, heavy strands. She felt like a bedraggled, wide-eyed cat—cornered but far from defeated. Her nails were still sharp and could scratch viciously.

Though the cold had taken root deep within her, she forced herself to sit upright, her blue eyes fixed on the two men across the table. Her defiance never waned.

The younger officer leaned forward, his elbows wet and glistening on the table's surface. "Have you had a nice bath?" he asked, his voice laced with cruel mockery.

Eileen locked eyes with him, the sting of her cheek a sharp reminder of the blows he had inflicted earlier—the same hand that had nearly drowned her in the water. Hatred swelled in her chest, an animosity more potent than anything she'd ever felt before.

Her voice, though croaky and strained, emerged with deliberation. "Excellent. I will be complaining at the Town Hall about what you have done to me."

Silence filled the room. The younger officer raised an eyebrow, clearly taken aback by her response. He shifted uneasily in his chair, and Eileen caught the flicker of uncertainty in the glance he exchanged with his colleague.

Good. Keep them guessing.

The older officer cleared his throat, his tone shifting to something more measured, more professional. "Tell us more about this businessman," he said. "The one you claim to be working for."

Aha, so this was the tactic now. Eileen felt a flicker of grim satisfaction. They had gained nothing from the *baignoire*, and now they hoped to corner her through the invented employer. But she was ready. The story had been carefully crafted for months; in case she ever needed it. And that moment was now.

She brushed a damp strand of hair out of her eyes, then hesitated deliberately, letting the pause settle as a hook. With a weary sigh to underscore how tiresome her job-seeking struggles had been, she began.

"I was bored at home and wanted to come to Paris to look for work, but when I got here, I couldn't find anything to do. Every day, I went to a café and bought a drink to have while I looked at the vacant jobs in the newspaper."

She let her gaze flick toward the older officer, who didn't meet her eyes, too absorbed in scribbling down her every word in his notebook.

"I was desperate," she continued. "Then one day, I had almost run out of money and was thinking I must go back home. There was a man in the café who kept staring at me."

The younger officer's eyes narrowed. "What man?"

Eileen gave him a look that spoke volumes. *Now, do you want to hear the story or not? If so, stop interrupting me.*

"I didn't know what the man wanted, so I didn't look at him," she said in a level voice. "But then he came to the table and said, 'You are worried? Are you alright?'"

She allowed a tiny, sad smile to ply on her lips, as if fondly remembering that moment of kindness. "I told him I was looking for a job and said I couldn't find one and had no more money. So, he said he might be able to help. He bought me a drink and sat down with me, and we spoke."

The younger officer moved as if to interrupt again, but the older man raised a hand, stopping him. Eileen noted the small power shift, and pressed on, unperturbed.

"He said, 'I am a businessman, and I need help with my business. I won't tell you what it is now, but I will later. I don't like people to talk about my business—it's not good. But I think I can help you.'"

She paused, letting the silence hang just long enough for the Germans to wonder where the story was going.

"He gave me some money to get by and said he would see me in a few days at the café." Eileen's face was the picture of supreme innocence, though every muscle in her body ached from the strain of holding herself together.

Inwardly, she sagged under the weight of keeping her composure, but outwardly, Jacqueline du Tertre remained unshaken, her story as steady as her gaze.

Now the older man interrupted her. "Don't you think it odd, *Mademoiselle*, that a stranger would offer you a job and then give you money before you had done anything for him?"

Eileen allowed a thoughtful pause as though genuinely considering the question. "No. He said he would be back, and I said I would be there. I was desperate, with no money, until he gave me some. So, I went back because I wanted to work for him. There was nothing else I could do." Her reply had just the right amount of naivety, and almost defensively, she added. "And he was nice to me. He was very polite, you see."

The German studied her for a long moment. Before she could gauge his conclusion, he abruptly changed the subject.

"How did you learn to use a wireless set?"

She didn't even blink. Her flawless preparation and mental rehearsals kicked in, ingrained in her for months. Though she'd never thought she'd have to use her fabricated story.

"I worked for the post office at home. They trained me to transmit messages using the wireless and Morse code. It's normal procedure in a French post office."

The Gestapo officer narrowed his eyes. "Normal procedure?" he repeated.

"Yes," she lied with conviction, giving him a look as if the question itself was offensive. "Every post office operator must know how to transmit and receive telegrams. It's part of the job."

He hesitated, then nodded slowly, appearing, if not entirely convinced, at least mollified for the moment.

The younger German, however, was clearly losing patience. His voice sharpened as he leaned toward her. "Do you know about the British spies in the country?" he barked.

Eileen blinked, her features shifting into a puzzled look. "I don't know what you mean," she replied primly.

The man slammed his hand on the table, the sharp sound reverberating through the confined space. Eileen flinched despite herself, the sudden noise catching her off guard. "You are a very stupid girl! That man you were sending messages for—he is a British spy! He used you to save himself!"

Eileen stared at him in disbelief, then shook her head. "No, you are mistaken. He is a French businessman..." she began, then her voice trailed off.

Though her expression remained stunned, she let them believe his words were slowly dawning on her. As if confronted with painful betrayal, she let her gaze drop to her lap, whispering to herself. "*C'est pas possible*. It can't be. It can't be."

Through her eyelashes she could see the Germans exchange a glance. And how their initial exasperation began to change into a smug triumph.

Eileen raised her eyes again to meet theirs. Her voice was soft now, regretful and trembling. "I had no idea. Truly not. If he used me, how would I have known? He said it was business. And I believed him."

Stay close to the truth but always stay one step ahead. The best lies are the ones that almost feel real.

Hadn't Colonel Buckmaster told her she was the best liar of them all? An unspoken and invisible smile spread through her. The victory was hers, not theirs. She'd skirted the truth so closely it wrapped itself around her lies like armor. She, the captive, had her captors exactly where she wanted them. At least for now.

The questioning resumed, the older officer scribbling in his notebook while the younger one paced behind her like an agitated wolf.

"What is your boss's address?" the older one demanded.

Eileen hesitated long enough to suggest discomfort, then gave a shrug. "He said it was 68 *Rue des Capucines*, but I've never been there. He said it was better that way—for business, you see."

The younger officer halted mid-step. "You've never been there?"

"No. We always met in a cafe."

Tapping his pen against the notebook, the other probed. "When's your next meeting with him?"

"Seven o'clock this evening." It came out as smooth as melted butter. She knew they would pounce on her answer, so she added quickly, "At a café opposite *Gare Saint-Lazare*. It's where we always meet."

"Excellent." The older man checked his watch. "Let's see if your story holds up."

Before she could reply, she was yanked out of her chair, the rough hands of the younger officer propelling her toward the door. "We leave now," he barked.

With her clothes still wet and clinging to her skin, Eileen was bundled into a car, flanked on either side by her captors. As they sped toward Gare Saint-Lazare, her mind raced. *They'll realize soon enough no one is coming. What then? How do I get out of this?*

The café was bustling with the evening rush as they arrived, the clatter of dishes and hum of conversation masking the tension that thrummed in Eileen's veins. She was ushered to a small table near the window in view of the station.

"When he arrives," the older officer instructed. "Do not alert him to our presence." He gestured toward a table not far from hers, where he and his colleague would be sitting. "We'll be watching. And listening."

Eileen nodded, feigning indignation as she smoothed her damp dress. "Of course, I won't tell him. He's made a fool of me!" she exclaimed, her voice rising with frustration. Then, as if an afterthought, she added, "But if I'm to sit here, I'll need to buy a drink. I can't just sit without one, but I have no money on me."

The Gestapo frowned but reached into his pocket and handed her a few francs. She took the money with a tight-lipped smile and ordered a cognac, her hands trembling as she picked up the glass. But its warmth and strength did wonders for her bruised body.

As she sipped, she could feel their eyes boring into her back. She forced herself to focus, to maintain her role. *You've outwitted them this far. Keep going.* But the minutes dragged on, and no one arrived. Her carefully constructed story was crumbling with every second that passed.

Suddenly, she stood up. Her chair scraped loudly against the floor, drawing the attention of the officers. The younger one jumped to his feet, reaching her in a few quick strides.

"Where are you going?" he demanded, his voice low and threatening.

"To the lavatory," she said sharply, lifting her chin. "Surely even you don't expect me to sit here forever without relief?"

The officer's jaw tightened. "I'll accompany you."

He followed her closely as she entered the narrow corridor leading to the lavatory. Inside, she locked the door behind her and immediately scanned the small, dingy space for an escape route. The only window was too high and far too small for her to squeeze through. Her heart sank. What now?

She unlocked the door slowly, composing herself as she prepared to step back into the lion's den. Just as she opened it, an air-raid siren wailed, its eerie, rising pitch cutting through the noise of the café. The officer stepped back, startled, and Eileen seized the moment.

"Well, it's too late for him now," she said, her voice laced with irritation as she brushed past him. "He won't come if there's an air raid, you know. The man's a lying coward, anyway."

The officer scowled but said nothing as they ushered her back out the door and she realized they were returning to 10 Rue des Saussaies. For now, the air raid had bought her some time, but she knew she was treading on borrowed ground.

THE GAME WASN'T OVER, but the stakes had just risen.

45

THE VERDICT

Back at Gestapo Headquarters in Rue des Saussaies, Eileen was shoved into an empty office, the door slammed shut behind her. She was left alone with a guard—a young, sharp-featured Frenchman with an air of arrogant indifference. His uniform, the dark blue of the Milice, marked him as a collaborator. He lounged against the wall, his rifle cradled loosely in one hand, smoking a German cigarette with the other as he watched her with idle amusement.

Eileen was ordered to sit on the wooden chair and not move. Her damp dress felt stiff and clammy against her skin. The air was thick with the acrid smell of cigarettes and stale coffee. Her captors had left to verify the address she'd given them—an address as real as the "businessman" she had conjured out of thin air.

The minutes dragged by, stretching into what felt like hours. Eileen's mind churned, while her stomach growled. She'd only had breakfast in the morning and a cognac in the café. She yearned for a cigarette but was too proud to beg the nasty Frenchman, who'd be delighted to refuse her one.

To pass the time she replayed every word she'd said during her interrogation. Had she slipped up? Had they seen through her lies? The time in the *baignoire* was a blur and she didn't exactly remember if she'd said one word there, but she was almost certain she had kept silent.

Stay calm. You've convinced them.

At last, the door opened, and the two Gestapo officers who'd pestered her all day entered.

"The address you gave us doesn't exist." The older man said flatly.

"Well, that proves it then," she retorted with conviction. "He must be an agent. Why else would he give me a false address? Why would I give you a fake address that you could prove doesn't exist?"

The younger officer's lips twisted into a scowl, ready to bite back but the older man shook his head, as if weary of her relentless defiance. "We are going to give you the benefit of the doubt."

Hope sprang up in Eileen's chest as the beginnings of a smile spread across her face. But his next words cut through her like a knife.

"We're sending you to a concentration camp," he said coldly. "You'll have a good laugh there. Yes, it won't be like here—it will be your punishment for having worked against us."

The smirks on their faces were wide and cruel as they watched her reaction. The Frenchman joined in their glee. Eileen's stomach churned, and her sense of triumph was pulverized into a handful of dust and blown away on an angry gust of wind within seconds.

A concentration camp. *This is it. The end.* The bravado she'd carefully constructed throughout her ordeal began to waver under the realization of this verdict. What good had it all done? She had fooled her captors, misled them at every turn—but she was still their prisoner. Her work as a wireless operator was over, and her fate now lay far beyond her control.

A new, deeper dread took hold of her. Would she ever see her sister again? The thought pierced her heart like a blade. She could picture Jacqueline's face contorted in anguish when she learned of her capture, the guilt and grief Jacqueline would carry. It was unbearable to imagine.

If only I hadn't sent that message from Bourg-la-Reine. If only I had gone straight to the new house in Le Vésinet.

But regret, she knew, was useless now. There was one small solace, faint but undeniable: she had betrayed no one. Not Alcide, not Armand, not Arnaud, not Blaise. She had said nothing of Louise or her sweet family. She'd done all that had been in her power to keep them safe.

Her lips pressed into a thin line, her chin lifting slightly. Inside, she was a storm of fear and despair, but outwardly, she was composed, defiant.

The older officer barked to the guard. "Take her away. To Fresnes prison."

Eileen stood, her legs trembling beneath her, but she forced her legs to obey, her head high as she was led from the room, one last deadly gaze at her torturers.

The car rattled through the streets of Paris, the silence inside broken only by the occasional muttered exchange between her guards and the hum of the engine. Eileen sat stiffly in the back seat, her eternally damp dress clinging to her skin as she gazed out of the window. Every familiar sight of the city felt like a knife to her chest, a sharp reminder of all she might never see again.

As they sped along Rue du Faubourg Saint-Honoré, her heart clenched. She had walked this street so many times, the energy of her important work pressing her on. Now, it felt like someone else's city—distant, unreachable, slipping away.

The car turned right onto Rue Royale, and Eileen twisted in her seat, straining to look back. In the opposite direction, she caught a fleeting glimpse of the magnificent Church of the Madeleine. Its neoclassical columns stood stoic against the evening light, a beacon of Heaven in a world that felt increasingly like hell.

The car jolted as it turned onto the Place de la Concorde. Eileen's eyes darted to the grand fountains and the towering obelisk at the square's center, bathed in the warm hues of the setting sun. She swallowed hard, fighting the urge to cry. *Is this the last time I will see it?*

They crossed the bridge over the Seine, the river glinting in the fading light, and merged onto Boulevard Saint-Germain. As the car passed close to Louise's apartment, Eileen forced her eyes away, focusing instead on the street ahead. *Don't look. Don't give them any reason to suspect you know someone here.* Memories of walking by that building, knowing that the people inside cared for her, tightened her chest like a vice.

The car forked right, heading south along Boulevard Raspail. The streets began to blur as despair wrapped itself around her, heavy and suffocating. She had lied, deceived, and endured the horrors of interrogation, but what good had it done? Fresnes awaited her now—a gateway to the concentration camps where survival was, at best, a faint hope.

A wave of misery swept over her, and for a moment, she allowed herself to sink into the depths of her predicament. *This is it. There is nothing left for me.*

But as the despair threatened to consume her, Eileen clasped her hands tightly in her lap and began to pray silently. The words came in a rush, tumbling through her mind, pleading with God for strength. Strength to endure, to resist, to fight. The prayers calmed her trembling hands and steadied her breathing, and with each repetition, she felt a small ember of hope begin to flicker deep within her.

As they approached Fresnes, the prison walls looming like a

dark shadow on the horizon, Eileen lifted her chin slightly. If she was to survive—if she was to overcome this—she had to remain optimistic. She couldn't afford to succumb to despair.

Plan. Focus. Escape.

Her mind turned to the task ahead, mapping out the possibilities. Every locked door had a weakness, every guard had a blind spot. She would find them. She had to.

As the car pulled to a stop in front of the imposing gates of Fresnes, Eileen clenched her fists, her resolve hardening. The guards hauled her out of the car, but she didn't flinch. Instead, she stepped forward, her gaze steady.

This isn't the end. Not yet.

PART XIII

~MIA~ TORQUAY, SEPTEMBER 2007

46

BACK IN THE NOW

2 Lisburne Crescent, Torquay, September 2007

Mia focused on the quiet ticking of the clock on the wall, its steady rhythm like a metronome to Eileen's heartbeat. She slipped back into her own armchair noiselessly, observing her client with the calm intensity of a watchful guardian.

Eileen sat trancelike, her breathing steady and even. The faint flicker of movement beneath her eyelids signaled a meditative state, her body at ease despite the weight of the memories she had just revisited.

Eileen had relived her arrest, her desperate playacting, and the guilt that had haunted her over that fateful last transmission. But something had shifted—was it the small, almost translucent smile on the old lady's face, a certain contentment around the always-pressed lips?

Mia watched closely as subtle changes swept over Eileen's face. The small muscles around her scalp and cheeks softened, the harsh lines of tension smoothing into tranquility. A delicate pink flush returned to her cheeks, and a faint curl of her lips suggested the shadow of a smile.

Feel it, Aunt Didi, Mia thought, her heart swelling with quiet pride for the resilient woman before her. *Feel that you were triumphant in your own way. You betrayed no one. You endured the terrors of torture without breaking. You didn't need your L-pill. Your prospects were grim, but you fared better than most captured agents. You misled the Gestapo enough to escape prolonged torture, and in doing so, you preserved the SPRITUALIST network. The work could continue because you made yourself the only sacrifice.*

Time moved fluidly as Eileen rested in her armchair, her rosary beads slipping rhythmically through her fingers, the soft purring of Whiskey at her feet blending into the ticking clock.

Mia marked the moment Eileen's eyelids fluttered, the trance loosening its hold. Her voice was soft but deliberate as she spoke. "Miss Nearne—Aunt Didi—how are you feeling?"

Eileen's brow furrowed slightly, the question drawing her back to the present. She didn't open her eyes immediately, her fingers continuing to roll over the rosary beads, as though anchoring herself in the here and now. Finally, she looked up, her blue eyes meeting Mia's.

Mia caught her breath. The eyes that had once seemed perpetually troubled were now clear, their blue brilliance undiminished by the years. They held strength, defiance, and a vivid spark that spoke of the indomitable spirit of Eileen Nearne.

In that moment, Mia saw not just her client, but the woman who had faced down the Gestapo and emerged triumphant in her own way.

"This time..." Eileen paused, searching for the right words. "It felt different."

Mia tilted her head, encouraging her to continue.

"I've told the story of my arrest so many times," Eileen said thoughtfully. "First, during the debriefing after the war. Then to doctors in various institutions over the following ten years. To journalists, biographers, historians, over the decades." She waved a hand, dismissing them all as if they were no more than ghosts. "The story had worn thin, become jaded. I was so done with it. But this time..." Her voice trailed off.

"This time?" Mia prompted.

"This time, I was there," Eileen said in a quiet voice. "Really there. I could feel it all again—the dingy interrogation room, the sting of that German's slap, the icy water from the *baignoire*. The rushing through Paris in that black car, my wet dress clinging to me. It was light-blue dress with a small belt." She hesitated again. "But at the same time..." She searched for the right words, her hands fluttering in the air.

"It was like I wasn't entirely there. It was like I was watching myself from above, outside of it all. I saw myself in that room, enduring it, but there was a sense of..."

"Protection?" Mia offered softly.

"*Ah oui, c'est ça. Protection*," Eileen replied in French. "Like I was being held, looked after, as if God Himself was shielding me."

Mia nodded. The EMDR techniques she had quietly employed during Eileen's storytelling seemed to have allowed her a level of detachment—a way to process without being consumed.

"And how do you feel now?" Mia asked.

Eileen took a deep breath. "Suffocated," she admitted. "I'd like some fresh air. I think I need it."

Mia rose, smoothing her skirt. "Let's go for a walk then," she said. "Fancy a stroll on the beach? It's sunny and warm, even for September."

Eileen's face softened into a smile, the first real smile since she had begun her tale that afternoon. For a moment, Mia glimpsed the vivacious girl Didi must have once been—dreamy but spirited, enjoying a family outing to the beach in Boulogne-sur-Mer, crayons and sketchbook in hand, a white hat perched on her dark curls, and another cat named Whiskey trailing behind.

"Yes, the sea air always does wonders," Eileen said, rising stiffly from the chair she'd been sitting in for far too long. Suddenly, she eyed Mia with amusement. "But, dear, how are you going to walk the beach on those stilts?" She pointed to Mia's four-inch designer heels, her grin widening.

Mia wasn't without spirit herself. With one quick, fluid movement, she slipped off the heels and quipped, "Like this, Aunt Didi—bare toes in the sand. I prescribe the same treatment for your dainty feet."

Eileen roared with laughter, the sound rich and unrestrained, filling the small flat. "You'd be surprised, girl, what this old aunt is capable of! We'll be the dotty duo of Torquay, if you'll have me."

Mia giggled, slipping the shoes into her bag, and offered her new aunt an arm as they stepped out into the balmy afternoon air.

The hum of traffic on Lisburne Crescent gave way to the soothing rhythm of waves in the distance. The warmth of the September sun brushed against their faces, and the salty tang of the sea filled the air.

As they walked side by side toward the shore, Mia couldn't help but notice the way Eileen's posture seemed to relax, her expression softening with each step. A lightness settled over her, as if the weight of the past had momentarily lifted.

Mia smiled inwardly, silently thanking God for EMDR. It didn't always work, and she'd been nervous—Eileen's trauma was so deeply rooted, so intricately layered after years of failed treatments. But today, it had worked.

. . .

"WOULD you care for a cup of tea at Pier Point to admire the view, Aunt Didi?" Mia asked as she noticed Eileen breathing more heavily beside her. Trudging through the sand had clearly taken its toll on the eighty-six-year-old.

"Why not? But I was more thinking of a sherry," Eileen said with a playful wink.

"A sherry for you, and a tea for me," Mia agreed. "I still have work to do tonight."

"Do you never stop working, Mia? Are you truly all work and no fun at... what are you—25?" Eileen shook her head, her voice carrying a teasing lilt.

"Twenty-six, actually." Mia replied. "But think of what you'd already lived through at my age, Aunt Didi. You'd escaped from France, worked as an operator at Bingham's unit, been a secret agent in France, arrested, tortured and survived concentration camps. You really didn't have much of a youth, did you?"

Eileen's smile faded, replaced by a reflective calm. "I had no choice, my dear. Those were different times. If I were young now, I'd enjoy peacetime and have fun." A wistful edge crept into her voice. "I've always wanted to have fun, you see. Just fun."

She fell silent and her gaze wandered to the horizon, following the seagulls that swooped low over the water before soaring back into the sky. The rhythmic crash of waves against the pier's pillars seemed to echo a timeless refrain, a reminder of life's enduring cycles.

"I like my job," Mia said, though Eileen's words stirred something deeper. "But it's true—I do tend to bury myself in it. There's always so much to do that I don't want to leave for the next day. I suppose I should take a day off now and then, but... yeah, I guess you could call me a workaholic."

Eileen studied her with those clear blue eyes, their depth sharper than Mia sometimes expected. "Tell me, dear," she said suddenly, setting her sherry glass down with a deliberate clink. "What do you know about Sebastian Stone?"

Mia was startled. "Sebastian Stone? Not much. Why do you ask?" She tried to keep her tone neutral, but curiosity—and a touch of unease—crept into her voice. Where was Eileen steering the conversation now? Did she have some trick up her sleeve? Had someone seen her dining with him at No. 7 and reported back to Eileen? It seemed unlikely, but in Torquay, people knew both her and Sebastian. Could Sister Damian have mentioned something?

Eileen waved a dismissive hand, scattering Mia's racing thoughts. "Well, I'll admit, I've always avoided reading that Torbay Weekly nonsense he writes. Stone's Throw, by the way—I find the name of that column rather cheeky. And it's all gossip and fluff, really. Celebrity divorces, who wore what. Utter rubbish." She paused, giving Mia a sly glance. "But when I read the paper this morning, I must say, I was pleasantly surprised. Seems the man's branching out."

Mia raised an eyebrow. "Branching out? Into what?"

"Serious topics," Eileen replied, leaning toward her in a conspiratorial way. "He's written a whole article about Torbay war veterans, who've come home from Afghanistan and found real help at Hope Haven Community Health. Your center."

Mia blinked, caught off guard. "Hope Haven? Sebastian wrote about my center?"

"Oh yes, and not just a blurb in his gossip column," Eileen said. "It was a full middle-page article. Apparently, his father was a war veteran with PTSD as well, but for him, help came too late. He took his own life." She shook her head sadly. "Must have been horrible for the Stone family. But he wasn't asking for pity. He was quite candid, talking about the importance of timely treatment for the military men and women who come back from war zones."

Mia listened intently, feeling shocked and surprised. Why hadn't

Sebastian mentioned the article when they met? Or told her about his father? The weight of this new information about his family added an another layer to her slowly evolving understanding of him. No wonder he'd been so downcast having freshly relived his loss to write the article—on top of the news that this Cindy was taking his son to America.

"I haven't seen today's paper," Mia admitted, still processing what she'd heard. "I left the center early this morning. Otherwise... I'm sure my colleagues would have mentioned it."

She fished her BlackBerry from her bag and tapped through her messages. Almost immediately, an email from Alexandra popped up, forwarding the article.

"Yes, my colleague sent me a copy." Mia held up the screen briefly before tucking the device back into her bag. "I'll read it later."

Eileen's eyes lingered on Mia as if reading her thoughts.

"Anyway, you seem to have taken quite an interest in our local reporter," Mia said, trying to pinpoint Eileen's reason for bringing him up.

The mischievous twinkle in Eileen's eye deepened. "Not quite *in* him, dear," she replied smoothly. "But it reminded me of something Sister Damian once mentioned about his mother, Mrs. Stone. I've seen her at church regularly, but I've never spoken with her. When I read the article, it all came back to me—Sister Damian said the family is part of one of her charity projects."

"Charity?" Mia asked, intrigued.

"I had no idea before, but apparently, the family's had a rough time. No breadwinner, and living off a war pension—well, I can tell you from experience, that doesn't add up to much. And Sister Damian mentioned an invalid daughter, so that must be your Mr. Stone's sister."

"He's not *my* Mr. Stone! Nowhere near," Mia protested, though she frowned thoughtfully. "I hadn't realized..."

"Well, now you do. And since we're on the topic, next time you meet him, just look past his bravado. Men haven't changed much over the years, my dear. They still put up a brave front when they're jelly inside." Eileen finished her sherry in one bold gulp and dabbed her mouth with her serviette, her expression as calm as a general surveying a battlefield.

"Now, take me home, dear. It's time for me to warm some of that soup you brought and turn in early. I need to sleep off all this talking."

Mia signaled to the waiter, but when she attempted to pay, Eileen wouldn't hear of it.

"The treat's on me, Doctor Mia," Eileen declared, pressing a ten-pound note into the startled waiter's hand.

"It's too much, Madam," the young man stammered.

"Then do something sensible with it, young man." Eileen gave him a firm nod of approval.

Arm-in-arm, they returned to Lisburne Crescent, walking slowly as the evening light faded and the gentle hum of nighttime settled over Torquay.

At the door, Eileen paused, turning to let Mia kiss her cheek.

"I suppose you'll be back for the story of my time in Fresnes and beyond, soon?" she asked, her voice carrying a faint sigh.

"Only if you want, Aunt Didi. I'd never push you."

Eileen's blue eyes locked on Mia's with a quiet intensity. "I don't think this is about wanting, my dear. It's about common sense. You're helping me prepare for my final years on this earth with a calmer conscience. And that's something God has wanted for me for a long time."

"So... the answer is yes?" Mia gave her another kiss.

Eileen's lips curled into a mischievous smile. "See you soon, *chérie*. And don't do anything I wouldn't do."

Mia laughed. “That leaves plenty of room for mischief, Aunt Didi.”

As Eileen opened the door, she turned back, her voice light with humor. “You do nothing out of the ordinary, but don’t worry—your old aunt will help you loosen up in time.”

Her soft giggle as she disappeared inside was music to Mia’s ears, leaving her smiling as she walked away into the night.

PART XIV

~EILEEN~ FRANCE/GERMANY JULY 1944 –
APRIL 1945

47

FREEDOM STOLEN

France, 15 August 1944

It had been three weeks. Weeks of waiting and not knowing. Eileen paced the cramped confines of her cell in Fresnes prison, her ears straining for anything that might hint at what lay ahead, any sound at all. A familiar voice, perhaps—one of her fellow agents—or, God willing, the Allies coming to liberate her. Or worse, the Gestapo carrying out their threat to send her east, to the camps.

Her thoughts swung wildly, hope rising one moment, only to crash into despair the next. Hunger gnawed at her constantly. She was filthy, bone-tired, yet still vigilant. Still defiant. Still eager to escape.

Every creak of a door in the corridor, every barked command outside, she noted. Could it be Armand and her comrades coming to rescue her? After all, she'd handed him London's coded request to raid Fresnes prison. But much as he'd wanted to carry out the order, even SPIRITUALIST's dare-devilish organiser had been doubtful.

"It's a fortress, to say the least, Rose. It's sheer suicide the Firm is asking of us. The place would need to be bombed from above before we could storm it. Allied planes would have to join the attack—and with that comes the risk of even more casualties among our ranks."

But still, if Armand knew she had been captured, maybe he'd reconsider?

Sleep came in fits and starts on the straw-stuffed mattress. The food—if it could even be called that—was barely enough to sustain her: a crust of bread, watery soup, weak coffee. Only the occasional cigarette offered her a fleeting sense of solace.

No one had come to question her again. Days blurred into each other, heavy with silence and solitude. She tried not to think about what London must think of her now—her capture was surely reported by now—or to dwell too long on her family and friends. But the dark nights were another matter. They gripped her like icy hands, cold and suffocating, dragging her into a gloom she could barely resist.

It's a good thing I've always been a bit of a loner, she told herself more than once. *Or I wouldn't be able to bear this isolation.*

To keep despair at bay, she filled her mind with activity: painting vivid images in her head, praying for hours, even composing imaginary coded messages to London. And she paced. Endlessly.

Her once-smart light-blue summer dress was torn and filthy, its hem trailing like a rag. She glanced down at it with disgust.

"If I survive this," she muttered hoarsely, her voice cracking from disuse, "I'll never wear a light-blue dress again."

Whispers of the outside reached her even through the closed gates and high walls of Fresnes. The Allies were close—very close. She could hear the rumble of artillery in the distance and the low roar of planes overhead. But it wasn't only the sounds of war that hinted at change. It was the guards—their furtive glances, their clipped whispers. The tension among them was palpable. The liberators were advancing; the Resistance was growing stronger by the day.

Even the failed assassination attempt on Hitler, news of which had seeped through the prison walls, gave Eileen a sliver of hope that the war's end was near.

But then, there were the gunshots.

They echoed through the prison grounds, each sharp crack splintering her fragile hope. Prisoners—her fellow *résistants*—were being executed almost hourly. Every shot was a grim reminder of the stakes, a warning of how close death truly was.

Eileen sat on the edge of the narrow cot in her cell, her fingers brushing the coarse, threadbare rag that served as a blanket. It was itchy and torn, but focusing on its texture kept her from falling apart. She closed her eyes, whispering the Lord's Prayer silently to herself, clinging to its words as a lifeline.

"*Notre Père, qui es aux cieux...*"

A loud clang jolted her from her prayer. Heavy boots stomped down the corridor, each step accompanied by the bark of German orders.

Her breath caught in her throat, ears pricked up. *What's happening now? Is it my turn to be shot?*

"*Aufstehen!* Get up!"

The cell door rattled open, and two guards filled the frame, their dark uniforms blending into the dim corridor. One gestured sharply with his rifle. "You. Out!"

With her heart pounding in her throat, Eileen obeyed, feeling naked in her vulnerability. All she had was the dress on her back—dirty, torn, and clinging to her skin. *Well, it's all I'll need,* she thought grimly. *To face the firing squad. My dignity and my God.*

She stepped into the corridor, blinking in the dim light. Around her, other prisoners—men and women alike—were being herded from their cells. Their faces were pale, their expressions blank, their eyes hollow.

"Where are they taking us?" she whispered to the woman beside her, red-haired with sunken cheeks and a nervous tremor in her hands.

"I don't know," the woman replied, her voice trembling. "I heard someone say it's a transport. To where—no one knows."

A transport. Eileen's stomach dropped. *The camps.*

Would that be better or worse than a firing squad? Perhaps worse. The thought made her chest tighten, but she forced herself to keep moving. The guards' rifles were raised, their shouts echoing down the corridor. There was no room for hesitation.

The prisoners were marched in single file to the courtyard, where a line of buses waited in the pre-dawn gloom. The air was damp with dew, though it promised to turn into a warm summer's day. The streets, silent before curfew was lifted, were eerily still. A thin mist blurred the outlines of buildings, softening the edges of reality and making everything feel strangely dreamlike.

Eileen climbed onto one of the buses, like most of the prisoners, with nothing but the clothes on her back. As long as nobody discovered her true British nationality—and there was nothing now that could demonstrate that—she believed she might have a chance of survival. This conviction wasn't based on logic—just pure instinct. But Eileen trusted her instincts.

The metal railings inside the bus were cold under her hands, and the space was packed too tightly with bodies. She slid onto a wooden bench near the back, squeezed between two other women whose shoulders pressed against hers.

The bus jerked forward, rattling and swaying as it sped through the streets. Eileen craned her neck to see out of the grime-streaked windows, desperate to understand where they were being taken.

Through the dirty glass, she caught fleeting glimpses of familiar

Parisian streets. The Rue du Faubourg Saint-Honoré. The Place de la Concorde. The grand boulevards and historic buildings she had once walked with a quick step, having work to do. Now, they seemed to mock her captivity, their beauty a cruel contrast to the harsh reality of the bus and its unknown, yet certainly horrible, destination.

The convoy continued north, past the heart of the city, away from the Allied forces that were closing in from the west and south. The distance from freedom was growing, and with it, the knot in Eileen's stomach tightened.

"Where do you think they're taking us?" whispered the woman beside her—a middle-aged woman with a long, thin face. She wore a hat with a feather and a black winter coat with a fur collar, though it was summer. How she wished she had that coat herself!

Eileen murmured back, "Nowhere good, that's for sure." Her gaze shifted to the armed guards at the front of the bus—Germans with sleek mustaches and cold, hostile faces.

The bus jerked to a halt at the Gare Église de Pantin. Just as Eileen had feared. This was where the trains bound for the east departed, heading toward Strasbourg and Mulhouse.

Shouted orders filled the air as the prisoners were herded off the buses. The first rays of sunlight broke over the railway station, their golden glow falling on a line of cattle cars waiting on the tracks.

Eileen's breath hitched. The sight of those cars—dark, foreboding, with their small, barred windows—confirmed her worst fears.

She glanced at the guards, their rifles slung casually over their shoulders. Their faces were impassive, their eyes like stone.

"*Die Züge sind abfahrbereit!* The trains are ready to depart!" one of them barked, his voice cutting through the early morning air.

Eileen drew a shaky breath and whispered to herself, "*Seigneur, donnez-moi la force...* Lord, give me strength."

Shuffling one foot at the time in the slow-moving line, Eileen's eyes darted over the platform. The inside of the station resonated with panicked voices and the clatter of boots on stone. As they passed a group of well-dressed men standing near the edge of the platform, Eileen frowned. These were no ordinary German officers. Their tailored suits and polished shoes set them apart from the guards who barked orders and swung rifles.

"What's this about?" she whispered to the woman in the black coat beside her.

The woman leaned close, her voice low. "Someone said that's the Swedish consul… and the president of the French Red Cross."

"Why would they be here to wave us off?" She remarked, sarcasm getting the better of her. The dignitaries stood stiffly, their faces blank, taking in the proceedings as though this were an orderly evacuation instead of what it so obviously was. If their presence was meant to reassure the prisoners and give them a false sense of security all was well, Eileen wasn't fooled.

Her eyes flicked to the line of cattle cars ahead. Dark, hulking shapes on the tracks, their barred windows hinting at the misery awaiting inside. This spectacle—the polished men, the whispered reassurances—didn't align with the grim reality of what she was seeing. She tightened her jaw. Whatever story they were trying to sell, she wasn't buying it.

Her turn came. A guard gestured sharply with his rifle, motioning her toward one of the freight wagons. With head held high, she ignored his barked commands to hurry on and climbed inside.

There were no seats, just bare wooden floors already crowded with people. Most clung to their small bundles of belongings, pressing them close as though the possessions might shield them from whatever lay ahead. Eileen had nothing but the clothes on her back, not even her false French papers to prove who she was or wasn't. The lack of belongings allowed her one advantage—she could shuffle around without worrying about leaving anything unattended.

She found a small space near the wall and sank down, tucking her knees to her chest. Others jostled to stand near the small, barred openings at the top of the wagon, desperate for air.

"Do you think we're going to Germany?" A thin and anxious voice next to her asked.

"Surely not," another replied. "There are no lavatories on board. It should be a short trip, but heaven knows where to."

The murmurs ebbed and flowed, hope and doubt battling for control. Eileen kept silent, her gaze fixed on the tiny sliver of daylight visible through the window.

By mid-morning, the train still hadn't moved. The heat inside the wagon was becoming unbearable. The sun blazed down, turning the steel exterior into an oven. People shifted uncomfortably, their faces flushed and shining with sweat. Pleas for water rose from the crowd, but the guards outside ignored them, as they smoked and chatted and drank their coffee or Schnapps.

Eileen stood and maneuvered her way toward the small opening, managing to gulp in a few breaths of fresh air. Her heart ached at the sight beyond: the platform now empty of dignitaries, the bustling station quieting as the day dragged on. The contrast between the bright sky and the stifling darkness inside the wagon was almost too much to bear.

By evening, tempers were fraying. The oppressive heat, the cramped conditions, and the gnawing hunger were pushing people to their limits. Eileen pressed her back against the wall, closing her eyes as she tried to block out the rising voices and the low, broken sobs that punctuated the air.

"Ready for departure," Eileen whispered grimly to herself, "sure. The lies come so easily to them!"

Just before midnight, a jolt ran through the wagon as the train finally began to move. The wheels screeched against the tracks, the motion throwing some of the standing prisoners off balance.

Eileen opened her eyes, staring into the dim, sweltering space around her. She didn't need to see the faces of the others to know what they felt. The fear. The despair.

She whispered another prayer under her breath, clutching at the faint hope that she might survive whatever came next.

48

FREEDOM SO CLOSE

As the train pulled out of Pantin Station just before midnight, Eileen pressed herself into the small space she had managed to claim near the train car wall. For over eighteen hours, she and her fellow prisoners had been crammed into the sweltering freight cars without food, water, or any semblance of sanitation. The stench of sweat, urine, and despair drowned out all the air.

The night had brought a small reprieve from the searing heat of the day, but the wagon was still suffocating. In the oppressive darkness, the only sounds were the rhythmic clank of the train wheels on the tracks. The sound translated to only one thing for Eileen.

Escape. Escape. Escape.

Her body ached, her throat burned with thirst, but she refused to succumb to despair. *As soon as the opportunity presents itself...* She clung to the thought like a lifeline, her gaze darting toward the small, barred window high on the wall.

The train continued its relentless journey through the night, its steel frame groaning with the weight of its human cargo. Some prisoners slumped against each other in a stupor of exhaustion and dehydration, while others, like Eileen, sat upright, their minds focused only on survival.

As dawn broke, a dull glow filled the solitary window, revealing the haggard faces around her. The temperature began to climb again, and with it came renewed suffering. People groaned and shifted uncomfortably, their clothes sticking to their sweat-soaked bodies.

Then, amidst the clanking of wheels and the hissing of steam, the train shuddered and came to a sudden halt. The jolt sent a ripple of unease through the wagon.

"What's happening?" someone whispered hoarsely.

Eileen strained to listen as the sound of guards shouting orders outside reached her ears. Moments later, the heavy doors of the wagon were dragged open, letting in a blinding flood of sunlight.

"*Raus! Alle raus!*" The command came harshly, and the guards gestured sharply with their rifles. "Everyone out!"

Eileen stumbled to her feet, her legs stiff and unsteady from hours of sitting. She joined the tide of prisoners spilling out onto the dusty ground, the sunlight searing her eyes after so long in darkness.

The scene that greeted them was one of chaos. The train had stopped at a rural station—Lagny, she overheard someone whisper—just 35 miles from Paris. The reason for the halt became clear as whispers spread: the Resistance had blown up part of the rail line ahead. The tracks were mangled and impassable.

The prisoners stood in stunned silence, many too dazed and dehydrated to comprehend what was happening. Some older men and women collapsed onto the ground, their bodies unable to endure the ordeal any longer.

Eileen's mind, however, held a single, all-consuming thought: *This may be my chance.*

Beyond the platform at Lagny, Eileen's eyes fixed on a patch of open field bordered by a thin line of trees. The trees looked impossibly far, but to her, they were a promise—a barrier that might shield her from the nightmare she was living. She flexed her stiff legs, feeling the ache from hours crammed into the train's suffocating confines.

I can make it, she told herself. *I have to try.*

The guards were distracted, still shouting orders and herding other prisoners off the train. It wasn't a perfect opportunity, but it was the only one she could see. Her pulse thundered in her ears as she glanced around, gauging the distance and the guards' positions.

Without another thought, she launched herself forward, her feet pounding the hard earth as she sprinted toward the trees. Gasps and murmurs followed her, and she caught a glimpse of wide-eyed women staring after her, frozen in horror.

The wind rushed past her face, and for a fleeting moment, she felt a spark of exhilaration. Freedom was just a few dozen meters away. If she could reach the treeline, she might have a chance to disappear into the dense foliage.

Then came the shout.

"*Halt!*"

Eileen's heart sank, but she didn't stop. She pushed herself harder, her legs burning with effort.

The guard's voice came again, louder this time, harsh and edged with fury. "Stop, or I will shoot!"

The threat was real. She heard the unmistakable click of a rifle being cocked.

For one agonizing moment, Eileen considered pushing on. *If I can just make it...* But reason overrode instinct. Her legs could never outrun a bullet.

She stopped abruptly, skidding slightly on the dusty ground. Her chest heaved with the effort, her heart hammering against her ribs.

The guard was on her in seconds. His hand clamped down on her arm like the coil of a snake. He yanked her roughly, nearly knocking her off balance.

"You thought you could escape?" he snarled in German, his face twisted with rage. His grip tightened as he dragged her back toward the platform, his rifle swinging dangerously close to her side.

Eileen didn't respond. Her lips pressed into a thin line as she forced herself to meet his gaze with defiance.

When they reached the small group of frightened women, the guard thrust her forward, causing her to stumble.

"If any of you try this again," he shouted, "you'll be shot without warning!"

The women flinched, their eyes darting between Eileen and the guard.

Eileen straightened, her limbs trembling from the exertion and adrenaline. She had failed this time, but she didn't regret trying.

For a brief moment, she'd felt hope. Real hope. The thought of freedom, even fleeting, was worth the risk.

She glanced at the other women, their faces pale and drawn, and held her chin high.

"Not today," she whispered to herself. "But one day, I'll get out of this. I'll get out."

The journey resumed, but now as a march on foot--a ragged procession of prisoners shuffling along the dirt road that ran parallel to the ruined tracks. The morning sun rose higher, its heat pressing down on them as if mocking their suffering. The guards kept barking orders to keep moving, occasionally shoving a straggler back into line.

Eileen stumbled over a loose stone, her legs stiff and trembling from fatigue. She barely noticed her own discomfort, so focused was she on the desperate faces around her. The frail elderly, the gaunt young, mothers clutching children—each step seemed to sap more of their dwindling strength.

Then, unexpectedly, a figure appeared at the edge of the fields. A farmer, sun-weathered and dressed in simple overalls, stood watching them. He held a bottle of water, which he raised in offering.

The guards shouted, waving him off, but more farmers emerged, stepping closer despite the danger. A woman handed a jug to one of the prisoners at the edge of the group. Others tossed water bottles and passed cups of milk into the crowd, their eyes full of pity and defiance.

Eileen caught a bottle hurled in her direction. The cool glass felt miraculous in her hands. She unscrewed the cap and drank deeply, the water reviving her parched throat. She passed it to the woman beside her, who nodded in silent thanks.

The guards shouted again, this time firing warning shots into the air, scattering the farmers. The prisoners were hurried along, and Eileen glanced back to see one farmer standing resolute, his eyes blazing with indignation.

By midday, the group reached a part of the track that was still intact. A new train, its boxy silhouette looming dark against the horizon, waited for them. The guards wasted no time, prodding and shouting as they herded the prisoners into the freight cars with rougher hands than before.

Eileen climbed aboard, the crowded interior swallowing her whole. The stench of sweat and fear from the previous occupants lingered, and the heat inside was suffocating. She wedged herself into a corner, her back against the wooden wall, and hugged her knees to her chest.

A guard's voice echoed down the platform. "*Achtung*! Listen carefully!" He strode past the cars, his rifle slapping against the side of the wagons. “If anyone attempts to escape, not only will they be shot, but everyone in their wagon will be executed as well!”

Eileen froze. Around her, heads turned, eyes narrowing in her direction. The memory of her earlier attempt fresh in their minds.

“Don’t,” someone hissed. “Don’t try it again. Please.”

Eileen nodded, her throat tightening. She could feel the unspoken fear radiating from the others. She could face her own death, but to risk theirs? That she couldn’t bear.

Leaning her head back against the wall, she closed her eyes, swallowing the bitter frustration that surged within her. For now, she would have to abandon her plan.

But deep inside, the determination to escape still burned. It wasn’t a question of if—only when.

49

RAVENSBRÜCK

A few days later - Fürstenberg, Germany, 20 August 1944

As the train shuddered to a halt, Eileen leaned against the splintered wooden wall of the wagon, exhausted but alert. The doors screeched open, and sunlight poured in, blinding the prisoners as they stumbled out onto the platform. The air was sharp and cool, carrying the distinct scent of pine. It was almost September.

Eileen squinted at the scene before her. So, this was Germany? The country of the hated Huns? All she saw was the outskirts of a picturesque village, its name displayed on a sign: Fürstenberg. Elegant white villas sprawled amidst lush gardens that stretched to the edge of a tranquil lake. The pine trees around the lake mirrored in the still, deep waters. A trout leapt, its silver body gleaming in the sunlight.

"Lake *Schwedtsee*," someone whispered.

The scenery looked like a postcard, incongruously peaceful. Surely not the country of the monstrous Third Reich. Or was it a harsh mockery?

Eileen's gaze darted to the thick forest. *I could escape into that foliage with the ease of a child.* The trees seemed to beckon her, their green crowns reaching upward, serene and silent. She filed the thought away for now, glancing at the anxious, exhausted women around her. *Not now, but soon.* She tucked the idea into the corner of her mind where her constant escape plans simmered—quiet and persistent, like a pot of stew left to warm on the stove.

But the postcard-perfect scene transformed into a cruel memory as they reached the gates of Ravensbrück concentration camp. The clear blues, pristine whites, and deep greens of the idyllic landscape seemed to evaporate, replaced by a murky palette of gray, black, and brown. The camp loomed as a dark, suffocating colossus, swallowing the vivid colors that had momentarily dazzled Eileen's eyes.

The tall walls rose before them, at least five meters high, topped with electrified, barbed wire. As they passed through the gates, the acrid scent of smoke filled the air, catching in Eileen's throat. No trace of the pine's heavenly fragrance remained; the stench overpowered everything.

Where does it come from? she wondered, her gaze drawn to a narrow passage at the far end of the camp. A stone building stood there, its chimney releasing thick, greasy smoke that hung over the camp like a curse.

They were herded onto an open square that stretched out ahead of them. Rows of women in filthy, threadbare clothes were already there--stock-still, faces hollow and resigned. A guard shouted, the crack of a whip split the air, and a body fell to the ground, motionless in the dust.

"The *Appelplatz,*" someone whispered. "We'll get our share of that too."

Eileen tore her eyes from the grim spectacle, her stomach churning, and glanced to the left. Behind a barrier of barbed wire stood the SS dining hall. Through the windows, Eileen saw male and female guards comfortably sat at neatly-set tables, laughing and talking as if they were at a countryside inn. Gaunt prisoners, their faces pale and frightened, moved between them, carrying trays of food.

The stark contrast between the brutality of the Appelplatz and the casual indulgence of the dining hall felt like a disgusting trick of her mind. *Who could dine here with a view of the Appelplatz?*

Eileen's fists clenched in the pockets of her torn dress. The guards' smug faces imprinted themselves in her memory, a searing reminder of the madness of this place.

They were marched onto the Lagerstrasse, the camp's central road flanked by long wooden barracks. The rhythmic thudding of boots on dirt mixed with the occasional barked order. The prisoners' shuffling steps were punctuated by the clinking of chains and the groans of those too weak to walk properly.

Eileen was pointed toward a barrack at the far end of the Lagerstrasse. She stepped inside, and the stench of unwashed bodies, damp wood, and stale air overwhelmed her. Rows of wooden beds lined the walls, stacked three high, leaving barely enough room to move. The dim light filtering through the small, grimy slits high up made the space feel more oppressive.

She sank onto one of the wooden bunks, her body aching from exhaustion, hunger, and thirst. Around her, women shuffled quietly to their assigned places, their expressions blank, their movements mechanical.

Some sat staring into space, while others lay down immediately, curling into themselves as though seeking escape within their own bodies.

Eileen surveyed the barracks with a steely gaze. She felt her resolve harden as her surroundings pressed down on her. *I won't become like them. I won't let them break me. With God's help, I will survive this.*

She closed her eyes, clasped her hands together, and whispered the words that would remain her daily prayer in hell.

"*Seigneur, donnez-moi la force...*" Lord, give me strength.

IN THE DAYS THAT FOLLOWED, Eileen adapted to the grim rhythms of the camp. Roll call on the Appelplatz before dawn meant standing for hours in the cold, rain, or blistering sun as guards counted and recounted the prisoners with mind-numbing precision. The monotony was broken only by the occasional crack of a whip or barked order, both reminders of the razor-thin line she walked daily.

For a short while, Eileen was assigned to work in the camp garden, growing vegetables for the staff and prisoners, though the best of the produce went to the former. The work was grueling, but she didn't mind. She was outside, where, if the wind was favorable, the air carried a faint hint of pine and the sun occasionally touched her face.

When the guards weren't looking, she took daring risks—plucking a tiny carrot, burying the telltale green tops immediately, or nibbling the edge of a cabbage leaf. The stakes were high; she'd seen the punishments meted out to others caught stealing food. But she was fast, cunning, and determined.

Eileen observed everything. She studied the camp with the sharp eye of a survivor, noting the hierarchy among guards and prisoners, memorizing faces, routines, and weaknesses. Her knack for languages quickly proved invaluable as she picked up German. She strained to catch snippets of conversation, piecing together meanings and learning how to reply when necessary.

One morning during roll call, a guard shouted at her for pausing, shoving her roughly. She stumbled but quickly caught herself.

Without hesitation, she murmured, "*Pardon, Herr Offizier.*" Her tone was deferential, her expression carefully neutral, but her eyes gleamed with an indiscernible spark. The guard scowled, unsure whether to be irritated or placated, and moved on.

Later, another prisoner leaned in and whispered, "That was bold."

"Not bold," Eileen replied softly. "Calculated."

Her wit became her shield, her faith a sanctuary. She found small ways to bring light to the darkness. Quiet jokes whispered among prisoners brought fleeting smiles to weary faces. Small acts of kindness, like offering a reassuring word or a shared observation, became her way of resisting the all-encompassing despair.

When a young woman near her sobbed quietly over her missing family, Eileen leaned close and whispered, "If they knew you were here, they'd tell you to fight. So, fight for them."

The words weren't just for the woman—they were for herself as well. Every day, Eileen repeated her silent mantra: *God is with me. I am still alive. I will escape.*

Not long after arriving at Ravensbrück, Eileen was surprised to encounter a fellow secret agent she had trained with and knew only by her codename, Odette. Slim, dark-haired, and undeniably elegant, Odette radiated a natural grace and dignity, even in the dehumanizing environment of the camp. Another captured wireless operator.

"We have to be careful," Eileen whispered in rapid French as she pulled Odette behind one of the barracks for a furtive chat. "On the one hand, it's a relief to be surrounded by other French women, but they mustn't overhear us. Of course, they know we're political prisoners," she added, pointing to the red triangle stitched onto the sleeve of her dress, "but they don't need to know we're British. I don't trust anyone."

"Nor do I," Odette agreed, her voice low. "That's why I stick with my French alias, Mademoiselle Marie Bernier."

"Exactly." Eileen nodded firmly. "I'm Jacqueline, and you're Marie. We stick to that. I'm glad you see it the same way."

Their meeting, however, was all too brief. Odette had to return to her barrack, but their exchange brought Eileen a glimmer of hope in an otherwise bleak world. Knowing there was someone who shared her background, her training, and her caution gave her a renewed sense of purpose.

In her own barrack, Eileen found another connection in Geneviève Matthieu, who occupied the bunk above hers. A cousin of General de Gaulle, Geneviève carried herself with an air of refinement and a dash of freedom, contrary to the filth and misery of the camp.

"You must always look for ways to thwart the camp rules without getting caught, *ma chèrie*," Geneviève advised one evening. She pulled scraps of paper and a pencil from the hidden depths of her pocket, holding them up with a faint smile. "Poetry keeps the soul alive. They can strip us of many things, but not everything."

Eileen admired her resilience and stubbornness, traits that shone through even when Geneviève battled typhoid and barely survived. Her aristocratic composure never faltered, and her quiet strength inspired Eileen to hold on to her own sense of identity and purpose.

BEFORE LONG, Eileen's feeling of isolation was further eroded by more reunions. Three other SOE agents appeared in the camp: Nadine and Ambroise, both wireless operators, and the glamorous and spirited Louise, better known as Violette Szabo, another lovely Louise. Nadine was, in fact, Lilian Rolfe, and Ambroise was Denise

Bloch. Unlike Eileen, none of the three hesitated to use their real names now that they had been captured.

They openly identified as British, wearing the red triangles with the letter "E" that marked them as 'Englisch' prisoners. Their boldness stood in stark contrast to Eileen's carefully maintained cover as Jacqueline du Tertre. She spoke only French and broken German, blending into the background as a polite, unremarkable presence—a shadow among the chaos.

It was Violette who broke through Eileen's cautious distance with her characteristic directness. "They didn't touch me with a finger," Violette declared one afternoon, her luminous dark eyes fixed on Eileen. "Really, Rose, you're making it unnecessarily hard for yourself."

Eileen flinched at the use of her codename. "Call me Jacqueline, please," she whispered, her voice low and urgent.

Violette tilted her head, her lips curling into a wry smile. "Honestly, you should've said you were English in the first place. The Germans know better than to mistreat British agents. They're scared out of their wits about losing the war."

Eileen's stomach tightened at the reminder of her ordeal at the Rue des Saussaies. She forced herself to meet Violette's gaze, her expression calm but firm. "It's different for me, Violette. I've worked too hard to make Jacqueline du Tertre convincing. My alias is my armor—my survival depends on it."

Violette sighed, brushing a stray curl from her face. "But it's dangerous," she insisted. "They've already branded us as the 'little paratroopers' here in the camp. You're one of us whether you claim it or not. Why not stand with us?"

Eileen admired Violette's courage and conviction, but their openness unnerved her. She had spent months honing her alibi, carefully crafting her role as a Frenchwoman caught in the wrong place at the wrong time. Aligning too closely with the others could unravel everything she had worked so hard to maintain.

Even so, the presence of her fellow agents brought a bittersweet comfort. Their camaraderie and bravery were a balm to her spirit, but also a reminder of the peril they all faced. The Germans would not hesitate to execute them if they were unmasked as SOE operatives. Eileen resolved to stay on the periphery—close enough to benefit from their presence but distant enough to preserve her carefully woven cover.

For those fleeting moments when the weight of survival felt lighter, there was always Geneviève. The older woman, with her quiet defiance and aristocratic air, offered companionship without intrusion. She was as social and outgoing as Eileen was solitary, and yet her whispered wisdom brought solace.

Eileen stayed at Ravensbrück for only fifteen days before she and the little paratroopers —Lilian, Denise, Violette, and Geneviève—were transported to Torgau. The brief reprieve of shared familiarity and strength faded into uncertainty as the next chapter of Eileen's ordeal loomed.

50

THE PLAN UNRAVELS

Several weeks later - Fort Zinna Prison, Torgau, Germany, Autumn 1944

The munition factory buzzed with the hum of machinery, its clanking, grinding, and occasional hissing sounds filling the air. The lights cast long shadows over the work benches, and the acrid scent of gunpowder hung thickly in the air, coating everything in its metallic tang. Eileen sat at her station, her fingers deftly assembling components for artillery shells. Each movement was precise; one misstep could mean an explosion.

Across the workshop, Violette moved with a quiet determination, her dark hair tucked beneath a kerchief. She glanced around before approaching Eileen and perching on the empty stool next to her while the guards were scolding another prisoner.

"I've done it," Violette whispered, barely audible over the din of the factory.

Eileen didn't look up from what her hands were doing. "Done what?"

"I've got a key," Violette murmured in a voice laced with triumph. She tapped her pocket with her fingers.

Eileen's eyes widened. "A key for what?"

"Escape, silly. One on the locks of the gates."

"How did you get it?"

"Let's say someone owed me a favor."

Eileen glanced around nervously, her voice dropping to a near hiss. "Then let's go—tonight. Right now. This place is a powder keg, Violette. Every moment we stay, we risk our lives."

But Violette shook her head in a resolute manner. "We can't rush this. The guards will notice us missing within minutes. We need to plan, time it right. It's not just about getting out—it's about staying out."

Eileen clenched her fists, frustration rising. "Planning takes time we don't have! What if the chance slips through our fingers?"

Violette placed a steadying hand on Eileen's arm. "Trust me. I'll go over everything tonight. When the time comes, we'll all get out. Together."

Reluctantly, Eileen nodded, though every fiber of her being screamed to act immediately.

That evening, the group huddled in a shadowy corner of the barracks. Violette spread out a crude drawing of the camp she had sketched on a scrap of paper smuggled from the factory.

"We'll use this gate," she said, tapping the small X she'd marked on the edge of the wall. "The guards rotate every two hours, but there's a window just before dawn when the shift is at its weakest."

Eileen studied the plan, her brow furrowed. "And once we're out?"

"We head for the forest," Violette said firmly. "There's a contact there—a farmer sympathetic to the Resistance. He'll hide us."

Eileen was in awe. Violette really had it all planned.

The women agreed. For the first time in weeks, hope flickered in their eyes.

But their whispers carried farther than they realized. In the corner of the barracks, a figure shifted in the shadows. It was Hilde, a sallow-faced woman known for her sharp ears and sharper tongue. Her lips curled into a smile as she listened.

The next morning, the women returned to the factory, their nerves stretched taut. They would go that night. Eileen glanced at Violette as they worked, her movements mechanical, her thoughts consumed by the plan.

Suddenly, a fellow prisoner hurried over, her eyes wide with urgency. She leaned close to Violette and whispered, "Get rid of it. Now. Hilde heard you last night. She's already gone to the overseers."

The blood drained from Violette's face.

Eileen froze, gripping the edge of the workbench. "Are you sure?" she asked, trying hard to keep her voice down.

"Yes," the woman replied. "Hilde thinks she'll get extra rations or privileges for ratting you out."

Violette didn't hesitate. She reached into her pocket and pulled out the key. With one swift motion, she slipped it into the folds of her apron. "We'll deal with her later," she said through gritted teeth. "For now, we have to stay calm."

But Eileen's mind raced. Their best chance at freedom was slipping away, and there was nothing they could do.

That night the atmosphere in the barracks was tense. More guards than usual conducted a thorough search, their boots thudding heavily on the wooden floors, overthrowing mattresses, emptying suitcases. Violette sat still as a statue, her expression blank as the guards came close.

Eileen's heart pounded like a hammer as they stopped in front of Violette.

"You," one of them barked, "Get up so we can search you and your place."

He stared at her for a long moment, suspicion etched into his face. Eileen saw everything being overturned; Violette being touched everywhere. She didn't even flinch. Then, with a grunt, he moved on.

When the guards left, the women exhaled collectively, tension breaking like a dam.

Eileen turned to Violette. "Where's the key?"

"Gone." Her voice was flat. "I dropped it in the factory. We couldn't risk it. It's over."

Eileen stared at her, her throat tightening. The plan, their hope —it had all crumbled because of one loose tongue.

For the rest of the night, Eileen lay awake, staring at the ceiling. Escape was still at the forefront of her mind, but now it seemed further away than ever.

51

THE ENGINE OF DEFIANCE

Several months later - Abteroda Concentration Camp (BMW), Germany, late January 1945

The bitter cold of the January day seeped through the thin fabric of Eileen's striped dress as she stood at the assembly bench of the BMW factory in Berka/Werra. The factory was poorly heated and buzzed with the relentless grind of machinery, the air filled with the acrid smell of oil and burning metal.

Her fingers, nimble despite the bruises and cuts that lined them, struggled to fit together the intricate pieces of the Messerschmitt aircraft engines.

The twelve-hour shifts drained her, the clanging noise of the factory pounding in her ears long after she left each day. Her head ached constantly, and her vision blurred from the intense concentration demanded by the tiny parts. Hunger gnawed at her even in her sleep.

But it was more than physical exhaustion that weighed on her—

it was the grim knowledge that every engine she assembled would power planes used to destroy her own country.

One day, after a particularly grueling shift, Eileen wiped the grease from her brow and pushed back the tattered kerchief she wore to keep her curls from falling over her face. She turned to one of the French girls working beside her and muttered under her breath, "Why should I help them destroy us? I won't do it anymore."

The girl glanced back, wide-eyed. "Jacqueline, don't—"

But it was too late. Eileen shoved her tools aside and stood, her voice defiant as she addressed the nearest guard. "I won't work anymore."

The guard, a burly man with a scar running down his cheek, approached her. His rifle hung nonchalantly over his shoulder, and his eyes were cold and calculating. "What did you say?"

"I said I won't work," she repeated, crossing her arms. "Why should I build engines to fight my own people?"

The room seemed to freeze, the dull clatter of machinery disappearing in the distance in the face of so much defiance. All eyes were on Eileen. But she was past caring.

The guard sneered. "Then you'll be punished."

"What worse punishment could there be than living in this hell?" She held her chin high. Enough was enough.

"Don't say you didn't ask for it." As he said it, she was grabbed by two guards and dragged to a corner of the factory floor. They held her down as they snipped off her curls, the thick brown locks falling to the ground in uneven tufts. She heard an electric trimmer, and every last bit of her hair was shaved roughly, blood dripping into her eyes and down her neck. She clenched her jaw, blinking away the blood and tears but refusing to give them the satisfaction of seeing her cry.

When they were done, they hauled her back to her bench. She

felt her bald head and quickly hid it under the tattered kerchief. Her scalp pricked and burned where the blade had scraped too close.

"I told you, I won't do it," she said firmly.

This time, the scarred guard raised his rifle, pointing it directly at her chest. His voice was low and venomous. "You have twenty minutes to decide. Work or die."

Eileen stared down the barrel of the rifle, her heart thundering. Everyone, guards and prisoners alike, were holding their breath. She thought of her sister, Jacqueline, of her family, and of the war she so desperately wanted to see end. Was this the moment she would choose to die?

After a long pause, she lowered her gaze and muttered, "I'll work."

The guard smirked and lowered his rifle. "Good choice."

But as Eileen returned to the work on her bench, her mind seethed with defiance. If she had to work, she would do it her way.

IN THE WEEKS THAT FOLLOWED, Eileen kept finding small ways to resist. She worked slower than the others, drawing sharp reprimands from the guards. She deliberately assembled parts in the wrong way, or broke them, her hands finding ways to sabotage without drawing immediate suspicion.

When confronted, she feigned incompetence. "I'm sorry, *Herr Offizier*," she would say, her voice dripping with false sincerity. "I'm simply not very good at this sort of thing. I wasn't trained for it, you see. I'm a translator. Engineering goes right over my head."

Every time she managed to break or botch a part, the sabotage gave her a small sense of triumph, a spark of satisfaction that kept her spirit alive. But it also drew unwanted attention.

One day, a guard yanked her away from her bench, dragging her outside to face a line of armed men. Her pulse raced as she realized she'd probably gone too far this time.

"We've had enough of your mistakes," the guard spat. "Maybe we should send you somewhere worse."

The threat hung in the air, heavier than the snow clouds above. Eileen's knees trembled, but she forced herself to meet his gaze. "Do as you must," she said, "I can't help being useless for BMW." Though fear coiled in her chest, she swore he would never know it.

When the news came that she was being transferred to another camp, Eileen's emotions were a whirlwind. Relief at escaping the factory mixed with dread at the unknown. Had she pushed too hard? Would this new camp be even worse?

She sat with a small group of French girls she'd grown close to, their faces pale as they whispered their goodbyes.

"You'll be fine, Jacqueline," one of them said softly. "You're the bravest of us all."

She managed a small smile, though her heart ached at leaving them behind. As she climbed into the truck that would take her to her next destination, she cast one last glance at the BMW factory.

Wherever I go next, she vowed silently, *I'll find a way to resist. And I'll find a way to escape.*

The engine roared to life, and the truck rolled forward, carrying her into yet another chapter of her fight for survival.

52

THE END OF THE ROAD

Several Months later - Markkleeberg Concentration Camp, near Leipzig, Early 1945

The truck jolted to a halt. Eileen blinked against the brightness of the winter sun as she stepped down, her wooden clogs slipping on the frozen ground. Around her, women stumbled forward, their gaunt frames resembling black shadows against the white of the snow-covered earth.

Her knees trembled, not just from the cold, but from exhaustion. The journey from Abteroda had been brutal—a relentless blur of jolting transport and icy landscapes. Farther east, farther from freedom. For hundreds of miles, she'd scanned the terrain for any chance to escape, but the bitter truth had settled over her like the frost: deep in German territory, survival outside the camps was nearly impossible.

Each time the truck had slowed, her heart had leapt with a fleeting hope that an opportunity might arise—a distracted guard, an open stretch of forest, anything. But each time, the guards' sharp eyes and the vastness of the snow-covered fields had stifled her hope.

If I escape now, I'll be caught and shot within seconds. Not yet. I have to wait.

But escape had become an obsession for her, certainly now her chances of survival became slimmer with each passing day. Maybe to die in freedom was better than to die in captivity? But her mind still reasoned against dying either way. Not yet.

The landscape of Markkleeberg Concentration Camp was a stark gray-white, the frozen ground glistening under a pale winter sun that gave no warmth.

Like the other new arrivals, most of them French women, she was handed a uniform: dark-gray overalls, baggy and coarse, with long sleeves and buttons down to the waist. The red triangle on the left sleeve marked her again as a political prisoner. She pulled it on numbly, the rough fabric scratching her skin.

To her blurry eyes, all the camps looked the same now. Barracks squatted in neat rows, their windows frosted over, and the air carrying the acrid smell of burning coal from the guards' quarters. There was no smoke from the prisoners' barracks; no heat would be wasted on them.

Eileen tried to steady herself as she and the others were marched toward the worksite. The icy ground crunched beneath their wooden clogs, and her breath came in shallow puffs, each one harder to draw than the last. She could feel the weight of her exhaustion pressing down on her like an iron chain. Months of malnutrition and grueling labor had sapped her strength, and a dry cough rattled in her chest.

Her thoughts were fractured, her memories tangled. She couldn't recall the journey from Abteroda clearly, just a blur of jolting trucks and endless snow-covered fields. She wasn't sure how many days she'd been on the move, nor did she care to count. Each mile had been another piece of herself chipped away.

"Keep moving!" a guard barked, as he strode alongside the line of women. Eileen barely registered the command. Her feet moved automatically, dragging her forward through the snow like a marionette on frayed strings.

When they reached the worksite, the ground was frozen solid, unyielding to their meager tools. Eileen was handed a rusted shovel, its wooden handle splintered. She gripped it tightly, willing her trembling hands to steady, and struck the icy earth. The blade bounced back, barely scratching the surface.

She struck again. And again. Each blow jarred her arms, sending a sharp ache through her weakened muscles. Around her, women fell to their knees, their bodies too frail to endure the labor. A few were dragged away by guards, their fates unknown but not hard to guess.

Eileen's vision blurred as dizziness took hold. The cold, the hunger, the relentless monotony—it all pressed against her like a lead weight. She leaned on her shovel, trying to catch her breath, her thoughts slipping into confusion.

Where am I? Her mind darting to memories of other camps, other barracks, other horrors. *Abteroda? Ravensbrück?* They all bled together in her mind, a nightmarish collage of barbed wire, barking guards, and aching bones.

"Jacqueline," a voice hissed beside her, snapping her out of her daze.

She turned to see a fellow prisoner, her face shadowed with grime and fear. "Keep moving," the woman whispered. "They're watching."

Eileen blinked, trying to focus. The guard's eyes bore into her, cold and unfeeling. She nodded weakly and forced herself to strike the ground again. The frozen soil mocked her efforts, but she kept at it, her grip tightening on the shovel as though it were the only thing anchoring her to reality.

THAT NIGHT, lying on the wooden slats of her 'bed' in the barracks, Eileen stared at the ceiling, her breath visible in the freezing air. Her body ached, her hands blistered and raw, her bowels festering with dysentery, but she clung to one thought: escape.

She whispered her prayer into the darkness, her bloodless lips barely moving. "*Seigneur, donnez-moi la force...*" Lord, give me strength.

Though her mind swirled with despair, a flicker of defiance burned within her. She would not give up. Not yet. She had come too far to let this be the end.

The camp was a prison, yes, but it was not impenetrable. Somewhere beyond those walls, the war was nearing its end, and the world was waiting. She just had to survive long enough to see it.

For now, that thought was her fuel to carry her into one more day.

53

THE FINAL MARCH

Four months later - April 1945

As winter's icy grip loosened, giving way to the milder breezes of spring, the air became full of anticipation in the camp. Eileen huddled with a group of women near the edge of the barracks, their whispered conversations filled with rumors of liberation.

The signs were everywhere. The guards were more anxious than ever, their barked orders more hurried, their glances frequently darting nervously toward the horizon. The distant rumble of artillery fire could be heard at night, a low and steady thunder that spoke of the Allied advance. The Americans from the West. The Russians from the East.

Eileen's body was frail, her steps unsteady, but her spirit burned brightly. She clung to the thought she'd anchored in herself through countless days of suffering:

The most important thing is the will to carry on. I can never let them see that they are winning. I must cling to the will to live, however long it takes. I will always have the hope it will be over soon.

News spread quickly among the prisoners. "President Franklin Roosevelt is dead," a guard had announced earlier that day, his tone laced with a strange mixture of gloating and resignation. "The war will be over soon."

The two things he said didn't combine in Eileen's muddled brain, so she only listened to his last remark. "The war will be over soon."

She exchanged glances with the French women nearby, their expressions mirroring her own. If the guards were speaking of war's end, it meant liberation was close.

By evening, the camp was abuzz with rumors. "The guards are leaving," someone whispered. "We'll be free!"

The French women, ever bold, began to hum the first bars of *La Marseillaise*. The tune swelled as more voices joined in, their song defiant and jubilant. For the first time in months, laughter rippled through the barracks.

Eileen allowed herself a small smile, the sound of La Marseillaise stirring something deep within her. The women were raiding the kitchen, emerging with scraps of food and a few precious tins of soup. She clutched a stale piece of bread someone handed her and took a cautious bite, savoring the rare taste of hope.

Then, the siren wailed.

The sharp, mechanical sound cut through the camp, silencing the singing and laughter. Eileen froze, the bread still in her hand. Across the Lagerstrasse, guards emerged from their quarters, their boots pounding against the gravel.

"An order from Berlin!" the camp commandant's voice boomed over the loudspeaker, harsh and unrelenting. "We are leaving on foot in twenty minutes. Those who are sick will be taken by cart, and the rest of you will follow. No one is to remain in the camp."

The words sent a ripple of dread through the women. Eileen's heart sank. The promise of freedom, so close she could taste it, evaporated in an instant.

"Why are they moving us now?" one of the women whispered, her voice trembling.

"To cover their tracks," Eileen replied grimly. "They don't want us to be found here when the Allies arrive. They want no evidence of what they've done."

The barracks erupted into frantic activity as the women prepared to leave. Eileen grabbed her few belongings, tattered shoes and her hidden piece of bread.

Her mind raced. *This march could be my opportunity. A chance to escape.*

But as she stepped out into the cold evening air, her resolve wavered. The guards were everywhere, rifles slung over their shoulders, barking orders and shoving women into line.

"Stay close," Eileen whispered to Yvette, a young Frenchwoman, who'd been with her in all the camps since Torgau. "Let's stick together, keep each other alive."

Yvette nodded, clutching Eileen's arm as they moved toward the gate. The camp, once a hellish prison, now seemed almost safe compared to the uncertainty that lay beyond its walls.

Eileen's gaze drifted to the horizon, where the fading light of day bathed the landscape in hues of orange and pink. She inhaled deeply, the scent of spring filling her lungs.

The war will end soon, she reminded herself. *I just have to survive this march. Just a little longer.*

The commandant's voice barked again, ordering the women to form lines. As the gates creaked open and the column of prisoners began to shuffle forward, Eileen whispered another prayer, her voice barely audible over the sound of boots crunching against gravel.

"*Seigneur, donnez-moi la force...*" Lord, give me strength.

And with that, she stepped into the unknown, her heart a mix of fear and unyielding determination.

THE PRISONERS WERE TOLD they were marching to another camp, some seventy miles to the south. The news was met with muted despair; their emaciated bodies could barely endure standing, let alone such a grueling journey through the night.

Eileen received the message blankly. *Seventy miles? Another camp? What now?*

As the women trudged out of the camp gates and into the town, they pushed carts carrying those too weak to walk. The wooden wheels creaked and groaned under the weight, their sound mingling with the labored breaths of the prisoners and the barked commands of the guards.

The guards marched up and down the column. Occasionally, they jabbed prisoners in the back with the butts of their rifles, shouting for them to move faster.

Eileen's gaze flicked to the tree line just beyond the residential streets of Markkleeberg, the thick woodlands offering a tantalizing promise of cover. The trees were tall and dense, their branches stretching skyward in defiance of the horrors nearby. *They're perfect,* she thought, her heart quickening. *If I can reach the edge without being seen...*

She began to study the guards' movements with the precision of a wireless operator timing transmissions. They marched in a rhythm —one would pass her, then another a few moments later. If she could time her escape just right, slipping between them unnoticed...

She clenched her trembling hands into fists, digging her nails into her palms to steady herself. *This is it,* she told herself. *My chance.*

The guard in front of her passed, his rifle slung lazily over his shoulder. She waited, counting the seconds, her ears straining for the sound of the next guard's boots.

Now.

With a burst of adrenaline, Eileen veered sharply to the left, leaving the column. Her legs screamed in protest, her body weakened by months of malnutrition and labor, but she pushed forward. Each step toward the woods felt like a leap across a chasm.

The trees grew closer. The scent of pine filled her nostrils, mingling with the sour tang of fear. She reached the first tree, pressing her back against the rough bark, her chest heaving as she fought to catch her breath. She bit her lip, willing herself to remain silent.

Seigneur, donnez-moi la force...

54

A DARING ESCAPE

Eileen leaned her back against the tree, which stood solid as a sentinel behind her. The coarse bark pressed into her back as her heart thundered in her ears. Her chest heaved, each breath burning her raw throat. She expected to hear the bark of a guard's voice, or the crack of a rifle shot slicing through the air. Her trembling fingers clenched the fabric of her overalls

Please, no.

She knew that this was it. Life or death. Her last chance. There would be no more opportunities. She couldn't survive the seventy-mile march, her body wouldn't be able to withstand it. She knew the forest could swallow her whole, offering either sanctuary or a grave. But she had no other choice.

Her breath rasped so loudly she had to press her hand to her chest, willing herself to be silent. She strained to listen, catching the rhythmic stomping of German jackboots and the weary shuffle of the women's feet on the gravel road. The convoy dragged on and on, stomping, shuffle, stomping, shuffle. It seemed to last for eternity.

They'll miss me soon, she thought. *Any second now, they'll count and—*

Finally, the sounds of the guards' boots began to fade, the rhythm growing softer and more distant. She dared to peer around the edge of the tree, from where she caught glimpses of the column retreating further down the road, swallowed by the mist and the forest beyond.

She remained frozen, unable to move. Her legs felt like lead, while her mind couldn't grasp the enormity of the situation. Could it really be true? Could she have slipped away unnoticed?

The stillness around her became real. Only the occasional rustle of the wind in the treetops interrupted the silence. But still every nerve in her body screamed at her to stay hidden. The moments dragged on, each one an eternity, her breath now shallow and uneven.

And then the realization hit her like a thunderclap. For the first time since that cursed day in Paris in the summer of the previous year, she was no longer a prisoner.

I. Am. Free.

Tears welled in her eyes as she sank to her knees, her head resting against the tree that had sheltered her. Her shoulders shook with silent sobs, the emotions she had buried for months surging to the surface. The weight of captivity was lifted, now replaced by the fragile hope of freedom.

"*Merci, Seigneur,*" she whispered, her voice cracking with emotion. "*Merci pour cette chance.*" Thank you, Lord. Thank you for this chance.

Eileen froze as she felt eyes upon her. She turned her head sharply, her breath catching in her throat. Through the dim light filtering through the trees, she saw movement—two figures emerging cautiously from the shadows.

"Jacqueline?" a soft voice whispered.

It was Yvette. The recognition hit Eileen like a flood of warmth, dispelling the chill of the woods and in her bones. Yvette had been her stalwart companion since Torgau, and now, against all odds, she was here. The other figure stepped forward without making a sound, and Eileen recognized Suzanne, another prisoner whose quiet resilience had always struck her.

For a moment, they simply stared at one another, the enormity of their shared defiance beyond comprehension. Then, as if on instinct, they closed the gap between them, their arms wrapping tightly around one another in an embrace that was equal parts relief, gratitude, and fierce determination.

"You made it," Eileen's voice broke with emotion.

"We made it," Yvette corrected with a trembling voice. "We're free, Jacqueline. For the first time in... in months... we're free."

The word 'free' hovered between them, almost too fragile to believe. They clung to each other as if afraid the reality might dissolve if they let go. Their thin, bony frames pressed together, their warmth shared, a lifeline in the vast cold of the night.

The woodland around them was still, the only sound their ragged breaths and the faint rustle of branches above. For months, the rhythm of their lives had been dictated by guards' commands, the crack of whips, and the grinding monotony of survival. Now, for the first time, there was silence. And in that silence was possibility.

Eileen pulled back for a moment, her bony fingers gripping Yvette's equally bony shoulders as she looked into her friend's tired but determined eyes. "We've done the impossible. Now we have to keep going."

Suzanne, who'd remained quiet, chimed in. "Together," she said.

That single word – together - carried the weight of their shared struggle ahead and the bond formed in its crucible.

The three women turned their faces toward the forest, its dark expanse both a shield and a challenge. Despite the dangers she knew awaited them—starvation, exposure, the risk of recapture—there was a lightness in Eileen's heart that had been absent for so long. For the first time, no guard dictated their every movement, their every morsel of bread, when they might lay down their heads.

Standing in the quiet, peaceful woodland, they shared a moment of God's stillness. They had survived hell, and though the road ahead was uncertain, they were no longer bound by chains. Their arms around each other, they drew strength from their unity, their shared hope, and the spark of freedom that now burned in their chests.

Eileen glanced up through the treetops, the stars glittering faintly above. She whispered again her prayer of thanks, her voice barely audible but full of conviction. "*Merci, Seigneur, pour cette chance.*" Thank you, Lord, for this chance.

The three women began to move. With cautious steps, with resolute hearts. Each one carried a part of the other's strength, and Eileen knew that together they would face whatever came next. Because they were free. And the freedom of tyranny was worth everything.

EILEEN, Yvette, and Suzanne moved cautiously along the road, back in the direction of Markkleeberg. Their gray overalls blended into the thick of the night. Every step felt like a risk, every breath a gamble. The town loomed ahead, its buildings scarred by war, but still the town was a better chance of survival than a night in the freezing woods.

Eileen's eyes fixed on the ruin of a house near the outskirts, the roof partially caved in, and the walls pockmarked with shrapnel. It stood close to the remains of the Junkers factory, clearly bombed many times by the Allies. "There," she whispered, pointing toward the damaged building. "Let's try our luck there."

They climbed through a jagged hole in the wall with the rubble scraping against their already raw hands. Eileen winced as her knee banged against a broken beam. Once inside, the air was dank and stale, filled with the metallic tang of destruction.

She collapsed onto the floor, the cold seeping through her thin clothes. Her legs trembled from the strain of walking, her body weak from hunger and exhaustion. Yvette and Suzanne slumped close beside her. Their breaths labored as they huddled as closely as possible for a bit of warmth.

"We can't stay here long," Suzanne murmured in a hoarse voice.

"Just until we gather our strength," Eileen replied. Her gaze swept the room, taking in the shattered furniture and piles of debris. "We'll need to explore the place in a minute, see if there's anything useful."

The three women lay together, the ragged blankets they'd taken with them from the camp barely providing any relief from the bitter cold. All three women were simply too worn-out to get up. The April wind howled through the broken windows, and Eileen shivered as snowflakes drifted inside, settling on the floor like flaky-white intruders.

When some of their strength returned, they ventured cautiously through the house. When the floorboards creaked under their feet, they stopped to listen for a reaction as each sound seemed magnified in the eerie silence. Eileen's heart pounded as she opened a battered cupboard, finding nothing but dust. A broken chair leaned against the wall, its legs splintered. There was no food, no water—nothing to sustain them.

"Although there's nothing to feed us here, we'll stay for the night," Eileen decided. "In daylight we'll go looking for food. For now, we'll have to make do with melted snow."

They bundled together on the cold floor again, trying to conserve warmth. Sleep came in fitful bursts, interrupted by the sounds of vehicles and the scraping of boots outside. Eileen's mind kept replaying the moment she'd slipped from the marching column. Triumph about her deed and fear of what lay ahead struggled in equal parts. Had the other women reported their missing? Were guards searching for them?

The next morning, hunger gnawed at her stomach, a relentless ache that refused to be ignored. Eileen pressed a hand to her abdomen, willing the sensation away. "We need to find food," she said resolutely, "Or we'll still die here and now."

They climbed back through the hole and ventured onto the road. The icy wind stung Eileen's face, and her breath formed small clouds in the air. Her eyes scanned the ground, searching for anything edible. She spotted a patch of tiny dandelion leaves growing stubbornly by the roadside and crouched down, plucking them carefully.

"Here," she said, passing some to Yvette and Suzanne. The bitter leaves did little to satiate their hunger, but they were better than nothing. Snow clung to the edges of the road, and they carefully scooped up what they could, the icy crystals melting on their parched tongues.

Suddenly, a sharp bark pierced the air. Eileen's head snapped up. A big black dog appeared in the distance, its tail raised as it barked furiously in their direction. Panic surged through her veins.

"Back to the house," she hissed, grabbing Suzanne's arm. They ran as quickly as their weakened bodies allowed, slipping back through the hole just as the barking grew louder. Eileen pressed her back against the wall, her chest heaving as she listened for footsteps or voices. But the barking eventually faded, and no one came.

"We'll stay here another day and night," she whispered. "Right now, it's too dangerous for us to go out again."

55

THE ROAD TO FREEDOM

That night Eileen, Yvette and Suzanne talked about their lives in France. Though she trusted Yvette and Suzanne completely, Eileen stuck with her Jacqueline du Tertre name, weaving in the real stories of her childhood in France as they sat close together on the wooden floor in the abandoned house. Her memories were real, and her French impeccable, so there was no need for invention beyond the name.

And it wasn't just for herself that she kept her British nationality to herself. She was afraid that until they were really safe, her secret mission in France could endanger her friends as well. Still, it was marvelous to talk of happier times and dream about a possible future, in which they would stay in touch for as long as they lived.

"I think we should not stay in Markkleeberg, so close to the camp," Yvette suggested when they rolled into their blankets to catch some sleep. "Let's head towards Leipzig tomorrow. If the Americans haven't reached it yet, we'll find somewhere to hide until they do."

Twenty miles, Eileen thought. *I'm not sure I can make that.* But she didn't want to thwart Yvette's plan. After all it made a lot of sense to get away from this town.

THEIR BREATHS PUFFED VISIBLY in the chill morning air, and the snow beneath their feet crunched as they moved cautiously onto the deserted road at the first light of day.

Eileen remained silent, leaning heavily against the wall for support. Her body ached with an intensity that made every movement a struggle. Her legs felt like lead, her chest burned with every labored breath, and the persistent cough that had plagued her for weeks now rattled in her chest like chains.

She could see the worry in her friends' eyes as they glanced at her. "I'm fine," she croaked, her voice hoarse but firm. "Let's go."

The truth was, she wasn't fine. She felt weaker than she ever had, her strength drained by months of starvation and exhaustion. But the willpower that had carried her through the Gestapo Headquarters, Fresnes Prison, Ravensbrück, Torgau, Abteroda, and finally Markkleeberg flared up again, and she clung to her will to live like a buoy in stormy seas.

Every step counts, she told herself, *each one brings me closer to freedom.*

Yvette and Suzanne flanked her, their arms steadying her as they moved slowly down the road. The woods stretched out on either side of them, the trees standing tall and silent like solemn friends.

"For sure the Americans must be close now," Yvette said with optimism.

"They must be," Suzanne replied, her voice equally resolute. "We just have to keep moving."

Eileen listened to their hushed conversation, grateful for their company. Then another cough interrupted the moment, sharp and jarring. She doubled over, her hands braced on her knees as she struggled to catch her breath.

"Jacqueline, you can't go on like this," Yvette said in a voice full of concern.

"I can," Eileen rasped, straightening with effort. "I have to. I want to see the Americans. I want to see freedom."

Suzanne glanced nervously up and down the road, scanning for any signs of danger. "We can rest here for a moment. But not too long."

THE AIR WAS UNNATURALLY STILL as Eileen, Yvette, and Suzanne rounded a bend in yet another road. The red streaks of the setting sun filtered through the bare branches of the surrounding trees. Eileen stopped abruptly, squinting her eyes in the red sun. Then she saw them—German soldiers standing at a road junction up ahead.

"We can't turn back," Suzanne whispered in a trembling voice. "They've seen us already."

"Keep walking," Eileen murmured, panic surging through her veins. Her fingers tightened around the thin blanket draped over her shoulders, ensuring it covered the red triangle on her gray, camp overalls. "We'll pretend to be French workers. That's our story."

The three women moved forward, their steps slow and deliberate. The soldiers' chatter stopped as the women approached. One of them, a thin, tall man with a hard-set jaw, stepped forward and barred their way.

"*Halt!*" he barked. His gaze sweeped over them rather too intently, Eileen noticed.

She swallowed hard, willing her cough to silence. "*Guten Abend*," she said politely, her French accent unmistakable.

"Your identity papers," the soldier demanded on a sharp tone.

Eileen's mind raced for a lie and found it. "We... we don't have them yet," she said in the same polite tone. "We're French workers. Volunteers."

The soldier raised an eyebrow, clearly skeptical.

"We were told to come here," Yvette chimed in. "To join a work party. They said we'd receive our papers when we arrived."

The man's eyes narrowed as he studied them, his gaze lingering on their gaunt faces, their threadbare clothes, and the lice that crawled visibly on their blankets.

Eileen's chest tightened. He knows, she thought. He knows exactly who we are.

The soldier turned and spoke in rapid German to his comrades. The group huddled together, their voices low but intense. Eileen strained to catch fragments of their conversation, but her grasp of German wasn't enough to decipher the hurried exchanges.

"They're deciding what to do with us," Suzanne whispered.

Eileen glanced at her friends, their faces pale and etched with fear. She whispered a silent prayer, her lips barely moving. *Seigneur, donnez-moi la force...*

The soldier turned to face them again with an unreadable expression on his narrow face. Eileen braced herself, feeling her friends next to her doing the same. Now it came. *Freedom gone, back into capture.*

"You are free to go," he said gruffly, waving them forward.

For a moment, the three women stood frozen, unable to comprehend what they had just heard.

"Go!" the soldier barked, gesturing impatiently.

"*Danke*," Eileen murmured as they moved past the guards, her legs trembling uncontrollably. Relief and terror swept through her entire system.

The moment they were out of earshot, Yvette whispered, "Did that really just happen?"

"They knew," Eileen said, her voice tight. "They knew exactly who we were."

"Then why let us go?" Suzanne asked as her brow furrowed in disbelief.

Eileen glanced over her shoulder, making sure the soldiers were out of sight. "They don't want us on their hands with the Allies so close," she said. "We're more trouble than we're worth."

They quickened their pace, the woods looming ahead like a sanctuary.

As soon as they reached the cover of the trees, they collapsed onto the frozen ground. For a long time, none of them spoke, the weight of their near-capture pressing down on them like a physical force.

"We're still free," Eileen finally uttered. "We're still free."

Yvette reached out and clasped Eileen's hand, her grip firm despite her shaking fingers. "Let's keep it that way," she said. "No more public roads. From now on, we stick to the woods."

56

THE PRIEST'S MERCY

The night on the church grounds was a cruel irony, the graveyard serving as a refuge while the cold, damp ground seemed to pull warmth from their bodies, hastening the risk of freezing to death. The ancient tombstones stood half-sunken, half erect, their inscriptions weathered by time and softened by moss.

The French escapees huddled together under their thin blankets. Their skeletal frames shivering in the bitter April night. Eileen pressed her lips together to stifle a cough, but the sound escaped, a hoarse rasp that echoed among the graves.

"Try to rest, Jacqueline," Suzanne whispered. "Tomorrow we might be truly free."

But Eileen couldn't rest. The ache in her body was nothing compared to the gnawing hunger in her stomach, or the ceaseless churn of her thoughts. She gazed up at the steeple silhouetted against the darkening sky. The church bells hadn't tolled, but she found herself wishing for their sound—a sign of life, of sanctuary, of hope.

As dawn broke, the three women stirred from their fitful sleep, their joints stiff from the cold. The golden light of morning bathed the village in a fragile glow, but it did little to ease the shadows clinging to their hearts. They needed food, shelter, and most importantly, safety.

Eileen's weary eyes lingered on the church doors. "It is a Catholic church," she remarked.

Yvette and Suzanne exchanged hesitant glances, but Eileen straightened, summoning her dwindling reserves of strength. "We must trust the priest. He won't betray us."

"You're certain?" Yvette asked. The doubt in her voice was unmistakeable.

"No," Eileen admitted. "But I have faith."

The trio approached the doors with cautious steps, ready to scatter at the first angry shout. Inside the church, the air was warmer and laden with the scent of incense and beeswax candles. The scent alone almost brought Eileen to her knees to pray.

A priest with a crown of gray hair around a bald scalp was kneeling before the altar, his head bowed in prayer. His cassock was well-worn, and his hands rested lightly on a rosary.

"*Pardon, mon Père*," Eileen called out softly.

The priest turned, his watery blue eyes widening as he took in the sight before him: three gaunt women, their faces hollow with hunger and fatigue, their ragged gray overalls bearing the red triangle that marked them as political prisoners.

He stood slowly, his expression a mixture of horror and compassion. Without a word, he gestured for them to follow.

He led them through a side door and into the rectory, a modest space filled with simple furniture and the comforting clutter of a lived-in space. The warmth inside was a balm against the chill that had settled so deeply in their bones.

The priest spoke softly in German, gesturing to them to sit.

Eileen caught the word "*bleiben*"—stay—and her eyes filled with tears.

"*Komm mall her, Gretchen,*" the priest called through a door that obviously led to the inner house.

The housekeeper called Gretchen entered, a middle-aged woman with a kind face and hands calloused from years of labor. The priest spoke to her in hurried tones, pointing to the women. She nodded solemnly and disappeared again.

Moments later, she returned with a tray, and the smell hit Eileen like a wave of salvation. Bowls of thick, steaming soup, the aroma rich with herbs and vegetables. Fresh bread, soft and warm, its golden crust a promise of nourishment they hadn't dared to dream of.

Eileen felt her throat tighten as she accepted a bowl, the weight of it almost too much for her trembling hands.

"*Danke,*" she whispered, her voice breaking. With her head bowed she prayed thanks to God for the church, the priest, the housekeeper, and the meal.

The clergyman and his loyal housekeeper stepped back, watching as the three women ate in silence, their tears mingling with the broth. The bread was unlike anything Eileen had tasted in her entire life—soft, sweet, and comforting, as if each bite carried with it the kindness of those who had prepared it. But her stomach was full so quickly, her mind and her eyes wanted to continue but her body couldn't take in the entire portion. Not all of it, not at once.

Her faith and her instinct had been rewarded. As she glanced at the priest, her heart swelled with gratitude. He risked himself to save them, and in doing so, had rekindled a spark of hope in the goodness of German people.

Gretchen bustled about the rectory with quiet efficiency, her kind face alight with care and sorrow. After the women had eaten their fill of bread and soup, she led them to a modest bedroom with three narrow beds, their frames creaking softly as they sat down. For a moment, Eileen simply stared at the clean sheets, the crisp folds seeming almost too luxurious to touch.

"*Schlafen*," the housekeeper said, folding both hands by her ears and tilting her head, miming a head on a pillow. Then she gestured to the beds. Inviting them with a wave of her hand, she went through an adjacent door. "*Bad. Badetuch. Seife.*"

The three women exchanged glances, the concept of a bath both alien and intoxicating after months of filth. Suzanne rose first, hesitating at the bathroom door before peeking inside. Her sharp intake of breath said it all.

"There's a tub," she whispered, her voice tinged with awe. "And soap! And white towels."

Eileen felt tears prick her eyes as she followed, her knees wobbling beneath her. The sight of the pristine white tub, the neatly folded towels, and the bar of soap placed ceremoniously beside the sink seemed almost unreal. She reached out a trembling hand, running her fingers over the cool porcelain.

The housekeeper, seeing their hesitation, frowned. She mimed washing her face and hair, pointing insistently to the soap and tub. "For you," she said firmly before leaving the room to give them privacy.

Eileen turned to her companions. "Can you believe this? Actual soap. And it smells of roses."

Tears welled in Yvette's eyes. "Are we dreaming, or is this real?"

The three women took turns bathing, their laughter mingling with tears as the grime of months was finally scrubbed away. Eileen lingered in the tub, her chest heaving with each ragged breath. The hot water soothed her aching body, though her persistent cough refused to subside.

Over the next few days, the kindness of Pater Ernst and housekeeper Gretchen nurtured their battered spirits. They slept deeply, their bodies drinking in the safety of warm beds. Suzanne and Yvette began to regain their strength quickly, their cheeks regaining a faint flush of color. Eileen, however, struggled. Her cough worsened, her fever climbing as she drifted in and out of consciousness.

Pater Ernst, noticing her decline, fetched a doctor he trusted. The physician, a gaunt man with weary eyes, examined Eileen with great care. He prescribed medicine and left vials of precious antibiotics, instructing the housekeeper to administer them carefully.

Eileen lay propped up in bed while her breaths were shallow and labored. Yvette sat beside her. "Jacqueline, *ma chèrie*," she murmured over and over. "You're strong. You'll fight through this."

Eileen managed a weak smile, her voice a rasp. "I'll fight. I've come too far to die now."

And fight she did. With the housekeeper's tender care, the priest's prayers, and the doctor's medicines, Eileen began to recover. Slowly, her fever broke and her strength returned. By the time they heard the distant rumble of tanks and the rhythmic crunch of Allied boots, she was well enough to stand.

On the morning of April 19, the 2nd and 69th Infantry Divisions of the U.S. First Army marched in. The 'Stars and Stripes' fluttered in the spring breeze, a symbol of freedom Eileen had dreamed of for so long.

The three friends, their gray overalls now washed and pressed, and the hated red triangle gone, stood and watched as the Germans around them surrendered. Eileen's short hair, though uneven, framed her pale face like a halo. She clutched Yvette's arm for support as she was still too weak to stand for long.

She looked toward the horizon, where the road stretched out under the brightening sky. Though her body was frail, her spirit burned with renewed strength. For her, for her friends, the war was over. At least, they had survived.

But had she? Was her ordeal truly over?

PART XV

~MIA~ TORQUAY, SEPTEMBER 2007

57

THE SPACE BETWEEN

2 Lisburne Crescent, September 2007

The low-hanging, late-afternoon sun caught the white hair of the war heroine seated opposite Mia, creating a luminous halo that seemed almost otherworldly. Eileen sat hunched in her armchair, her hands gripping the edges as though bracing against an invisible storm. Her voice was coarse, as if still struggling for breath from a chest infection, but it carried a fervor that defied the frailty of her frame.

"*Nous avons survécu à tout, n'est-ce pas?* We survived it all, didn't we? But I might as well not have... I might as well." Her gaze was distant. A sharp desperation clung to every word. "They didn't believe me. They thought—"

Mia, knowing what was about to come as she had studied Eileen's file in detail, gently interrupted her in a steady voice. "Miss Nearne—Aunt Didi." She leaned forward, her hand resting lightly over Eileen's to draw her back to the present through touch. "You're here now. With me. Mia. You're safe, Aunt Didi. And we're not going to the Americans yet. Later, we will. But we'll go together. You and me."

At first, the words seemed to float past Eileen, as though she were too far away to catch them. Her lips moved silently, whispering fragments of painful thoughts from a time long gone. It wasn't unusual for survivors to slip into this space when recounting their past—a liminal place where memory blurred with reality.

Mia had seen it many times before, but with Eileen, the stakes felt higher. Watching her teeter at the edge of a storm so profound made Mia hyperaware of every detail. This trauma went deeper than any she had encountered in her career. She couldn't let Eileen slip. The next hour would be critical.

"I know you want to keep going," Mia continued softly. "And we will, I promise. But not right now. I need you here with me first."

Finally, Eileen blinked, her eyelids fluttering, her eyes filled with confusion as though she had just remembered where she was. Her frail, blue-veined hands gripped Mia's tightly, holding on as if Mia were an anchor in a storm. "But you don't understand," she murmured, her voice trembling. "There's more. So much more."

Mia allowed her hand to remain firmly within Eileen's grasp, steady and warm, a lifeline. "I do understand, Aunt Didi," she said softly. "That's why we need to pause. Just for a moment." She waited a beat, letting the silence settle like a calming balm. Then, in her gentlest tone, she added, "Listen to the clicking of the clock, Aunt Didi. Didn't you tell me it once belonged to your sister Jacqueline?"

For a fleeting moment, Mia thought Eileen might follow the cue, that her gaze might drift to the comforting metronome of the clock. Instead, her eyes snapped to Mia's with wild, desperate clarity. "Jacqueline!" she cried, the name tearing from her like a wound reopened. "That was the whole problem, don't you see? I was Jacqueline! Jacqueline, Jacqueline! I had trained myself to be her. How could I be Eileen again? How could I?"

Mia held steady as Eileen's anguish surged, her outburst raw and unfiltered. Inwardly, Mia cursed the shortsightedness of the Firm all those years ago. What had they been thinking, giving Eileen Nearne an alias bearing her beloved sister's name? Did they not consider the psychological toll it might take on a young woman already risking everything for them?

But now was not the time to dwell on their failures. Mia was here to deal with what was in front of her—not with mistakes buried in the past. Her only task was to safeguard the fragile trust Eileen had placed in her. Tentative as it was, that trust was still intact. As long as it held, Mia believed she could navigate Eileen even through this iceberg of pain and guilt.

"Aunt Didi," Mia said in a pacifying voice. "It's all right. You don't have to be anyone but yourself anymore. Not Jacqueline, not anyone else. Just you. And I'll help you find her again."

She kept her gaze locked with Eileen's, her tone firm but infused with compassion. Slowly, she felt the tension in Eileen's grip ease, though the storm in her eyes still raged. It wasn't resolution—not yet—but it was a step. A small one, but a step, nonetheless.

"Let's come back to it this afternoon and now have a cuppa?" Mia suggested. She straightened in her seat, her tone even and soothing. "I think we've earned that, don't you? And you know what? We'll make it together. Wouldn't it be nice if you showed me how to make a strong cup of tea? I'm one of these modern chicks who only drinks chamomile tea, but I'd love to see how you do it."

Eileen stared at her as if she'd lost all her senses. For a moment, Mia wondered if she had overstepped, but then Eileen's lips curved into what resembled a sardonic smile.

"Chamomile tea?" Her voice edged with disbelief. "What's that supposed to do—soothe your nerves or your conscience? Real tea isn't made with flowers, my dear—it's made with leaves and backbone. Now get up, and I'll show you how to make a proper brew."

Mia couldn't help but laugh, relief washing over her. Eileen was fully back in the moment, her wit as sharp as ever. "All right, Aunt Didi," she said, standing. "Lead the way. Show me how it's done."

Eileen gave a curt nod. Her strength seemed to return as she pushed herself up from the armchair with practiced determination. "Just don't expect me to go easy on you. If you're going to learn, you'll do it right."

In the kitchen, the tension of the earlier session faded into the background and was replaced by the practical steadiness of a new ritual—one that, in its simplicity, felt like healing in action.

As they settled back down, Eileen grumbled about too much milk and not enough sugar, her tone brusque but familiar. Mia allowed herself a small smile, grateful for the return of her sharp-witted client. Still, the air between them felt charged, and Mia knew she couldn't delay any longer. She needed to address what had just happened.

But, as usual, Eileen was quicker.

"Why did you do it?" she asked abruptly.

"Do what?" Mia replied, momentarily puzzled.

"Don't play dumb with me, girl." Eileen's blue eyes fixed on her, sharp and demanding. "You interrupted the last part of my story. When I wanted to tell you what happened with the American Intelligence Service. I wanted to have it over and done with, you see."

"I know, Aunt Didi," Mia said, uneasy under Eileen's stare. "And it's not my usual practice to interrupt a session like this. But I had a good reason."

"Being?" Eileen's eyes narrowed, bordering on anger. It wasn't just impatience; Mia could see the desperation behind them. She clearly wanted—needed—to unburden herself of this pain. Mia swallowed hard, doubting herself for a brief moment before she explained.

"What happened to you, Aunt Didi, right at the moment you

were finally safe, is, in my opinion, criminal. And I believe it's your deepest scar."

The sharpness in Eileen's eyes softened slightly as Mia continued. Her voice trembled with the intensity of her conviction.

"There is no stronger woman than you, Aunt Didi. All the humiliation, the pain, the hunger, the illness, the cold, the inhuman treatment you endured during those nine months of captivity—you took it in your stride. All of that, you survived because you believed in something bigger than yourself: good over evil. And you won, Aunt Didi. You triumphed.

"But the moment the 'good guys'—the ones who were supposed to be your allies—didn't believe your story and turned you over to the bad guys again..." Mia paused, her voice almost breaking. "That's when I believe your spirit broke. And anyone's spirit would have. That should never have happened—to you, to anyone. It's appalling beyond words."

Mia stopped, her throat tight with anger and sorrow. She hadn't meant to let so much of her frustration spill out, but she couldn't help it.

Eileen gazed at Mia in surprise. "I'm sure it wasn't intentional, dear," she said almost apologetically. "Those were very chaotic times." She hesitated, her expression darkening. "But you're right. I've never looked at it that way. The Americans did break my spirit. Their actions made me doubt my faith, my loyalties. Doubt why I had fought so desperately for the cause I thought we both stood for."

"That's why I had to stop you, Aunt Didi," Mia said in a voice that sounded dejected. "I needed to make you aware that we're entering the most crucial part of your healing. You must see that this part of your war memory is different from the rest. I truly believe it's this pain point that has traveled with you through the decades. We have to take the sting out of it. I hope—" Mia's voice faltered briefly, her own emotions threatening to surface. “I hope you’ll feel freer after.”

For a long moment, Eileen didn’t respond. Her gaze drifted toward the window, her expression unreadable. The clock ticked softly in the background, filling the silence. Then, slowly, she nodded.

“All right,” she replied in a low voice. “But you have to promise me... promise me it won’t make me... worse. I couldn’t handle that.”

Mia leaned forward to take Eileen’s hands in hers. “I can promise you this: it won’t make you worse, Aunt Didi. But I believe it will make you better. I can’t guarantee it. Though, by God, I wish I could.”

Eileen exhaled shakily, taking her hands back.

“Let me finish this awful cup of tea first.” The mockery in her tone, the sly smile--all great survival tactics--disappeared as she closed her eyes and leaned back into the armchair. Mia watched her closely and saw something flicker across her face, something she hadn’t seen before.

Non-resistance.

For the first time, Eileen didn’t fight the weight of her trauma. She wasn’t ready to let it go, not yet. But she wasn’t pushing it away either.

And that was enough for now.

PART XVI

~EILEEN~ GERMANY / ENGLAND 16 APRIL - 23 MAY 1945

58

SURELY, THIS WAS THE FINAL STRETCH?

U.S. Interrogation Camp, Leipzig, 19 April 1945

For ten days, the rectory and Pater Ernst's Catholic church on the outskirts of Leipzig had been a haven of warmth for Eileen, Yvette, and Suzanne. Amidst the chaos of a broken world and the ordeals they'd endured—too raw to even begin processing—they had found the peace and mercy of God, reflected in the goodness of two brave German souls.

Pater Ernst had been their protector, and Gretchen their nurturer, both risking their lives to shelter concentration camp refugees. The shield they'd offered from the ever-present threat of death and danger was beyond words.

Now, with the American army in control of the area, it was time for the girls to take their leave. Yet, as they stood before the priest and housekeeper, words seemed insufficient for the depth of their gratitude.

"Pater Ernst," Eileen said, her voice almost choking with emotion as she reached for his flabby white hand, adorned with the ruby ring that had so often clasped a prayer book. Summoning her best German, she said, "*Ihre Güte und Ihr Mut—Gott wird es nie vergessen. Danke.*" Your kindness and your courage—God will never forget it. Thank you.

Pater Ernst folded her small hand tightly between both of his and gave her a somber nod. "You owe me nothing, children. You owe God your survival. I am only His instrument. Go home. Live well. And always thank the Lord. His justice will reign."

Beside him, Gretchen dabbed at her eyes with the corner of her apron, her usual no-nonsense practicality cracking under the weight of the moment. "You poor lambs. I'll never forget the sight of you three that first night," she said with a sniffle. Then, fixing her stern gaze on Eileen's gaunt frame, she added, "You eat, my lamb. Eat everything you can get your hands on. And stay out of trouble for the rest of your lives. You must promise me."

"We promise," Yvette said, smiling through her tears. "And we'll remember you every day."

Suzanne stepped forward, clutching Gretchen's hands tightly. "*Danke*," she said through a tight throat. "*Merci*. Thank you. For everything."

Eileen turned to take one last look at the rectory, the graveyard where they'd hidden that first night, and the golden cross that crowned the church. This had been their sanctuary—a stepping stone to real freedom.

As she stepped into the street, wrapped in the love of faith and hope, her heart lifted. Surely now, with the Americans here, the hardest part was over.

The American soldiers were easy to spot—loud, confident, their khaki uniforms clean and crisp compared to the bedraggled survivors around them. Eileen straightened her back and approached the nearest one, her step determined despite the uncertainty curling in her stomach.

"I am English. Can you please show me where the Red Cross is?" she announced in a careful but firm voice. It had been so long since she'd spoken her father tongue that the words felt foreign on her lips. Still, she was determined—*from now on, I'll be my real self. Goodbye, Jacqueline du Tertre. You served me well.*

The soldier blinked at her, startled by the polished British accent coming from someone so visibly worn by war. His sunburned face crinkled in surprise as he sized her up, his hands resting casually on his hips. Before he could respond, Yvette and Suzanne surged forward, their expressions a mix of shock and confusion.

"*Comment ça, tu es anglaise?*" Yvette demanded. "How can you be? Who are you? Where do you come from?"

Eileen turned to them, switching effortlessly into French. "I didn't lie to you about my youth. I *did* grow up in France, but my father was English, so that makes me—"

Before she could explain further, the soldier interrupted. "Now hold on there, missie," he drawled, his voice carrying the cadence of the American South. "I got no idea what you're talkin' 'bout, bouncin' between English and French like a rabbit in a briar patch. Makes my head spin. I'm just a plain ol' boy from Texas tryin' to do my job. Y'all want the Red Cross, huh?"

Yvette and Suzanne stared at him, bewildered, while Eileen nodded. The soldier's tone softened as he saw the state they were in. "Look, ma'am, my job is real simple: make sure former camp prisoners like y'all got a roof over your heads tonight. You'll be safe now, I promise. We'll sort out all the where-ya-come-froms and where-ya-goin's tomorrow."

He fished into his pocket, pulling out a crumpled pack of Lucky Strikes. "Care for a cig, ladies? Good ol' American welcome."

Without hesitation, they each took one. Yvette's hands trembled as he gave her a light. Suzanne didn't seem a real smoker but joined in, nonetheless. Eileen inhaled deeply, the smoke curling around her face, like relief made tangible.

The soldier grinned, tipping his helmet back. "There ya go. Now, if y'all can quit all that French jabberin' for a spell, I'll show you to one of our safe houses. Got beds, blankets, even hot water if you're lucky. Reckon that'll do ya better than standin' out here tryin' to explain things I don't rightly understand."

Eileen couldn't help but smile at the man's easy manner. His accent was as far from the clipped tones of her father or the lilting French of her childhood as she could imagine, but his warmth and practicality cut through the surreal nature of the moment.

"Thank you," she said, giving him a warm smile. "And thank you for liberating us."

"Don't mention it, missie. Seeing the state you gals are in, reckon we're just in time." He motioned for them to follow, his boots crunching on the gravel.

As they walked, Yvette began again in a tone tinged with disbelief. "*Anglaise?* Truly? After all this time?"

Eileen glanced at her friend and felt clumsy and vulnerable now her secret was laid bare. "Yes," she replied softly. "I'm sorry. I'll explain."

"What's your real name then?" Suzanne asked.

Eileen hesitated, taking a moment, as it seemed so solemn. The three words almost felt alien, outside of her. "Eileen Mary Nearne."

But when she heard her own name aloud, after so many months of secrets and subterfuge, her feet suddenly touched solid ground. The name was hers—unshaken, unbroken, and undisputed.

THE NEXT DAY, the three girls were taken to a building the U.S. Army had commandeered and was now using as a temporary prison camp for presumed Nazi criminals. Eileen entered the barracks with a steady flame of hope in her heart. Her strength was bolstered by the idea that she would soon be heading home—to England, to Jacqueline, and eventually to her family in France.

In a small, makeshift room, an American captain sat across from the three women, a cluster of SS officers ominously standing to one side.

Yvette and Suzanne spoke first, explaining in French and broken English that they had worked for the French Resistance before being captured and transported to Germany. The captain listened intently, jotting down every detail. Then he turned to Eileen.

"And you?" he asked. "Your story?"

"I am ... I was a British agent with the SOE, the Special Operations Executive. I worked as a W/T Operator for a resistance network that operated in the Paris region," Eileen said clearly, meeting his gaze without hesitation. "I was captured by the Gestapo in Paris in July last year and have been in various German concentration camps since August."

As she spoke, she felt the piercing eyes of the SS officers on her, and her discomfort grew. It was deeply unsettling to be in their presence again after everything they'd done. Her skin prickled with unease. *Why are they here? What could they possibly have to do with me now?*

When the captain finally addressed the SS officers, her discomfort turned to dread.

"You treated these women horribly," the captain said coldly, his disdain evident. "You will pay for it."

One of the officers raised his hands in mock protest, his expression calculated and unrepentant. "We know nothing about those women," he said smoothly. "I've never seen them before." His oily tone filled the room, and Eileen understood all too well the game they were playing.

"*Wir haben es nicht gewusst*," he added, the first layers of 'we didn't know' settling like smoke over the room, suffocating and vile.

Eileen's hands tightened into fists, but she forced herself to stay calm. She was a British citizen, after all. Surely, this was just a formality, a necessary step before she was allowed to go home.

"You," the captain commanded, pointing to Yvette and Suzanne, "you'll be joining other French nationals in the Red Cross transit camp before going back to France."

Then his gray eyes, framed by bushy eyebrows, shifted to Eileen. "Your story sounds odd to my ears. I've never heard of this Secret Operations Executive that you claim to be working for. We need more information, so I'm sending you to another camp for further questioning."

Eileen's heart plummeted. Was her British citizenship—her truth—going to be her undoing now, at the very end? Should she have clung to her French persona a little longer? The thought flickered briefly, but she pushed it aside. These were her liberators. Surely the truth needed to come out now.

She stood frozen, stunned by the captain's words, unable to fully process them. It wasn't until Yvette tugged hard on her sleeve that she registered the voice beside her.

"We need to say goodbye for now, *chérie*. We're going."

Eileen turned sharply to face her friends, tears already welling in her eyes. Their goodbye was sudden and brutally unexpected, like a piece of herself being ripped away. The bond they had forged through escape and survival was unbreakable, yet here they were, being torn apart. They had endured trials that few could understand, only to be cast back into uncertainty once again.

"No," Eileen whispered, her voice trembling as she clung to Yvette. "Don't go yet. I need you."

Suzanne stepped forward, wrapping her arms around both of them. Together, the three women stood like this, holding on to each other as if their very lives depended on it. In that moment, they didn't care about the American captain's impatience or the sneering SS officers watching nearby. Their shared grief outweighed everything else.

Yvette pulled back, gripping Eileen's hands as tight as she could. "Say it again," she insisted, her voice low but fierce. "You must remember my address. I don't want to lose you."

Eileen swallowed the lump in her throat and repeated it. "I'll remember," she said, choking on the tears that threatened to spill. "I promise. I'll write as soon as I can. *Au revoir, mes amies. Je vous aime pour toujours.*"

When they hugged for the last time, it was fierce and desperate, a moment suspended in time. Then, reluctantly, Yvette and Suzanne turned to follow their escorts.

Eileen stood rooted in place, watching as their gray-overalled figures grew smaller with every step, until they disappeared entirely.

Her chest ached as she realized she was alone again. Not completely—she still had her strength and her will—but the loss of her friends felt like losing pieces of her armor.

And now, uncertainty loomed larger than ever.

THAT EVENING, Eileen was taken to another camp. The buildings were different, the atmosphere heavier, colder.

She was to be questioned further, they told her, about her role as a British agent.

Eileen's hope wavered but held. She clung to the thought of home, of Jacqueline. Soon, she thought. Soon, this will all be over.

She closed her eyes, letting the image of Jacqueline's face fill her mind. It was the only thing keeping her fears at bay. She had survived so much already. Surely, this was the final stretch.

59

NOT BEING BELIEVED

The next day - Another American Camp, Germany, April 1945

Eileen sat stiffly on the hard wooden chair in her gray overalls, her hands clenched in her lap. Across the table, the American officer, a sharp-eyed man in his thirties with a clipped manner, shuffled a stack of papers. The room was small, cold, and filled with the faint smell of damp concrete.

"Name?" the officer asked, not looking up.

"Eileen Mary Nearne," she replied, wondering why he asked if she could see her full details clearly spelled out on the file in front of him.

"Number?"

"I don't have a number," she said quietly.

Now the officer glanced up and frowned. "No number? Everyone's got a number. What camp were you in?"

"Ravensbrück." Eileen tried to keep her voice from catching in her throat, "and then I was transferred to Torgau. But I wasn't registered. I—"

The officer interrupted. "You weren't registered? That's convenient."

Eileen bristled. "I wasn't registered because I wasn't supposed to survive. I was a *Nacht und Nebel* prisoner—a 'Night and Fog' detainee. Do you know what that means?"

The officer leaned back in his chair, his skepticism evident. "Go on."

"I'm a British agent," she said firmly. "I worked as a wireless operator for the Special Operations Executive—the SOE. I was arrested by the Gestapo in Paris in July last year. My papers were confiscated. I was interrogated, tortured—"

"Papers," the officer cut her off, holding up his hand. "You got *anything* to prove that?"

Eileen's breath hitched, but she forced herself to stay calm. "No. As I said, the Gestapo took them when I was arrested."

"No papers, no number, no nothing," the officer muttered, scribbling something in his notebook. He looked up sharply. "Who was your commanding officer?"

"Colonel... Max Baxter, no that's not right...," Eileen blurted out, her voice faltering as soon as the words left her lips. She froze. It should have been Maurice Buckmaster.

The officer's pen stopped mid-stroke. "Colonel Max Baxter? Never heard of him." He folded his arms and stared her down. "Funny story. Never heard of SOE."

Eileen's chest tightened. "I—"

"Let me get this straight." The officer's voice was cold and sharp. "You're claiming to be some British secret agent, dropped into occupied France in the dead of night, working radios, dodging the Gestapo—and you don't even remember the name of your superior?"

"It was a mistake," she said desperately. "I'm tired. I've been through—"

He slammed his hand on the table, making her flinch. "Enough!"

The silence that followed broke Eileen's heart into a hundred pieces.

"Listen," he said, his tone now low and menacing. "Your story doesn't add up. No papers, no number, no proof. And you can't even keep your story straight. If you're not lying, you're hiding something."

"I've signed the Official Secrets Act," Eileen protested, her voice trembling. "I can't—"

"Secrets, huh?" The officer smirked. "Let me tell you what I think. I think you're a German spy. And until we can figure out what to do with you, you're going somewhere where you can't cause any trouble."

Eileen's blood ran cold. "No," she whispered. "You don't understand. I'm telling the truth! I'm British—"

"Enough," he snapped again, motioning to a soldier standing by the door. "Take her away."

The soldier stepped forward, grabbing Eileen roughly by the arm.

THE CELL DOOR slammed shut behind her and Eileen was once again a prisoner. Vaguely registering German voices around her, she sank down to her haunches against the grimy wall. Not looking up, curling into herself.

As she sat on that cold floor, too dazed to comprehend how it had all gone so wrong, despair flooded over her in waves. Her thoughts tripped over themselves, unable to form a coherent picture.

Surely, that well-fed man—that American officer—must have seen how malnourished she was. Did he not notice the gaunt hollows of her cheeks, the sallow pallor of her skin? Did the threadbare camp uniform not speak for itself?

How could he not see? How could anyone look at me and think— Her breath hitched. *A traitor? A German spy? After all I've endured?*

The thought cut her like a knife. Her hands shook as she clutched the fabric of her uniform, her fingers digging into the coarse material as if trying to tether herself to reality.

Even if he found my story suspicious, she thought, her mind clawing for logic, *could he not have waited? Could he not have checked with London first?*

Her voice had trembled when she mentioned the SOE. She realized now how it must have sounded to him: distant, unsure, and inconsistent. And yet, how could it not? After everything—after Ravensbrück, after Torgau, after the constant threat of death—she was barely holding herself together.

She'd tried pleading with the Americans who took her away. Her voice had cracked as she begged, her eyes wide and desperate. But their responses were the same—always the same.

"We're sorry," one of the soldiers said. "With so many German agents around, we just can't take any chances."

Another added, "Even if you had a message saying you were English, it wouldn't prove anything. These German spies are clever—they'd try anything."

Their words played over and over in her mind, a cruel litany she couldn't escape. Her heart sank deeper with each repetition, as if a weight pressed her into the ground. *Just swallow me whole. I'm ready*, she thought in her despair.

For the very first time in her life, Eileen was angry with God.

Her lips moved soundlessly at first, forming the words she could not speak aloud. Her mind screamed them instead: *Why, God? Why did You let me survive everything—the pain, the hunger, the cold, the humiliation—to bring me to this?*

She pressed her palms to her temples, trembling, her breath shallow and ragged. "Why?" she whispered, the word tearing from her like a sob. "Why did You save me, only to bring me here, to this shame?"

Tears streamed down her cheeks as she sat hunched and small, her body rocking as though trying to soothe a pain no comfort could touch.

"I have not yielded," she whispered. "I have kept my faith in You. I've endured everything. What more do You want me to do?"

Her words echoed in the empty space where her heart once was, unanswered, swallowed by His silence. She clenched her fists, her knuckles pale, her despair spiraling. *What more, God? What more?*

All she wanted now was to be left alone. To curl into herself, to fade into nothing, to simply die. She would die here, in shame and disbelief.

The thought felt oddly comforting, a release from the torment of being doubted, of being cast aside. She closed her eyes, her head leaning against the cold wall of the cell. In that moment, she wanted nothing more than oblivion.

Then, faintly at first, she heard voices. She looked up, her vision blurry from tears, and saw them. The German women—the camp overseers, unmistakable in their sharp postures and cruel smirks—were gathered at the other end of the barracks. They were laughing, their voices lilting in mock sweetness as they flirted shamelessly with the American soldiers.

One of the women, her blonde hair neatly combed and her cheeks powdered, leaned closer to a young soldier, brushing her hand against his arm. He grinned boyishly, handing her a cigarette from a pack of Lucky Strikes.

Another overseer, dark-haired with icy eyes, held a tin of food, the corners of her mouth curled in triumph as she slipped it into her pocket.

Eileen blinked while she caught her breath.

They're getting food? Cigarettes? Privileges?

She watched in disbelief as the soldiers—barely older than boys—laughed with the women, seemingly oblivious to the atrocities they had committed. These women, who had tormented her and countless others, now stood there charming her liberators.

The fury came slowly at first, like an ember smoldering in her chest.

How dare they.

Eileen sat up straighter, her mind beginning to clear. Her hands clenched into fists as the ember flared into a spark, then into a roaring flame.

These women—who starved us, beat us, humiliated us—are now laughing and eating while I sit here, accused of being a spy?

Her heart pounded with indignation, her despair burned away by the sheer injustice of it all. She felt the strength returning to her limbs, her back straightening as the spark inside her reignited something she thought had been lost forever.

I am not having this.

The words echoed in her mind, fierce and resolute. She pushed herself to her feet, the weight of hopelessness replaced by the fire of righteous anger.

I will not be degraded to their level. I have fought too hard, sacrificed too much, to let them win now.

She took a deep breath, her thoughts sharpening with clarity. The Americans had to know the truth—not just about her, but about these women who had fooled them so easily.

Eileen squared her shoulders and marched toward the nearest soldier. "I need to speak with your commanding officer."

The soldier blinked, startled by her sudden presence. "What for?" he asked. He sounded hesitant.

"Because you are letting yourselves be fooled," she said sharply, pointing toward the overseers. "Those women—do you know who they are? They were camp overseers. Guards. They tormented prisoners—starved us, beat us, killed us. And now they stand there laughing with you, taking your food and your cigarettes, while I sit here being accused of being a spy for the enemy I fought against."

The soldier looked between her and the women. Eileen didn't flinch.

"I demand to see a senior officer," she said, her voice ringing with conviction. "Someone who will listen. Someone who can do something about this."

The soldier opened his mouth as if to protest, but the intensity in her eyes stopped him. He nodded with reluctance. "All right. Stay here."

As he walked off, Eileen stood tall, her chin lifted. Her heart still pounded, but it wasn't with fear. For the first time since being accused of being on the wrong side, she felt alive again.

I will fight this.

Her spirit, broken only hours ago, now burned brighter than ever. She would not let this stand—not for herself, and not for all the others who had suffered.

Not today. Not ever.

60

FINALLY, JUSTICE

The office was sparse but orderly: a wooden desk cluttered with papers, a half-empty bottle of whiskey, and a pack of Lucky Strikes sitting beside a small ashtray. The American intelligence officer leaned back in his chair, the smoke from his cigarette curling lazily into the air. His uniform, though neatly pressed, showed signs of long days and late nights—a frayed edge on his sleeve, scuffed boots.

Eileen stood before him, her back straight and her hands clasped tightly to keep them from trembling. She was exhausted, her body cried out for rest, but her inner resolve burned brightly.

The officer took a long drag on his cigarette, his eyes fixed on her through the smoke. "Well, ma'am," he said, his Southern drawl softened with fatigue. "You don't look like you're gonna budge until I hear you out. So, go on. What's got you so fired up?"

"Those women." She pointed through the window in their direction. "The ones who were laughing and smoking with your men—they're camp guards. SS overseers. They tortured prisoners—starved us, beat us, humiliated us."

He raised an eyebrow, blowing out a slow stream of smoke. “You’re tellin’ me those ladies out there,” he gestured vaguely with his cigarette, “are war criminals?”

“Yes,” Eileen snapped. “And they’ve been using your soldiers’ kindness to get privileges they don’t deserve. Food, cigarettes, whatever else they can charm out of them. While I—” She stopped herself, swallowing the lump in her throat. “While I, a British agent who served your cause, sit accused of being a German spy.”

He held her gaze, but his expression was unreadable. Then he stubbed out his cigarette with deliberate care and leaned his elbows on the desk. “All right. Tell me everything.”

Eileen took a deep breath and began recounting her story with a clarity born of desperation. “My name is Eileen Mary Nearne. I was trained at Beaulieu in England as a wireless operator for the Special Operations Executive. I was flown into France by Lysander on the night of 2 March 1944. I worked in occupied France under the alias Jacqueline du Tertre, sending coded messages back to London. I was arrested in July last year, interrogated by the Gestapo, and sent to Ravensbrück. I’ve been in camps ever since.”

The officer’s eyes narrowed slightly. “This Special Operations Executive you’re talkin’ about—how come I’ve never heard of it?”

Eileen’s jaw tightened. “It’s a secret organization. You wouldn’t have heard of it. But if you contact Colonel Maurice Buckmaster or Flight Officer Vera Atkins in London, they’ll confirm everything I’ve told you.”

“And where am I supposed to find these folks?” he asked, leaning back again.

She hesitated. “I don’t know where the headquarters is exactly,” she admitted, “but the Hotel Victoria on Orchard Street in London is where they operate from.”

The officer rubbed his temple, his disbelief evident. “Hotel Victoria,” he muttered, half to himself. “Lady, you’re askin’ me to believe we've been droppin' women into occupied France by plane in the middle of the night. That sounds like something' outta Hollywood."

"It's the truth," Eileen said firmly, though cringing at the sting of his skepticism. There it was again. *When would they listen?*

He studied her for a long moment, then sighed heavily, reaching for his whisky. "All right," he said, taking a sip. "Here's what I'll do. I'll look into your case, see if I can get someone higher up to make contact with London. But you gotta understand, we're drowning in cases here—refugees, prisoners, spies, folks we can't even figure out what to call. You're just one of many."

Eileen nodded, swallowing her disappointment. "I understand. But please, don't delay. I've survived too much to be left in limbo any longer."

The officer's face softened. "I'll make sure you're moved somewhere better," he said. "You've been through hell. I can see that much. No more sittin' with those Nazi guards. You've got my word on that."

"Thank you," Eileen said in her quiet, sincere voice.

Later that day

Eileen stood at the edge of the camp, watching as a group of female Nazi guards, their heads freshly shaved, were marched behind barbed wire by American soldiers.

Her eyes narrowed as she spotted the familiar faces of the overseers who had tormented her. The blonde one clutched her gray dress, looking small and insignificant without her uniform. The dark-haired one kept her head high, her icy stare intact despite her shaved scalp.

The American soldiers who had once laughed and flirted with the German women were nowhere to be seen. A small, grim satisfaction stirred in Eileen's chest. It wasn't justice—not yet—but it was something.

She turned away from the sight, her shoulders stiff but her steps lighter. Her new barracks were different—cleaner, quieter. There was a proper bed, though the mattress was thin, and she had more privacy. It was still captivity, but it was better than the grim corners she'd occupied before.

As she placed her packet of cigarettes and sandwiches on the bed, a voice broke the silence.

"*Je m'appelle Paulette. Et toi?*"

Eileen turned to see a woman sitting cross-legged on the neighboring cot, her elbows resting on her knees. Paulette was petite but wiry, her dark hair tied back in a messy braid that hung over one shoulder. Her olive-toned skin was marked with faint scars, and her large, watchful eyes held a wary curiosity. She looked as though she had seen more of life's hardships than any woman her age should have.

For a moment, Eileen froze, instinctively reaching for the persona she had lived under for so long. *Jacqueline du Tertre,* the name hovered on her lips. But then she caught herself, straightened, and spoke the truth, "Eileen. Eileen Mary Nearne."

Paulette tilted her heady. "*Tu n'es pas Française?*"

"No," Eileen affirmed on a here-we-go-again tone. "I grew up in France, but I'm British."

"British?" Paulette looked surprised, then shrugged. "Well, you speak French like one of us. Why are you here, Eileen?"

Eileen hesitated. Telling her story had become almost mechanical by now, but the looks of disbelief that invariably followed made it no easier. Still, she told Paulette of her time as a wireless operator for the SOE, her capture, and the long months in the camps.

Paulette listened intently, her sharp eyes never leaving Eileen's face. When Eileen finished, she shook her head angrily. "And the Americans don't believe you? After all that?"

Eileen gave a bitter laugh. "They think I'm a German spy. And you?"

Paulette crossed her arms over her chest, a deep frown between the clear eyes. "I was with the French Resistance. Carrying messages, helping sabotage the Germans. Then I was caught and thrown in a camp." Her voice hardened. "Now, they don't believe me either. Can you imagine? The Americans think I'm a spy too. They say we need to prove our stories."

Eileen's jaw clenched. "Prove?! After everything we've done, everything we've been through? Shouldn't surviving be enough?"

"Exactly," Paulette said fiercely. "They have no idea what it's like —what we've been through. We risked everything for them. For *their war.* And this is how we're treated?" She gestured angrily at the barracks around them.

Eileen's anger flared up again. "It's appalling. We fought for the same cause. We suffered for it. And yet, here we are—treated like criminals while the real ones get away."

Paulette sighed, her anger giving way to exhaustion. "At least," she said, her tone softer now, "they're not locking us up with those Nazi women anymore."

"No," Eileen agreed, glancing at her new surroundings. "It's a bit better here. And at least we can talk. In French."

Paulette gave her a faint smile. "*C'est vrai.* Talking helps. And it's nice to have someone who understands. The Americans mean well, maybe, but they don't understand. Not really."

Eileen sat on the edge of her bed, her shoulders slowly relaxing. "No," she agreed. "I guess we have to believe they mean well, but how can they be so ignorant?"

The two women sat in companionable silence for a moment,

glancing at each other, glad to no longer be so terribly alone and misunderstood.

Fifteen days later - 12 May 1945

Eileen sat on the edge of her bunk, absently tracing the faded pattern of the thin blanket beneath her. The news of the German surrender spread through the camp like wildfire. The war was over, they said, but for Eileen, nothing had changed.

Three weeks in custody had stretched endlessly, her pleas and explanations falling on deaf ears. Even now, the taste of indignation lingered, bitter and unrelenting. She had spent so long fighting for their cause—for freedom—and yet here she remained, under suspicion.

The guard's voice broke her from her thoughts. "Nearne. Office. Now."

She blinked, startled. Her name was rarely spoken with anything other than dismissal or disdain. Rising to her feet, she smoothed her camp-issued dress and followed the guard down the dimly lit hallway.

The small office was as nondescript as the others she had been summoned to before—bare walls, a desk, and a single chair. But the man standing behind the desk was different. His uniform was sharply pressed, the insignia on his shoulder gleaming in the dim light. He was tall, with a square jaw and a calm but commanding presence.

As soon as she entered, he stepped forward and extended his hand.

"Miss Nearne," he said warmly, his American accent clear but tempered with a professional formality. "I'm Major Denis Newman. It's an honor to meet you."

Eileen stared at his hand for a moment, stunned, before hesitantly taking it. The handshake was firm. It grounded her in the reality of the moment.

"Please, sit." He gestured to the chair.

She lowered herself as she was told. "Major Newman," she asked cautiously. "What is this about?"

The Major leaned against the desk with a worried expression on his clean-shaven face. "I'm here to apologize, Miss Nearne. For everything. The treatment you've endured, the suspicion you've been subjected to—it never should have happened."

Eileen felt as if her breath had stopped. The words, though true, sounded surreal, as though she'd conjured them in a desperate dream.

"We received a report from London," Newman continued, "in response to your earlier interrogations. When our interrogation report crossed Flight Officer Vera Atkins' desk, she acted immediately. She knew who you were and understood what had happened. Miss Atkins has been working tirelessly to locate you, and once the details matched your profile, she sent me to find you. She's been working with Colonel Buckmaster to clear your name and bring you home."

Eileen stared at him, dumbfounded. She opened her mouth to speak but found herself unable to form words.

The Major said in a soft voice, "We've already confirmed with London that you were captured after working in France for 5 months. The Gestapo and the camps—everything you've endured—was corroborated by your records and by those who worked with you. Miss Atkins wanted me to assure you personally that you are believed, and every effort is being made to set things right."

Eileen's lips started to tremble. She'd braced herself for harsh judgments of her person for so long that this sudden affirmation felt almost incomprehensible. "You—you believe me?" she whispered, tears spilling over her cheeks.

"Absolutely," Newman said, offering her his clean handkerchief. "And I'm here to make sure you're treated with the respect you deserve."

Her eyes filled with tears, and she dabbed them, inhaling a vague scent of the Major's eau de cologne. After all these weeks of humiliation and doubt, the shift was overwhelming. She sat up straighter, her composure returning as she absorbed his words.

"Thank you," she said quietly. "Thank you for coming. Thank you for believing me. It's all I asked for."

Newman's expression was solemn. "You'll be leaving this camp immediately. I've arranged for you to be billeted at the Christliche Hospice nearby. You'll have proper accommodation, food, and rest. You'll also be given fresh clothes and whatever else you might need while we finalize your return to London."

Eileen tried to take it all in, but her mind had difficulty catching up to the moment. "The hospice," she repeated, almost as if testing the words. It sounded far removed from the grim barracks she'd grown used to.

Newman stood, offering his hand again. "Let's get you out of here, Miss Nearne. You've waited long enough."

This time, Eileen took his hand without hesitation.

"I'll ...I'll be needing to say goodbye to Paulette. She... she was in the same boat as me, just on the French side of the Resistance. I don't suppose...?" She looked at the American Major as if he might help her new friend as well.

"That's all sorted too, thank God." He said in a chirpy voice, "Paulette will be leaving for France soon."

61

THE ECHO OF VALOR

Christliche Hospice, Germany, 12 May 1945

The Christliche Hospice stood tall and intact amidst the rubble of war-torn Germany, a stoic testament to its Christian origins. Its weathered stone walls radiated a quiet dignity, and the 'Stars and Stripes' flying atop its roof left no doubt about who now held authority in the area.

"Go on, Miss Nearne, after you," Major Denis Newman said, holding the heavy oak door open.

Before stepping inside, Eileen glanced at the tall American officer beside her and caught the subtle reverence in his demeanor. From the beginning, Newman's attitude towards her had been different from the mistrust, even contempt, she'd encountered from the Americans before, and it held something deeper—a genuine admiration tinged with protectiveness.

Inside, the air was warmer, smelling of wood smoke, leather polish and cigarettes. It was clean, orderly, and wonderfully quiet—

the opposite of the crowded, grim barracks in which they had locked her up.

"It's very much a bachelor's digs, I'm afraid," Newman said with an apologetic smile. "Not exactly the Ritz, but I couldn't stand leaving you in that camp for even one more day. I promise you, though, we're respectable gentlemen, and we'll do our best to make you comfortable. Even if hosting a female secret agent is a first for us."

Eileen laughed, her voice light for the first time in what felt like months. "Don't worry, Major Newman," she said. "I have two older brothers and spent most of the war working with men. I think I can manage."

Newman chuckled, his eyes sparkling with warmth. "Call me Denis," he said. "And truly, Miss Nearne, you're something else. I've never clapped eyes on a female secret agent before, and now I find myself escorting one who escaped from a concentration camp. Miss, you're my heroine."

Eileen felt a blush rise to her cheeks and lifted a hand self-consciously to her short curls. "Please, call me Eileen. And I just did my duty. I never expected to get caught, much less... well, all the rest of it."

Denis's green eyes held her gaze as he said in a soft, admiring tone. "And yet, you came through it all. Magnificently, I might add. Not many can say that, Eileen."

"Stop it, or I really will start blushing," she said, laughing, but her voice was warm, and her cheeks held a faint pink glow.

As they moved farther inside, a kind-faced nurse approached them, her uniform bearing a small US flag logo. Newman gestured to her. "Beryl, before you go back to the hospital, could you show Miss Nearne to her room and make sure she has everything she needs?"

Beryl gave Eileen a warm smile. "Of course, Major. Miss Nearne, if you'll come with me?"

"Come back down when you're ready," Newman said as he turned back to Eileen. "No pressure, but I'd love to introduce you to the boys. We usually play a hand of cards or a game of chess before dinner. They'll be dying to meet you—a modern Joan of Arc, if I might say so."

Eileen grinned, her confidence rising under his easy charm. "How long will I be staying here... Denis?" she asked. She liked the sound of everything so far, but she ached to return to England, to find her sister, and to finally go home.

"Two nights, at least," he said. "We're working on getting you a flight. It all depends on which airfield we can send you out from. Will that be all right?"

"Of course," she said. "I'll see you later."

With that, Eileen followed Beryl up the staircase, feeling relieved. But there was also the germ of something else. For the first time since her capture, she felt truly seen—not just as a woman who had endured unspeakable trials, but as someone worth admiring for who she was, what she stood for. Alcide had looked at her that way and so had Armand. Men she held in high esteem.

Major Denis Newman had made her feel worthy again. And though she wasn't quite sure how to process it, she couldn't help but smile.

Beryl wasn't particularly talkative, her clipped instructions and hurried movements making it clear she was under a heavy workload. Sensing the strain, Eileen stayed quiet, suppressing the many questions she wanted to ask. Instead, she followed the nurse silently to a small room at the end of the hall.

"This is yours for now," Beryl said briskly, motioning toward the bed. On it lay a neatly folded pile of clothes: a khaki uniform, sturdy and practical, with the stars-and-stripes on both lapels. Beside it sat a cream-colored blouse, its fabric crisp and clean, even a tie and the funniest little cap Eileen had ever seen.

"I hope they fit at least somehow," Beryl sighed. Her gaze lingered on Eileen's gaunt frame. "You're still terribly thin, but it's all we've got. No seamstresses around to take it in and all I had was this new WAAC uniform, you see."

Eileen reached out and ran her fingers over the fabric of the blouse, savoring the feeling in her fingertips. She swallowed hard as unexpected emotions rose in her chest. The uniform wasn't her old WAAF attire, but it was close enough to stir something deep within her—a sense of dignity she hadn't felt in what seemed like a lifetime.

"Thank you so much. It will do fine," Eileen said, trying to speak over the lump forming in her throat. "I'll be proud to wear it."

Beryl sighed again. "It's not exactly by the book, Miss Nearne, but it'll make sure you don't run into trouble when flying out. That dress you've got on now would... raise a few eyebrows."

Eileen nodded, still running her fingers over the blouse. To wear proper clothes again—a uniform, no less—felt like stepping back into the world she had almost forgotten existed. It wasn't just fabric; it was a symbol of restoration, of regaining her place as a human being. As a war veteran.

"Thank you," she said softly, glancing at Beryl. "Truly."

"There's a bathroom next door," Beryl continued in her brisk yet not unkind voice. "You can have a wash if you'd like. I've laid out underwear, stockings, a brush, comb, toothpaste, soap—whatever you might need. And when you leave, you can take that small suitcase."

Eileen's eyes widened at the sight of the battered brown suitcase tucked neatly in the corner. Tears welled up before she could stop them, and she quickly looked away, blinking furiously.

It wasn't just the suitcase. It was what it represented. Since her arrest, no—since she had boarded the Lysander that fateful night—she, *Eileen*, had owned nothing. No clothes of her own, no possessions to hold onto, just carefully selected items to reinforce her persona as Jacqueline du Tetre. And those were abruptly lost with her arrest, leaving her with absolutely nothing. It had stripped away a part of her, dehumanizing her in ways she hadn't fully realized until this moment.

And now, here was a suitcase. And clothes. And toiletries. Simple, ordinary things that made her feel like a person again.

"Thank you," she repeated, unable to suppress her voice from trembling. She turned back to the bed, her fingers lingering on the US flag on the uniform. "I'll... I'll try it on now."

Beryl gave Eileen a curt nod, the sharpness of her business-like face softening as she stepped toward the door. "I'll leave you to it, Miss. Take your time. When you're ready, just go down the corridor and down the stairs. You'll find the boys in the dining room."

Eileen watched the American nurse leave, the soles of her sturdy shoes squeaking on the polished floor of the hallway. For a moment, Eileen remained still, staring at the neatly folded garments on the bed and the small suitcase in the corner. They still seemed out of place, tokens of normalcy in a life that had become anything but. She still had to find a way to own them, to grow back into normalcy.

She picked up the uniform jacket and held it before her chest. It was going to be too wide for now but not terrible.

"I have to grow into it," she murmured. The fabric was sturdy and familiar, its sharply cut lines evoking memories of another uniform, another life. Clutching blouse, jacket, and skirt, she resolutely walked to the bathroom. As she closed the door behind her, she caught sight of her reflection in the mirror above the sink.

She froze.

The woman staring back at her was a stranger. Her cheeks were hollow, her blue eyes shadowed with exhaustion. Her short curls framed a face etched with lines of suffering and resilience. It was a face that carried the weight of secrets, of fear, of survival—but also the quiet strength of someone who had endured the unthinkable and was still standing.

Eileen laid the uniform carefully on the chair beside the bath, her movements deliberate. Then, her hands rose to touch her reflection, her fingertips hovering just above the cool glass.

She traced the lines of her face, studying herself as though seeing the contours of her soul for the first time. Her reflection seemed to shift and ripple, each version of herself from the past twenty-four years gliding into view, one after the other, glimmering and fading like shadows on water.

"First, I was Didi," she whispered, her voice trembling under the weight of memory. "The baby of the family. The dreamer. Ditzy Didi. The painter. The girl who could communicate with cats. Impractical, unworldly, not much to be expected of." Didi was innocence and youth, carefree and untouched by the cruelty of war, a girl who vanished the moment the Germans and Italians marched into France and her world fell apart.

"Then I became Miss Eileen Nearne," she continued, her voice steadying. "Fleeing France with my sister. Sowing the first seeds of resistance and strength." Gone was Ditzy Didi, the girl who wanted to paint pictures and live in a house full of cats. In her place stood someone different—someone harder, more determined.

She paused, her fingers brushing the glass as if to summon the next iteration of herself. "After that came Rose," she murmured, her lips curving faintly. "The resistance fighter. The enigma. The shadow of myself." Rose was fun. She was strong, independent, yet dependable. "I loved being Rose. She felt free, bold. She was my shield."

Her tone shifted, sharpening as the next name fell from her lips. "And then, finally, Jacqueline du Tertre." Her voice was now tinged with hesitation. “I don’t know what to think of her. I always thought she was my strongest shield, but now...” Eileen frowned. “Perhaps she was a burden.” She was an actress, a pragmatic liar, someone who could never be trusted with the truth.” *Was she really me? Or just a mask I wore to survive?*

Her reflection seemed to shimmer, and for a moment, she thought she caught a flicker of Jacqueline’s dark eyes, bold and defiant.

Don’t discard me too easily, Eileen, the phantom of her alter ego seemed to whisper. *I protected you with my Frenchness, my quick wit, my impossible schemes. It was I who pulled you through the camps. You’ll see that soon enough. Be kind to me—I am part of you, too.*

Eileen took a step back and gripped the edge of the washbasin as the realization swept through her.

“I’m all of them,” she said aloud. “I have been and always will be.”

This truth was both magnificent and scary, a burden and a balm. Didi, Eileen, Rose, Jacqueline—they weren’t separate. They were facets of the same person. Each had played their role, carried her through the unthinkable, and now they were handing her the reins.

Turning away from the mirror, she let the hot water run in the bath, steam curling into the air. She quickly stripped off the tattered remnants of her old life and stepped into the soothing heat, closing her eyes as the tension melted from her body.

I am me. I am free.

When she emerged, she reached for the uniform. The silk chemise and blouse felt like a soft caress against her skin, and as she buttoned the khaki jacket, each movement felt like a small act of reclamation. The belt of the skirt cinched her waist, holding her together. The stars-and-stripes on the lapels gleamed faintly in the lamplight, a reminder of the new chapter waiting for her.

When she was fully dressed, her hair combed and her teeth brushed, she turned back to the mirror.

The woman who stared back at her now wasn't a stranger. She was still gaunt, her body marked by months of starvation and suffering, but she stood tall, her shoulders squared. Her reflection radiated something she hadn't seen in years: belonging, strength, quiet, unyielding pride.

"I'm going to make something of myself in the years that God still grants me," she told her mirrored self in a voice that was firm and clear.

Her reflection didn't answer, but it didn't need to. She met her own gaze, and for the first time, she saw everything she was.

Ditzy Didi. Brave Rose. Quick-witted Jacqueline. Stubborn, God-fearing Eileen.

She was all of them.

She was the echo of valor.

PART XVII

~EILEEN & MIA~ TORQUAY, SEPTEMBER 2007

62

LIGHT-BLUE TOMORROWS

2 Lisburne Crescent, Torquay September 2007

The light in Eileen's flat seemed brighter, the atmosphere lighter. Whisky, her beloved tabby, purred more contentedly on the windowsill, and Jacqueline's clock ticked with a rhythm that felt almost upbeat.

Eileen Nearne, white-haired, wrinkled, and frail, sat in her armchair, radiating an unexpected vibrancy. Her blue eyes, as clear and deep as a Swiss lake, glimmered with life as she regarded Dr. Mia Thompson sitting across from her.

The young woman shifted slightly, clearly hesitant to break the moment of calm, yet eager to ask her questions.

I am you as well, Mia Elaine Thompson, Eileen thought as she studied the dark-haired beauty opposite her. *I've always had the gift of caring, just like you. I cared for my dear Maman, my Abuela, Father, and Fred. And didn't I look after Jacqueline in her final months? And all the years I worked my shifts at the Branch Hill care home in London. The same sweet thread of caring for others runs through us.*

"What's going on in your mind?" Mia's gentle voice broke through Eileen's reminisces.

Eileen smiled at her. "Ah, dear, getting all that off my chest was a good thing. I hope it wasn't too gruesome for you?"

Mia hesitated before answering carefully. "It was tough, Aunt Didi. To hear how the U.S. Army didn't believe you… I can't say it didn't touch me deeply."

"True, true," Eileen nodded. "It's haunted me all this time. I simply couldn't let go of the split reaction I've always had to those weeks. You see, in the camps, in those last weeks, we did nothing but talk about the Americans coming. We whipped ourselves up with visions of chocolate, cigarettes, and these heroes who would sweep us off our feet. No—actually, it started earlier."

Mia leaned in, her pen poised in her hand.

"When I was training at Beaulieu, we knew the Americans were joining our side. We built this magical picture of what liberation would look like. So, when they treated me the way they did, I couldn't reconcile it with the fantasy I had created in my head."

"And can you now?" Mia's eyes were filled with hope.

Eileen paused, then smiled with quiet confidence. "Oh yes, girl. Not just because of those wonderful men at the Christliche Hospice, but because of all the Americans I've met since. Through Jacqui, when she worked for the United Nations in New York—I met such capital people. Truly. I long ago forgave those first officers. They were only doing their job, even if they got it wrong. What I hadn't done," she added softly, "was come clean with the pain inside myself."

Mia nodded but when she didn't speak, Eileen continued.

"I feel freer than I've ever felt. Quite chipper, actually. I think I'm done drowning in the past."

"That's fantastic, Aunt Didi," Mia said warmly, closing her notebook. "I'm so happy to hear that. Any idea what brought it on?"

Eileen waved her hand dismissively, but there was a twinkle in her eye. "Oh, you shrink, always another question, right? Time, memories, talking—perhaps even you." She offered a sly smile. "But enough of that. I'm done dwelling. I've decided to make something of myself in the days God still grants me. We never know how long or how short that may be."

"That's wonderful, Aunt Didi." Mia's smile was warm, and Eileen could see how touched she was, knowing her therapy had been successful. "Any idea what you'd like to do next?"

Eileen's expression lit up, her hands lifting in a flutter of excitement. "First, let me tell you an anecdote about Americans—about Rollo and Denis. Such charming young men."

"Were they the American officers at the hospice near Leipzig?" Mia asked.

"Yes, yes, dear, the very same. Major Denis Newman and Captain Rollo Young—they were charming, just charming—looked after me as if I were royalty."

Mia tilted her head, her curiosity piqued. "You did mention Denis comparing you to Joan of Arc, but I don't recall a Rollo?"

Eileen's laughter bubbled up, light and infectious. "Oh, Rollo was a bit cheeky, but in the best way. And Denis, well, he was kind and respectful, but I could tell he was a little in awe of me. Can you imagine?" Her laughter deepened, a sound so youthful and carefree that Mia couldn't help but join in.

"I made them supper, you know," Eileen went on, her hands miming the memory as she spoke. "In that hospice kitchen, with proper copper pans and a real stove. I hadn't been near one in years! I simply couldn't resist making those eggs. Eggs! Can you imagine? A farmer had brought us fresh ones, and it felt like treasure."

"What did they say about you cooking?" Mia asked, captivated by the joy radiating from her client.

"Oh, they let me!" Eileen said with a dramatic flair, her voice rising with delight. "I asked them, 'Could I do that? It will be heaven to be in a proper kitchen again.' And do you know, they handed me a real apron—yes, over my WAAC uniform!—and let me get to it. I fried those eggs with butter and a pinch of salt. Oh, it was such fun, Mia. Such fun!"

Mia chuckled. "I can picture that scene like it was yesterday."

"It was yesterday," Eileen beamed, "well sort of." Then she leaned closer, lowering her voice conspiratorially. "Before I left, Rollo handed me a note. He insisted—protection of sorts, you see, so that I wasn't to be harassed anymore on my way home."

She got up with some difficulty and made her way to a nearby drawer where she pulled out a neatly folded piece of paper without any difficulty finding it. Her hands trembled slightly as she handed it to Mia.

"You read it. I don't know where my glasses are."

Mia read the faded typewritten words:

The bearer, Cadet Ensign Eileen Nearne, is a British Officer employed by MO-I (SP) War Office. She has been given instruction by me to report back to London and, in view of the treatment she received while a prisoner in German hands, may she be given every help, please. Her credentials may be verified by telephoning Major Sherren at Welbeck 7744 London.

R.S. Young, CAPT. (BR), T Force, Att.12 Army.

"That's incredible," Mia said, handing it back. "So, you flew straight to England after that?"

"Not quite." Eileen shook her head. "First to Brussels, then finally to Croydon on 23 May 1945. But, no more trouble on the way. Thanks to Rollo's sweet note. I had no passport, you see."

"And when you landed?" Mia prompted her.

Eileen waved a hand, her smile turning mischievous. "Oh, let's not get into all that. Too many questions, not enough time. I want to talk about *now*—the present, the future!"

She noticed the hesitation in Mia's expression, the professional instinct to probe deeper warring with a gentle understanding. But then Mia let it go, at least for now.

"All right, what's on your mind, Aunt Didi?"

Eileen's eyes lit up like stars. "I've thought about it long enough, and now I know for sure. I want to go to the Special Forces Club dinner on 11 November. With you."

"That's a wonderful goal," Mia said warmly. "But... with me?"

"Yes, of course with you! I'm far too old to be traipsing all the way to London by myself. You can drive me."

Mia laughed softly. "I'd be honored, Aunt Didi. But would they let me in? I'm not a member."

"Of course, I can bring a guest! Heavens, I'm one of the last SOE dinosaurs around. If they can't make room for my crowd, who's left to invite?" Eileen giggled. "But I need you there for more than just the driving, you know. To shield me a bit from too many nosy people. You'll be part driver, part bodyguard. All right?"

She could see Mia thrived on the trust put in her.

"Again, Aunt Didi, I'd be honored to accompany you. And I'd be honored to do anything you ask of me."

"I'm not finished!" Eileen declared, raising a finger. "I want a light blue dress for the occasion. The most beautiful light blue you've ever seen. I haven't worn that color since..." Her voice softened, trailing off as her gaze grew distant. "Since my arrest. But this time, I'll wear it for Jacqueline du Tertre. To honor her. She deserves it."

"Light blue sounds perfect, Aunt Didi," Mia said warmly. "It's a profound way to reclaim your past. Now, will that be all, or do you have more on your wishlist?"

Eileen's smile turned wistful. "Yes, I want to meet Sebastian Stone."

Mia's expression turned deadpan, just as Eileen had expected. She could practically see Mia thinking, *here we go again.*

Before Mia could say a word, Eileen waved her hand dismissively. "Maybe it's reclaiming another part of my youth, dear. It's really for me. I think he reminds me of a boy I once knew in Grenoble."

Eileen noticed the way Mia leaned towards her, her interest piqued. "I remember you mentioning a young student in one of our earlier talks. Who was he again?"

"Andy," Eileen said, her face lighting up as the memory surfaced. "I don't remember his last name. He was funny, a bit footloose and fancy-free. I met him during a protest meeting at the University of Grenoble. Jacqui had dragged me along, of course." A chuckle bubbled up. "Andy was quite the dandy."

The rhyme amused her even more.

"I've always liked a bit of a wild streak in a man," Eileen continued. "Gives them some flavor, don't you think? Never been keen on the pinstriped suit, bowler hat, umbrella type." She rolled her eyes for emphasis. The gesture earning a smile from Mia. "Andy made me laugh despite the gruesome war we were living through. Having had to leave our beautiful villa in Nice for that drafty old castle in Grenoble, I desperately needed that laughter."

Mia's eyes seemed to brighten too. "Didn't you mention he was a musician?"

She nodded. "Yes, he played the bass in a jazz band—quite well, too. But he also studied engineering. Such a clever boy. He and I only went out for a couple of weeks before Jacqui and I decided to leave Grenoble for England." In a softer voice she added. "I've often wondered what might have been if I'd stayed."

The room fell quiet. A tinge of melancholy in the air. Whiskey stretched and yawned on the windowsill. Eileen could feel Mia mulling over the question she expected.

"You never married?"

She met Mia's gaze briefly before looking out the window. "No, it never came to that. A shame, really. I'd have loved to have a family of my own." She paused, her lips pressing together in a wistful smile. "Didn't happen."

Turning her gaze back to Mia, she noted the attentive expression on her young friend's face. "Now, dear, we can't have you in that same boat," she said, her tone light but her words deliberate. "You probably don't call it 'spinster' these days anymore, which is all the better—it's a horrible word—but..." She trailed off, studying Mia's reaction.

Mia's lips curved into what Eileen guessed was an attempt to deflect. "We call it 'happily single,' Aunt Didi."

"Hogwash!" Eileen's voice rose with playful indignation. She straightened in her chair, her old stubbornness rekindled. "God didn't create us to go through life alone."

"So, that makes you a matchmaker now?" There was a hint of humor in Mia's hazel eyes.

Eileen's smile faltered for a moment. Then she shook her head. "I seriously think I blew my one chance at happiness when I left Andy," she admitted quietly. "A man who has a flair for living life to the fullest is as rare as hen's teeth. And..." Her words lingered in her mind before she spilled them forth. "I don't know him yet, but I think Sebastian Stone might have that quality."

She noticed Mia's posture shift ever so slightly. For the first time, the composed and unflappable Dr. Thompson seemed unsettled. There was a faint tension in her shoulders, the smallest hesitation in her movements, and Eileen knew she was on the right track.

Mia was as terrified of love as Eileen had been. Being strong and surviving was one thing—vulnerability was another matter entirely. Love required opening your heart, and for someone like this kind, beautiful, but deeply-guarded young woman opposite her, that meant risking the pain of being hurt all over again.

A pause settled between them, stretching out just long enough to carry unspoken truths. But Eileen didn't feel the need to fill it. She simply smiled; her expression serene as she watched Mia process Eileen's words in that thoughtful, professional way of hers.

You'll see, Eileen thought, her heart lifting with quiet certainty. *I'm not wrong about this.*

63

CIRCLES OF DOUBT

A few weeks later - Torquay, October 2007

Mia sat in her black Mini Cooper outside 2 Lisburne Crescent, staring at the leather steering wheel as though it might somehow provide the answers she couldn't seem to find. She'd cracked the window to let in some fresh air, and the autumn breeze carried the distinct smells of fallen leaves and roasted chestnuts. Sunlight slanted through the windshield, highlighting the displays on the dashboard.

Beyoncé's *Irreplaceable* played softly through the speakers, a catchy backdrop to her restless thoughts, as she finished the last of her Starbucks latte—picked up earlier in Fleet Street when the day still felt full of promise.

Her visit to Eileen had been lighthearted, full of jokes and playful banter. It was the kind of day that should have felt hopeful.

Instead, Mia's thoughts spun in relentless circles.

The blue dress was already hanging in Eileen's wardrobe, ready for its grand debut at the Special Forces Club dinner next month. Invitations had been accepted, logistics sorted, and Eileen was positively glowing with anticipation. Every Tuesday, when Mia visited her under the guise of "checking in," she marveled at the transformation.

Eileen Nearne—Aunt Didi—the indomitable SOE agent, was ready to step back into the light. She'd even taken up collecting donations for Animals in Distress again, making her rounds to the local pubs with her tin collection box in hand.

And Mia?

She was stalling.

Indecisiveness gnawed at her. She'd promised Eileen she'd bring Sebastian Stone for a visit soon. In a moment of eagerness to feed Eileen's curiosity about the reporter, she'd even mentioned he had something to share about her sister, Jacqueline.

"Oh? And what might that be?" Eileen had perked up immediately, the blue eyes sharp and alive with interest.

Mia had stumbled over her reply, suddenly regretting the slip. Knowing full well that Sebastian's gift—the first edition School for Danger 1948 docudrama starring her sister and Harry Rée—was sitting in her bag, she'd practically slapped herself on the forehead for not simply handing it to Eileen then and there, as Sebastian had suggested. That ship had sailed now.

And Eileen wouldn't let it rest. Anything to do with her beloved sister was urgent to her.

With that knowing twinkle in her eye, she'd asked different variations of: Still keeping that boy all to yourself, dear? You might as well admit you like him.

Mia had laughed it off, dismissing it as one of Eileen's playful jabs, but the truth was more complicated.

It wasn't just the fear that Sebastian, ever the journalist, might accidentally prod at the wrong parts of Eileen's past. It wasn't even the worry that Eileen and Sebastian would gang up on her with their matching charm and irreverence.

It was that Mia wasn't sure she wanted to let Sebastian closer to herself.

She could already hear Alexandra's voice, sharp and disapproving. Her best friend's opinion was rooted in personal bitterness, of course—one of Sebastian's past entanglements that hadn't ended well. Alexandra's harsh dismissal of him still echoed in Mia's mind: "Sebastian Stone? Really? The man's a mess. A walking emotional minefield. Spare yourself, Mia."

Even if he was interested in me, Mia thought for the hundredth time, gripping the steering wheel tighter, *he doesn't have the substance I'm looking for in a man. I need someone solid. Not someone as messed up as I am relationship-wise.*

And yet...

There were moments—small, fleeting moments—when she wondered if she was wrong. When she thought, *what if Eileen is right?*

The way his gaze lingered on her, just a second longer than necessary. The quiet attentiveness in his voice when he asked about her work or her life. The way he had genuinely wanted to meet Eileen—not as a journalist chasing a story, but as someone who truly respected her legacy.

And then there were the things that didn't fit the narrative of him being 'substance-less.' His relentless determination to fight for his son, despite the odds. His apparent quiet financial support for his mother and disabled sister, something he never boasted about. Was it fair to dismiss all of that because of a few high-profile affairs? Or was she trying to make him out to be something he wasn't, simply to shield herself?

The thought made her stomach twist.

Am I wrong about him? Or just afraid to find out?

With a frustrated sigh, Mia pushed the thoughts aside. There was too much to do—too much to focus on for herself, for Hope Haven, and for Eileen.

Eileen.

Mia's lips curved into a faint smile as she thought of her client's growing energy and zest. Eileen had even brought up the idea of speaking to one of the veterans' groups at Hope Haven, not as a participant, but as someone who could share her reflections on her wartime experiences and the healing she'd sought afterward.

The idea had stuck with Mia.

Wouldn't it be extraordinary to see Eileen standing in front of those veterans? To see the woman who had once been locked in a prison camp for her heroism now inspiring others to reclaim their lives?

Mia's mind flitted to the center itself. *Hope Haven Community Health.* It had always been a name she was proud of, but lately, she'd been toying with an idea.

The Eileen Nearne Rehabilitation Centre.

The name felt right. Perfect, even. But she knew Eileen wouldn't accept such a thing now—not when she was still rediscovering her sense of worth. Perhaps after the Special Forces dinner, after seeing how much everyone thought of her now as the "Queen of SOE", she would understand how exceptional she truly was.

But that was for later.

For now, Mia needed to face the reality she'd been avoiding. She needed to invite Sebastian to Eileen's home. To bring him into this delicate, personal circle. And to accept whatever feelings—hers and his—might come with it.

With a deep breath, Mia finally turned on the engine and drove towards Torbay Weekly's office on Windsor Road.

She parked in front of Sebastian's office and took a deep breath. Though almost certain she would regret this visit, Eileen's stubborn determination left her little choice. That lady had a way of wearing down even the most steadfast resistance.

Stepping out of her MINI, Mia smoothed the checkered skirt of her suit, adjusted the strap of her shoulder bag, and strode toward the entrance on her high heels with more confidence than she felt.

Inside, the receptionist was as nonchalant as ever, popping her gum and typing furiously while cradling a phone between her ear and shoulder. She caught sight of Mia, flashed a thumbs-up, and pressed the intercom button without missing a beat.

Seconds later, Sebastian appeared at the top of the staircase, tall, broad-shouldered, and with that disheveled, just-out-of-bed look that seemed annoyingly effortless. His reddish-blond hair was tousled, and his wide smile lit up the room as he ambled down the steps.

For a fleeting moment, Mia hesitated. A small, irrational part of her wanted to turn on her heels and bolt. *Why does he have to be so darn attractive?* she thought, half annoyed. It wasn't just his sharp jawline, the unruly hair, or the frame that somehow managed to be both lanky and commanding. It was the way he *was.*

Energetic. Charismatic. Utterly at ease in his own skin.

And that, she thought with an inward sigh, *is what makes this so impossible.*

"Mia, my favorite English Riviera citizen!" Sebastian called out, his grin widening. "I thought you'd forgotten all about me. Haven't seen you in..."

"A week, Sebastian," Mia interrupted drily, raising one of her dark eyebrows.

"Well, it seems like forever to me." His green eyes glinted with a teasing warmth, but he checked himself quickly, redirecting his tone. "Come into my office. Same old mess, I'm afraid, but not everyone can be as on top of things as you." The apologetic smile he flashed her sent an unwelcome lurch through her chest.

"I can only stay for a minute, Sebastian."

"No problem, a minute is better than nothing. Care for a glass of my finest bubbly water?"

"No thanks, I just had a latte."

He turned halfway up the stairs, his hand on the railing, giving her a look of surprise. "So, you do drink coffee? For some reason, I pegged you as a tea-only kind of girl."

"Yes, I drink coffee," Mia replied with amusement. "And I'm a shopaholic so I sin daily. I'm not the Holy Mary you seem to take me for."

"Gosh, welcome to my world," Sebastian laughed. "Good to know there's no need to dust the pedestal then."

In his office, he swept a stack of papers off a chair opposite his desk and patted the seat. "Here, take a load off." For a moment, he towered close to her, his cologne—*was it Hugo Boss?*—lingering in the air. It was disarming.

Then the moment passed. He swooped behind his desk with that signature blend of energy and ease, settling into his chair and fixing her with a curious look.

Leaning forward, elbows on the desk, Sebastian fixed her with an inquisitive smile. "So, what brings you to my little corner of the world?"

Mia shifted in her chair, fidgeting with the strap of her bag. She tried to keep her tone professional, but her nerves betrayed her. "I need to ask you something."

"Fire away," he said easily, his green eyes gleaming. "Though I should warn you—I've got some news too."

Mia hesitated one final time, then dove in. "I'd like you to come to Miss Nearne's flat. She's been asking about you, and I think it's time you met her."

Sebastian's face lit up, his grin as wide and unguarded as a child's. "Really? Miss Nearne wants to meet me? You're not just pulling my leg, are you?"

"No, truly," Mia said, and she couldn't help but notice the sheer joy radiating from him. "She's quite curious about you—and about the thing you said you had for her regarding Jacqueline."

"So, you still haven't given her the tape?" His tone was gently teasing.

"I didn't think it was my place," Mia replied, an edge of defensiveness creeping into her voice.

"It doesn't matter now, because wow—this is incredible. I am honored." His tone carried a reverence that surprised her. "I mean it, Mia. She's a legend. At least to me. And to be invited into her home —thank you."

Mia smiled despite herself. Under so much enthusiasm it was hard to keep up her guarded exterior. "I have to warn you, though. She's quite the character. But I think you and she might actually get on well."

"You think so? Why?" The boyish delight in Sebastian's expression tugged at something inside her.

"Well," Mia suppressed a smirk, "you both seem to have a tendency to color outside the lines, if you understand what I'm saying."

"You mean we're quirky, bordering on the eccentric?" He raised one of his reddish eyebrows.

"Your words, not mine," Mia shot back, now fully unable to hide her amusement. "So, shall I arrange it with Eileen?"

"Gladly," Sebastian grinned. "But you'll be there too, right? To keep us both coloring within the lines, Dr. Thompson."

"I will," Mia replied in her calm therapist voice. "Don't worry, Mr. Stone. I've got you both under control."

Sebastian's grin softened, shifting into something more reflective. "I've been having a pretty good day, actually. And this invitation just makes it better."

"Good news?" Mia prompted.

"Great news." Sebastian's green eyes flickered with optimism. "My lawyer thinks I've got a real shot at getting custody of my son, Adam. Cindy's husband—that Benson Bennison III—is apparently in jail now in Michigan for real estate corruption. It's not clear if she's involved, but she's being questioned. That could change everything for Adam and me."

Mia blinked, taken aback. "That's... that's huge, Sebastian. I mean... actually looking after him?"

"Maybe." His expression grew more serious, and his voice dropped a notch. "I'm still processing it. I've never really been a dad, and Adam hardly knows me. Should I? Shouldn't I?"

Mia instinctively slipped into her professional tone. "From what you've told me, Cindy hasn't exactly given him a stable life so far. And he's still young—what is he, five?"

"Four—well, nearly five now," Sebastian corrected, his tone contemplative. "Anyway, it's early days, but I'm mentally preparing myself for a complete overhaul of my life."

Mia nodded. "Looking after a child would be a huge responsibility."

His grin returned, boyish and infectious. "Yeah, give up the bachelor lifestyle, you mean?"

"Your words, not mine." Mia raised her hands in mock defense. "I'm not judging. Besides, I have no experience with kids that young, so I couldn't advise you." She stood, ready to leave. "I really ought to be going. Would next Tuesday suit you to come for tea at Miss Nearne's? Say two o'clock?"

"Sure, sure!" Sebastian said eagerly, rising to his feet. "I'll wait for you at her door. But hey, I've got more news."

Mia, already halfway to the door, turned back. "Being?"

Sebastian combed a hand through his unruly locks, which fell instantly back into place. "The Guardian has offered me a history column. Every Saturday. A dream gig—writing about the past, making it relevant. It's what I've always wanted to do."

"Oh my!" Mia felt a genuine surge of happiness for him. "That's wonderful, Sebas. Congratulations!"

"Thanks." For a moment, he looked almost shy, his usual confidence tempered by something more vulnerable. "It's been a long road, but maybe things are starting to turn around. I guess I really need to finish that PhD, now."

He walked her to the front door, and as they descended the stairs, Mia found herself thinking, *he's a chameleon.* Shifting between roles so effortlessly—gossip columnist, historian, father-to-be, journalist. But not just any chameleon. *A very lively, very good-looking chameleon.*

"*Just what you need,*" Eileen's voice seemed to whisper to her. Mia shook her head almost imperceptibly, dismissing the thought. *I'm not ready yet.*

At the door, Sebastian hesitated, catching her gaze with an expression she couldn't quite read. "Thanks for coming by, Mia. Really. And for the invite. And sorry for dumping all my news on you. I should ask about your life, too."

"It's okay, Sebas," she said lightly. "I don't talk much about my own life, I guess."

"Well," he said with a crooked smile, "we'll have to change that, won't we?"

He leaned in slightly, as if to kiss her cheek, but caught himself and instead gave her shoulder a friendly pat, his warmth lingering like an old friend's.

"See you Tuesday. Can't wait!"

"Looking forward to it," Mia replied, her voice steady even as her heart wavered.

As she stepped out into the crisp autumn air, she felt the familiar tug of her internal battle.

Him and me. It's impossible, she told herself. *Especially if he's got a child in tow.*

And yet...

64

VULNERABLE TRUTHS

One week later - 2 Lisburne Crescent, Torquay, October 2007

Mia perched on the edge of Eileen's well-worn sofa, her notebook balanced on her knee—not for taking notes, but as a sort of security blanket. Across the room, Sebastian Stone sat hunched over a cup of tea, his tall frame awkwardly compressed into the delicate armchair, which seemed far too small to accommodate him.

Eileen, by contrast, sat straight-backed in her favorite chair, the light catching her white curls, styled with noticeable care. She wore a pair of old-fashioned spectacles perched on her nose, through which she regarded Sebastian with a shrewd yet welcoming gaze. A faint hint of pink on her lips suggested she'd applied lipstick, and her burgundy jumper and matching skirt lent a dignified elegance to her frail, almost translucent, skin.

Even in old age, Eileen Nearne radiated a quiet beauty. There was something regal in her proud bearing, a trace of the aristocratic blood that coursed through her veins.

Mia couldn't help but marvel at the queenlike posture of her formerly-withdrawn client. The transformation was astonishing. And yet, beneath the polished exterior, she sensed something deeper—a nervousness, perhaps. It was as though Eileen was stepping into a role, one she hadn't played in years, and was bracing herself to meet its demands.

Never trust a stranger. The old suspicion seemed to hum beneath Eileen's poised exterior, mingling with something else, something softer, more wistful. Was it possible that having the dashing Sebastian Stone sitting opposite her reminded Eileen of her youth? Of Andy? Of those fleeting, romantic days she had recently spoken of so fondly?

For a moment, Mia wondered if Eileen herself was unsure how to handle the rush of memories, the stirring of old feelings she thought she'd long buried.

It was always a wonder to Mia what went on inside that remarkable mind. But today, the mystery felt even more profound. And it was contrary to what she'd expected.

As Eileen had requested the visit herself, she'd expected sparks to fly—Eileen's sharp wit colliding with Sebastian's irreverent humor. But the air between them was surprisingly serious, almost heavy. It made Mia feel like an intruder in a conversation that neither participant entirely knew how to navigate.

Setting down his teacup and maneuvering rather awkwardly in the delicate chair, Sebastian reached into the inside pocket of his jacket. He wore a black corduroy ensemble that, to Mia's eye, seemed slightly overdressed for the occasion. His unruly hair was kept in place with a tad too much gel, and a faint scratch on his jaw suggested a rushed morning shave.

With a diffident smile, he retrieved a round metal case and held it in both hands, almost like a schoolboy offering a prized drawing to his teacher.

"Miss Nearne," he began, his voice reverent, "I managed to find something a couple of weeks ago that made me think of you immediately. So, I purchased it and would love to give it to you."

"What is it, Mr. Stone?" Eileen asked, her curiosity clearly piqued, "I love unexpected presents."

"Oh, please call me Sebastian, ma'am." He smiled, then extended the case toward her. "Here—it's a first edition of the 1948 docudrama your sister starred in."

Eileen's eyes lit up as she took the case into her frail hands, her fingers trembling slightly as they traced the embossed title. "*School for Danger: Now It Can Be Told*. Oh, yes. Heavens, it's been decades since I saw this." Her voice was tinged with nostalgia.

"But I don't think I have the proper equipment to watch it, do I, Sebastian?" she asked, pronouncing his name with a delicate French lilt that caught Mia's ear.

Sebastian's grin widened, boyish and a little awkward. "No, it's more of a keepsake. But if you'd like to watch the movie again, it's actually been uploaded to YouTube, on the internet. I could bring my laptop sometime and show it to you."

Eileen laughed softly, shaking her head. "I have no idea what you're talking about, my dear young man. You'll have to explain this modern wizardry to me. But I'll hold you to that offer. I'd love to see Jacqui play Miss Williams again." And her voice grew more wistful as she added, "Oh, she was so good. A natural talent. We saw the movie together at the Regal Cinema in London, just before she sailed off to work for the United Nations in New York."

"And you haven't seen it since?" Sebastian asked gently.

Eileen shook her head, her expression softening. "No. It's one of those things... life takes over. And later, after my sister passed and I was asked to talk more about the war, I just couldn't face seeing her move and talk as if she was still here." She paused, her voice quiet but steady. "But, I think I can now."

Sebastian nodded, and Mia could see his usual enthusiasm bubbling to the surface. "Well, I have to say, both the movie and the actors have lost none of their freshness and originality. It's timeless, really. Your sister was remarkable in it—absolutely captivating."

Eileen's smile deepened, though Mia didn't miss the flicker of sadness that crossed her face. "Thank you, Sebastian. It means a great deal to me that you thought of this. But we don't need to talk about Jacqueline now," she added, her voice firm but not unkind. "She's had her moment."

With that, Eileen's smile faded, her expression becoming unreadable. She set the case gently on the side table next to her, her hands lingering on it for just a second too long before she folded them in her lap. The silence that followed felt heavy, almost tangible.

Mia kept her eyes on Eileen, wondering what had caused the shift. Was it simply the mention of Jacqueline? The pain of seeing her sister immortalized in a role that kept her forever vibrant and alive? Or was it something deeper—perhaps the shadow of their post-war relationship, with Jacqueline soaring to brilliant heights in New York while Eileen remained in the shadows, working quiet, low-profile jobs?

Mia made a mental note to unravel the bond between the sisters when the time was right. Eileen had often spoken of Jacqueline with pride, but there were layers beneath the surface—unspoken comparisons, the weight of living in someone else's shadow.

Mia recalled the sad face with which Eileen had told her the soft spot Colonel Buckmaster had had for Jacqueline, while about Eileen he'd written on her file, even after the debacle with the Americans, *'Not the same stamp as her sister.'*

Whatever the root cause, Mia could see that Eileen was deflecting, steering the conversation away from a subject that cut too close.

Sebastian, sitting across from her, looked uncertain. He glanced between Eileen and Mia, clearly unsure whether to speak or let the silence linger. His usual confidence seemed to falter as he picked up the teacup which was already empty.

In an atmosphere caught between vulnerability and avoidance, Mia wondered if she should step in, but part of her also knew this was a moment best left to unfold naturally—or not at all.

Eileen turned her sharp gaze toward Sebastian again and said in her soft but deliberate voice. "How's your family, Sebastian? I sometimes see your mother at Mass."

Sebastian shifted in his seat, his expression momentarily guarded, then softening. "Mother is slowly recovering, thank you. It's been two years now since..." He hesitated.

"...your father... passed?" Eileen finished for him, her tone neither blunt nor hesitant, but compassionate.

Sebastian cleared his throat, his fingers gripping the edge of his chair. "Yes. It wasn't completely unexpected, but it... uh... still hit us hard. It was awful."

Eileen nodded knowingly, her gaze steady. "Sister Damian mentioned your father fought in Afghanistan?"

"Yes, he did. He was a helicopter pilot. But he must have been in some terrible situations there. He just never talked about them. Only got more and more depressed."

Eileen sighed. "It's hard to talk about war when you come back. People don't understand that the noises terrify you, the memories haunt you. They just don't understand." Her voice was very soft, not accusatory—more matter-of-fact, showing she was speaking from a deep well of personal knowledge.

Sebastian's jaw tightened as he nodded. "True. Mother comes from a military family—her father was in the Navy—but she'd never experienced anything like what happened with Dad. He was... became unreachable... most of the time. And I was away at university when things got really bad. She was left to handle everything at home, including Mimi, who needed all her attention."

"Mimi?" Eileen asked gently. "Your younger sister?"

"Yes." A flicker of tenderness passed through his expression. "She suffered oxygen deprivation at birth and has needed a lot of help throughout her life. It's been... a challenge."

"But she's doing better now?" Eileen prompted.

"She's finally in a good care center, thank God," Sebastian's tone grew lighter. "It's a wonderful place. She's made friends there, and the staff are amazing. Mother worried herself sick for years about Mimi, especially after Dad... after he passed. But now that Mimi's settled, it's been a huge weight off her shoulders."

Eileen fixed him again with her blue stare. "That must cost quite a bit. You take care of all that, don't you?"

Sebastian flushed, looking down at his hands. "Most of it, yeah. But the nuns at Our Lady Help of Christians & St. Denis have been incredibly generous. Sister Damian's been amazing—she even found grants to help cover some of the costs. I don't know how she does it."

Eileen's lips curved into an appreciative smile. "Good nuns have a way of working miracles."

"They certainly do," Sebastian agreed with a small laugh.

Mia, who'd been quietly observing the interactions between them, felt a mix of emotions stir within her. This was another side of Sebastian she hadn't seen before—a man carrying the weight of family responsibility, doing what he could to support those he loved despite his own struggles. She'd always seen him as a lively, irreverent presence, but here he was, earnest and deeply vulnerable.

He's a chameleon, she thought again, her earlier impression solidifying. He shifted seamlessly between roles—charming journalist, dedicated son, loving brother—all with a sincerity that left her unsettled.

Mia glanced at Eileen, who was nodding approvingly. The older woman seemed to understand Sebastian on a level that surprised her, as though she could see straight through his bravado to the man beneath.

Eileen broke the silence, her tone thoughtful. "Family is everything, you know. Even when the world turns against you, they're still your anchor."

Sebastian's expression grew distant. "Yes, I've come to realize that more and more. For years, I just wanted to live my life—have fun, be young. But the ties that bind you to blood relations are..."

"...unseverable," Eileen finished for him, her voice carrying the quiet authority of someone who has lived it.

Mia sat quietly, observing the moment. She realized she was learning more about Sebastian's complex background than she ever imagined. The Sebastian she saw now—vulnerable, grounded—was light years from the slick charmer Alexandra had described.

"I like you, Sebastian," Eileen said suddenly, a small smile breaking across her face. "Just as I thought I would. You've got a proper heart beating inside that impressive chest of yours. Or, as we say in French, *Vous avez le cœur à la bonne place.*"

Sebastian gave her one of his warm, generous smiles. "Thank you, Miss Nearne. That means a lot coming from you."

Eileen tilted her head and winked. "Then perhaps you'd consider calling me Aunt Didi, like Mia does. I hate being addressed as Miss Nearne, with a vengeance. It's so formal and not me at all."

Sebastian chuckled. "Aunt Didi, it is! Is that really what you call her?" He turned to Mia for the first time, including her in the conversation.

Mia nodded. "Yes, it's a privilege, really."

"And very unprofessional," Eileen interjected with a mock sternness, wagging a finger at Mia. "But I'm far too old to care, and Mia would never misuse her position. I'm absolutely certain of that."

Her smile widened, and her tone turned decisive. "And I've decided something else, Sebastian. I'd like you to come with Mia and me to the Special Forces dinner in London on 11 November. Do you own white-tie?"

Mia straightened in her seat, startled. "Wait, Aunt Didi—what?"

"Oh, don't look at me like that, Mia," Eileen said with a mischievous twinkle in her eye. "I've made up my mind. Sebastian here should see the Special Forces Club. And besides," she added, her tone light but resolute, "we could use a dashing young man to escort us, couldn't we?"

Sebastian looked between them, his grin widening as he took in the moment. "I'd be honored," he said earnestly. "Honestly, I can't think of anything better. And don't worry about white tie—I'll find one, even if I have to fly to Paris for it."

Eileen let out a soft laugh. "That won't be necessary, young man. Mr Reginald on Fleet Street will have a perfectly-fitting white-tie, even for someone your size."

Mia sighed, half-exasperated, half-resigned, though the corners of her lips twitched in amusement. "Of course you'd have that ready, Aunt Didi. I knew you had another trick up your sleeve."

Eileen reached for her tea, her expression innocence-personified. "It's settled, then."

Mia had to laugh despite herself.

Aunt Didi, matchmaker extraordinaire, she thought. *She always gets her way.*

65

DOORS TO THE FUTURE

One week later - Hope Haven Community Health, Torquay, October 2007

For Mia, this gray October day, windy and wet, felt like her own D-Day. More significant, perhaps, than even the day she received her Doctorate in Clinical Psychology from the University of Exeter just five months earlier.

Today, everything she'd worked for, everything she'd envisioned for her trauma work, was coming together. This center—her center—was alive with purpose, a place where fractured lives found healing.

She stood before the mirror in the quiet, staff facilities, taking a rare moment to herself. The woman staring back at her was undeniably successful, the culmination of years of effort and resilience.

She noted the sleek, dark ponytail, the elegantly-styled, long fringe. Her almond-shaped, honey eyes were framed by subtle makeup, and her tailored blouse and trousers fitted her figure perfectly. She was polished, poised, accomplished—someone who had built a life others might envy.

And yet, in the corners of her eyes, she caught the shadow of a little girl, small and shivering, hugging her knees as the walls of her world crumbled around her.

Mia closed her eyes, but the memories came anyway. She was back in that house, barely five, hearing deafening screams from the room next door. The loud bangs. The door flying open. A hand gripping her arm too hard, pulling her away, her own small fists hitting out in defiance.

The scene shifted. Now she was older, huddled beneath Princess Pier, blowing on her frozen fingers, hungry, angry, forgotten. Her stomach ached with emptiness, her heart with betrayal. The only constant was the voice in her head, whispering: *Survive. Just survive.*

Mia opened her eyes and took a deep breath, grounding herself in the present. *We've been there. Let's not go back now.*

But she knew why the memories had surfaced. They weren't here to haunt her; they were here to anchor her. To remind her, as they always did, of where she had come from. They kept her high heels planted firmly on the ground, a quiet voice ensuring no amount of success would ever go to her head.

She thought of Miss Elsie, the one foster carer who had shown her kindness. Who taught her to read and let her sleep with the light on when the nightmares came. She thought of the pain of losing her too soon, the years of darkness that followed, and the battle to climb out of it.

Her gaze returned to the mirror, and for a moment, she wasn't sure who she saw. The polished, professional woman staring back at her seemed at odds with the broken, furious girl still hiding in the shadows of her mind.

Am I relationship material? The thought crept in unbidden, sharp and invasive. *Could I ever let someone in enough to know all this? Would he even want to?*

She shook her head, dismissing the thought. Today wasn't about her doubts. It wasn't about her, at all.

Today was about Eileen Nearne, the indomitable woman who had trusted Mia, opened up to her, and inspired this community with her courage. Mia smiled as she thought of her. Eileen, with her wit, her sharp mind, and her unstoppable will, had become a part of Mia's life that she couldn't imagine losing.

Her BlackBerry buzzed in her pocket, pulling her from her thoughts. A text from Sebastian flashed on the screen:

> Pouring cats and dogs. Can I bring Aunt Didi in my MG? Or is that insane? Wish I had a proper car, but we'll be drenched otherwise.

Mia typed a quick reply:

> Of course. She'll love the sports car. Just don't let her think you're rescuing her—she's not big on being saved.

Sliding her phone back into her pocket, Mia glanced at her reflection one last time. *Let the past anchor you, not weigh you down,* she reminded herself.

Straightening her shoulders, she stepped out of the quiet room and into the bright, bustling hallway of the center she had created. The storm might rage outside, but inside these walls, there was hope. For everyone.

Ronald, her handyman and loyal shadow, stood waiting for her in the hallway. His lean frame shifted slightly as she approached, his hands fidgeting behind his back. Ronald had always been like this—quiet, observant, and meticulous. They'd been through fire together during their years on the streets, and now he was her steadfast supporter, as reliable as the rising sun.

"Everything ready for our important guest of the day, Ron?" Mia asked, her tone light, but warm.

He gave a small nod, his dark-gray eyes darting toward hers for only a moment before flitting away. "I think so, Mi. But..." He hesitated. "I wasn't sure if Miss Nearne would like a microphone. That's what I wanted to ask you."

Mia smiled gently, sensing his nervousness. "Have you got one on standby, Ron?"

"Of course." His gaze flicked up again, just briefly, as if offended she'd even think he might overlook such a detail.

"You know what?" Mia said, her voice soft with affection. "Just ask her when she's seated in her chair. My guess is she'll call it 'modern rubbish' and say, 'I've got a good enough voice, thank you.' But it's thoughtful of you to consider it."

Ronald's hands stilled, his shoulders relaxing slightly. "For you, always, Mi. I put carafes of water on the tables. Glasses too."

Mia's heart swelled. She reached out and lightly touched his arm. "I love you, Ronnie."

They exchanged their quick, practiced high-five, the one they'd invented long ago, a symbol of their bond.

As Ronald turned and headed back toward the therapy room, Mia watched him go, warmth in her heart. She knew he'd monitor the event with the precision of a general surveying the battlefield. Ronald never missed a thing, not when it came to her.

How she loved him. Ronald was her little brother in every way that mattered, tied not by blood but by shared trials and triumphs that had forged them into family.

The next person Mia bumped into was her right-hand woman, Alexandra Torres, carrying a stack of files as though they weighed nothing. Petite but formidable, with olive skin and sharp, dark eyes that missed nothing, Alexandra stopped mid-stride.

"Mia, you look like you're about to confess to a murder?"

Mia brushed her fringe aside and met her best friend's gaze. "Alex, there's something I need to tell you before you hear it from anyone else."

Alexandra's eyebrows arched to her hairline as only she could do. "Okay, now I'm intrigued. What is it?"

Mia hesitated, glancing toward the door of the therapy room. The thought of Alexandra walking in unprepared and seeing Sebastian did not seem like a good idea. "Sebastian is coming here today." Her voice was completely steady, but her gaze wasn't.

Just as she expected Alexandra froze, the dark eyes narrowing. "Sebastian? As in *that* Sebastian?"

Mia nodded, her lips pressed into a thin line.

"Why? Mia, why is he coming here? And why am I only hearing about this now?" Alexandra's voice was controlled but not free of frustration.

Mia took a step towards her, lowering her voice. "I know I should have told you earlier, but I wasn't sure how to bring it up. He's been helping me with Miss Nearne."

"With Miss Nearne?" Alexandra couldn't keep her voice down now. "You let *him* into her orbit? Mia, you were the one who said he couldn't be trusted around her."

"I know," Mia admitted, holding up a hand to calm her friend. "I said that because I didn't know him, I had no experience to go on for myself. But he's... different, Alex. He's not the same guy you knew two years ago."

Alexandra shifted the pile of files from one hip on the other, looking defensive. "Different how? Enlighten me."

Mia took a breath to search for the right words. *Why was this so difficult?*

"When you were... uh ... involved with him, his dad had just died... killed himself. The guy was a mess—running wild, denying everything, trying to escape. I know that's never an excuse, but he's learned some lessons since. He's changed. More grounded, thoughtful, and genuinely trying to put his life together. He's not the man who broke your heart, Alex. And he's been nothing but respectful and helpful with Miss Nearne."

Alexandra's jaw tightened, her dark eyes boring into Mia's. "And what about you? Are you sure this isn't about more than just Miss Nearne? I know the type, Mia."

Mia flushed, caught off guard by the question. "I... don't know. Maybe. But that's beside the point right now. This *is* about Miss Nearne, who's coming here today, and she likes him, Alex. She *wanted* to meet him."

Alexandra's expression softened just a fraction, though her guard remained up. "And you? Do you trust him?"

Now Mia nodded without hesitation. "I do. I know it sounds crazy, but yes, I really trust him."

Alexandra studied her for a long second. "Darling, if there's one person in this world who's never reckless, it's you. I've not seen you do one thing out of the ordinary since we've known each other. Which is a good five years now. If you're saying Slick Sebas is different, I'll trust you on that. But..."

"But what?" Mia prompted.

"But I'm not rolling out a red carpet for him. He hurt me, and I'm not going to forget that overnight. I'll be civil, but I'll be watching."

"That's fair," Mia said softly. "And for what it's worth, I think he regrets how things ended with you. He was in a bad place, Alex. We've all been there in one form or another."

Alexandra's lips quirked into a small, wry smile. "You're too kind for your own good, you know that?"

Mia smiled back, feeling relief flooding through her. "And you're too fierce for yours, Alex my dear. That's why we work so well together."

"Don't push it," Alexandra teased, before glancing toward the therapy room. "Let's see how he handles himself. If he's as changed as you say, I'll keep an open mind. But he gets no free passes."

"Understood." Mia gave her a quick, grateful nod. As Alexandra strode away, her files tucked under her arm, Mia let out another big breath of relief.

Mia opened the door to the largest room of the rehabilitation centre, a warm, welcoming smile carefully fixed on her lips. The muted green and cream walls, chosen for their calming effect, were lined with photographs of veterans—snapshots of camaraderie, resilience, and the shared struggles that tied them together.

The hum of conversation filled the air, mingling with the occasional clink of coffee cups on saucers and bursts of laughter. It was a lively, comforting sound, yet Mia couldn't fully shake the tightening in her chest as she surveyed the room where Aunt Didi would soon make her entrance.

There were at least fifty people present: veterans, staff, and a few family members who had gathered to hear Eileen Nearne speak. A mix of anticipation and curiosity seemed to ripple through the crowd, yet Mia's focus caught on the quieter moments, the unspoken burdens carried by those who sat scattered around the room.

Near the back, a man in a wheelchair, his lower legs missing, leaned forward as he told a story to the younger veteran beside him. His gestures were so animated that his words seemed to leap off his lips, bringing a spark of life to their corner of the room. Across from them, a woman sat quietly, her military uniform immaculate and medals shining on her chest. The left side of her face was unrecognizable, the scars of war etched into her skin, but she listened intently, tilting her one good ear toward the group she sat with.

Mia felt a pang in her chest. It was, of course, nearly impossible to show mental trauma on the outside. Physical wounds could be seen, but others were hidden, gnawing away quietly in the recesses of the mind. Those scars were no less real, no less painful, and she knew the room was full of them.

Yet, there was connection here, a sense of unity. Hope Haven was alive this afternoon, a sanctuary not just of healing, but of shared understanding.

She made her way toward the front of the room, her heels clicking softly against the polished floor. Her glance danced over the room as she felt eyes being drawn to her. Her heart swelled with both pride and nerves. Eileen's transformation over the past months had been remarkable, but public speaking was another hurdle entirely.

Still, if anyone could do it, it was Eileen Nearne. Mia thought of the light in the older woman's eyes when they'd spoken of this event, of the determination that had carried her through so much. Eileen's strength would certainly shine through today.

Mia cleared her throat. "Good afternoon, everyone," she began in her warm, steady voice that instantly hushed all other conversation. "As you probably all know, I'm Mia Thompson and this is my center. It's wonderful to see so many of you here today. As always, your presence makes this center what it is—a place of resilience, connection, and growth. Today, we have the honor of welcoming a very special guest. Miss Eileen Nearne, who has graciously agreed to join us and share her story."

She paused, her smile deepening as she met a few familiar faces in the crowd. "She'll be here shortly, and I promise, she's worth the wait."

66

A NAME TO HONOR

Mia sat in the front row, her hands resting on her notebook. She had no intention of taking notes—holding it was simply a habit, a comfort. Her gaze flicked to the door just as it swung open, and in came Eileen, arm-in-arm with Sebastian.

At barely five feet, Eileen was no match for Sebastian's towering 6'4" frame, but in presence, she outshone him completely. Regal and commanding, she walked with the dignity of a queen stepping into her court.

Dressed impeccably in her burgundy jumper and skirt, her two medals pinned side-by-side, her white curls perfectly styled, Eileen looked every inch the war heroine. But then she paused in the doorway, lifting a hand with mock exasperation.

"Beastly weather," she declared, her voice ringing out like a bell. "The kind of weather that grounded Lysanders and kept us waiting in safe houses, itching to be dropped into France. But nothing stops me now! I'd rather dodge raindrops than bullets, I think you'd all agree."

The room broke into warm laughter, and Mia felt herself relax. Eileen had the room in the palm of her hand already.

Sebastian guided her across the front of the room, his hand steady on her arm. A comfortable armchair awaited, set up as if it were a throne.

Mia stepped forward with a wide smile. "Aunt Didi, you've already won them over, and you haven't even started."

Eileen winked at her. "Charm and a lifetime of improvisation, my dear. Now, let's see if I can actually sit without ruining the illusion."

Sebastian helped her settle into the chair, crouching as he adjusted the cushions behind her. "You're all right like this, Aunt Didi?" he asked, his voice full of warmth and admiration.

"Perfectly all right, thank you, young man," she replied, patting his arm. "More space than in that dinky toy you call a car."

Sebastian laughed, retreating to lean against the wall as Eileen surveyed the room with sharp eyes. The chatter quieted, and Ronald appeared, shuffling toward the front with a portable microphone in hand.

His face was slightly flushed, his hands cradling the sleek black device as though it were a fragile relic. "Miss Nearne," he began, his voice a little too high-pitched, "I've got the microphone here... if... uh, you want to use it."

Eileen eyed the microphone as if it might bite her. "Doesn't it need to be plugged in somewhere?"

"No, ma'am," Ronald stammered. "It... it operates on batteries."

"Aha!" Eileen exclaimed, her eyes gleaming with mischief. "Well, let's be fancy for once. I'll probably be rubbish at it, but I hope it won't zap me."

Mia bit back a smile, nodding at Ronald to proceed.

He demonstrated the controls. "Y-you just press this button here to turn it on, but it's already live, so you don't—"

Too late. Eileen pressed the button with confidence and lifted the microphone to her lips. "*Merde alors*!"

The exclamation rang out, amplified for everyone to hear. A stunned silence hung in the room for half a second before the laughter started—first a chuckle, then a full wave of it rolling through the crowd.

Eileen blinked, then grinned, thoroughly unbothered by her gaffe. "Well, there we have it. I've officially sworn in French for an audience—no going back now!"

Sebastian, who'd laughed along with the rest, said. "I think it's a perfect icebreaker, Aunt Didi, but you may have to explain it to the audience."

Eileen fixed him. "So, you knew it was the last thing we said to each other before we went on a mission?"

He just bowed, reverently.

Eileen's expression became more reflective as she adjusted the microphone. "Perhaps I do need to explain. It was our way of saying, as agents, to one another, 'Here we go, and damn the risks.' A reminder to be brave, even when we were terrified."

The room quieted as her words settled over them, the weight of her history and the significance of the moment sinking in.

"And now, Aunt Didi? How does it feel to say '*Merde alors*' here, today?" Mia asked.

Eileen smiled as her gaze swept over the room. "Today, it feels right. Because it's not just about bravery. It's about moving forward, no matter what. Whether you're jumping into enemy territory or stepping into a room like this, it's the same."

Mia watched the faces of the veterans around her—some smiling, others nodding, all captivated by Eileen's words. For a woman who once struggled to speak of her past, Eileen was commanding the room with a grace and ease that was breathtaking.

Mia felt herself relax. Eileen had them. A little later, she noticed

Alexandra slip in through the back. Her petite frame was just visible beyond the rows of chairs, her sharp eyes scanning the room before settling on Sebastian. For a moment, her expression tightened, but then she nodded briefly at Mia and found a spot to stand quietly near the door.

At least she came, Mia thought, relieved. She hoped Alexandra would see what she already had—that this wasn't the Sebastian of two years ago.

"Let's try again," Eileen said, her voice steadier as she adjusted the microphone. "Good afternoon, everyone. My name is Eileen Nearne, but I think you probably knew that."

A soft chuckle rippled through the room, easing some of the tension.

"Though I've lived in Torquay for nearly twenty years, few people knew I had been a secret agent during World War II. And I wanted to keep it that way. I still want to keep it that way, to be honest. I have no intention of giving talks on television or blabbing with journalists."

Her gaze swept the room, landing briefly on Sebastian with a knowing twinkle.

"I agreed to speak today for one reason," she continued. "Because Doctor Mia—whom I suspect you all already adore—is a phenomenon when it comes to PTSD.

THAT'S something I didn't even know I had until a few months ago."

A murmur of recognition rippled through the crowd. Eileen nodded, her expression reflective.

"Suffering as we do," she said, her blue eyes shining with a mix of empathy and resolve. "Inside of us. Quietly. Out of sight. And the suffering doesn't just go away because the war does. We all know that."

More nods, some murmurs of agreement.

"So, let me be clear," Eileen went on. "This talk isn't about banging myself on the chest for how brave I was or recounting extraordinary things I might have done decades ago."

She tapped her chest with a small smirk, making her medals clink. The audience chuckled.

"No," she said with a gentle smile. "I'm here because I wanted to sit among people who understand where my pain comes from. People like you. And to share a glimpse of what I've learned. That even at my age, you can still come to terms with some of it. Not all of it—those scars will always be there. But truly, if you'd asked me this summer if I'd be here, in my best dress, making a fool of myself chatting into an amplifier, I'd have told you that you were out of your mind."

Laughter filled the room, warm and genuine.

Eileen adjusted the microphone in front of her mouth as her expression turned more thoughtful. "Now, I'm not much of a speechmaker. I'd rather have a conversation. So instead of boring you with my stories, how about this? Let's make it a conversation. Ask me anything you like—about my experiences, my recovery, or what life looks like after it all. I'll do my best to answer, and maybe, just maybe, we'll all leave here feeling a little lighter."

The room buzzed with energy as heads turned, and a few hands tentatively rose. Eileen glanced at Mia, who gave her an encouraging nod.

"Right then," Eileen said, her voice carrying a touch of mischief. "Who's going to be brave enough to go first?"

A young veteran raised his hand. "What was it like to arrive in France during the war? Were you scared?"

Eileen smiled. "Terrified but also full of anticipation. I had waited for that moment for almost two years, you see. We flew low, in a little Lysander, landed in a pitch-black field, and the pilot barely waited for me to grab my bag before taking off again. Efficient, but not exactly reassuring."

She paused for a moment. "I wasn't alone, fortunately. I was with my organizer, Maître William Savy. An international lawyer in his other life, though I only knew him at that time by his codename, Alcide. He was experienced—this was already his second mission—and a proper grown-up at thirty-eight, while I was just twenty-three, fresh-faced and trying to act like I knew what I was doing."

The audience smiled, the picture of contrast clear in their minds.

"Luckily, our reception team were members of the French Resistance. That night went as planned, but I knew well enough how easily things could go wrong. Many of my fellow agents weren't so lucky, especially by 1944. The Gestapo had become very... efficient... at sniffing us out."

A shadow passed across her face at mentioning the Gestapo. But then she said, brighter and determined. "Still, you don't let fear have the last word. You remind yourself why you're there, and you keep moving."

A staff member raised her hand next. "How did you manage to keep your cover when you were surrounded by danger?"

Eileen's lips curved into a faint smile. "Ah, well, as a wireless operator, I wasn't often in the thick of the fight, so to speak. My job was more solitary—I picked up coded messages and sent them back to London from whichever house my set was hidden in. Lonely work, really. Most of the time, I hardly saw anyone, and when I did, they only knew me by my codename, Rose."

She paused, glancing at the room before continuing. "My identity papers said I was Jacqueline du Tertre, a Frenchwoman. In England, during our training, we drilled our false identities until they became second nature. Every detail—your hometown, your family, your schooling—had to be ingrained. So, when the time came, you didn't hesitate. You became that person."

Her tone grew more somber. "It wasn't until I was captured that I truly had to live as Jacqueline. She had to be convincing, every moment. And that's where the training came in—it gave me the confidence to act my role, even when fear threatened to undo me."

Eileen leaned back in her chair. "So, yes, the key was preparation. And a bit of acting skill. I'd like to think I could've made a decent stage career of it if things had been different."

The wife of a veteran raised her hand. "What was the hardest part about being captured?"

Eileen's expression grew distant, her eyes unfocusing for a moment. "Honestly? The silence. When the questioning stopped, when the cell door closed, and I was left alone with my thoughts. The what-ifs, the could-have-beens—they played over and over in my mind like a broken record."

She paused, her hands resting on her lap. "At least when they were shouting or bullying me, I had something to focus on, something to fight against. But the silence? That's when your fears creep in, and you start to doubt everything."

She took a breath before she added, "But even then, I clung to the one victory I had—I'd outwitted them. The Gestapo believed I was just a foolish Frenchwoman, not a British agent. My alias, Jacqueline du Tertre, held up. They never uncovered the truth."

"But that same lie, that same success, almost became my undoing. After the camps, even the Americans didn't believe I was who I really was. To go through all that, only to have your own allies doubt you... that was a different kind of pain."

A young therapist in the audience was next: "What would you say to someone who's just starting their journey of healing from trauma?"

Eileen thought for a moment. "Be kind to yourself. Healing isn't a straight road—it's a winding path with bumps and detours. Don't rush, and don't do it alone. Find people who will walk with you," her eyes settling on Mia for a moment, "who will remind you that you're more than your pain. And don't be afraid of falling back. I think healing is a path of two steps forward and one step backwards."

After a series of heartfelt and profound exchanges, Sebastian raised his hand. "Aunt Didi, what's the most ridiculous thing that ever happened to you during the war?"

Eileen chuckled, a playful twinkle lighting up her eyes. "Of course, that question would come from you, you rascal." She paused for dramatic effect, her gaze sweeping the room. "Ah, it must have been rather at the beginning of the war, when my sister Jacqueline and I fled France for England to join the war effort in 1942."

She leaned forward as though sharing a delicious secret. "After many detours, we landed in Lisbon and managed to board a merchant ship bound for Gibraltar, from where we could sail to Glasgow. Now, this merchant ship was owned by a skipper named Thompson—what's in a name, huh?" She shot a wink at Mia, drawing a ripple of laughter from the room.

"Well, Captain Thompson was as gruff as you'd expect, but he had a certain... flair. As he welcomed us aboard, he said, 'She ain't no luxury liner, but she'll hold her own. I've never had passengers before, mind ye, especially young ladies. But don't fret, lassies—I'll make sure yer comfortable.'"

Eileen mimicked the skipper's rough accent, her voice dropping into a gravelly tone, earning more chuckles from her audience.

"Now, as he led us aboard, I couldn't believe my eyes. The ship was covered—absolutely covered—in mismatched flowers. Bouquets, pots, even tin cans stuffed with blossoms were scattered all over. And what does dear Captain Thompson say? 'Thought ye'd appreciate a wee touch of color. Not much for decoratin' but figured lassies might like it.'"

She leaned back, her shoulders shaking with laughter. "So, there we were, Jacqueline and I, swaying on a creaky old ship on the wild

Atlantic, surrounded by flowers. Bouquets sliding from one side of the deck to the other every time the ship rocked. It was like traveling in a floating garden."

Amidst the roar of laughter, Mia rose and stepped forward, standing beside Eileen. She could see the slight sag in the elderly lady's shoulders, a reminder of her age despite the sparkle in her eyes.

"Thank you, Aunt Didi, for sharing your incredible stories with us today. Your courage, humor, and wisdom have been nothing short of inspiring. You've reminded us all of the resilience we carry within us."

Eileen raised a finger, her face alight with mock indignation. "Oh, are you shooing me off already? I was just getting started!"

The room erupted in another wave of laughter, and Mia's smile widened. "You've held us spellbound, Aunt Didi. But I think you've earned yourself a nice glass of sherry and some nibbles—and perhaps save the rest of your amazing life for next time."

Eileen straightened in her chair. "Next time, eh? So, I haven't worn out my welcome?"

The room responded with another ripple of laughter and affectionate murmurs. "She's wonderful! And "Of course, we want her back!"

Before Mia could speak her closing words, an elderly veteran in the back of the room rose to his feet. His medals gleamed against his blazer, and the weight of his presence alone silenced the room. His deep, resonant voice carried across the space.

"Miss Nearne, you are not just welcome here—you are needed here. And not just as a guest. What you've shared today has reminded all of us that healing takes bravery. You've shown us what it means to carry pain with grace and still move forward."

The room fell utterly silent, the gravity of his words sinking in like ripples in still water.

He turned to Mia. "Dr. Thompson, with all due respect, I think this center ought to bear her name. The Eileen Nearne Rehabilitation Centre. What better name for a place dedicated to resilience and healing?"

Gasps and murmurs spread through the room, followed by a swell of applause. Mia, caught off guard, felt the words of her own dream suddenly given life. She glanced down at Eileen, who looked stunned, her hands fluttering as if searching for her rosary.

"Oh, heavens, no!" she exclaimed with conviction. "That's far too grand for me. I'm just an old lady with a few stories to tell."

A young veteran in the front row stood up. "But those stories, Miss Nearne, have changed the way I see my own struggles. You've given us something priceless today—something that will stay with us forever."

Sebastian came to stand next to Eileen's chair to offer his support. "Aunt Didi, it sounds like you're becoming the legend Mia and I already knew you were. Please accept it. This is your place now, too."

Eileen's cheeks flushed pink, her fingers brushing the medals on her chest as if seeking comfort. "Oh, stop it, all of you. You'll make me cry, and I can't have that. Not in front of all these fine people."

Mia stepped to her side, placing a reassuring hand on her shoulder. "Aunt Didi, you cannot know how glad I am to hear Fred and Terry voice this idea. Thank you, gentlemen. This plan has been on my mind ever since I saw Eileen begin to heal."

She knelt to be level to Eileen's gaze. "Listen to me. Whether you want the honor or not, you've earned it. You've given so much of yourself, even when it was difficult, even when it hurt. This is the least we can do for you. And if everyone here agrees..." Mia glanced around the room, catching nods and murmurs of agreement rippling through the crowd. "And, with your blessing, I think it's time I order a new sign for the front of the building."

Applause erupted, a wave of emotion that seemed to lift everyone in the room. Eileen, though still protesting faintly, couldn't hide the tears welling in her bright blue eyes. She dabbed at them with a trembling hand, murmuring in French, "*Vous êtes tous trop gentils*. You're all too kind. Far too kind."

Sebastian leaned in, his voice low, meant only for her and Mia. "Aunt Didi, kindness has nothing to do with it. It's about respect, and you've earned every bit of it."

Eileen looked between him and Mia, her gaze full of something unspoken but deeply felt. Flanked by them both, she glanced around the room at the faces watching her with admiration, gratitude, and love. She reached for the microphone one last time.

"Well," she said in a voice laced with emotion, "I suppose I'll have to accept, then. *Merde alors*!"

For a moment, the room was silent, and then, as if cued by some unseen conductor, the crowd erupted in laughter and a unison cry: "*Merde alors*!"

Eileen chuckled, setting the microphone down as if passing the moment back to the room. She leaned back in her chair, the weight of decades lifting from her shoulders.

Mia caught Sebastian's eye over Eileen's snowy-white curls and saw her own tears reflected in his eyes as well. Love and courage—both ran so deep, so unshakably strong.

For Mia, the room seemed to blur through her tears, her emotions cresting. Eileen had found her place, her name, her legacy. And Sebastian, standing beside her with that mixture of strength and vulnerability, felt more like a partner than she ever would have expected.

PART XVIII

~MIA~ LONDON, 11 NOVEMBER 2007

EPILOGUE

A few weeks later - The Special Forces Club, London – 11 November 2007

The Special Forces Club stood quietly in Knightsbridge, its red-brick facade offering no hint of the extraordinary stories it sheltered within. Only the brass lion's head door knocker, polished to a shine and glinting in the light, hinted at the legacy behind the discreet, members-only entrance.

Inside, the air was steeped in dignified tradition. The space was larger than the unassuming exterior suggested, with rooms dedicated to countries that had contributed to the clandestine fight during the war.

Each room bore the personal touch of its benefactors: the Danes honored Ebbe Munck, the man who sparked Denmark's armed resistance; the Americans created the Donovan Room, named for William J. Donovan, head of the wartime OSS. Elsewhere, there were tributes to the Belgians, Poles, Australians, and Canadians, all carefully curated by members of their respective nations. The

Norwegians had refurbished the Linge Room, a solemn tribute to Martin Linge, the founder of the Norwegian Independent Company.

But no section loomed as large as the French wing. Nearly 500 secret agents had served under SOE's French department, organizing, training, and arming Resistance fighters across occupied France. The walls here practically vibrated with their legacy, the faces of the agents gazing out from framed photographs—many encircled in black to mark their ultimate sacrifice.

The Club had been founded in 1945 at the urging of General Colin Gubbins, the wartime chief of SOE. His vision was for a meeting place where those who'd served in the shadows could find fellowship, share memories, and quietly honor the lives of comrades who had not returned. For decades, the legendary agents had passed through these halls, their footsteps now faint echoes in the corridors. Only a handful of them remained, but the Club endured —a testament to its importance. Funds and respect flowed freely, ensuring the weight of these agents' stories would not fade into the silence of history.

The wood-paneled walls bore plaques and photographs, black-bordered for those who didn't survive. Artifacts, from resistance armbands to clandestine wireless sets, told their stories in muted whispers. It was a space of reverence, commemorating men and women who had risked everything and, in many cases, given all.

This was not a place of ostentation but of quiet honor. Even the details—the worn Persian rugs underfoot, the faint scent of aged wood and polish—spoke of a legacy preserved, a duty never forgotten.

THE GLEAMING, red MG pulled to a stop outside the Special Forces Club, its vintage engine purring to a halt as heads turned toward the striking sight. Sebastian stepped out first, his white tie and tails immaculate, his unruly hair tamed for once. He moved quickly to the passenger side, unwinding the plaid blanket from Eileen's lap before offering her a steady hand to exit the low-slung sports car.

As she emerged, Mia couldn't help but shake her head in disbelief. The November wind bit at their cheeks, and she tugged her cashmere coat tighter around herself as she stepped out of her MINI, parked just behind Sebastian and Aunt Didi.

It had been a short drive from their nearby hotel, but the weather was enough to put anyone on edge—especially with Eileen's fragile lungs. "It's madness," Mia had muttered earlier, trying to reason with the former agent. "You can't ride in that wind tunnel, Aunt Didi. Your cough has only just settled."

"Nonsense," Eileen had shot back, waving off their protests. "This old bronchitis comes and goes. A souvenir from the war. Nothing to worry about."

But both Mia and Sebastian had worried. At 86, Eileen's health was not something they could afford to take lightly, and the MG was hardly the ideal vehicle for a cold, damp, November night. Its thin roof barely kept out the chill, let alone the possibility of rain.

Now, standing before the Club, Eileen adjusted her short white mantel over her dazzling, calf-length light-blue dress. She looked as regal as ever, her white curls impeccably styled, pearl earrings in her ears, her presence commanding despite the cold.

"Was it worth the fuss?" Sebastian teased, his tone light but his eyes filled with genuine concern as he steadied her.

Eileen cast him a withering look. "Don't be daft, young man. It's a marvelous car. Besides, you wouldn't deny an old lady her joy, would you?"

Mia joined them, still reeling between fond exasperation and relief. "At least we booked the hotel for three nights," she said under her breath to Sebastian. "One more night for the weather to improve and her to recover. And, no way is she riding back in that contraption. She's coming with me in the MINI."

Sebastian grinned but wisely kept his thoughts to himself.

Eileen turned toward the brass lion's head knocker on the door, pausing as if the weight of her memories rested just beyond the threshold. For a moment, her gaze became distant, before she straightened her shoulders and went up the steps.

"The last time I was here, I was with Vera," she murmured. "She passed in 2000, you know. Now I'm one of the last still standing. It's odd... Jacqui's been gone almost twenty-five years. We used to come here together every time she was back from the States." She stopped, then shook her head briskly and announced in her brisk way. "Ah well, shall we dears? I can't stand out here all night reminiscing while the good wine gets poured without me."

Mia and Sebastian exchanged a glance—equal parts love, reverence, and awe—before following Miss Eileen Nearne up the steps, into the hallowed halls of history.

Eileen let the knocker fall once, its clang sharp in the evening's air, and the door swung open almost immediately. A uniformed attendant greeted them with a warm smile, stepping aside to usher them in.

"Miss Nearne, what an honor. I can tell you we were all thrilled to see your name on this year's list."

"Thank you, Jeremy," Eileen replied with a friendly nod. "It's good to see you're still here as well."

Jeremy's smile widened. "I can assure you, ma'am, everyone wanted to work tonight when they heard you were coming."

"Ho, ho, young man." Her tone teasing. "Now you're exaggerating."

Their coats were handed to the attendant, and Eileen, flanked by Mia and Sebastian, made her way toward the hum of conversation, the clinking of glasses, and the unmistakable buoyancy of military camaraderie. As they entered the main room, a quiet stir rippled through the crowd, heads turning toward them as recognition dawned.

"Miss Nearne," a clear, authoritative voice rang out. Princess Anne, The Princess Royal the Club's patron, stepped forward, dressed in a sharply tailored navy suit, her own medals gleaming against her breast pocket. "What an honor to have you with us tonight."

Eileen curtsied as her hand rested on Sebastian's arm for balance. "Your Royal Highness, the honor is mine," she said in a tone as poised as ever.

Mia, standing next to Eileen, felt a lump rise in her throat. This was Eileen's moment—the one she had resisted for so long. To see her standing tall, commanding respect and admiration in a room filled with military legends, was nothing short of awe-inspiring.

After the formalities of the welcome, Eileen whispered in Mia's ear.

"I want to show you my friends. The ones who are no longer here." She led them into the 'Hall of Fame' where she moved very slowly, her hand brushing the polished wood of the gallery railings as she spoke in a quiet, measured tone.

"They called this the silent service," she began. "But here, in these faces, the silence speaks."

She stopped before a trio of black-rimmed portraits—Violette Szabo, Denise Bloch, and Lilian Rolfe. Their expressions were solemn, their eyes fierce with resolve.

"I met them in Ravensbrück," Eileen said softly. "They believed their British citizenship would protect them. It didn't. The Nazis were determined to erase any trace of what we were." She paused, her voice catching. "They were brave—braver than I'll ever be. But I survived because I stayed Jacqueline du Tertre, the silly Frenchwoman. It was the only way."

Sebastian's voice was hushed. "You were brave too, Aunt Didi. Don't diminish what you did."

Eileen nodded, but her gaze remained fixed on the portraits. "They paid the highest price. That's what I call bravery."

They moved on, Eileen stopping again before another series of portraits.

"Alcide," she said, pointing to William Jean Savy's face. "My first organizer. Only after the war did I learn his real name. I knew he was an international and well-respected lawyer in Paris, but to me, he was simply Alcide. Though apparently, he was also a masterful cook—hence the *Maître* often added before his name. A man of many faces, but above all, a man who believed in justice, even in the shadows. He passed in 1993."

She gestured to the portrait of René Dumont-Guillemet, whom she had known as Armand. "Playboy-turned-patriot," she said with a bittersweet smile. "He was my second organizer. All charm and wit —but fearless when it counted. Died in 1980."

"And this," she continued, pointing to a third portrait, "is Adrien Grafeuille, my fellow W/T operator, Arnaud, who was wise enough to move to the house in *Le Vésinet*. Lost sight of him after the war. He was born the same year as I was, so he might still be alive."

She paused before the next portrait. "Antoine Diacono, the Maltese agent I knew as Blaise. He's still around, but I've never seen him here."

As they moved down the hall, Eileen's steps slowed. When they reached the portrait of her sister Jacqueline, she stopped entirely. The room seemed to fall away as Eileen reached out a trembling hand to touch the edge of the frame.

"*Ma chère sœur*," she whispered. "We did it, Jacqui, as we promised each other in Grenoble that Easter in 1942. We made it through."

Mia stepped closer, her heart tightening at the raw tenderness in Eileen's words. Sebastian placed a steadying hand on Eileen's back, his usual charisma subdued in the presence of such deep emotion.

Eileen turned to them both, her blue eyes glistening but resolute. "She always said the fight was worth it. And she was right. For all of us. For the peace the world so desperately needed."

Then, straightening, she turned her back on the portraits and spoke in her usual clipped voice, carrying that unmistakable French undertone.

"*Alors, mes enfants*, time for dinner and champagne. I'm here to celebrate, not to mourn. I've done enough of that for several lifetimes."

Seated at the table of honor, Eileen glanced around, taking it all in. The room buzzed with a tapestry of voices sharing stories of the past, tributes to those absent, and laughter born of shared understanding. The atmosphere was warm and buoyant—a testament to the respect and resilience of those gathered.

On Eileen's right sat 85-year-old Yvonne Baseden Burney, petite, elegant, and composed, her determination still evident in her sharp, lively eyes. The two women exchanged warm smiles, their bond forged in the crucible of Ravensbrück, where both had narrowly escaped death. Like Eileen, Yvonne had survived by pretending to be French—a ruse that had saved her life but left scars that only those who'd lived it could truly understand.

On her left sat the inimitable Australian Nancy Wake, the 'White Mouse' herself, now 95. Nancy's hearty laugh still filled the air as she recounted a particularly audacious tale of outwitting the Gestapo, her French-accented English delivered with a mischievous glint in her eye.

She leaned toward Eileen, patting her hand affectionately. "And here you are, *chérie*. Outshining us all tonight, eh?"

Eileen chuckled, shaking her head. "Nonsense, Nancy. They're here to see you, the legend who took down the enemy with her bare hands."

Nancy winked, her laughter ringing out again as she took a generous gulp of champagne. "Oh, I'll take the compliment, but we all know you're the quiet storm they admire most."

Eileen turned to Yvonne and said in a soft voice. "Do you remember the nights in Ravensbrück when we talked about this moment? Dreaming of being free and celebrating? Back then, it seemed impossible."

Yvonne nodded. "It did. But we're here now, Eileen. And tonight, we celebrate the impossible."

"I heard Pearl Witherington Cornioley wanted to come, but she's poorly," Nancy remarked in a more somber tone.

Eileen agreed. "It's not the same without Pearl. All she's done for us SOE agents Section F post-war should never be forgotten."

"I went to the Valençay Commemoration service last year," Yvonne added, "but the traveling gets into one's bones, doesn't it?"

"I'm not moving anymore." Nancy shook her white head with conviction. "I've traipsed around the world, but enough is enough."

"Phyllis Latour is still alive in New Zealand," Yvonne disclosed, her encyclopedic memory on display. "But it's too far for her to come to London, now."

"You know, she's only three weeks younger than me," Eileen quipped, her lips curling into a playful smile. "Quite the baby."

As the three women sat together, chatting, eating and drinking, they seemed quite unaware of the attention they drew, or perhaps they simply didn't care. Around them, whispers of admiration floated between tables as others stole glances, marveling at the sight of these living legends.

From across the room, Mia and Sebastian observed the trio. Sebastian leaned in and whispered, "They don't even realize the weight of their presence, do they?"

"No," Mia replied, her voice filled with awe. "But that's what makes them who they are—why they're so extraordinary. It's not about recognition for them—it's about the work they did, the people they were, and the bonds they forged. It was all self-evident to them. The attitude of one of the strongest generations ever to grace the earth. We're lucky to still witness it with our own eyes."

Eileen caught their gaze and lifted her champagne flute toward them in a small, knowing salute before turning her attention back to her companions. Her cheeks were slightly flushed, her blue eyes brighter than ever, and her medals gleamed in the warm light of the room.

The three lady agents continued their conversation, their elderly voices mingling into the warm hum of the room as the Special Forces annual dinner carried on—a celebration of resilience, courage, and lives lived with unwavering purpose.

It was, without a doubt, a night to remember.

As the evening wound down, Eileen sought out her younger companions again. Sebastian returned from the bar, balancing three cups of tea. "I've been informed by Her Majesty"—he gestured toward Eileen—"that another drop of alcohol would be her undoing."

Eileen chuckled, her wit undimmed. "Indeed. Even a queen has her limits."

Sebastian handed a cup to Mia, then placed the last one in front of Eileen. He raised his own cup with a flourish. "To Aunt Didi—the Queen of SOE."

"To Aunt Didi," Mia echoed, her voice warm and full of love.

Eileen shook her head, though her smile was radiant. "What an odd business, raising cups," she teased, her tone laced with humor. "But who cares? I'll drink to whatever comes next."

As their cups clinked, the moment felt timeless—an intersection of history, reverence, and love, woven together in the simplest yet most profound of acts.

"So, my dears," Eileen announced, a twinkle in her eyes that immediately put Mia and Sebastian on alert. "My niece in Italy has written with some very good news."

Mia leaned forward, intrigued. Eileen rarely mentioned her niece. "Is that Odile?"

"Yes, of course. Who else?" Eileen said with mock impatience, though her tone was laced with affection. "She's been such a blessing, always trying to set things right where others gave up. For decades, she's been working on reclaiming the family house on the *60 bis Avenue des Arènes de Cimiez* in Nice."

"The house you left in 1940 when you fled to Grenoble?" Mia asked.

Eileen's expression softened with nostalgia. "Yes, the very same. It was rented out during the war, but the tenant refused to leave when we wanted it back. Then her daughter did the same, stubborn as a mule. The French authorities were no help, absolutely useless. But now, Odile has managed it. The house is ours again."

"That's incredible news, Aunt Didi!" Mia exclaimed.

"It is," Eileen agreed, though her tone carried a bittersweet note. "But I'm too old to travel now. Oh, how I would love to see the place with my own eyes again. I always dreamed of retiring there. And Odile, bless her heart, has her hands full with her family and her health."

"So, what happens now?" Sebastian asked, his curiosity evident.

Eileen's eyes sparkled with that familiar mischief. "That's as clear as day, young man. You and Mia will go on my behalf. Inspect the house, assess its condition, and report back. I expect photographs. Lots of them."

Sebastian raised an eyebrow, clearly caught off guard. "You want us to go to Nice? Together?"

"Precisely," Eileen said, her tone as matter-of-fact as if she were assigning a simple errand to the corner shop. "See my house. Tell me if it still holds its charm. I spent some of the happiest years of my life there."

Mia hesitated, her brow furrowing. "Aunt Didi, I can't just take time off. What about my clients?"

Eileen waved a hand as if to dismiss Mia's worries. "It will only be for a week. And it's all arranged. Check your phone, Mia. Alexandra will have sent you the replacement list by now."

Mia pulled out her Blackberry, her jaw dropping as she read the message. "She... she actually did. How on earth did you arrange that?"

"I have my ways," Eileen replied with sly amusement. "Your colleague is almost as impressive as you are, Mia. And she knows when to listen to her elders."

She turned her gaze to Sebastian with a glimmer of triumph in her eyes. "And your Chief Editor told me you can work from anywhere, young man."

Sebastian chuckled, running a hand through his hair. "He's not wrong. I can."

He turned to Mia, trying to lighten the moment with a playful grin. "Well, Doctor Mia, it seems the Queen has spoken. Shall we embark on this royal inspection?"

Mia glanced between them, taking a deep breath before finally nodding, a reluctant but genuine smile breaking across her face. "I suppose we shall."

Eileen watched the exchange with satisfaction. "And do stay close, my dears. It might be chilly this time of year, even on the Côte d'Azur, and the house may be in a dilapidated state. No need for either of you to catch a cold."

Mia flushed slightly. "Aunt Didi, are you matchmaking again?"

Eileen tilted her head, the picture of innocence. "Matchmaking?

Me? I wouldn't dream of it. I'm simply ensuring that two sensible people do something splendid together. And who knows? Maybe the Riviera air will work its magic."

Sebastian's grin widened. "Magic or not -- MG or plane, Mia?"

"Plane!" she cried, "I don't want to freeze my legs off."

Eileen let out a contented sigh. "Off you go, my loves. The world waits for no one. And neither does France. *Je vous embrasse avec tout mon cœur!*"

Before Mia or Sebastian could respond, Eileen pulled them into a warm embrace, her frail arms strong with emotion. It was a gesture of trust, of love, and of faith in what was to come.

THANK YOU FOR READING ***The Echo of Valor***! I hope you've enjoyed Mia's and Eileen's stories in the second *Timeless Agents* instalment!

NOW JOIN MIA AND SEBASTIAN ON THEIR TRIP to Eileen's flat in Nice. A rocky flight, a broken high heel and Edith Piaf await you!

I'D LOVE TO WELCOME YOU on my newsletter here to continue the journey! If you're already a subscriber, don't worry—our system recognizes you. These bonus chapters are ALSO FOR YOU as my loyal readers.

Happy reading,

Hannah

https://www.hannahbyron.com/bonus-teov

AUTHOR'S NOTE

Eileen's later years, as described in the novel, are not reflective of her real life. She lived her final years largely in solitude, and while she received widespread recognition upon her passing, she did not experience the kind of celebration and support in life that I have imagined for her. The therapy sessions between Eileen and Mia, as well as the character of Mia herself, are entirely fictional. I am in no way a professional in PTSD treatment, and these elements are included purely as a narrative tool to explore Eileen's inner world and struggles. This story is my way of imagining what her life could have been if her courage had been fully acknowledged during her lifetime.

Here's where I've deviated from the historical records to add fictionalized elements.

Youth Chapters

The chapters covering Eileen's youth are largely fictional, though based on historical records of her early life. Eileen was born in 1921 in London to an English father, John Nearne, and a Spanish mother, Countess Marie de Plazoala. She was the youngest of four children, with an elder sister, Jacqueline, and two older brothers, Francis and Frederick.

In 1923, the family moved to France, and Eileen grew up more French than English, though she remained fluent in both languages and spoke English with a French accent throughout her life. The family lived in various locations, including Boulogne-sur-Mer, Nice, and Grenoble, where Eileen's parents stayed after the war.

Aliases and Travel Documents

In the spring of 1942, I depict the Nearne sisters traveling from Grenoble to Lisbon under the fake surname "De Bonville." This name is fictional, and sources differ on whether they used aliases or traveled under their real names. Their journey was undoubtedly fraught with danger, and they were reportedly sent back to Grenoble at one point before continuing on.

Eileen's two field aliases, Alice Wood and Jacqueline du Tertre, are both historically accurate. However, for narrative clarity, I have only used the latter, which is sometimes spelled as "Dutertre" in historical records.

William Savy, Eileen's "chef" of the WIZARD Network used two codenames in the field: Alcide and Regis. He probably used Regis for WIZARD but as readers may remember him as Alcide in the first book The Color of Courage as Lise de Baissac's pre-war friend, he's Alcide here too.

Training and SOE Assignments

Historical accounts conflict on whether Eileen trained with SOE immediately after her 1942 interview with Selwyn Jepson or if she was first assigned to Bingham's Unit to train as a wireless operator. For simplicity, I have chosen to merge these elements into a cohesive timeline.

Fictionalized Scenes and Characters

London Hosts: Eileen and Jacqueline stayed with a couple named George and Odile upon their arrival in London, but their surname is unknown. I have used the fictional name "Bennett."

Hotel Victoria's Black Bathroom: The meeting between Eileen and Maître William Jean Savy (codenamed Alcide) in the famous black bathroom is fictional. Historical records confirm their meeting but not its location.

GREYHOUND Reception Team: The names "Marc" and "Frederick" for the GREYHOUND Network members who met Eileen and Savy are fictional.

Louise and Her Family: While Eileen stayed with a woman named Louise in France, details about their interactions are sparse, and the discussions depicted in the novel are fictional.

Landlord: this meeting at Eileen's rented room in Porte de Champerret is fiction.

Dubois family: It is unclear whether the Dubois family who owned the house in Bourg la Reine were sometimes present or not.

Skeds: I don't know what Eileen's schedule was to come 'on the air' for her transmissions.

Departure Savy for London: I changed Savy's sudden departure for the sake of storytelling but he did leave Eileen in France without a network

Wristwatch Gift: While female SOE agents did receive gifts from Colonel Buckmaster, I do not know if Eileen specifically received a wristwatch.

Paulette: The young French woman Eileen met while detained by the Americans was named Paulette but her description is fictional.

Sidney Jones aka Felix

The friend Armand (René Dumont-Guillemet), the organiser of the SPIRITUALIST Network talks about who is missing, was Sidney Charles Jones (Felix). He was betrayed by double agent Roger Bardet and executed in Mauthausen in September 1944.

Fresnes, Transport, and Camps

Last Message from Bourg-la-Reine: The content of Eileen's final transmission before her arrest is fictional.

False Papers: It is unclear whether Eileen had false papers with her during her transport from Fresnes to Germany.

Priest and Housekeeper: The identities of the Catholic priest and housekeeper who sheltered Eileen near Leipzig are unknown, so I have created fictional versions of them.

Post-Liberation Events

After her escape, Eileen was detained for a couple of weeks by the Americans, who mistook her for a collaborator. This profoundly affected her and contributed to her lifelong struggles. While I chose to focus on a more celebratory narrative for her later years, this omission does not diminish the importance of her actual experiences.

This novel is my way of imagining a world where Eileen Nearne received the recognition she so deeply deserved during her life. It is my tribute to her, as well as to the countless other men and women of the SOE who fought, suffered, and sacrificed for the cause of freedom. Their stories deserve to be remembered, shared, and celebrated.

WHO IS HANNAH BYRON?

I'm Hannah Byron, and I've been telling stories since I could hold a pen, though I never dared to dream anyone would actually want to read them. Born in Paris in the mid-1950s to a British mum and a Dutch dad, I grew up with strong ties to three countries that continue to inspire my work—France, the UK, and Holland. It's no surprise that most of my novels are set right here in Western Europe, where history and culture run deep.

For decades, I balanced life as a mother, a university professor and a translator, but now I'm a full-time author, and it feels like I've finally come home. My first dip into the publishing world came in 2010, but life threw me a curveball in 2014 when I lost my brave daughter after a battle with cancer. That devastating loss, followed by a few more rough years, made me step away from writing.

By 2019, I was ready to pick up the pieces. Armed with determination—and my big-girl pants—I dove back in, this time with a clear vision of what I wanted to write: stories of resistance women and romance set during WWII. Maybe not the most commercial choice for an independent author, but one I'm deeply passionate about. These women's courage and resilience are endlessly fascinating to me, and they inspire everything I write.

These days, life is smiling again. My eldest son is part of my business (you can thank him for this lovely website!), and my youngest son is a proud dad to my adorable granddaughter, with another little one on the way. Being a granny is absolutely wonderful—I'm loving every moment of it.

So, grab a cup of tea (or something stronger!) and dive into my world of WWII heroines and timeless love stories. I hope you find as much joy in reading them as I do in writing them.

WHAT ELSE DO I WRITE?

HISTORICAL FICTION
The Resistance Girl Series

DUAL TIME-LINE NOVELS
Timeless Agents Series

AS HANNAH IVORY
The Mrs Imogen Lynch Series

Printed in Great Britain
by Amazon